DEADLY ACCUSATION

"You killed Wilkins," Polti growled harshly, and triumph shone in his eyes. "Somebody search his saddlebags! You all knew Wilkins had him some gold dust he used to carry around. I bet we'll find it."

"You seem right shore," Lance suggested. "Did you put it in my bag while I was in the Trail House? I saw you slippin' out."

"Tryin' to get out of it?" Polti sneered. "Well, you won't. I'm goin' to search them bags here and now."

Lance was very still, and his green eyes turned hard and cold. "No," he said flatly. "If anybody searches them bags, it won't be you, and it'll be done in the presence of witnesses."

"I'll search 'em!" Polti snapped. "Now!"

He wheeled, but before he could take even one step, Lance moved. He grabbed the thin man and spun him around. With a whining cry of fury, Polti went for his gun, but his hand never reached the holster....

Other *Leisure* books by Louis L'Amour:

THE SIXTH SHOTGUN
THE GOLDEN WEST (Anthology)
THE UNTAMED WEST (Anthology)

LOUIS L'AMOUR

A MAN CALLED TRENT

LEISURE BOOKS   NEW YORK CITY

A LEISURE BOOK®

August 2006

Published by special arrangement with Golden West Literary Agency.

Dorchester Publishing Co., Inc.
200 Madison Avenue
New York, NY 10016

ISBN 0-8439-5600-3

The name "Leisure Books" and the stylized "L" with design are trademarks of Dorchester Publishing Co., Inc.

Printed in the United States of America.

Visit us on the web at www.dorchesterpub.com.

TABLE OF CONTENTS

EDITOR'S NOTE

Very early in his career as a pulp writer, in the period just prior to the outbreak of the Second World War, Louis L'Amour created a series character named Pongo Jim Mayo, the master of a tramp steamer in Far Eastern waters, in L'Amour's words "an Irish-American who had served his first five years at sea sailing out of Liverpool and along the west coast of Africa's Pongo River, where he picked up his nickname. He's a character I created from having gotten to know men just like him while I was a seaman in my yondering days." After the war, when L'Amour began to specialize in Western fiction, he wrote most frequently under the pseudonym Jim Mayo, taking it from this early fictional character. One of L'Amour's earliest series characters in his Western fiction was the gunfighter Lance Kilkenny, who figured in two of his early pulp short novels. "The Rider of Lost Creek" by Jim Mayo appeared in *West* (4/47). It was expanded and changed when it subsequently was published as an original paperback in 1976.

"A Man Called Trent" by Jim Mayo appeared in *West* (12/47). L'Amour subsequently reworked "A Man Called Trent" into *The Mountain Valley War*, published as an original paperback in 1978.

This edition marks the first time "The Rider of Lost Creek" as originally published has ever appeared in paperback since its first magazine publication. There is a special magic in these original short novels, and it has been a pleasure for me to have gathered these fine Western stories together in book form.

The Rider
of Lost Creek

I

A lone cowhand riding a hard-pressed horse reined in at the hitching rail before a Dodge barroom. Swinging from saddle, he pushed through the batwing doors, slapping the dust from his hat.

"Make it rye," he said hoarsely, as he reached the bar.

When the raw, harsh liquor had cut the dust from his throat, he looked up at a nearby customer, a man known throughout the West as a gun expert—Phil Coe.

"They've begun it," he said, his voice rough with feeling. "They're puttin' wire on the range in Texas."

"Wire?" A burly cattle buyer straightened up and glared. "Huh, they won't dare! Wire ain't practical! This here's a free range country, and it'll always be free range!"

"Don't make no difference," the cowhand who had just entered insisted grimly. "They're a-doin' it." He downed a second shot, shuddered, then glanced up slantwise at Coe. "You seen Kilkenny?"

He spoke softly, but a hush seemed to fall over the room, and men's eyes sought each other questioningly. Somewhere chips clicked, emphasizing the stillness, the listening.

"No," Coe said after a minute, "and you better not go around askin' for him."

"I got to see him," the cowpuncher insisted stubbornly. "I been sent to find him, and I got to do my job."

"What you want with Kilkenny?" demanded a short, wide-faced young man with light hair and narrow, pig-like eyes.

The cowpuncher glanced at him and his own eyes darkened. Death, he knew, was never far away when anybody talked to this man. Along with Royal Barnes, Wild Bill Hickok, and Kilkenny himself, this Wes Hardin was one of the most feared men in the West. He was said to be fast as Hickok and as cold-blooded as the Brockman twins.

"They want guns in the Live Oak country, Hardin," the cowpuncher said. "There's a range war comin'."

"Then don't look for Kilkenny," Coe said. "He rides alone, and his gun ain't for hire."

"You seen him?" the cowpuncher persisted. "I got word for him from an old friend of his."

"I hear tell he tied up with King Fisher," someone said.

"Don't you believe it," the cattle buyer stated flatly. "He don't tie up with nobody." He hesitated, then glanced at the cowpuncher. "I did hear tell he was down in the Indian Territory a while back."

"Who'd you get the word from?" Coe asked the cowpuncher quietly. "Might be somebody here knows Kilkenny and could pass the word along."

"Just say Mort Davis is in trouble. Kilkenny won't need no more than that. He sticks by his friends."

"That's right." The cattle buyer nodded emphatically. "Mort nursed him through a bad time after Kilkenny gunned down the three Webers. Mort stood off the gang that come to lynch Kilkenny. Iffen Kilkenny hears Mort needs help, he'll ride."

"Funny Royal Barnes never hunted Kilkenny for killin' the Webers," someone suggested. "With Barnes bein' half-brother to the Webers and all,"

"That'd be somethin' . . . Barnes an' Kilkenny," another agreed. "Two of the fastest gunmen in the West."

Conversation flowered in the room, and through it all the name of Kilkenny was woven like a scarlet thread. One man had seen him in Abilene. Two men had cornered him there, two bad men trying to build a tough reputation. They had drawn, but both had died before they could fire a shot. Another man said he had seen Kilkenny hold his hand out at arm's length with a poker chip on its back. Then he had tipped his hand slowly, and, when the chip fell free, he had drawn and fired before the chip reached the level of his waist.

"He's faster'n Hickok," someone else said dogmatically, "and he's got the nerve of Ben Thompson."

"What's he look like?" still another demanded. "I never seen the feller."

"Nobody agrees," the cattle buyer said. "I've heard a dozen descriptions of Kilkenny, and no two alike. He never makes hisself known until the guns start shootin', and he fades right after. Nobody knows him."

"This wire won't last in Texas," a lean, raw-boned

Texan changed the subject to say. "That Live Oaks country nor this 'n', either, they ain't made for wire. It's free range and always will be. The buffalo was here before the longhorn, and it was free grass then. It always has been."

"I don't know," someone else said doubtfully. "There's farmers comin' out from the East. Hoemen who'll fence their own ground and break the sod for crops."

"This country ain't right for farmin', I tell you," a young cowhand said. "You ever foller a trail herd? Iffen they ever plow this plains country up, it will blow clean to Mexico!"

But even as the men in Dodge talked and condemned wires, along the right way in Botalla, in the Live Oak country, lay huge reels of it, gleaming and new. Literally miles of it, on great spools, unloaded from wagon trains and ready to be strung. Reports implied there would soon be a railroad in Texas. Fat beef, good beef, would soon be in great demand. In this year of 1880, 40,000 tons of steel barbed wire of the Haish and Glidden Star varieties were to be sold to Texas ranchmen.

In the bar of the old Trail House in Botalla, rancher Webb Steele smashed a ham-like fist upon the bar. "We're puttin' it up!" he shouted. "Hoss high, pig tight, and bull strong! If them who don't like it want war, it's war they'll get!"

"Who fences Lost Creek Valley?" some hardened soul demanded. "You or Chet Lord?"

"I'm fencin' it!" Steele declared, glaring about the room. "And if necessary my riders will ride the fence with rifles!"

Outside the barroom a tall man in black trousers,

black shirt, and a worn buckskin vest walked a rangy yellow horse down the one street of Botalla, then swung down in front of the Trail House. The buckskin relaxed, standing tree-legged, head hanging in weariness. The tall man loosened the cinch, taking in the street with quick, alert eyes.

It was merely the usual double row of false-fronted buildings he saw, almost every other one a saloon. He knew that men along the walk were looking at him, wondering about him, but he seemed not to notice.

He could feel their eyes, though, like a tangible touch, lifting from his low-slung, tied-down guns to his lean brown face and green eyes. They were noting the dust in the grain of his face, the dust on his clothing, the dust on the long-legged buckskin. They would know he had traveled far and fast, and that would mean he had traveled for a reason.

When he stepped up on the walk, he closed his eyes for an instant. It was a trick he had learned that would leave his eyes accustomed to inner dimness much more quickly than would otherwise be the case. Then he stepped through the doors, letting his eyes shift from left to right, taking in the room in one swift, comprehensive glance. There was no one he knew. No one here, he was sure, knew him.

Webb Steele, brawny and huge, strode past him through the doors, his guns seeming small, buckled to his massive frame.

"I'll have a whiskey," the tall man said to the bartender. He took off his flat-crowned black hat to run his fingers around the sweaty band, then through his black curly hair. He replaced the hat, dropped his right hand to the bar, then glanced about.

Several men leaned on the bar nearby. The nearest,

a man who had walked to the bar as Steele left, was a slim, wiry young fellow in a fringed buckskin jacket and black jeans stuffed into cowhide boots.

The young man had gray, cold eyes. He looked hard at the stranger. "Don't I know you?" he demanded.

The green eyes lifted in a direct expressionless look. "You might."

"Ridin' through?"

"Mebbe."

"Want a job?"

"Mebbe."

"Ain't you a cowhand?"

"Sometimes."

"I'll pay well."

"What outfit you with?"

"I'm not with any outfit," the young man said sharply. "I *am* the Tumblin' R."

"Yeah?"

The young man's face flamed and a queer, white eagerness came into his eyes. "I don't like the way you said that!" he snapped.

"Does it matter?" drawled the tall man. For an instant the young rancher stared as if he couldn't believe his ears, and he heard men hurriedly backing away from him. Something turned over inside him, and with a sickening sensation in the pit of his stomach he realized with startling clarity that he was facing a gun battle, out in the open and alone.

An icy chill went down his spine. Always before when he had talked, loud and free, the fact that he was Chet Lord's son had saved him. Men knew his hard-bitten old father only too well. Then, there had been Bonner and Swindell. Those two men had affronted Steve Lord and later both had been found dead in the trail, gun in hand.

Suddenly the awful realization that he must fight swept over Steve Lord. Nothing his father might do afterward would do any good now. He stiffened. His face was tense and white as he stared into the cold green eyes of the stranger.

"Yeah," he snapped, "it matters, and I'll make it matter!"

His hand hovered over his gun. For an instant, the watchers held their breaths. The tall man at the bar stared at Steve Lord coolly, then Steve saw those hard green eyes change, and a glint of humor and friendliness came into them.

With a shrug the stranger turned away. "Well," he drawled, "don't kill me now. I hate to get shot on an empty stomach." Deliberately he turned his back and looked at the bartender. "How about another whiskey? The trail shore does make a feller dry."

Everyone began talking suddenly, and Steve Lord, astonished and relieved, dropped his hand to his side. Something had happened to him and all he knew was that he had narrowly escaped death from a shoot-out with a man to whom blazing guns were not new.

The tall man at the bar lifted his eyes to the mirror in time to see a thin-bodied fellow with close-set eyes slide quietly from his chair and go out the side door. No one seemed to notice him go except the tall stranger who noted the intentness of the man's eyes, and something sly in his movements.

The stranger swallowed his drink, turned on his heel, and walked outside. The thin man who had left the Trail House was talking with three men across the street in front of the Spur Saloon. The tall man saw the eyes of the three pick him up. Swiftly screening their faces, he strolled on.

Idling in front of the empty stage station a few minutes later, he saw Steve Lord coming toward him. Something about the young man disturbed him, but although his eyes lifted from the cigarette he was rolling, he said nothing when Steve stopped before him.

"You could have killed me," Steve said sharply, staring at him.

"Yeah." The tall stranger smiled a little.

"Why didn't you? I made a fool of myself, talkin' too much."

The stranger smiled. "No use killin' a man unnecessarily. You may be Chet Lord's son as I heard, but I think you make your own tracks."

"Thanks. That's the first time anybody ever said that to me."

"Mebbe they should have." The stranger took a long drag, and glanced sideward at Steve. "Knowin' you're pretty much of a man often helps a feller be one."

"Who are you?" asked Steve Lord.

The stranger shrugged. "The name is Lance," he replied slowly. "Is that enough for you?"

"Yeah. About that job. We'd like to have you. I may not be gun slick but I know when a man is."

"I don't reckon I'll go to work just now," observed the man who said his name was Lance.

"I'd rather have you on our side than the other," Steve said honestly. "And we'll pay well."

"Mebbe I won't ride for either side."

"You got to! Those that ain't for us are against us."

Lance smoked quietly for a moment. "Tell me," he finally said, "what kind of a scrap is this?"

"It's a three-cornered scrap actually," Steve said. "Our outfit has about forty riders, and Webb Steele has about the same number. We split the Live Oak country between us. By the Live Oak, I mean the territory between the two ranges of hills you see out east and west of here. They taper down to a point at the border. Webb Steele and us Lords both have started puttin' up wire, and no trouble till we get to Lost Creek Valley, the richest piece of it all. Good grass there, and lots of water."

"You said it was three-cornered. Who's the other corner?"

"He don't matter so much." Steve shrugged. "The real fight is between the two big outfits. This other corner is a feller name of Mort Davis. Squatter. He come in here about three year ago with his family and squatted on the Wagontire water hole. We cut his wire, and he cut ours. There she stands right now."

Lance studied the street thoughtfully, aware that while he was talking with Steve Lord, something was building up down there. Something that smelled like trouble. The three men with whom the thin man had talked had scattered. One was watching a boy unloading some feed, one was leaning on the hitch rail, another was studying some faded medicine show posters in a window.

Abruptly Lance turned away from Steve. There was something behind this, and he intended to know what. If they wanted him, they could have him.

II

Lance had started strolling carelessly toward the Spur Saloon when he heard a sudden rattle of wheels and racing hoofs behind him, and sprang aside just in time to escape being run down by a madly careening buckboard. The driver—a girl—stood up, sawing the plunging broncos to a halt, then wheeling the buckboard to race them back at a spanking trot. She brought them up alongside of Lance and her eyes were ablaze with irritation.

"Will you please stay out of the street?" she demanded icily.

Lance looked at her steadily. Red-gold hair blew in the wind, and her eyes were an amazingly deep blue. She was beautiful, not merely pretty, and there was in her eyes the haughty disdain of a queen who reprimands a clumsy subject.

"Pretty," he drawled slowly, "pretty, but plumb spoiled. Could be quite a lady, too," he added regretfully. Then he smiled and removed his hat. "Sorry, ma'am. If you'll let me know when you expect to use the street for a racetrack, I'll keep out of the way. I'll do my best to keep everybody else out of the way, too."

He turned as if to go, but her voice halted him.

"Wait!"

She took a couple of quick turns with the lines, jumped to the street, and marched up to him. Her eyes were arrogant and her nostrils tight with anger. "Did you mean to insinuate that I wasn't a lady?" she demanded. She held her horsewhip in her right hand, and he could see she intended to use it.

He smiled again. "I did," he said quietly. "You see, ma'am, it takes more than just beauty and a little money to make a lady. A lady is thoughtful of other people. A lady don't go racing around running people down with a buckboard, and, when she does come close, she comes back and apologizes."

Her eyes grew darker and darker and he could see the coldness of fury in them. "You," she snapped contemptuously, "a common cowpuncher, trying to tell me how to be a lady!"

She drew back the whip and struck furiously, but he was expecting it, and without even shifting his feet he threw up an arm and blocked the blow of the whip with his forearm. Then he dropped his hand over and grasped the whip. With a quick twist he jerked it from her hands.

The movement tilted her off balance and she fell forward into his arms. He caught her, looked down into her upturned face, into her eyes blazing with astonishment and frustrated anger, and at her parted lips. He smiled. "I'd kiss you," he drawled, "and you look invitin', and most like it would be a lot of fun, but I won't. You spirited kind kiss much better if you come and ask for it."

"Ask?" She tore herself free from him, trembling from head to foot. "I'd never kiss you if you were the last man alive."

"No, ma'am, I reckon not. You'd be standin' in line waitin', standin' away back."

A hard voice behind Lance stopped him short.

"Seems like you're takin' in a lot of territory around here, stranger. I'd like to ask you a few questions."

Lance turned slowly, careful to hold his hands away from his guns.

The thin-faced man was standing close by, his thumbs hooked in his belt. Two of the other men had spread out, one right and one left. The third man was out of sight, had circled behind him probably, or was across the buckboard from him.

"Let's have the questions," he replied calmly. "I'm right curious myself."

"I want to know," the man demanded, his eyes narrow and ugly, "where you was day before yesterday."

Lance was puzzled. "The day before yesterday? I was ridin' a good many miles from here. Why?"

"You got witnesses?" the thin man sneered. "You better have."

"What you gettin' at?" Lance demanded.

"I s'pose you claim you never heard of Joe Wilkins?"

Several men had gathered around now. Lance could hear them muttering among themselves at the mention of that name.

"What do you mean?" Lance asked. "Who is Joe Wilkins?"

"He was killed on Lost Creek trail the day before

yesterday," the fellow snapped. "You was on that trail then, and there's them that think you done him in. You deny it?"

"Deny it?" Lance stared at the man, his eyes watchful. "Why, I never heard of Joe Wilkins, haven't any reason to kill him. 'Course, I haven't seen him."

"They found Wilkins," the thin man went on, his cruel eyes fastened on Lance, "drilled between the eyes. Shot with a six-gun. You was on that road, and he'd been carryin' money. You robbed him."

Lance watched the man steadily. There was something more behind this bald accusation than appeared on the surface. Either an effort was being made to force him to make a break so they could kill him, or the effort was to discredit him. If he made a flat denial, it would be considered that he was calling the fellow a liar, and probably would mean a shoot-out. Lance chuckled carelessly. "How'd you know I was on Lost Creek trail?"

"I seen you," the man declared.

"Then," Lance said gently, "you were on the trail, too. Or you were off it, because I didn't see you. If you were off the trail, you were hiding, and, if so, why? Did you kill this Wilkins?"

The man's eyes narrowed to slits, and suddenly Lance sensed a hint of panic in them. They had expected him to say something to invite a fight. Instead, he had turned the accusation on his accuser.

"No! I didn't kill him!" the man declared. "He was my friend!"

"Never noticed you bein' so friendly with him, Polti," a big farmer declared. "If you was, I don't think he knowed it."

"You shut up," Polti, the thin man, snapped, his eyes blazing. "I'll do the talkin' here."

"You talked enough," Lance replied calmly, "to make somebody right suspicious. Why are you so durned anxious to pin this killin' on a stranger?"

"You killed Wilkins," Polti growled harshly, and triumph shone in his eyes. "Somebody search his saddlebags! You all knew Wilkins had him some gold dust he used to carry around. I bet we'll find it."

"You seem right shore," Lance suggested. "Did you put it in my bag while I was in the Trail House? I saw you slippin' out."

"Tryin' to get out of it?" Polti sneered. "Well, you won't. I'm goin' to search them bags here and now."

Lance was very still, and his green eyes turned hard and cold. "No," he said flatly. "If anybody searches them bags, it won't be you, and it'll be done in the presence of witnesses."

"I'll search 'em!" Polti snapped. "Now!"

He wheeled, but before he could take even one step, Lance moved. He grabbed the thin man and spun him around. With a whining cry of fury, Polti went for his gun, but his hand never reached the holster. Lance's left hit Polti's chin with a crack like that of a blacksnake whip, and Polti sagged. A left and a right smashed him down, bleeding from the mouth.

"This don't look so good for you, stranger," the big farmer stated fearlessly. "Let's look at them bags."

"Right," Lance replied quietly. "An honest man ain't got anything to fear, they say, but it wouldn't surprise me none to find the dust there."

Watching him closely, the crowd, augmented now

by a dozen more, followed him to his horse. Suddenly he stopped.

"No," he said, "a man might palm it if it's small." He turned to the girl who had driven the buckboard, and who now stood nearby. "Ma'am, my apologies for our earlier difficulty, and will you go through the bags for me?"

Her eyes snapped. "With pleasure! And hope I find the evidence!"

She removed the articles from the saddlebags one by one. They were few enough. Two boxes of .45 ammunition, one of rifle ammunition, some cleaning materials, and a few odds and ends of rawhide.

As she drew the packet of pictures out, one of them slipped from the packet and fell to the ground. The girl stopped quickly and retrieved it, glancing curiously at the picture of an elderly woman with a face of quiet dignity and poise. For an instant she glanced at Lance, then looked away.

"There is no gold here," she said quietly. "None at all."

"Well," Lance said, and turned, "I guess. . . ."

Polti was gone.

"Puts you in the clear, stranger," the big farmer said. "I wonder where it leaves Polti?"

"Mebbe he'd've tried to slip it into the saddlebag when he searched it," somebody suggested. "Wouldn't put it past him."

Lance glanced at the speaker. "That implies he has the gold dust. If he has, he probably killed Wilkins."

Nobody spoke, and Lance glanced from one to the other. A few men at the rear of the crowd began to sidle away. Finally the big farmer looked up.

"Well, nobody is goin' to say Jack Pickett lacks nerve," he said, "but I ain't goin' to tackle Polti and them gun-slick *hombres* he trails with. It's like askin' for it."

The crowd dwindled, and Lance turned to find the golden-haired girl still standing there.

"I'm still not sure," she said coldly. "You could have buried it."

He grinned. "That's right, ma'am, I could have."

He turned and walked away. The girl stared after him, her brows knit.

Lance led the buckskin slowly down the street to the livery stable. He walked because he wanted to think, and he thought well on his feet. This thing had a lot of angles. Polti was mean and cruel. The man was obviously a killer who would stop at nothing. For some reason he had deliberately started out to frame Lance. Why, there seemed no reason. He might, of course, know why he had come to Live Oak and the town of Botalla.

In the livery stable Lance was rubbing down the buckskin when he heard a voice speak from the darkness of a stall behind him.

"Busy little feller, ain't you?"

The speaker stepped out of the stall into the light. He wore a battered hat, patched jeans, and a hickory shirt. Yet the guns on his hips looked business-like. Powerfully built, he had brick-red hair, and a glint of humor in his sardonic blue eyes.

"Name of Gates," he said. "They call me Rusty."

"I'm Lance."

The eyes of the stranger in Botalla took in the cowpuncher with quick intelligence. This man was rugged and capable. He looked as if he would do to ride the river with.

"So I heard." Rusty began making a smoke. Then he looked up, grinning. "Like I say, you're busy. You invite Steve Lord to a shootin' party, then side-step and let him off easy. A lot of people are askin' why. They want to know if you've throwed in with Chet Lord. They want to know if you was scared out. Then you tangle with that wildcat, Tana Steele. . . ."

"Webb Steele's daughter? I thought so. Noticed the name of Tana Steele on a package in the buckboard."

"Yeah. That's her, and trouble on wheels, pard. She'll never forgive, and, before she's through, she'll make you eat your words. She never quits."

"What do you know about this *hombre*, Polti?" asked Lance.

"Bert Polti? He's a sidewinder. Always has money, never does nothin'. He's plumb bad, an' plenty fast with that shootin' iron."

"He hangs out at the Spur?"

"Mostly. Him and them pards of his . . . Joe Daniels, Skimp Ellis, and Henry Bates. They're bad, all of them, and the bartender at the Spur is tough as a boot."

Lance started for the door. Rusty stared after him for an instant, then shrugged.

"Well," he said, "I'm buyin' a ticket. This is one ride I want to take." And he swung along after Lance.

Lance walked up on the boardwalk and shoved open the batwing doors of the Spur. Bert Polti had been looking for trouble, and now Lance was. Slow to anger, it mounted in him now like a tide, the memory of those small, vicious eyes and the tenseness of the man as he stood, set to make a kill.

Never a troublemaker, Lance had always resented being bullied, nevertheless, and he resented seeing others pushed around. It was this, as much as a debt to pay, that had brought him to Botalla. There was as yet no tangible clue to what the trouble here was all about. He had only Steve Lord's version, one that seemingly ignored the rights of Mort Davis. Yet now Polti was buying in. Polti had deliberately tried to frame him with a killing. Lance hadn't a doubt but that Polti had planned to plant gold dust in his saddlebags.

III

A half dozen men were loitering about the bar when Lance walked in, turned, and looked around.

"Where's Polti?" he demanded.

One of the men he had seen talking to Polti was sitting at a table nearby, another stood at the bar.

There was no reply. "I said," Lance repeated sharply, "where's Polti?"

"You won't find out nothin' here, stranger," the seated man drawled, his tone insulting. "When Polti wants you, he'll get you."

Lance took a quick step toward him and, catching a flicker of triumph in the man's eye, wheeled to see an upraised bottle aimed at his head. Before the man who held it could throw, Lance's gun fairly leaped from its holster. It roared and the shot caught the bottle just as it left the man's hand.

Liquor flew in all directions, and the man sprang back, splattered by it.

Holstering his gun, Lance stepped in and caught the man by the shirt and jerked him around. Instantly the fellow swung. Turning him loose, Lance hooked a short left to the chin, then stabbed two fast jabs to the face. He feinted, and threw a high hard right. The fellow went down and rolled over on the floor.

Without a second's warning, Lance whirled around and grabbed the wrist of the man at the chair, spun him around, and hurled him to the floor.

"All right!" he snapped. "Talk, or take a beatin'! Where's Polti?"

"The devil with you!" Lance's latest victim snarled. "I'll kill you!"

Then Lance had him off the floor, slammed him against the bar, and proceeded to slap and backhand him seven times so fast the eye could scarcely follow. His grip was like iron, and before that strength the man against the bar felt impotent and helpless.

"Talk, cuss you!" Lance barked, and slapped him again. The man's head bobbed with the force of the blow. "I'm not talkin' for fun!" Lance said. "I want an answer!"

"Apple Cañon," the man muttered surlily, "and I hope he kills you."

Lance slammed him to the floor alongside the first man, then spun on his heel, and walked out. As he came through the door, he saw Rusty Gates standing outside, hand on his gun. Gates grinned.

"Didn't take long," he said dryly. "You operate pretty fast, pardner."

"Where's Apple Cañon?" Lance demanded.

"Well," Gates said, and rolled his quid of chewing in his jaws, "Apple Cañon is almost due south of here, down close to the border. That's where Nita Riordan hangs out."

"Who's she?" Lance wanted to know.

"Queen of the Border, they call her. Half Irish, half Mexican, and all dynamite. The best-looking woman in the Southwest, and a tiger when she gets started. But it ain't her you want to watch. It's Brigo. Jaime Brigo is a big Yaqui half-breed who can sling a gun as fast as the Brockmans, track like a bloodhound, and is loyal as a Saint Bernard. Also, he weighs about two pounds less than a ton of coal."

"What's the place like . . . a town?"

"No. A bar, a bunkhouse, and three or four houses. It's a hang-out for outlaws. And, feller, it ain't no place for a man t'go lookin' for Bert Polti. That's his bailiwick."

Lance saddled Buck, his buckskin, and headed south, leaving Rusty at the stable, staring thoughtfully after him. The day was beginning to fade now, and he could see the sun grow larger as it slid away toward the western mountains. There was still heat. It would not be tempered until after the sun was gone, until the long shadows came to make the plains cool.

The bunch grass levels were dotted with mesquite and clumps of prickly pear, and Lance rode on through them, letting the buckskin have his head on the narrow winding trail. Prairie dog towns were all about, but they disappeared as the rocks grew closer. Once he saw a rattler, and there were always buzzards, circling on slow, majestic wings above the waste below.

When he had gone no more than two miles, he left

the trail and started cross-country, still thinking of Polti. He did not trust this man. He began to dig and pry in his memory, trying to uncover some clue as to Polti's actions. But more and more it became apparent that the secret of all the trouble lay in something he did not know.

The dim trail he had taken when he left the main trail to Apple Cañon was lifting now, skirting the low hills, steadily winding higher and higher. The story that he was going to Apple Cañon was a good one. It would cover up what he actually intended to do. And soon he would go to Apple Cañon.

Polti was dangerous. He knew that. Nor did he underrate the two men he had beaten up in the Spur. Their kind were coyotes who would follow a man for months for a chance to pull him down.

There was menace in this country, an impending sense of danger that would not leave him. There was more here than met the eyes, more than the smile on tall, handsome Steve Lord's face, more than the sullen anger of the lovely, pampered Tana. There was death here, death and the acrid smell of gunpowder.

What did they know? What was behind the message he had received that had brought him here? Was it just another range war, or was it more?

Yet anyone who had lived in Texas through the Taylor and Sutton feud knew that range war could be deadly. And in Texas these days men rode with awareness. The wire was stirring up old feelings, old animosities. The big ranches were all stringing wire now. The smaller ranches were doing likewise. Starved for range for their herds, and pinched down to small areas, they saw extinction facing them if they did not fight. And they had neither the wealth to hire gunmen, nor the strength to fight without them unless they banded together.

Joe Wilkins, who Lance had learned was a nester, had been slain. The mention of his name and the quick surge of feeling had been enough to indicate that submerged fires burned here, and close to the surface. Any little spark might touch off an explosion that would light a thousand fires along the border, and turn it into an inferno of gunsmoke. Men were all carrying guns. They were carrying spare ammunition, too. They were ready, one and all. They rode the range, or rode fence with rifles across their saddle bows, and their keen eyes searched every clump of mesquite or prickly pear. Joe Wilkins had died, fences had been cut, and the ugly shape of war was lifting its head.

It was a time when men shot first and asked questions afterward. The notorious outlaw, Sam Bass, was riding the trails, robbing banks and trains. John Wesley Hardin was running up his score of twenty-seven men killed. King Fisher had 500 men riding to his orders on both sides of the border, King Fisher with his tiger-skin chaps and silver-loaded sombrero. Wild Bill Hickok, Bat Masterson, Billy Tilghman, Ben Thompson, and a hundred other gun slicks and toughs were riding the trails, acting as marshals in towns, or gambling.

The long fences were cutting down the range. The big ranches would still have range, but there would be too little grass for the cattle of the small ranchers. For them it was the end, or a battle for survival, and such a battle could have but one result. Yet the small ranchers were banding together. They were wearing guns.

From the crest of a ridge, Lance looked over the

valley of Lost Creek and could see the long silvery strands of barbed wire stretching away as far as the eye could reach.

"I don't know, about this wire business," he mused, patting the buckskin on the shoulder. "I don't know who's right. There's arguments for both sides. It gives everybody a chance to improve breedin' and have crops, and anybody can see the longhorn is on the way out. Too little beef. These whitefaces now, they have something. They carry a lot more beef than a longhorn. You an' me, Buck, mebbe we're on the way out, too. We're free, and we go where we please, and we don't like fences. If they build fences, this country is finished for us. We'll have to go to Dakota, or mebbe to Mexico or the Argentine."

The buckskin turned down the little trail through the tumbled boulders and cedar, a dim, concealed little trail that the sure-footed mountain horse followed even in the vague light of late evening. This was not an honest man's trail, but Lance was not worried for he knew the manner of man he rode to see. That man who would never be less than honest, but he would fight to the last ditch for what he believed to be his own.

The trail dipped into a hollow several hundred yards across, and, when Lance had ridden halfway across it, he dismounted and led his horse into a sheltered position behind a boulder. It would be a long wait, for he was early. Sitting against a boulder, he watched the declining sun fall slowly westward, watched the shadows creep up the rocky walls, and the sunlight splash color upon the cliffs.

He must have fallen asleep, for when he awakened

the stars were out, and he judged several hours must have passed.

It was quiet, yet when Lance lifted his eyes, it was in time to catch the gleam of starlight on a pistol barrel aimed over a rock. Then, even as he moved, the muzzle flowered with flame. As he hurled himself desperately to one side, he heard the bullet strike, then again, and something struck him a wicked blow on the back of the head. He tumbled on his face among the boulders. In his fading consciousness he seemed to feel something hot and sticky along his cheek. . . .

The first thing Lance knew, a long time later, was the throbbing pain in his skull as though a thousand tiny iron men were hammering with red-hot hammers at the shell of his skull, pounding and pounding. He opened his eyes to see a distant star shining through a crevice in the rocks across the hollow. Then he saw something long and dark lying upon the ground. It was like the body of a man.

Turning over painfully, Lance got his hands under him and pushed himself up to his knees. For a long time then he was still, and his head swayed and seemed like an enormous, uncontrollable thing. He forced his eyes to focus, but the starlight was too slight to help him to see more than he had.

Then he got a hand on the rock beside him, and pushed himself to his feet. There he remained, leaning against the rock. One hand dropped instinctively to his gun on the right side, then he felt for the other. Both were there.

The first shot, if there had been more than one, had

missed him. It had either ricocheted off a rock then and hit him, or else the unseen killer had fired again. He apparently had been left for dead. Feeling of his skull, he could understand why, for his hair was matted with blood.

Feeling around, his head throbbing fiercely, he found his hat and hung it around his neck by the rawhide chin strap. His head was too swollen for him to wear the sombrero. Stumbling to where he had left his horse, he found Buck waiting patiently. The yellow horse pricked up his ears and whinnied softly.

"Sorry, Buck," Lance whispered. "You should've been in the stable by now, with a good bait of oats."

He had swung into the saddle and turned down into the hollow before he remembered the shape on the ground. Then he saw it again.

There was more than the shape, for there was a standing horse. He dismounted and, gun in hand, walked cautiously over to the body. It was that of a stranger. In the vague starlight he could see only the outline of the man's features, but it was no one he knew. Then he saw the white of the envelope.

Stooping, his head pounding, he picked it up. There was writing on the back. By the light of a shielded match, he read a painful scrawl:

Mort needs help bad. I wuz dry-gulched. He koodnt kum.

It was written on the back of a letter addressed to Sam Carter, Lost Creek Ranch. Scratched by a dying man.

Thrusting the letter into his pocket, Lance wheeled his horse and rode away down the trail.

Lost Creek Ranch lay ahead and to the south, but he turned the buckskin again and rode away from the trail, skirting a cluster of rocks and heading for the ranch, whose position he had ascertained from Rusty, and knew from a map that had been sent him. He drew his rifle from its boot and put it across his saddle bow.

Still several miles away, he saw a glow in the sky. A glow of burning buildings. His eyes grew hard, and he spoke urgently to Buck. The long-geared yellow horse quickened his pace.

Lance passed what must have been Mort Davis's fence, but some of the posts were down, and the wire was gone. Lance refrained from watching the fire, keeping his eyes on the surrounding darkness. Maybe he was too late. A house was burning, and perhaps Mort Davis was dead. Suddenly he saw a man run out of the shadows.

"That you, Joe?" the man shouted.

Lance reined in, and swung his horse on an angle to the man. The fellow came closer.

"What's the matter?" he demanded. "Can't you hear me?"

The speaker was one of the two men Lance had whipped in the bar earlier that day. They recognized each other at the same instant. With a startled gasp the fellow went for his gun. Lance pulled the trigger without shifting the rifle, and the man grabbed his stomach, sliding from the saddle with a groan.

IV

Without looking down, Lance started toward the glow of the fire, his face set and angry. Had they killed Mort?

They had not. Lance was still several hundred yards away when he saw a rifle flash and heard the heavy bark of Mort's old Sharps. Several shots replied.

Touching spurs to the buckskin, Lance whipped into the circle near the flames at a dead run, snapping three quick shots into a group of men near a low adobe wall. It was a gamble at that speed, but the attacking group was bunched close. There was a cry of pain, and one of them whirled about. He was fully in the light and his chest loomed up. Lance put a shot into him as he flashed abreast of the man, heard a bullet whip past his own ear. Then he was gone into the darkness beyond the light of the flames.

Sliding from saddle, Lance put the rifle to his

shoulder and shot twice. Reloading in haste, he began smoking up every bit of cover near the burning house, taking targets when they offered, and seeking the darkest spots of cover at other times. When his rifle was emptied, he dropped it to his side and opened up with a six-gun.

Men broke from cover and ran for their horses. The old Sharps bellowed in protest at their escape, and one of the men fell headlong. He scrambled up, but made only three steps before he pitched over again, dangerously near the flames.

Again Lance reloaded, then walked forward.

"Mort!" he called. "Come out of there, you old wolf! I know your shootin'!"

A tall, dark-bearded man in a battered black felt hat sauntered down from the circle of rocks at the foot of the cliff.

"Looks like you got here just in time, friend," he said. "You see Sam?"

Briefly Lance explained. Then he jerked his head in the direction the attackers had taken. "Who were they?" he asked.

"I don't know. Mebbe Webb Steele's boys. Him and Lord want me out of here, the worst way." He scratched the stubble on his lean jaws. "Let's have us a look."

Three men had been left behind. With the man Lance had killed out on the prairie, that made four. It had been a costly lesson. Well, Lance told himself, they should have known better than to tackle an old he-wolf like Mort Davis.

A lean, gangling sixteen-year-old strolled down from the rocks. He carried a duplicate of his father's Sharps. He stood beside his father and stared at the bodies.

"Don't look like nobody I ever seen," Mort said thoughtfully, "but Webb and Chet both been a-gettin' in some new hands."

"Pap," the youngster said, "I seen this one in Botalla trailin' with Bert Polti."

Lance studied the man's face. It wasn't one of the men he knew. "Mort," he asked, "where do the Brockmans figger in this?"

The old man puckered his brow. "The Brockmans? I didn't know they was in it. Abel Brockman rode for Steele once, but not no more. He got to sparkin' Tana, and the old man let him go. He didn't like it none, neither."

"It don't look right," Lance said as he rubbed his jaw reflectively. "Lord and Steele are supposed t'be fightin', but so far all I've seen is this gang that trails with Polti. They jumped me in town."

"Watch them Brockmans," Mort said seriously. "They're poison mean, and they never fight alone. Always the two of 'em together, and they got this gunfightin' as a team worked out mighty smooth. They always get you in a spot where you can't get the two to once."

Lance looked around. "Burned all your buildin's, didn't they? Any place you can live?"

"Uhn-huh. We got us a little cave back up here. We lived there before we built us a house. We'll make out. We're used to gettin' along without much. This here's the best place we had for a long time if we can keep it."

"You'll keep it," Lance promised, his face harsh and cold.

Mort Davis had done his share in making the West a place to live. He was getting old now, and deserved the rewards of his work. No big outfit, or outlaws either, was going to drive him off, if Lance could help it.

"Who knew this Sam Carter was to meet me?" he asked. "Or that you were?"

"Nobody I know of," said old Mort. "Carter's a 'puncher who started him a little herd over back of the butte. We worked together some. He was settin' for chuck when them riders come down on us. I asked him to get you."

Lance sketched the trouble in Botalla, then added the account of his run-in with Tana Steele. Mort grinned at that.

"I'd a give a purty to seen that," he said. "Tana's had her head for a long time. Drives that there buck-board like a crazy woman! At that, she can ride nigh anythin' that wears hair, and she will! Best lookin' woman around here, too, unless it's Nita Riordan."

"The woman at Apple Cañon?" Lance asked quickly.

"Yep. All woman, too. Runs that shebang by her-self. Almost, that is. Got her a Yaqui half-breed to help. Ain't nobody to fool with, that Injun."

"You better hole up and stay close to home, Mort," Lance said after a minute. "I'm dead tired, but I've some ridin' to do. I caught a couple of hours' sleep back in the hollow before the trouble."

He swung into saddle and started back over the trail. It was late and he was tired, but he needed more information before he could even start to figure things out. One thing he knew. He must talk to Lord and Steele and try to stop the trouble until they could get together. And he must get more information.

Four of the enemy had died, but even as he told himself that, he remembered that none of the dead men had been in any sense a key man. They were just straw men, men who carried guns and worked for hire, and more could be found to fill their places.

And then Sam Carter was gone. A good man, Sam. A man who could punch cows, and who had enough stuff in him to start his own place, and to fight for what he knew was right. No country could afford to lose men like that.

Suddenly, on the inspiration of the moment, Lance whirled the buckskin from the trail and headed for the Webb Steele spread. He could try talking to Steele, anyway.

He was well into the yard before a man stepped from the shadows.

"All right, stranger! Keep your hands steady. Now light, easy-like, and walk over here."

Lance obeyed without hesitation, carefully keeping his hands in front of him in the light from the ranch house window. A big man stepped from the shadows and walked up to him. Instinctively Lance liked the hard, rugged face of the other man.

"Who are you?" the man demanded.

"Name of Lance. Ridin' by and thought I'd drop in and have a talk with Webb Steele."

"Lance?" Something sparked in the man's eyes. "You the gent had the run-in with Miss Tana?"

"That's me. She still sore?"

"Lance"—the older man chuckled—"shore as I'm Jim Weston, you've let yourself in for a packet of trouble. That gal never forgets! When she come in this afternoon, she was fit to be tied!" He holstered his gun. "What you aimin' to see Webb about?"

"Stoppin' this war. Ain't no sense to it."

"What's your dicker in this?" Weston asked

shrewdly. "Man don't do nothin' unless he's got a angle somewheres."

"What's your job here, Weston?" Lance said.

"Foreman," Weston announced. "Why?"

"Well, what's the ranch makin' out of this war? What are you makin'?"

"Not a cussed thing, cowboy. She's keepin' me up nights, and we got all our 'punchers guardin' fence when they should be tendin' to cows. We're losin' cattle, losin' time, losin' wire, and losin' money."

"Shore. Well, you don't like that. I don't like it, either. But my own angle is Mort Davis. Mort's a friend of mine, and, Weston, Mort's goin' to keep his place in Lost Creek. He'll keep it, or, by glory, there'll be Lord and Steele 'punchers planted under every foot of it."

"Think you're pretty salty, don't you?" Weston demanded, but there was a glint of understanding in his eye. "Well, mebbe you are."

"I've been around, Weston. But that don't matter. You and me can talk. You're an old trail hand yourself. You're a buffalo hunter, too. What you got against Mort?"

"Nothin'. He's a sight better hand and a whole lot better man than lots of 'em ridin' for this ranch now." He shook his head. "I know what you mean, mister. I know exactly. But I don't make the rules for the ranch. Webb does . . . Webb, or Tana."

They stepped inside the ranch house, and Weston tapped on an inner door. At a summons, he opened it. Big Webb Steele was tipped back in his chair across the table from the door. His shirt was open two buttons, showing a hairy chest, and his hard level eyes seemed to stare through and through Lance. To his right was Tana, and, as she saw Lance, she came to her feet instantly, her eyes blazing. Across the table was a tall, handsome man in a plain black suit of fine cut, a man with blue-gray eyes and a small, neatly trimmed blond mustache.

"You!" Tana burst out. "You have the nerve to come out here?"

"I reckon, ma'am," Lance drawled, and he smiled slyly. "I didn't reckon you carried your whip in the house. Or do you carry it everywhere?"

"You take a high hand with my daughter, Lance, if that's your name," Webb rumbled, glancing from Tana to Lance and back. "What happened between you two?"

"Steele," Lance said, grinning a little, "your daughter was drivin' plumb reckless, and we had a few words in which I attempted to explain that the roads wasn't all built for her own pleasure."

Webb chuckled. "Young feller, you got a nerve. But Tana can fight her own battles, so heaven have mercy on your soul."

"Well," Lance said, "you spoke of me takin' a high hand with your daughter. If my hand had been applied where it should have been, it might've done a lot more good."

Webb grinned again, and his hard eyes twinkled. "Son, I'd give a hundred head of cows to see the man as could do that. It'd be right interestin'."

"Father!" Tana protested. "This man insulted me."

"Ma'am," Lance interrupted, "I'd shore admire to continue this argument some other time. Right now I've come to see Mister Steele on business."

"What business?" Webb Steele demanded, cutting short Tana's impending outburst.

"War business. You're edgin' into a three-cornered war that's goin' to cost you plenty. It's goin' to cost Chet Lord plenty, too. I come to see about stoppin' it. I want to get a peace talk between you and Chet Lord an' Mort Davis."

"Mort Davis?" Webb exploded. "That no-account nester ain't goin' to make no peace talk with me! He'll get off that claim or we'll run him off!" Webb's eyes were blazing. "You tell that long-geared high-binder to take his stock and get!"

"He's caused a lot of trouble here," the man with the blond mustache said, "cutting fences and the like. He's a menace to the range." He looked up at Lance. "I'm Victor Bonham," he added. "Out from New York."

Lance had seated himself, and he studied Bonham for an instant, then looked back at Webb Steele, ignoring the Eastern man.

"Mister Steele," he said, "you've got the rep of bein' a square shooter. You come West with some durned good men, some of the real salty ones. Well, so did Mort Davis. Mort went farther West than you. He went on to Santa Fé and to Salt Lake. He helped open this country up. Then he finds him a piece of ground and settles down. What's so wrong about that?" Lance shifted his chair a little, then went on. "He fought Comanches and Apaches. He built him a place. He cleaned up that water hole. He did things in Lost Creek you'd never have done. You'd never have bothered about it but for this fencin' business. Well, Mort Davis moved in on that place, and he's a-goin' to stay. I, for one, mean to see he stays." He leaned forward. "Webb Steele, I ain't been here-abouts long, but I been here long enough to know something mighty funny is goin' on. Mort Davis was burned out tonight, by somebody's orders, an' I don't think the orders were yours or Chet Lord's, either. Well, as I said, Mort stays right where he is, and, if he dies, I'm goin' to move in an' bring war to these hills like nobody ever saw before."

"You talk mighty big for a loose-footed cowhand," Bonham said, smiling coldly. "We might decide not to let you leave here at all."

Lance turned his head slowly at the direct challenge and for a long minute he said nothing, letting his chill green eyes burn into the Easterner. "I don't know what your stake is in this, Bonham," he said evenly, "but when I want to leave here, I'm goin' to. I'll leave under my own power, and, if I have to walk over somebody in gettin' out, I could start with you."

"Better leave him alone, Bonham," a new voice interrupted. "He means what he says."

They all looked up, startled. Rusty Gates stood in the doorway, a sardonic smile on his hard red face.

"I was ridin' by," he explained, "and thought I'd rustle some coffee. But take a friendly tip."

Bonham laughed harshly. "I. . . ."

"Better shut up, New York man," Gates said. "There's been enough killin' tonight. You keep talkin', you're goin' to say the wrong thing." Rusty smiled suddenly, and glanced at Lance, his eyes twinkling. "Y'see"—he lighted his smoke—"I've heard Lance Kilkenny was right touchy about what folks said of him."

V

The name dropped into the room like a bombshell. Tana's hands went to her throat, and her eyes widened. Webb Steele dropped his big hands to the table and his chair legs slammed down. Jim Weston backed up a little, his tongue wetting his lips.

It was Bonham, the man from New York, who Lance Kilkenny was watching, and in Bonham's eyes he saw a sudden blaze of white, killing rage. The man's lips drew back in a thin line. If ever lust to kill was in a man's face, it was in Victor Bonham's then. An instant only, and then it was gone so suddenly that Kilkenny wondered if it had not been a hallucination.

"Did you say . . . Kilkenny?" Webb Steele demanded. "The gunfighter?"

"That's right." Lance's voice seemed to have changed suddenly. "My name is Lance Kilkenny. Mort Davis was in trouble, so I came to help him." He glanced up at Webb. "I don't want trouble, if I can avoid it, but they tried to burn out Mort and wipe him out."

"What happened?" Bonham demanded.

"Four men died," Lance said quietly. "They were not men anybody ever saw ridin' with Steele or Lord." He smiled a little. "Mort's still around, and still able."

Bonham was staring at him. "Yes, I seem to recall something about a man named Kilkenny being nursed by Davis, after a fight."

Lance got up. "Think it over, Mister Steele. I'm not ridin' for war. I never asked for trouble with any man. But Mort's my friend. Even with two old prairie wolves like you and Chet Lord there can be peace. You two should get together with Mort. You'd probably like each other."

Kilkenny stepped backward out of the door and went down the steps to the buckskin. Tana Steele stood there beside the horse. He had seen her slip from the room an instant before he left.

"So," she said, scorn in her voice, "you're a gunman. I might have known it. A man who shoots down other men, less skilled than he, then holds himself up as a dangerous man."

"Ma'am," Kilkenny said quietly, taking the bridle, "I've killed men. Most of 'em needed it, all of 'em asked for it. What you say doesn't help any, or make it worse." He swung into the saddle. "Ma'am," he added softly, "you're shore pretty in the moonlight . . . where a body can't see the meanness in you. You've either got an awful streak somewhere to make you come out here and say somethin' unpleasant, or else"—he grinned impudently—"you're fallin' in love with me."

Tana started back angrily. "In love with you? Why . . . why, you conceited, contemptible. . . ."

But the buckskin swung around and Lance dropped an arm about her waist and swung her from the ground. He was laughing, and then he kissed her. He held her and kissed her until her lips responded almost in spite of themselves. Then he put her down and swung out of the ranch yard at a gallop, lifting his voice in song.

> *Old Joe Clark has got a cow*
> *She was muley born.*
> *It takes a jaybird forty-eight hours*
> *To fly from horn to horn.*

Tana Steele, shaking with anger or some other emotion less easily understood, stood staring after him. She was still staring when his voice died away in the distance.

Then she heard another horse start up, and watched it gallop down the trail after Lance Kilkenny.

It was several minutes before the rider caught up with Kilkenny, and found him, gun in hand, facing downtrail from the shadows at the edge. It was Rusty Gates. "What do you want?" Kilkenny demanded.

Rusty leaned forward and patted his black on the neck.

"Why, I reckon I want to ride along with you, Kilkenny. I hear you're a straight shooter, and I guess you're the only *hombre* I ever met up with could get into more trouble than me. If you can use a man to side you, I'd shore admire to ride along. I got an idea," he added, "that in days to come you can use some help."

"Let's ride, Rusty," Kilkenny said quietly. "It's getting late. . . ."

When Lance Kilkenny rolled out of his blankets in the early dawn, he glanced over at Gates. The redhead was still snoring. Kilkenny grinned, then shook his boots carefully to clear out any wandering tarantulas or scorpions that might have holed up for the night. Grimly he contemplated a hole in his sock. No time for that now. He pulled the sock down to cover the exposed toe, and slid the boot on. Then he got up. Carefully he checked his guns.

He moved quietly out of camp. For ten minutes he made a painstaking search of the area. When he returned to camp, he saddled his horse and rode quietly away. He was back, and had bacon frying when Rusty awakened and sat up.

They had camped on a cedar-covered mountainside with a wide view of Lost Creek Valley. From the ridge above they could see away into the purple distance of the mountains of Mexico. The air was brisk and cool with morning.

Coffee was bubbling in the pot when Rusty walked over.

"You get around, pardner," he said. "Shore, I slept like a log. Hey!" He looked startled and pleased. "You got bacon!"

"Got it last night from that Mexican where we got the *frijoles*. He's got him a half dozen hogs."

Rusty shook himself, and grinned. Then he looked up, suddenly serious.

"Ever see this *hombre* Bonham before?" he asked.

"No." Kilkenny glanced sideward at Gates. "Know him?"

"No. He ain't from around here."

"I wonder."

"You wonder? Why? They said he was from New York. He looks like a pilgrim."

"Yeah, he does." Lance poured coffee into two cups. "But he knew about Mort carin' for me after the fight with the Webers."

"Heard it around probably. I heard that myself." Rusty grinned. "You're too suspicious."

"I'm still alive." Lance Kilkenny grinned wryly.

Rusty nodded. "You got something there. Don't pay to miss no bets. Who you think Bonham is?"

Lance shrugged. "No idea."

"You had an idea last night. You said this fightin' wasn't all Lord an' Steele."

"You think it is?" asked Kilkenny.

Rusty shook his head. "No. Can't be. But who?"

"You been here longer than I have. How does she stack up to you? Who stands to gain but Steele and Lord? Who stands to gain if they both get gunned out or crippled?"

"Nobody. Them two have got it all, everywheres around here. Except for Mort, of course, but Mort ain't grabby. He wants his chunk of Lost Creek Valley, that's all."

"Rusty, you ever see a map of this country?"

"Map? Shucks, no! Don't reckon there is one. Who'd want a map?"

"Maps are handy things," Kilkenny said, sipping his coffee. "Sometimes a country looks a sight different on a map than you think it does. Sometimes, when you get a bird's eye view of things, you get a lot of ideas. Look here."

Drawing with his finger in the sand, Lance Kilkenny drew a roughly shaped V showing the low mountains and hills that girded the Live Oak country. Off to one side he drew in Lost Creek Valley.

"Right here, where it opens on the main valley," he said, "is where Lord and Steele's fence lines come together."

"That's right, plumb right," Rusty agreed. "That's what all the fuss is about. Who gets the valley?"

"But notice," Lance said, "this V-shaped valley that is half Steele's and half Lord's runs from the point of the V up to the wide cattle ranges of Texas. And up there are other cow outfits, bigger than even Lord's and Steele's. Fine stock, too. I come down through there a while back and rode over some fine range. Lots of whiteface bulls brought in up there. The stock is bein' improved. In a few years this is goin' to be one of the greatest stock-raisin' countries in the world. The fences won't make much difference at first except to limit the size of the roundups. There won't be no more four county roundups, but the stock will all improve, more beef per steer, and a bigger demand for it. The small ranchers can't afford to get good bulls. They'll cut fences here and there, as much to let bulls in with their old stock as anything. But that's only part of it. Look at all these broad miles of range. They'll be covered with fat stock, thousands upon thousands of head. It'll be fat stock, good grass, and plenty of water. They'll shift the herds and feed the range off little by little. You've punched cows long enough to have rustled a few head. Huh, we all have now and again. Just

think now, all this is stock country up here above the
V. Now foller my finger." He drew a trail in the dust
down through the point of the V into the country below. "See?" he asked.

Rusty furrowed his brow and spoke thoughtfully.
"You mean somebody could rustle that stock into
Mexico? Shore, but they'd have to drive rustled cows
across the Steele and the Lord spreads, and. . . ." His
eyes narrowed suddenly. "Say, pardner, I get it. You
mean, if Lord and Steele was both out of it, whoever
controlled that V could do as he danged well pleased
down there. Right?"

Kilkenny nodded. "What's this place at the point of
the V?"

"That's Apple Cañon. It's the key to the whole
country, ain't it? And it's a hang-out for outlaws!"

"Shore, Apple Cañon. The Live Oak country is like
a big funnel that will pour rustled stock down into
Mexico, and whoever controls the Live Oak and Apple Cañon controls rustlin' in all this section of
Texas!"

"Well, I'll be durned!" Rusty spat into the dust.
"And that's where Nita Riordan lives!"

Kilkenny got up. "That's right, Rusty. Right as rain,
and we're ridin' to have a little talk with Nita. We're
ridin' now."

Llano Trail lifted up over the low hills from the Live
Oak country and headed down again through Forgotten Pass, winding leisurely across the cactus-
studded desert where only the coyotes prowled and
rattlesnakes huddled in the shade of boulders, and
the chaparral cock ran along the dim trails. Ahead
of the two horsemen, lost like motes in a beam in all

the vast emptiness of the desert, could be seen the great, ragged rocks of the mountains. Not mountains of great height, but huge, upthrust masses of rock, weirdly shaped as though wrought by some insane god.

It was a country almost without water, yet a country where a knowing man might live, for barrel cactus, the desert reservoir, grew there. One might cut a hole in the cactus and during the night or in a matter of an hour or so considerable liquid, cool and fresh, would gather. Always sufficient for life.

The buckskin ambled easily, accustomed to long trails, and accustomed to having his head in pacing over the great distances. His was a long-stepping, untiring walk that ate up the miles.

The sun lifted from behind a morning cloud, and started climbing toward noon. Buzzards wheeled lazily, their far-seeing eyes searching the desert in an endless quest for food.

Slouching in his saddle, his hard face burned almost as red as his hair, Rusty Gates watched the rider ahead of him. It was easy to admire a fighting man, he thought. Always a fighter himself, Rusty fought because it was easy for him, because it was natural. He had punched cows, ridden the cattle trails north. He had, one time and another, tried everything, been everywhere a man could go on a horse. Usually he rode alone. But slowly and surely down the years he began picking up lore on Lance Kilkenny. He had it at his fingertips now.

VI

Everyone, Rusty Gates thought, knew about Hickok; everyone knew about John Wesley Hardin, and about Ben Thompson and his partner, Phil Coe. Not many knew about Kilkenny. He was a man who always moved on. He stayed nowhere long enough to build a solid reputation. Always it seemed, he had just gone. There was something so elusive about him, he had come to seem almost a phantom. Someone picked trouble with him, someone was killed, and Kilkenny was gone. Once they tried to rob him in a gambling den in Abilene. Two men had died. Apaches had cornered him in a ruined house in New Mexico, and, when the Apaches had drawn off, they had left seven dead behind them. In a hand-to-hand fight in Trail City he had whipped three men with fists and chairs. Then, when morning came, he was gone.

The stories of the number of men he had killed varied. Some said he had killed eighteen men, not counting Indians and Mexicans. The cattle buyer back in Dodge, who had made a study of such things, said he had killed not less than twenty-nine. Of this Kilkenny said nothing, and no man could find him to put the question.

"You know," Rusty said suddenly, breaking in on his own thoughts of Kilkenny, "the Brockmans hang out in Apple Cañon."

"Yeah." Kilkenny sat sideward in the saddle, to rest. "I know. We might run into 'em."

"Well," Rusty said, and he rolled the chew of tobacco in his jaws and spat, "there's better places to meet 'em than Apple Cañon. There'll be fifty men there, mebbe a hundred, and all friends of the Brockmans."

Kilkenny nodded and rolled a smoke. Then he grinned whimsically. "What you worried about?" he asked. "You got fifty rounds, ain't you?"

"Fifty rounds?" Gates exclaimed. "Shore, but shucks, man, I miss once in a while." He looked at Kilkenny speculatively. "You seen the Brockmans? They'll weigh about forty pounds more'n you, and you must weigh two hundred. I seen Cain Brockman shoot a crow on the wing!"

"Did the crow have a gun?" drawled Kilkenny.

That, decided Rusty, was a good question. It was one thing to shoot at a target even such a fleeting one as a bird on the wing. It was quite something else when you had to shoot at a man with a flaming gun in his fist. Yes, it made a sight of difference.

"By the way"—Kilkenny turned back in his saddle—"I want the Brockmans myself."

"Both of 'em?" Rusty was incredulous. "Listen, I. . . ."

"Both of 'em," Kilkenny said positively. "You keep the sidewinders off my back."

Rusty glanced up and saw a distant horseman coming toward them at an easy lope. He was still some distance away.

"Somebody comin'," he told Kilkenny. "One man."

"It's Steve Lord," Kilkenny said. "I picked him up a couple of miles back."

"Don't tell me you can see his face from here!" Rusty protested. "Why I can barely see it's a man!"

"Uhn-huh." Kilkenny grinned. "Look close. See the sunlight glintin' on that sombrero? Steve has a hatband made of polished silver disks. Not common."

Rusty spat. Easy enough when you figure it out, he thought, but not many would think of it. Now that it was mentioned he recalled that hatband. He had seen it so many times it no longer made an impression.

Suddenly he asked Kilkenny: "About that Mendoza deal. I was in Sonora after you killed him. I heard he was the fastest man in the world with a gun, then you beat him to it. Did you get the jump or was you just naturally faster?"

Kilkenny shrugged. "Didn't amount to much. He beat me to the draw, though."

"I didn't think anybody ever beat you," observed Rusty.

"He did. Mebbe he saw me a split second sooner. Fact, I think he did."

"How come he didn't kill you?" Rusty glanced at him curiously.

"He made a mistake." Kilkenny wiped sweat from Buck's neck. "He missed his first shot. Never," he added dryly, "miss the first one. You may not get another."

Steve Lord came up at a gallop and reined in

sharply. "You!" he said, as he glanced sharply from one to the other. "Didn't know you was interested down thisaway."

"Takin' a look at Apple Cañon," Rusty said. He grinned widely. "I'm a-goin' to interduce Kilkenny to Nita."

"I heard you was Kilkenny," Steve said, and looked at him curiously. "I've talked to five men before who claimed to know you. Each gave a different description."

"Steve," Lance said, "this fight ain't goin' to do you or your old man any good. I had a talk with Webb Steele. I think we need a meetin' between your dad, Webb Steele, and Mort Davis to iron this trouble out."

"Mort Davis?" Steve exploded. "Why, Dad's threatened to shoot him on sight. They'd never dare get in the same room."

"I'll be there," Kilkenny said dryly. "If any shootin's done, I'll do it."

Steve shook his head doubtfully. "I'll talk to him, but it won't do any good. He's too hard-headed."

"So's Webb Steele," Rusty agreed, "but we'll bring him around."

"No need for anybody to fight," Kilkenny said. "I came in this to help Mort. You and your dad stand to lose plenty if this war breaks wide open. Why fight when it's to somebody else's interest?"

Steve's head jerked around. "What you mean by that?" he demanded.

Kilkenny looked up mildly, then drew deeply on his cigarette, and flicked off the ash before he replied. "Because there's somebody else in this," he said then. "Somebody who wants Lord and Steele out of the way, somebody who stands to win a heap. Find out who that is, and we'll know the reason for range war."

Steve's face sharpened. He wheeled his horse. "You won't find anybody at Apple Cañon!" he shouted. "I saw the Brockmans there!" Then he was gone.

"Scared," Rusty Gates suggested. "Scared silly."

"No," Kilkenny said, "he ain't scared. It's somethin' else."

Yet, as he rode on, he was not thinking of that, or of anything that had to do with this trouble except in the most remote way. He was thinking of himself, something he rarely allowed himself to do beyond caring for the few essential comforts of living, the obtaining of food and shelter. He was thinking of what lay ahead, for in his own mind he could see it all with bitter clarity.

This was an old story, and a familiar one. The West knew it, and would know it again and again in the bitter years to come. Struggle was the law of growth, and the West was growing up the hard way. It was growing up through a fog of gunsmoke, and through the acrid odor of gunpowder, and the sickly sweet smell of blood. Men would die, good men and bad, but strong men all, and a country needed its strong men. Such a country as this needed them doubly bad. Whether it would be today he did not know, but he knew there must be a six-gun showdown, and he had seen too many of them. He was tired. Young in years, he had ridden long on the out trail, and knew only too well what this meant. If he should be the best man, he would live to run again and to drift to a new land where he was not known as a killer, as a gunman. For a few days, a few months, all would go well.

Then there would come a time, as it was coming now, when it was freedom and right, or a fight to the death. Sometimes he wondered if it was worth it.

There was something familiar about this ride. He remembered it all so well. Ahead of him lay trouble, and going to Apple Cañon was typical of him, just what he would do. It was always his method to go right to the heart of trouble, and Apple Cañon seemed to be the key point here.

There was so much ahead. He did not underrate Bert Polti. The snake-eyed gunman was dangerous, quick as a cat, and vicious as a weasel. The man would kill and kill until he was finally put down full of lead. He would not quit, for there wasn't a yellow thing about the man. He would kill from ambush, yes. He would take every advantage, for he did not kill from bravado or for a reputation. He killed to gain his own ends, and for that reason there would be no limit to his killing. Yet at best Polti was a tool. A keen-edged tool, but a tool nevertheless. He was a gunman, ready to be used by a keener brain, and such a brain was using him now. Who it was, Kilkenny could not guess. Somehow he could not convince himself that behind the bluff boldness of Webb Steele lived the ice-cold mind of a killer. Nor from what he could discover was Chet Lord different.

No, the unknown man was someone else, someone beyond the pale of the known, someone relentless and ruthless, someone with intelligence, skill, and command of men. And afterward there would be only the scant food, the harsh living of the fugitive, then again a new attempt to find peace in new surroundings. Someday he might succeed, but in his heart he doubted it.

He was in danger. The thought impressed him little, for he had always been in danger. The man he sought this time would be aware by now that he knew the danger lay not in Steele or Lord, but outside of them. Yet his very action in telling them what he thought might force the unknown into the open. And that was what he must do. He must force the play until at every move it brought the unknown more and more into the open until he was compelled to reveal himself.

The direct attack. It was always best with the adroit man. Such a man could plan for almost anything but continuous frontal attack. And he, Kilkenny, had broken such plots before. But could he break this one? Looking over the field, he realized suddenly that he was not sure. This man was cool, deadly, and dangerous. He would anticipate Kilkenny's moves, and from the shelter of his ghost-like existence he could hunt him, pin him down, and kill him—if he was lucky.

Kilkenny looked curiously at the mountains ahead. Somewhere up there Forgotten Pass went over the mountains and then down to the Río Grande. It wasn't much of a pass, as passes go, and the section was barren, remote. But it would undoubtedly be an easy route over which to take cattle to Mexico, and many of the big ranches down there were buying, often planning to sell the rustled cattle they bought back across the border.

It was almost mid-afternoon before the two riders rounded the shoulder of rock and reined in, looking down the main street of the rickety little town of Apple Cañon. Kilkenny halted his horse and studied the situation. There were four clapboard buildings on one side of the street, three on the other.

"The nearest one is the sawbones," Rusty explained. "He's a renegade from somewheres, but a good doc. Next is the livery stable and blacksmith shop all in one. The long building next door is the bunkhouse. Forty men can sleep there, and usually do. The place after that is Bert Polti's. He lives there with Joe Deagan and Tom Murrow. On the right side the nearest building is Bill Sadler's place. Bill is a gambler. Did a couple of stretches for forgery, too, they say. He cooks up any kind of documents you want. After his place is the big joint of Apple Cañon, the Border Bar. That's Nita's place. She runs it herself. The last house, the one with the flowers around, is Nita's. They say no man ever entered the place. You see"—Rusty glanced at Lance—"Nita's straight, though there's been some has doubted it from time to time. But Nita, she puts 'em right."

"And the place up on the cliffs beyond the town?" Kilkenny wondered. "Who lives there?"

"Huh?" Rusty scowled his puzzlement. "Where you mean?"

Kilkenny pointed. High on a rocky cliff, in a place that seemed to be secure from all but the circling eagles, he could dimly perceive the outline of some sort of a structure. Even in the bright light, with the sun falling fully on the cliff, it was but a vague suggestion. Yet, even as he looked, he caught a flash of light reflecting from something.

"Whoever lives there is a careful man," Kilkenny said dryly. "He's lookin' us over with a glass!"

Rusty was disgusted. "Well, I'll be hanged! I been here three times before, and once stayed five days, and never knowed that place was there."

Kilkenny nodded understandingly. "I'll bet a pretty

you can't see it from the town. I just wonder who it is who's so careful? Who wants to know who comes to Apple Cañon? Who can hide up there and remain unknown?"

"You think . . . ?"

"I don't think anything . . . yet. But I mean to find out, some way. I'm a curious *hombre*, Gates."

VII

Kilkenny was in the lead by a dozen paces as the two rode slowly down the street. A man sitting before the Border Bar turned his head and said something through the window, but aside from that there was no movement.

Yet Kilkenny saw a man with a rifle in some rocks at the end of the street, and there was a man with a rifle in the blacksmith shop. The town, he thought grimly, was well guarded.

They walked their horses to the hitching rail and dismounted. The man sitting on the porch looked at them curiously and spat off the end of the porch. His eyes dropped to Kilkenny's tied-down guns, then strayed to his face. His attention seemed to sharpen, and for an instant his eyes wavered to Rusty.

They stepped up on the porch and Kilkenny pushed through the batwing doors. Rusty loitered on the porch, brushing dust from his clothes.

"Travelin's dry business," he muttered.

"Risky, too," the watcher replied softly. "You're askin' for trouble comin' here with him. The word's out."

"For me, too, then," Rusty said. "We're ridin' together."

"Like that, huh? Can't help you none, cowboy."

"Ain't askin'. Just keep out of the way."

Rusty stepped inside. Kilkenny was standing at the bar. The bartender was leaning or the bar farther down, doing nothing. He was pointedly ignoring them.

As Rusty stepped through the doors, he heard Kilkenny say in a deceptively mild voice:

"I'd like a drink."

The bartender did not move a muscle, and gave no evidence that he heard.

"I'd like a drink," Kilkenny said, and his voice was louder.

The three men sitting in the room were covertly watching. Two of them sat against the west and south walls. The third man was across the room, almost behind Kilkenny, and against the east wall. The bar itself covered most of the north wall except where a door opened at one end. It apparently led to a back room.

"I'm askin' once more," Kilkenny said. "I'd like a drink."

The burly bartender turned toward him then, and his stare was hard, ugly.

"I don't hear you, stranger," he said insultingly. "I don't hear you, and I don't know you."

What happened then was to make legend in the border country. Kilkenny turned and his hand shot out. It grasped the bartender's shirt collar, and jerked—so hard that the bartender slid over the bar and crashed on the floor outside of it.

He hit the floor all sprawled out, then came up with a choking cry of anger. But Kilkenny was ready for him. A sharp left lanced at the bartender's eye, and a wicked right hook in the ribs made his mouth drop open. Then Kilkenny stepped in with a series of smashing, bone-crushing punches that pulped the big man's face and made him stagger back, desperately trying to protect his face with crossed arms. But Kilkenny was remorseless. He whipped a right to the midsection to bring the bigger man's arms down, then hooked a left to the chin that dropped the bartender to all fours.

Stopping quickly, Kilkenny picked the man up and smashed a looping right to the chin. The bartender staggered back across the room and hit the floor in a heap against the far wall.

It was over so suddenly, and Big Ed Gardner, the barkeep, was whipped so quickly and thoroughly that it left the astonished gunmen present staring. Before they could get set for it, Kilkenny sprang back.

"All right!" Kilkenny's voice cracked like a whip in the dead silence of the room. "If you want Kilkenny, turn loose your dogs!"

The name rang like a challenge in the room, and the three men started. The gunman against the west wall touched his lips with a nervous tongue. In his own mind he was sure of one thing. If they went through with their plan he himself was going to die. No one had told them the man they were facing was Kilkenny.

It caught them flat-footed. They sat deathly still, their faces stiff. Then, slowly, the man against the south wall began letting his hand creep away from his guns.

"All right, then," Kilkenny said evenly. "What was you to do here? Gun me down?"

Nobody spoke, and suddenly Kilkenny's gun was in his hand. How it got there no man could say. There was no flicker in his eyes, no dropping of his shoulder, but suddenly his hand was full, and they were looking down the barrel of the .45.

"Talk," Kilkenny said. "You, against the west wall. Tell me who sent you here, and what you was to do. Tell me, or I start shootin' your ears!"

The man swallowed, then wet his lips. "We wasn't to kill you," he said hoarsely. "We was to make you a prisoner."

Kilkenny smiled then. "All right. Mexico's south of here. Travel!"

The three men hit the door in a lump, struggled madly, then all three got out, swung onto their horses, and hit the road on a run.

A rifle cracked outside. Kilkenny stiffened, and stared at Rusty. It rang out twice more. Two neat, evenly spaced shots!

Kilkenny stepped quickly to a place beside the window. One of the fleeing gunmen had been shot down near the end of the street. The others, at almost equal distances, lay beyond.

"Who done that?" Rusty questioned.

"Evidently the boss don't like failure," Kilkenny suggested, thin-lipped. He shrugged. "Well, I still want a drink. Guess I'll have to pour it myself."

"It won't be necessary," said a smooth feminine voice.

Both men turned, startled.

A girl stood at the end of the bar, facing them. She stood erect, her chin lifted a little, one hand resting on the bar. Her skin was the color of old ivory, her hair jet black and gathered in a loose knot at the nape of her neck. But it was her eyes that were most noticeable—and her mouth. Her eyes were hazel, with tiny flecks of a darker color, and they were large, and her lashes were long. Her lips were full, but beautiful, and there was a certain wistfulness in her face, a strange elusive charm that prevented the lips from being sensual. Her figure would have wrung a gasp from a marble statue, for it was seductively curved, and, when she moved, it was with a sinuous grace that had no trace of affectation.

She came forward, and Kilkenny found himself looking into the most amazingly beautiful eyes he had ever seen.

"I am Nita Riordan," she said. "Could I pour you a drink?"

Kilkenny's expression did not change. "Nita Riordan," he said quietly, "you could."

She poured two drinks and handed one to each of them. She did not glance at Big Ed who was beginning to stir on the floor.

"It seems you have had trouble," she said.

"A little . . . hardly worth mentionin'," Kilkenny said with a shrug. "Not so much trouble as any man would cheerfully go through to meet a girl like you."

"You are gallant, *señor*," Nita said, looking directly into his eyes. "Gallantry is always pleasant, and especially so here, where one finds it so seldom."

"Yes," Kilkenny said quietly, "and I am only gallant when I am sincere."

She looked at him quickly, as though anxious to find something in his face. Then she looked away quickly. "Sincerity is difficult to find in the Live Oak, *señor*," she said. "It has little value here."

"It still has value to some," he said, letting his eyes meet hers. "It has to me." He looked down at Big Ed. "I don't like to fight," he said slowly, "but sometimes it is necessary."

Her eyes flashed. "That is not sincere, *señor!*" she retorted severely. "No man who did not like to fight could have done *that!*" With a gesture she indicated Big Ed's face. "Perhaps it is that you like to fight, but do not like *having* to fight. There is a difference."

"Yes." He hitched his guns a little, swallowed his whiskey at a gulp, and looked back at her. "Nita Riordan," he asked quietly, "who is the man in the cliff house above Apple Cañon?"

Her eyes widened a little, then her face set in hard lines. He saw her lips part a little, and saw her quick breath.

"I cannot answer that, *señor*," she said. "If there is a man there, he would resent it. You saw what happened to three who failed? I would not like to die, *señor*. There is much joy in living, even here where there are only outlaws and thieves. Even here the world can be bright, *señor*. For a cause, I can die. For nothing, no. To tell you now would be for nothing."

"They told me you were the boss at Apple Cañon," Kilkenny suggested.

"Perhaps. Things are not always what they seem, *señor*."

"Then I'll go talk to the man on the cliff," Kilkenny

said. "I'll ask him what he wants with Kilkenny, and why he prefers me alive rather than dead."

"Kilkenny?" Nita's eyes widened, and she stepped closer, her eyes searching his face. "You?"

"Yes. Are you surprised?"

She looked up at him, her eyes wide and searching. "I heard long ago, Kilkenny, that you were a good man. I heard that your guns spoke only when the need was great."

"I've tried to keep it that way."

"And you ride alone, Kilkenny?"

"I do.

"And are you never lonely, *señor?* For me, I have found it sometimes lonely."

He looked at her, and suddenly something in his eyes seemed to touch her with fire. He saw her eyes widen a little, and her lips part as though in wonderment. Kilkenny took a half step forward, and she seemed to lean to meet him. Then he stopped abruptly, and turned quickly, almost roughly away.

"Yes," he said somberly, "it has been lonely. It will be more so, now."

He turned abruptly toward the door and had taken three strides when her voice caught him.

"No! Not now to the cliff, *señor.* The time is not now. There will be many guns. Trust me, *señor,* for there will be another time." She stepped closer to him. "That one will be enough for you, *señor,* without others. He is a tiger, a fiend. Perdition knows no viciousness such as his, and he hates you. Why, I do not know, but he hates you with a vindictive hatred, and he will not rest until he kills you. Go now, and quickly. He will not shoot you if you ride away. He wants to face you, *señor.* Why, I do not know."

Kilkenny stopped and turned toward her, his green eyes soft, and strangely warm.

"Nita," he said softly, "I will ride away. He may be the man you love. Mebbe you're protectin' him, yet I don't believe either of them things. I'll trust you, Nita. It might be said that a man who trusts a woman is one who writes his name upon water, but I'll take the chance."

He stepped quickly from the door and walked to the buckskin. Gates, only a step behind, also swung into saddle. They rode out of town at a rapid trot.

"Whew!" Rusty Gates stared at Kilkenny. "Mister, when you try, you shore get results. I never saw Nita Riordan like she was today. Every man along the border's had ideas about her. She's hosswhipped a couple, knifed one, and Brigo killed a couple. But today I'd 'a' swore she was goin' t'walk right into your arms."

Kilkenny shrugged. "Never put too much weight on a woman's emotions, Rusty. They ain't reliable. . . ."

Behind them, in the saloon at Apple Cañon, a door slowly opened. The man who stood in the door looking at Big Ed was even larger than the bartender. He seemed to fill the open door, seemed huge, almost too big to be human. Yet there was nothing malformed about him. He was big, but powerfully, splendidly built, and his Indian face was dark and strangely handsome. He moved down the bar with no more noise than a sliding of wind along the floor, and stopped close to Big Ed.

The bartender turned his battered, bloody face toward him.

"No," Brigo said softly, "you will not betray the *señorita*." His black eyes were dark with intent as he stared into Big Ed's. "If one word of this reaches *him*, I kill you! And when I kill you, *amigo mío*, it will not be nice, the way I kill."

"I ain't talkin'," Big Ed said gruffly through battered lips. "I had enough."

VIII

Nita was standing in her garden, one hand idly fingering a rose, when Brigo came through the hedge. He looked at her, and his lips parted over perfect teeth.

"You have found him, *señorita*," he murmured. "I see that. You have found this man for whom you waited."

She turned quickly. "Yes, Jaime. It is he. But has he found me?"

"Did you not see his face? His eyes? *Sí, señorita*, Jaime think he find you, too. He is a strong man, that one. Perhaps"—he canted his head speculatively—"so strong as Jaime."

"But what of *him*?" Nita protested. "He will kill him. He hates him."

"*Sí*, he hates. But he will not kill. I think now something new has come. This man, this Kilkenny.

He is not the same." Brigo nodded thoughtfully. "I think soon, *señorita*, I return to my home. . . ."

Trailing a few yards behind Kilkenny, Rusty Gates stared up at the wall of the valley. A ragged, pine-spread slope fell away to a rocky cliff, and the sandy wash that ran at the base of it. It was a wild, lonely country. Thinking back over what he knew of this country, he began to see that what Kilkenny had said was the truth. Someone had planned to engineer the biggest rustling plot in Western history.

With this Live Oak country under one brand, cattle could be eased across its range and poured down through the mouth of the funnel into Mexico. By weeding the bigger herds carefully, they might bleed them for years without anyone finding out what was happening. On ranges where cattle were numbered in thousands, a few head from each ranch would not be missed, but in the aggregate it would be an enormous number. This was not the plan of a moment. It was no cowpuncher needing a few extra dollars for a blow-out. This was a steal on the grand scale. It was the design of a man with a brain, and with ruthless courage. Remembering the three men dead back at Apple Cañon, Rusty could see even more. The boss, whoever he was, would kill without hesitation, and on any scale.

Kilkenny was doing some thinking, too. The leader, whoever he was, was a man who knew him. Slowly and carefully he began to sift his past, trying to recall who it might be. Dale Shafter? No, Shafter was dead. He had been killed in the Sutton-Taylor feud. Anyway, he wasn't big enough for this. Card Benton? Too small. A small-time rustler and gambler. One by one he sifted their names, and man after man cropped up in his mind, men who had never rustled, men who were gamblers and gunslingers, men who had cold nerve and who were killers. But somehow none of them seemed to be the type he wanted. And who had fired at him that night in the hollow as he waited for Mort Davis? Who had killed Sam Carter? Was it the same man? Was he the leader? Kilkenny doubted it. This man wanted him alive, and that one had tried to kill him. Indeed, the man had left him for dead. Someone, too, had killed Joe Wilkins. That would take some looking into.

Kilkenny walked his horse down a weathered slide, and crossed a wash. The trail led through a low place walled on each side by low, sandy hills, covered with mesquite, bunch grass, and occasional prickly pear. This job of saving Davis's place for him was turning into something bigger than Lance Kilkenny had dreamed. It was becoming one of the biggest things he had ever walked into. One thing, at least—he had proved to himself that Steele and Lord were out of it. Now if he could bring them to peace with Mort Davis, the only thing left would be to fight it out with the mysterious boss of the gang.

Somehow, more and more, he was beginning to feel that there was more behind this plan than he imagined. This didn't seem like even a simple rustling scheme. Try as he might, he couldn't fit any man into it who he knew. Nor any he had heard of. Yet the fact remained that the leader knew him. Gun experts were as much a part of the West as Indians or cows. It was not an accident that there were so many. And they were, good and bad, essential to the making of the West. Kilkenny was one of the few who saw his own place in the scheme of things clearly. He knew just exactly what he meant, what he was.

Billy the Kid, Pat Garrett, Wes Hardin, Hickok, Ben Thompson, Tom Smith, Earp, Masterson, Tilghman, John Selman, and all the rest were a phase. Most of them cleared out badmen, opened up the West. They fought Indians and they were the tough, outer bark of the pioneering movement. The West was a raw country, and raw men came to it, but there had to be peace. These men, lawless as many of them were, were also an evidence of the coming of law and order, for many of them became sheriffs or marshals, became men who made the West safer to live in.

There could be an end to strife. It was not necessary to go on killing. It could be controlled, and one way to control it was to put the law in the hands of a strong man. Often he was himself a badman, and sometimes he killed the wrong man. But by and large, he kept many other gunmen from killing many more men, and brought some measure of order to the West. Yet this new outlaw leader, this mysterious man upon the cliff, this man who seemed to be pulling the strings from behind the scenes was not one of these. He was different, strange.

Shadows grew longer as the sun sank behind the painted hills, and a light breeze came from the south, blowing up from Mexico. There was a faint smell of dust in the air. Kilkenny glanced at Gates.

"Somebody fogged it along this trail not so long ago," he said. "Somebody who wanted to get someplace in a hurry."

"Yeah." Rusty nodded. "And that don't mean anything good for us."

"Whoever the big mogul in this game is," Kilkenny

said thoughtfully, "will try to break the trouble between Steele and Lord without delay."

"The worst of it is we don't know what he'll do, or where he'll strike next," Gates said.

They were riding at a steady trot toward Botalla when they saw a rider winging it toward them. Rusty flagged him down.

"Hey, what's the rush?" he demanded.

"All tarnation's busted loose!" the rider shouted excitedly. "Lord's hay was set afire, and Steele's fence cut. Some of Lord's boys had a runnin' fight with two of Steele's men, and in town there have been two gunfights!"

"Anybody killed?" Kilkenny demanded anxiously.

"Not yet. Two men wounded on Steele's side!" The cowboy put spurs to his horse and raced off into the night toward the Steele Ranch.

"Well, there goes your cattle war!" Rusty said. "This'll make Lincoln County look like nothin' at all! What do we do now?"

"Stop it, that's what."

Kilkenny whipped the buckskin around and in a minute they were racing down the road toward Botalla.

The main street was empty and as still as death when they dashed up, but there were lights in the Spur, and more lights in the bigger Trail House. Kilkenny swung down, loosened his guns in their holsters, and walked through the batwing doors of the Trail House.

Men turned quickly at his approach, and their voices died down. He glanced from one to the other, and his eyes narrowed.

"Any Steele men here?" he demanded. Two men stepped forward, staring at him, hesitant, but ready for anything.

"We're from Steele's," he said. "What about it?"

"There'll be no war," Kilkenny said flatly. "Neither of you men is firin' a shot at a Lord man tonight. You hear?"

The nearest cowpuncher, a hard-bitten man with a scarred face, grinned, showing broken yellow teeth. "You mean, if I get shot at, I don't fight back? Don't be foolish, *hombre!* If I feel like fightin', I'll fight. Nobody tells me what to do."

Kilkenny's eyes narrowed. "I'm tellin' you." His voice cracked like a whip. "If you shoot, better get me first. If not, I'm comin' after you."

The man's face paled. "Then you talk to them Lord men," he persisted stubbornly, backing off a little. "I ain't anxious for no gunslingin'!"

Kilkenny wheeled and crossed to the Spur. Shoving the doors open, he stepped in and issued the same ultimatum to the Lord men. Several of them appeared relieved. But one man got up and walked slowly down the room toward Kilkenny.

Lance saw it coming. He stood still, watching the man come closer and closer. He knew the type. This man was fairly good with a gun but he wanted a reputation like Kilkenny's, and figured this was the time to get it. Yet there was a lack of certainty in the man's mind. He was coming, but he wasn't sure. Kilkenny was. No man had ever outshot him. He had the confidence given him by many victories.

"I reckon, Kilkenny," the Lord cowpuncher said, "it's time somebody called you. I'm shootin' who I want to, and I ain't takin' orders from you. I hear you're fast. Well, fill your hand!"

He dropped into a gunman's crouch, then froze and his mouth dropped open. He gulped, then swallowed. The gun in Kilkenny's hand was leveled at the pit of his stomach.

Somehow, in the gunfights he'd had before, it had never happened like that. There had been a moment of tenseness, then both had gone for their guns. But this had happened so suddenly. He had expected nothing like that heavy .45 aimed at his stomach, with the tall, green-eyed man standing behind it.

It came to him abruptly that all he had to do to die was drop his hand. All at once, he didn't want to die. He decided that being a gun slick wasn't any part of his business. After all, he was a cowpuncher.

Slowly, step by step, he backed up. Then he swallowed again. "Mister," he said, "I reckon I ain't the *hombre* I thought I was. I don't think there'll be any trouble with the Steele boys tonight."

Kilkenny nodded. "No need for trouble," he said quietly. "There's too much on this range, anyway."

He spun on his heel and walked from the barroom.

For an instant all was still, then the big cowpuncher looked around, and shook his head in amazement.

"Did you see him drag that iron?" he asked pleadingly. "Where the devil did he get it from? I looked, and there it was!"

There was silence for a long time, then one man said sincerely: "I heerd he was gun swift, but nothin' like that. Men, that's Kilkenny!"

Rusty Gates grabbed Kilkenny as he left the Spur.

"Kilkenny," he said, "there's a stranger rode in today. He asked for you. Got somethin' to tell you, he says. Hails from El Paso!"

"El Paso?" Kilkenny scowled. "Who could want to see me from there?"

Gates shrugged. "Purty well lickered, I hear." He lighted a smoke. "But he ain't talkin' fight. Just insists on seein' you."

"Where is he now?"

Kilkenny was thoughtful. El Paso. He hadn't been in El Paso since the Weber fight. Who could want to see him from there?

"He was at the Trail House," Gates said. "Come in just after you took off. Tall, rangy feller. Looks like a cowhand, all right. I mean, he don't look like a gunslinger."

They stepped down off the walk, and started across the street. They had taken but three steps when they heard the sharp rap of a shot. Clear, and ringing in the dark street. A shot, and then another.

"The Trail House!" Gates yelled, and broke into a run.

Kilkenny made the door two steps ahead of him, shoved it open, and stepped in. A cowpuncher lay on his face on the floor, a red stain growing on the back of his shirt. A drawn gun lay near his hand. He was dead.

Slowly Kilkenny looked up. Bert Polti stood across the man's body, a smoking gun in his fist. He looked at Kilkenny and his eyes narrowed. Kilkenny could see the calculation in his eyes, could see the careful estimate of the situation. He had a gun out, and Kilkenny had not drawn. But there was Gates, and in his own mind, reading what the man thought, Kilkenny saw the momentary impulse die.

"Personal fight, Kilkenny," Polti said. "This wasn't no cattle war scrap. He knocked a drink out of my hand. I asked him to apologize. He told me to go to thunder and I beat him to it."

Kilkenny's eyes went past Polti to a cowpuncher from the Lord ranch.

"That right?" he demanded.

"Yeah," the cowpuncher said slowly, his expression unchanging, "that's about what happened."

Polti hesitated, then holstered his weapon and walked outside.

IX

Several men started to remove the body, and Kilkenny walked to the bar. Looking at the liquor in his glass, he heard Rusty speaking to him softly.

"The *hombre* that got hisself killed," Rusty said, "he was the one lookin' for you."

Kilkenny's eyes caught the eyes of the cowpuncher who had corroborated Polti and, with an almost imperceptible movement of the head, brought the man to the bar.

"You tell me," Kilkenny said. "What happened?"

The cowpuncher hesitated. "Ain't healthy to talk around here," he said doubtfully. "See what happened to one *hombre?* Well, he's only one."

"You don't look like you'd scare easy," Kilkenny said dryly. "You afraid of Polti?"

"No." The cowpuncher faced Kilkenny. "I ain't afraid of him, or of you, either, for that matter. Just ain't healthy to talk. Howsoever, while what Polti said was the truth, it looked powerful like to me that Polti deliberately bumped the cowboy's elbow, that he deliberately drew him into a fight."

"What was the 'puncher sayin'? Anythin' to rile Polti?"

"Not that I know of. He just said he had him a story to tell that would bust this country wide open. He did him a lot of talkin', I'd say."

So! Bert Polti had picked a quarrel with the man who had a message for Kilkenny, a man who said he could bust this country wide open. Kilkenny thought rapidly. What had the man known? And why from El Paso? Suddenly a thought occurred to him.

Finishing his drink, he said out of the corner of his mouth: "Stick around and keep your eyes open, Rusty. If you can, pick up Polti and stay close to him."

Stepping from the Trail House, Kilkenny walked slowly down the street, keeping to the shadows. Then he crossed the alley to the hardware store, and walked down its wall, then along the corral, and around it. He moved carefully, keeping out of sight until he reached the hotel.

There was no one in sight on the porch, and the street was empty. Kilkenny stepped up on the porch and through the door. His action seemed leisurely, to attract no attention, but he wasted no time. The old man who served as clerk was dozing behind the desk, and the proprietor, old Sam Duval, was stretched out on a leather settee in the wide, empty lobby. Kilkenny turned the worn account book that served as register, and glanced down the list of names. It was a gamble, and only a gamble.

It was the fifth name down:

Jack B. Tyson, El Paso, Texas.

The room was number 22. Kilkenny went up the stairs swiftly and silently. There was no sound in the hall above. Those who wanted to sleep were already snoring, and those who wanted the bright lights and red liquor were already at the Trail House or the Spur.

Somewhere in his own past, Kilkenny now felt sure, lay the secret of the man in the cliff house, and this strange rider out of the past who had been killed a short time before might be a clue. Perhaps—it was only a slim chance—there was something in his war bag that would be a clue, something to tell the secret of his killing. For of one thing Kilkenny was certain—the killing of Tyson had been deliberate, and not the result of a barroom argument.

The hallway was dark, and he felt his way with his feet, then when safely away from the stair head, he struck a match. The room opposite him was number 14. In a few minutes he tried again, and this time he found room 22.

Carefully he dropped a hand to the knob and turned it softly. Like a ghost he entered the room, but even as he stepped in, he saw a dark figure rise from bending over something at the foot of the bed. There was a quick stab of flame, and something burned along his side. Then the figure wheeled and plunged through the open window to the shed roof outside. Kilkenny went to the window and snapped a quick shot at the man as he dropped from the roof edge. But even as he fired he knew he had missed.

For an instant he thought of giving chase, then the idea was gone. The man, whoever he was, would be in the crowds around the Spur or the Trail House within a matter of minutes, and it would be a fool's errand. In the meantime, he would lose what he sought here.

There was a pounding on the steps, and he turned, lighting the lamp. The door was slammed open, and the clerk stood there, his old chest heaving. Behind him, clutching a shotgun, was Duval.

"Here!" Duval bellowed. "What the consarn you doin' in there? And who's a-shootin'? I tell you I won't have it!"

"Take it easy, Dad," Kilkenny said, grinning. "I came up to have a look at Tyson's gear and caught somebody goin' through it. He shot at me."

"What right you got to go through his gear your ownself?" Duval snapped suspiciously.

"He was killed in the Trail House. Somebody told me he had a message for me. I was lookin' for it."

"Well, I reckon he ain't fit to do no kickin'," Duval admitted grudgingly, "and I heard him say he had a word for Kilkenny. All right, go ahead, but don't be shootin'! Can't sleep no-ways."

He turned and stumped down the narrow stairs behind the clerk.

A thorough examination of the drifting cowpuncher's gear got Kilkenny exactly nowhere. It was typical of a wandering cowpuncher of the period. There was nothing more, and nothing less.

There was still no solution, and out on the plains he knew there had been no settlement of the range war situation. His own warnings had averted a clash tonight, but he could not be everywhere, and sooner or later trouble would break open on the range. Already, in other sections, there was fighting over the introduction of wire. Here, the problem was made worse by the plot of the rustlers, or what he believed was their plot.

He could see a few things. For one, the plan had been engineered by a keen, intelligent, ruthless man. That he had already decided. It would have gone off easily had he not suddenly, because of Mort Davis, been injected into the picture. The fact that the mysterious man behind the scenes hated him was entirely beside the point, even though that hate had evidently become a major motive in the mysterious man's plans.

Well, what did he have? Somewhere behind the scenes were the Brockmans. Neither of them was a schemer. Both were highly skilled killers, clansmen of the old school, neither better nor worse than any other Western gunmen except that they fought together. It was accepted by everyone that they would always fight together. The Brockmans he did not know. From the beginning he had accepted the fact that someday he would kill them. That he did not doubt. Few of the real gunfighters doubted. To doubt would have been to fail. There was the famous case of the duel between Dave Tutt and Bill Hickok as an example. Hickok shot Tutt and turned to get the drop on Tutt's friends before the man shot had even hit the ground. Bill had known he was dead.

The Brockmans no doubt felt as secure in the belief they would win as Kilkenny did. Somebody had to be wrong, but he could not make himself believe that was important. It was something he would have to live through, and it in no way could affect the solution of the plot on which he was working. True, he might be killed, but if so the solution wouldn't matter, anyway.

Every way he looked at it, the only actual member of the outlaw crew he could put a finger on was Bert Polti, and there was a measure of doubt there. He had not seen Polti at Apple Cañon. The man had a house there, but apparently spent most of his time at Botalla. Polti might have killed Wilkins and Carter. It seemed probable he had. Yet there was no proof. No positive proof.

Again and again Kilkenny returned to the realization that he must go up to the cliff house at Apple Cañon. He was not foolish enough to believe he could do it without danger. He had none of the confidence there that he would have in facing any man with a gun, for in the attack on the cliff house, an attack must be made alone. There were too many intangibles, too many imponderables, too many things one could not foresee. Lord and Steele might postpone their fighting for a day or two. They might never fight, but the problem of Lost Creek Valley would not be settled, and the man at Apple Cañon would try to force the issue at the first moment.

Standing in the dimly lit room, Kilkenny let his gaze drift about him. He had turned then, to go, when an idea hit him. The man who had fired at him before, and who had killed Carter, had stopped on the spot to reload. A careful man. But then, a smart man with a gun always was.

Carefully Kilkenny began to search the room, knowing even as he did that the search would be useless, for the man had left too quickly to have left anything. Then he went down the stairs and out back. With painstaking care, and risking a shot from the dark, he examined the ground. He found footsteps, and followed them.

Sixty feet beyond the hotel, he found what he sought. The running man had dropped the shell here, and shoved another into the chamber. Kilkenny picked up the brass shell. A glance told him what he had half expected to find. The unseen gunman was the man who had killed Sam Carter.

"Found somethin'?"

He straightened swiftly. It was Gates, standing there, his hand on his pistol butt, staring at him.

"A shell. Where's Polti?"

"Left town for Apple Cañon, ridin' easy, takin' his time."

"You been with him like I said?" Kilkenny demanded.

"Yeah." Rusty nodded. "He didn't do that shootin' a while ago if that's what you mean. I heard the shootin', then somebody come in and told us you was playin' target down here, and I'd had Polti within ten feet of me ever since you left me."

Kilkenny rubbed his jaw and stared gloomily into the darkness. So it wasn't Bert Polti. The theory that had been half formed in his mind that Polti was himself the unseen killer, and a close agent of the man on the cliff, was shattered.

Suddenly a new thought came to him. What of Rusty? Where had Rusty Gates been? Why had Rusty joined him? Was it from sheer love of battle and admiration for him, Kilkenny? Or for some deeper purpose?

He shook his head. He would be suspecting himself if this continued. Turning, followed by Gates, he walked slowly back to the street. He felt baffled, futile. Wherever he turned, he was stopped. There were shootings and killings, then the killer vanished.

The night was wearing on, and Kilkenny mounted the buckskin and rode out into the desert. He had chosen a place, away from the town, for his camp. Now he rode to it and unsaddled Buck. Within a few minutes he had made his camp. He lit no fire, but the moon was coming up.

It was just clearing the tops of the ridges when he heard a ghost-like movement. Instantly he rolled over behind a boulder and slid his six-gun into his hand. On the edge of the wash, not fifteen feet away, a man was standing.

"Don't shoot, Kilkenny," a low voice drawled easily. "This is a friendly call."

"All right," Kilkenny said, rising to his full height. "Come on up, but watch it. I can see in the dark just as well as the light."

The man walked forward and stopped within four feet of Kilkenny. He was smiling a little.

"Sorry to run in on you thisaway," he said pleasantly, "but I wanted a word or two in private, and you're a right busy man these days."

Kilkenny waited. There was something vaguely familiar about the man. Somewhere, sometime he had seen him.

"Kilkenny," the man said, "I've heard a lot about you. Heard you're a square shooter, and a good man to tie to. Well, I like men like that. I'm Lee Hall."

Lee Hall! The famous Texas Ranger, the man known as Red Hall who had brought law and order to more than one wild Texas cow town, and who was known throughout the border regions! He walked around a little, then stopped.

"Kilkenny," he said slowly, "I suppose you're wonderin' why I'm here? Well, as I said, I've heard a lot about you. I need some help, and I reckon you're the man. What's been happenin' down here?"

Briefly Kilkenny sketched in the happenings since his arrival, and what had happened before, from what he had heard. He advanced his theories about Apple Cañon.

"Nita Riordan?" Hall nodded. "I knew her old man. He came out from the East. Good man. Hadn't lived in Carolina long, came there from Virginia, but good family, and a good man. Heard he had a daughter."

"What did you want me t'do?" Kilkenny asked.

"Go ahead with what you're doin', and keep this cattle war down. I'm puttin' up wire on my own place now, and we're havin' troubles of our own. If you need any help, holler. But you're bein' deputized here and now. Funny thing," Hall suggested thoughtfully, "you tellin' me about the killin' of Wilkins and Carter. These ain't the first of the kind from the Live Oak country. For the past six years now people have been gettin' mysteriously shot down here. In fact, Chet Lord's half-brother was dry-gulched, and not far from Apple Cañon. Name of Destry King. Never found who did it, and there didn't seem any clue. But he told me a few days before he died that he thought he knew who the killer in the neighborhood was."

X

Hall left after over two hours of talk. Kilkenny stretched out with his saddle for a pillow, and stared up at the stars.

Could it be there was some other plot, something that had been begun before the present one? Could the old killings be connected with the new? There was only a hint. Destry King, half-brother to Chet Lord, had been killed when he had thought he had a clue. Had he confided in his half-brother?

It was high time, Kilkenny thought, that he had a talk with Chet Lord. So far circumstances had conspired to keep him so occupied that there had been no chance, and his few messages had been sent through Steve.

Long before daylight Kilkenny rolled out of his blankets and saddled up. He headed out for Cottonwood and the railroad and arrived at the small station to find no one about but the stationmaster.

Carefully he wrote out three messages. One of them was to El Paso, and one to Dodge. The third was to a friend in San Antonio, a man who had lived long in the Live Oak country, and who before that had lived in Missouri.

When he left Cottonwood, he cut across country to the Apple Cañon trail and headed for the Chet Lord Ranch. He was riding through a narrow defile among the rocks, when suddenly he saw two people riding ahead. They were Tana Steele and Victor Bonham.

"Howdy," he said, touching his Stetson. "Nice day."

Tana reined in and faced him.

"Hello," she said evenly. "Are you still as insulting as ever?"

"Do you mean, am I still as stubborn about spoiled girls as ever?" He grinned. "Bonham, this girl's shore enough a wildcat. Plenty of teeth, too, although pretty."

Bonham laughed, but Kilkenny saw his eyes drop to the tied-down guns. When they lifted, there was a strange expression in them. Then Bonham reined his horse around a bit, broadside to Kilkenny.

"Going far?" Bonham asked quietly.

"Not far."

"Chet Lord's, I suppose? I hear he's not a pleasant man to do business with."

Kilkenny shrugged. "Doesn't matter much. I do business with 'em, pleasant or otherwise."

"Aren't you the man who killed the Weber brothers?" Bonham asked. "I heard you did. I should think it would bother you."

"Bother me?" Kilkenny shrugged. "I never think of it much. The men I kill ask for it, an' they don't worry me much one way or the other."

"It wasn't a matter of conscience," Bonham replied dryly. "I was thinking of Royal Barnes. I hear he was a relative of theirs, and one of the fastest men in the country."

"Barnes?" Kilkenny shrugged. "I never gave him a thought. The Webers asked for it, an' they got it. Why should Barnes ask for anything? I've never even seen the man."

"He might," Bonham said. "And he's fast."

Kilkenny ignored the Easterner and glanced at Tana. She had been sitting there watching him, a curious light in her eyes.

"Ma'am," he said slowly, "did you know Destry King?"

"King?" Tana's eyes brightened. "Oh, certainly. We all knew Des. He was Chet Lord's half-brother. Or rather, step-brother, for they had different parents. He was a grand fellow. I had quite a crush on him when I was fourteen."

"Killed, wasn't he?" Kilkenny asked.

"Yes. Someone shot him from behind some rocks. Oh, it was awful. Particularly as the killer walked up to his body and shot him twice more in the face and twice in the stomach."

Bonham sat listening, and his eyes were puzzled as he looked at Kilkenny. "I don't believe I understand," he said. "I thought you were averting a cattle war, but now you seem curious about an outdated killing."

Kilkenny shrugged. "He was killed from ambush. So were Sam Carter and Joe Wilkins. So were several others. Of course, they all cover quite a period of time, but none of the killin's was ever solved. It looks a bit odd."

Bonham's eyes were keen. He looked as if he had

made a discovery. "Ah, I see," he said. "You imply there may be a connection? That the same man may have killed them all? That the present killings weren't part of the range war?"

"I think the present killin's was part of the range war," Kilkenny said positively, "but the way of killin' is like the killin's in them old crimes." He turned to Tana. "Tell me about Des King."

"I don't know why I shouldn't," she said. "As I told you, Des was a wonderful fellow. Everyone liked him. That was what made his killing so strange. He was a fast man with a gun, too, and one of the best riders on the range. Everyone made a lot of Des. Several riders had been shot, then an old miner. I think the first person killed was an old Indian. Old Comanche, harmless enough . . . used to live around the Lord Ranch. Altogether I think there were seven men killed before Des was. He started looking into it, having an idea they were all done by the same man. He told me once that I shouldn't go riding, that I should stay home and not ride in the hills. Said it wasn't safe."

"You rode a good deal as a youngster?"

"Oh, yes. There weren't many children around, and I used to ride over to talk and play with Steve Lord. Our fathers were good friends then, but it was six miles over rough country to his house then . . . wild country."

"Thanks. I'll be gettin' on. Thanks for the information, ma'am. Glad to have seen you again, Bonham."

Bonham smiled. "I think we may see each other often, Kilkenny."

Suddenly Tana put out her hand. "Really, Kilkenny," she said, "I'm sorry about that first day. I knew you were right that first time, but I was so mad I hated to admit it. I'm sorry."

"Shore." Kilkenny grinned. "But I'm not takin' back what I said about you."

Tana stiffened. "What do you mean?"

"Mean?" He raised his eyebrows innocently. "Didn't I say you were mighty pretty?"

He touched his spurs lightly to the buckskin's flanks and took off at a bound. After a brisk gallop for about a quarter of a mile he slowed down to a walk, busy with his thoughts.

Hall's information had been correct. Des King had had a theory as to who the killer was. He had been steadily tracking him down. Then the killer must have seen how near he was to capture, and had killed King. But what was the thread that connected the crimes? There was no hint of burglary or robbery in any of them. Yet there had to be a connection. The pattern was varied only in the case of King, for he had been shot several times, shot as if the killer had hated him, shot through and through. And why a harmless old Indian? A prospector? Several riders? Kilkenny rode on, puzzling.

Ahead of him the ground dipped into a wide and shallow valley down which led the cattle trail he was following. Nearby were rocks, and a wash not far away.

Kilkenny rolled a smoke and thoughtfully lighted it. He flipped the match away and shoved his sombrero back on his head. The situation was getting complicated, and nowhere closer to a solution. The Steele and Lord fight was hanging fire. Twice there had been minor bursts of action, and then both had petered out after his taking a hand, yet it wasn't fooling anybody. The basic trouble was still there, and Davis hadn't been brought together with Steele and Lord.

Above the Live Oak, the country was seething, too. Wire cutters were loose, and fences were torn down nightly. Cattle were being rustled occasionally, but in small bunches. There was no evidence they had come through the Live Oak country and down to Apple Cañon.

Kilkenny had almost reached the Lord ranch house when he saw Steve come riding toward him, a smile on his face. Steve looked closely at Kilkenny, his eyes curious.

"Didn't expect to see you over here," he said. "I figgered you was goin' back to Apple Cañon!"

"Apple Cañon?" Kilkenny asked. "Why?"

"Oh, most people who see Nita want to see her again," Steve said. "You lookin' for Dad?"

"That's right. Is he around?"

"Uhn-huh. That's him on the roan hoss."

They rode up to the big man, and Kilkenny was pleased. Chet Lord was typically a cattleman of the old school. Old Chet turned and stared at Kilkenny as he approached, then looked quickly from him to Steve. He smiled and held out his hand.

"Kilkenny, huh? I thought so from the stories I been hearin'."

Lord's face was deeply lined, and there were creases of worry about his eyes. Either the impending cattle war was bothering Chet Lord or something else was. He looked like anything but a healthy man now. Yet it wasn't a physical distress. Something, Kilkenny felt instinctively, was troubling the rancher.

"Been meanin' to see you, Mister Lord," Kilkenny

said. "Got to keep you an' Steele off each other's backs. Then get you with Mort Davis."

"You might get me and Webb together," Lord said positively, "but I ain't hankerin' for no parley with that cow-stealin' Davis."

"Shucks." Kilkenny grinned. "You mean to tell me you never rustled a cow? I'll bet you rustled aplenty in your time. Why, I have myself. I drove a few over the border couple of times when I needed a stake."

"Well, mebbe," said Lord. "But Davis come in and settled on the best piece of cow country around here. Right in the middle of my range."

"Yours or Steele's," Kilkenny said. "What the devil? Did you expect him to take the worst? He's an old buffalo hunter. He hunted through there while you was still back in Missouri."

"Mebbe. But we used this range first."

"How'd you happen to come in here? Didn't like Missouri?"

Chet Lord dropped a hand to the pommel of his saddle and stared at Kilkenny. "That's none of your cussed business, gunman! I come here because I liked it . . . no other reason."

His voice was sharp, irritated, and Kilkenny detected under it that the man was dangerously near the breaking point. But why? What was riding him? What was the trouble?

Kilkenny shrugged. "It don't mean anythin' t'me. I don't care why you came here. Or why you stay. By the way, what's your theory about the killin' of Des King?"

Chet Lord's face went deathly pale, and he clutched suddenly, getting a harder grip on the saddle horn. Kilkenny saw his teeth set, and the man turned tortured, frightened eyes at Kilkenny.

"You better get," Lord managed after a minute. "You better get goin' now. If you'll take a tip from a friendly man, keep movin'."

He wheeled his horse and walked it away. For a moment, Kilkenny watched him, then turned his head to find Steve staring at him, in his eyes that strange, leaping white light Kilkenny had seen once before.

"Don't bother Dad," Steve said. "He ain't been well lately. Not sleepin' good. I think this range war has got him worried."

"Worried?"

"Uhn-huh. We need money. If we lose many cows, we can't pay off some debts we've got."

After a few minutes' talk, Kilkenny turned his buckskin and rode away from the ranch. He rode away in a brown study. Something about Des King had Chet Lord bothered. Was Lord the murderer of his own step-brother? But no! Chet might shoot a man, but he would do it in a fair, stand-up fight. There was no coyote in Chet Lord any more than there was in Webb Steele or Mort Davis.

XI

More and more the tangled skein of the situation became more twisted, and more and more he felt the building up of powerful forces around him, with nothing he could take hold of. He was in serious danger, he knew, yet danger was something he had always known. It was the atmosphere he had breathed since he had gunned his first man in a fair stand-up fight at the age of sixteen.

There was something about Chet Lord's fear that puzzled him. Lord had seemed more to be afraid for him, than for himself. Why? What could have aroused Lord's fear so? And what had made the man so upset? Was he really in debt? Somehow, remembering the place and the fat cattle, and knowing the range as he did, Kilkenny could not convince himself that Steve's statement was true. It was a cover-up for something else. There was fresh paint, all too rare in the Texas of those days, and new barbed wire, and new ranch buildings, and every indication that money was being spent.

Yet somewhere on that range a killer was loose, a strange, fiendish killer. It was unlike the West, a man who struck from ambush, a man who would kill an old Indian, who would ambush a prospector, and who would shoot down lonely riders. Somewhere, in all the welter of background, there was a clue.

Kilkenny lifted his head and stared gloomily down the trail. He was riding back through the shallow valley and down the cattle trail along which he had just traveled. He looked ahead, and for some reason felt uneasy.

Lord's gettin' his fear into me, he told himself grimly. *Still, in a country like this a man's a fool to ride twice over the same trail.*

On the impulse of the moment, he wheeled his horse and took it in two quick jumps for the shelter of the wash. As the horse gathered himself for the second jump, a shot sounded, and Kilkenny felt the whip of the bullet past his head. Then another and another.

But Buck knew what shooting was, and he hit the wash in one more jump and slid into it in a cascade of sand and gravel. Kilkenny touched spurs to the horse and went down the wash on a dead run. That wash took a bend up above. If he could get around that bend in a hurry, he might outflank the killer.

He went around the bend in a rush and hit the ground running, rifle in hand. Flattening himself behind a hummock of sand and sagebrush, he peered through, trying to locate the unseen rifleman. But he moved slightly, trying to see better, and a shot clipped by him, almost burning his face. A second shot kicked sand into his eyes. He slid back into the wash in a hurry.

"The devil!" he exploded. "That *hombre* is wise! Spotted me, did he?"

He swung into saddle and circled farther, then tried again from the bank. Now he could see into the nest of rock where the killer must have waited and from which the first shot had come. There was no one in sight. Then he saw a flicker of movement among the rocks higher up. The killer was stalking him!

Crouching low, he waited, watching a gap in the rocks. Then he saw the shadow of a man, only a blob of darkness from where he huddled, and he fired. It was a quick, snapped shot and it clipped the boulder and ricocheted off into the daylight, whining wickedly.

Then it began—a steady circling. Two riflemen trained in the West, each maneuvering for a good shot, each wanting to kill. Twice Kilkenny almost got in shots, and then one clipped the rock over his head. An hour passed, and still he had seen nothing. He circled higher among the rocks and, after a long search, found a place where a man had knelt. On the ground nearby was a rifle shell, a shell from a Winchester carbine, Model 1873.

Mebbe that'll help, he told himself. *Ain't too many of 'em around. The Rangers mostly have 'em. And I've got one. I think Rusty still uses his old Sharps, and I expect Webb Steele does. But say!* He stopped, scowling. *Why, Tana Steele has a 'Seventy-Three! Yeah, and if I ain't mistaken, so has Bonham!*

This couldn't continue. Three times now the killer had tried shots at him, if indeed all had been fired by the same man. Bonham was in the vicinity, but why should Bonham shoot at him? Tana Steele was near, also, and Tana might have a streak of revenge in her system. But Chet Lord wasn't far away, either, and there were other men on the range who might shoot. Above all, this was an uncertain country where every man rode with an itch in his trigger finger these days.

One thing was sure. He was no nearer a solution than he had been. He had shells from the killer's six-gun and now from a Winchester 1873. Yet he had no proof beyond a hunch that the attempts at killing had been made by the same man.

The mysterious boss of Apple Cañon apparently had not wanted him killed. Hence, why the attempts now, if he were responsible? Or had the attempts, as he had suspected before, been the work of different men? But if not the Apple Cañon boss, and if not Bert Polti, then who? And why? Who else had cause to kill him?

Yet, so far as he knew, many of the mysterious killings in the past had been done without cause. At least, there had been no reason of which he was aware. Underneath it all, some strange influence was at work, something cruel and evil, something that was not typical of the range country where men settled their disputes face to face.

Kilkenny kept to back trails in making his way back to Botalla. The thing now was to get Steele, Lord, and Davis together and settle their difficulties if they could be settled. Knowing all three men, and knowing the kind of men they were, he had little doubt of a settlement.

The two bigger cattlemen were range hungry and Davis was stubborn. Like many men, each of them wanted to work his own way, each was a rugged individualist who had yet to learn that many more things are accomplished by co-operation than by solitary efforts.

Botalla lay quietly under the late sun when the buckskin walked down the street. A few men were sitting around, and among them were several cowpunchers from the Lord and Steele spreads. Kilkenny reined in alongside a couple of them. A short cowpuncher with batwing chaps and a battered gray sombrero looked up at him from his seat on the boardwalk, rolled his quid in his jaws, and spat.

"How's it?" he said carefully.

"So-so." Kilkenny shoved his hat back on his head and reached for the makings. "You're Shorty Lewis, ain't you?"

The short cowpuncher looked surprised. "Shore am. How'd you know me?"

"Saw you one time in Austin. Ridin' a white-legged roan hoss."

Lewis spat again. "Well, I'll be durned! I ain't had that hoss for three year. You shore got a memory."

Kilkenny grinned and lighted his cigarette. "Got to have, livin' like I do. An *hombre* might forget the wrong face!" He drew deeply on the smoke. "Shorty, you ride for Steele, don't you?"

"Been ridin' for him six year," Lewis said. "Before that I was up in the Nations."

"Know Des King?" Kilkenny asked casually.

Lewis got to his feet.

"Just what's on your mind, Kilkenny?" he asked. "Des King was a half-brother of Lord's, but we rode together up in the Nations. He was my friend."

Kilkenny nodded. "I thought mebbe. Lewis, I got me a hunch the *hombre* that killed Wilkins and

Carter also killed Des King. I got a hunch that *hombre* tried to kill me."

"But King was killed some time ago," Lewis protested. "Before this fight got started."

"Right. But somebody is ridin' this range that has some other reason for killin' men. Somebody who's cold-blooded and vicious like nobody you ever seen, Shorty. Somebody that's blood-thirstier than an Apache."

"What kind of man would be killin' like that?" Lewis demanded. Then he nodded. "Mebbe you got somethin', feller. Nobody would've shot into Des after he was down, mebbe already dead, except somebody who hated him poison mean, or somebody who loved killin'."

"There was an old Indian killed, and a prospector," reminded Kilkenny. "Know anything about them?"

"Yeah. Old Yellow Hoss was a Comanche. He got to hittin' the bottle purty hard and Chet Lord kept him around and kept him in likker because of some favor the old Injun done for him years ago. Well, one day they found him out on the range, shot in the back. No reason for it, so far's anybody could see. The prospector's stuff had been gone over, but nothin' much was missin' except an old bone-handled knife . . . a Injun scalpin' knife he used to carry. Had no enemies anybody could find. That seems to be the only tie up betwixt 'em."

"Where were they killed?"

"Funny thing, all of 'em were killed betwixt Apple Cañon and Lost Creek Valley. All but one, that is. Des King was killed on the Lord range not far from Lost Creek."

Kilkenny nodded. "How about you tellin' Chet to

come in tomorrow mornin' for a peace talk, Shorty? I'll get Webb and Mort Davis in."

After he had told some of the Steele hands that he wanted to see Webb, Kilkenny rode down to the general store. Old Joe Frame was selling a bill of goods to Mort Davis's boy. Through him word was sent to Mort.

Rusty was waiting on the boardwalk in front of the Trail House when Kilkenny returned. He looked up and grinned.

"If you swing a loop over all three of 'em," he said, "you're doin' a job, pardner. It'll mean peace in the Live Oak."

"Yes," Kilkenny said dryly, "peace in the Live Oak after the gang at Apple Cañon is rounded up."

Gates nodded. Touching his tongue to a cigarette paper, he looked at Kilkenny. "May not be so hard. You been makin' friends, pardner. Lots of these local men been a-talkin' to me. Frame, Winston, the lawyer, Doc Clyde, Tom Hollins, and some more. They want peace, and they want some law in Botalla. What's more, they'll fight for it. They told me I could speak for 'em, say that when you need a posse, you can dang' soon get it in Botalla."

"Good." Kilkenny nodded with satisfaction. "We'll need it."

"Think any effort'll be made to break up your peace meetin'?" Rusty asked. "I been wonderin' about that."

"I doubt it. Might be. They better not, if they are goin' to try, because I got us a plan."

Morning sunlight bathed the dusty street when the riders from the Steele Ranch came in. There were just Webb, Tana, Weston, and two Steele riders. One of them was Shorty Lewis.

Rusty and Kilkenny were loafing in front of the Trail House.

"She's shore purty," Rusty said thoughtfully, staring after Tana as she rode toward the hotel. "Never saw a girl so purty."

Kilkenny grinned. "Why don't you marry the gal?" he asked. "Old Webb needs him a bright young son-in-law, and Tana's quite a gal. Some spoiled, but I reckon a good strong hand would make quite a woman of her."

"Marry *her?*" Rusty exploded. "She wouldn't look at me. Anyway, I thought mebbe you had your brand on her."

"Not me." Kilkenny shook his head. "Tana's all right, Rusty, but Kilkenny rides alone. No man like me has a right to marry and mebbe break some woman's heart when someday he don't reach fast enough. No, Rusty, I've been ridin' alone, and I'll keep it up. If I was to change, it wouldn't be Tana. I like to tease her a bit, because she's had it too easy with men and with everything, but that's all."

He got up, and together they walked down the street toward the hotel. Webb Steele and Tana were idling about the lobby. In a few minutes, Chet Lord came in, followed by Steve. Then the door opened, and Mort Davis stood there, his tall, lean figure almost blocking the door. He stared bleakly at Steele, then at Lord, and walked across the room to stand before the cold fireplace with his thumbs hooked in his belt.

"Guess we better call this here meetin' to order," Kilkenny suggested, idly riffling a stack of cards.

"The way I hear it, Steele an' Lord are disputin' about who fences in Lost Creek, while Mort here is holdin' Lost Creek."

"He's holdin' it," Steele said harshly, "but he ain't got no right to it."

"Easy now," Davis said. "How'd you get that range of your'n, Steele? You just rode in an' took her. Well, that's what I done. Anyway, I figgered on Lost Creek for ten year. I come West with Jack Halloran's wagon train fifteen year ago and saw Lost Creek then."

"Huh?" Webb Steele stiffened. "You rode with Halloran? Why, Tana's mother was Jack Halloran's sister."

Davis stared. "Is that a fact? You all from Jackson County?"

"We shore are! Why, you old coot, why didn't you tell me you was *that* Davis? Jack used to tell us about how you and him. . . ." Webb stopped, looking embarrassed.

"Go right ahead, Steele," Kilkenny said dryly. "I knew if you and Mort ever got together and quit fightin' long enough to have a confab, you'd get along. Same thing with Lord here. Now, listen. There ain't no reason why you three can't get together. You, Steele, are importin' some fine breedin' stock. So is Lord. Mort hasn't got the money for that, but he does have Lost Creek, and he's got a few head of stock. I don't see why you need to do any fencin'. Fence out the upper Texas stock, but keep the Live Oak country, this piece of it, as it is. Somebody has moved into Apple Cañon and has gathered a bunch of rustlers around. Well, they've got to be cleared out. Lock, stock, and barrel. I'm takin' that on myself."

"We need some law here," Webb Steele said suddenly. "How about you becomin' marshal?"

"Not me," Kilkenny said. "I'm a sort of deputy now. Lee Hall dropped by my camp the other night and he gave me this job. Makes it sort of official. But before I leave here, I'm goin' to take care of that bunch at Apple Cañon. Also," he added, "I'm goin' to get the man responsible for all these killin's."

His eyes touched Chet Lord's face as he spoke, and the big rancher's face was ashen.

Steve spoke up suddenly. "You sound as if you believed there's no connection between the killin's and this fight?"

"Mebbe there is, mebbe there isn't. What I think is that the man who's doin' the killin' is the same man who killed Des King, the same who killed old Yellow Horse."

XII

Chet Lord was slumped in his chair and Kilkenny thought he had never seen a man look so old. Tana Steele was looking strange, too, and Kilkenny, looking up suddenly, saw that her face was oddly white and puzzled.

"I think," Kilkenny said, after he had made his disturbing accusation about the mysterious killer, "that Des King knew who the killer was. He was killed to keep him from exposing that rattler, and also, I believe, because the killer hated King."

"Why didn't he tell then?" Steve Lord demanded.

Kilkenny looked up at Steve. "Mebbe he did," he said slowly. "Mebbe he did."

"What d'you mean by that?" Webb Steele demanded. "If he told, I never heard nothin' of it."

Kilkenny sat quietly, but he could see the tenseness in Tana's face, the ashen pallor of Chet Lord, slumped in his chair, and Steve's immobile, hard face.

"Des," Kilkenny said slowly, "had a little hangout in the hills. In a box cañon west of Forgotten Pass. Well, Des kept a diary, an account of his search for the killer. He told Lee Hall that, and Lee told me. Tomorrow I'm goin' to that cabin in the cañon and get that diary. Then I'll know the whole story."

"I think . . . ," Tana began, but got no further because suddenly there was a hoarse yell from the street and the sharp bark of a six-gun. Then a roll of heavy firing.

Kilkenny left his chair with a bound and kicked the door open. There was another burst of firing as he lunged down the steps. His foot caught and he plunged headlong into the dust, his head striking a rock that lay at the foot of the steps.

Rusty and the others plunged after him. They were just in time to see two big men lunging for their horses while rifles and pistols began to bark from all over town. One of the big men threw up his pistol and blazed away at the group on the porch. Rusty had just time to grab Tana and push her against the wall as bullets spattered the hotel wall.

Kilkenny, his head throbbing from the blow of his fall, crawled blindly to his feet, eyes filled with dust. There was a wild rattle of hoof beats, then horses charged by him. One caught him a glancing blow with its shoulder and knocked him flat again. There was another rattle of gunfire, and then it was over.

Kilkenny got to his feet again, wiping the dust from his eyes.

"What was it?" he choked. "What happened?"

Frame had come running up the street from the general store carrying an old Sharps rifle.

"The Brockmans!" he shouted. "That's who it was!

Come to bust up your meetin' and wipe you out, Kilkenny. Jim Weston, Shorty, and the other Steele rider tried to stop 'em."

Webb Steele stepped down, eyes blazing. "So that was the Brockmans that rode by! Cussed near killed my daughter!"

"Yeah," Frame agreed. "They got Weston. Lewis is shot bad, and they got the other boy . . . O'Connor, I think his name was. Weston never had a chance. He dropped his hand for his gun and Cain drilled him plumb center. Abel took Lewis, and they both lowered guns on the last one. It was short and bloody, and I don't think either of them got a scratch."

"This busts it!" Steele shouted. "We'll ride to Apple Cañon and burn that bunch to the ground! They've gone too far!"

Tana Steele was straightening up. She looked at Rusty. "You saved my life," she said quietly. "If you hadn't thrown yourself in front of me, I might have been killed."

Rusty grinned, and suddenly Kilkenny saw blood on his shirt.

"You better take him inside, Tana," he said. "He's hit."

"Oh!" Tana caught Rusty quickly. "You're hurt!"

"It ain't nothin'," Rusty, said. "Shucks, I. . . ." He slumped limply against the wall.

Steele and Frame picked him up and started inside. The Lords, father and son, headed down the street.

Suddenly Kilkenny heard the porch boards creak, and a low voice, Bert Polti's, spoke.

"All right, Mister Lance Kilkenny, here's where you cash in."

As Kilkenny recognized the voice, he whirled and

drew. Polti's gun flamed as Kilkenny turned, and he felt the hot breath of the bullet. Then he fired.

Polti staggered, but caught himself. His head thrust forward, he tried to squeeze off another shot, but the six-gun wouldn't come up. He tried, then tried again, but slowly the gun muzzle lowered, he toppled, and fell headlong.

Steele came charging to the door, gun in hand. He took one look, then holstered his gun.

"Polti, huh? He's had it a comin' for a long time. How come he drew on you?"

Kilkenny explained briefly. Steele nodded. "Figgered with your back turned he had a chance to get you. Well, he didn't make it. Good work, son! You beat the rope for him with that bullet." He looked down at the fallen man. "Plumb center, too. Right through the heart."

Kilkenny looked up. "Steele, get your boys ready and stand by. Have Lord do the same. I'm goin' after the Brockmans myself, and, when I come back, we're goin' t'clean up Apple Cañon. Right now the main thing is to get the Brockmans out of the way."

"You goin' after 'em alone?" Steele was incredulous. "They just gunned down three men!"

"Uhn-huh." Kilkenny grinned, without humor. "But there's only two of 'em. I'll go after 'em. You see that somebody takes care of Rusty."

Steele grinned then. "I reckon Tana's doin' that."

A half hour later, stocked with grub for three days, Kilkenny rode out of town on the trail of the Brockmans. For the first half mile they had ridden hard, then had slowed down, saving their horses when they noticed no pursuit. They were both shrewd riders and they would save their horses while confusing their trail.

Three miles from town they had turned from the trail and taken to the rough country toward the lava beds. The trail became steadily more difficult, and wound back and forth across the desert, weaving around clusters of boulders and following dry washes. They had used every trick of desert men to lose their trail, and yet it could be followed. Still, time and again, Kilkenny was compelled to dismount from his horse, search the ground carefully, and follow as much by guess and instinct as by sight or knowledge.

It became evident the Brockmans were traveling in a big circle. Picturing the country in his mind, Kilkenny began to believe they were heading for Cottonwood. But why Cottonwood? Could they by chance know of the wires he had sent? Were they afraid of what those wires might mean to them? Or were they watching the station on orders from the unknown in the cliff house?

On impulse, Kilkenny swung the buckskin from the trail and cut across country for Cottonwood. Now he kept to the cover, and rode steadily by gulch and by cañon, toward the little station.

That night he bedded down on the same creek that ran into Cottonwood, but about six miles upstream from the town. His camp was a dark camp, and he tried no fire, eating a cold supper and falling asleep under the stars.

With daylight he was up. Carefully he cleaned his guns and reloaded them. He knew the Brockmans, and was under no misapprehension as to their skill. They were good, and they were dangerous together. If only by some fortune or stratagem he could catch each one alone. It was a thought, but the two ate together, slept beside each other, walked the streets together, and rode together.

It was almost nine o'clock before he saddled up and rode into town. If his calculations were correct, he was still ahead of the Brockmans. He would still make Cottonwood first, but, if not first, at almost the same time.

When he reached town, he tied Buck under the trees on the edge of the stream, and walked across the little log footbridge to the street. There was nothing much in Cottonwood. On one side of the street was the little stream, never more than six feet wide, and a row of cottonwood trees backed by some bunches of willow beyond the stream. On the opposite side were the telegraph office and station, a bar, a small store, and four or five houses. That was about all. Kilkenny walked into the station.

"Any messages for me?" he asked.

The stationkeeper nodded and stretched. "Yeah. Just come in. Three of 'em."

He passed the messages across to Kilkenny, broke a straw off the broom, and began to chew it slowly and carefully, glancing out the window occasionally.

"Reckon there'll be some fireworks now," he said, nodding at the messages. "It shore beats the devil."

Kilkenny pocketed the messages without glancing at them, left the station, and crossed the street to the willows, after a brief glance into the bar. On the far side of the bridge he lay down on the grass and began to doze.

He was still there an hour later when the stationmaster came to the door. "Hossmen comin' out of the brakes, stranger!" he called out. "They look powerful like the Brockmans!"

Kilkenny got up slowly and stretched. Then he leaned against the trunk of a huge cottonwood. Waiting.

The riders turned into the road leading to Cottonwood at a fast trot. There were three of them now. Kilkenny did not know the third man. They came on at a fast trot. As they reined in suddenly in front of the bar, Kilkenny stepped out and walked across the bridge.

Abel Brockman had swung down. Hearing the footsteps on the bridge, he turned and glanced over his shoulder. His hand stiffened, and he said something, low-voiced, and began to turn. The Brockmans had been caught off side.

Kilkenny stepped out quickly from under the trees. "All right!" he yelled.

Up the street a man sitting on a bench in front of a door suddenly fell backward off the bench and began to scramble madly for the door. Cain Brockman was still in the saddle, but he grabbed for his gun. As Abel's hand moved, Kilkenny's hand whipped down in the lightning draw that had made him famous. His gun came up, steadied, and even as Abel's six-shooter cleared his holster, Kilkenny fired.

Walking toward them he opened up with both guns. Abel got off a shot, but he had been knocked off balance by Kilkenny's first shot, and he staggered into the hitch rail. Cain's horse reared wildly, and the big man toppled backward to the ground. Kilkenny walked on, firing. Abel went to one knee, swung up, lurching, and his guns began to roar again.

Unbelieving, Kilkenny stopped and steadied his

hand, then fired again. He was sure he had hit Abel Brockman with at least four shots.

Abel started to fall, and, swinging on his heel, Kilkenny tried to get a shot at the third man. But, grabbing Cain Brockman, the fellow dragged him around the corner out of sight. One of the horses trotted after them. Gun in hand, Kilkenny walked up to Abel.

Lying on his back in the dust, hand clutching an empty gun, his chest covered with blood, Abel Brockman stared at him.

"Cain'll kill you for this!" he snarled, his eyes burning. "Cain'll . . . oh!" Abel's face twisted with agony. "Cain . . . where's . . . ?"

One hand, thrust up and straining, fell into the dust, and Kilkenny, who had lifted his eyes toward the corner, started toward it.

Then he heard a sudden rattle of hoofs, and he broke into a run.

The third man, whoever he had been, with Cain Brockman across his saddle was taking off up the trail.

Kilkenny stared after them a moment, then shrugged, and walked back. He didn't think he had hit Cain Brockman. Probably he had been thrown from his horse and knocked cold.

Kilkenny retrieved Buck and swung into the saddle. Then he rode back by the station. The stationmaster thrust his head out.

"Didn't think you could do it, mister!" he said. "Some shootin'!"

"Thanks. And thanks for the warnin'." Kilkenny jerked his head back at Abel Brockman's body. "Better get that out of the street. He's pretty big and he'll probably spoil right fast."

He turned Buck toward the Botalla trail, and started down it. Well, it wouldn't be long now. He slapped Buck on the shoulder and lifted his voice in song:

> *I have a word to speak, boys, only one to say,*
> *Don't never be no cow thief, don't never ride*
>   *no stray.*
> *Be careful of your rope, boys, and keep it on*
>   *the tree,*
> *But suit yourself about it, for it's nothin' at all*
>   *to me!*

Yet, even as he sang, he was thinking of the problems ahead. It was the time to strike now before anything else was done by the man at Apple Cañon to stir up strife between the Steele and Lord factions. If he and the ranchers and Botalla men could attack Apple Cañon and rout out the rustlers living in the long house there, and either capture them or send them over the border, much of the trouble would be over.

The cowpunchers of the two ranches would still have hard feelings, all too easily aroused if the proper stories were circulated and there should be more killing. Kilkenny realized that. So the thing to do was to strike before the man at the cañon could direct another move. That meant they must move at once—now!

XIII

Polti was dead. Abel Brockman was dead. That much at least had been done. Cain Brockman was alive. How would he react? Would he come out to kill Kilkenny as Abel had maintained? Would he flee the country, harassed by the thought of his brother's being gone? Would his confidence be ruined? There was no guessing what the man might do, and, despite the death of Abel, Kilkenny knew that Cain Brockman was still a dangerous man. Then two others remained, for Kilkenny was convinced that the unknown killer on the range and the man at Apple Cañon were not one and the same. Two men left, and no hint of who either one was.

On a sudden hunch, Kilkenny turned the buckskin and took a cut-off across the hills toward Apple Cañon. Another talk with Nita might give him some clue. Or was he fooling himself? Was it simply because he wanted to see the hazel-eyed girl who had stirred him so deeply?

He rode on, his face somber, thinking of her. A man who rode the lonely trails had no right to talk love to a woman. What did he have to offer? He had nothing, and always in the background was the knowledge that someday he would be too slow. He couldn't always win. Confident as he was, certain as he was of his skill, he knew that a day must come when he *would* be too slow. Either that, or it would be a shot in the back by an enemy, or a shot from someone who wanted to be able to say he was the man who killed Kilkenny. That was what any gunman of repute had always to fear. For there were many such.

More, there was that curious thing that made gunmen seek each other out to see who was fastest. Men had been known to ride for miles with only that in mind. Sometimes those meetings had come off quietly and without actual shooting. Sometimes it was a matter of mutual respect, as in the case of Wild Bill Hickok and John Wesley Hardin. Some gunmen did live together, some were friends, but they were the exception, and there was always the chance that some ill-considered remark might set off the explosion that might leave a dozen men lying in death.

No, men who lived by the gun died by the gun, and no such man had any right to marry. No matter where he might go in the West, there would always be someone, sometime, who would know him. Then his name would become known again, and he must either fight or be killed. Billy the Kid, Wild Bill, Ben Thompson, King Fisher, Phil Coe, and many another were to prove the old belief in dying by the gun. One day the time would come for him, too, and, until then, his only safety lay in moving on, in being what he had always been, a shadow on the border, a mysterious, little-known gunman who no man could surely describe.

The buckskin skirted the base of a hill, and came out among some cedars. Below lay Apple Cañon.

Thoughtfully Kilkenny studied the town. It seemed quiet, and there was no telltale flash from the cliff house. It might be that he could visit the town without being seen.

Carefully, keeping to cover of the scattered groves of cedar, Kilkenny worked his way along the mountainside, steadily getting closer and closer to the bottom. There was no sign of life.

Finally, close to the foot of the hill, he dismounted and tied the buckskin to a tree with a slipknot. Enough of a tie to let the buckskin know he should stand, but not enough to hold him if Kilkenny should whistle for him. Then, keeping the saloon between himself and the livery stable, Kilkenny walked casually out of the trees toward the back of the bar.

The biggest chance of being seen would be from the Sadler house, or by someone walking down the short street of the town. He made the trees around Nita's house without being seen. Carefully he placed a hand on the fence, then vaulted it, landing lightly behind the lilacs.

Inside the house someone was singing in a contralto voice, singing carelessly and without pretense as people sing when the song is from the heart more than the brain. It was an old song, a tender song, and for a long time Kilkenny stood there by the lilacs, listening. Then he moved around the bushes and stopped by the open window.

The girl stood there, just inside, almost within the reach of his arm. She had an open book in her hands, but she was not reading, she was looking out at the hills across the valley, out across the roof of the livery stable at the crags.

"It's a lovely picture," he said softly, "a mighty lovely picture. Makes me regret my misspent life."

She did not jump or show surprise, nor at first did her head turn. She kept her eyes on the distant crags, and smiled slowly.

"Strange that you should come now," she said softly. "I had been thinking of you. I was just wondering what you were like as a little boy, what your mother was like, and your father."

Kilkenny took off his hat and leaned on the window sill.

"Does it matter?" he asked softly. "No man is anything but what he is himself. I expect his blood has something to do with it, but not so much. It's what he does with himself, afterward. That's what matters. And I haven't done so well."

"No? I would say, Kilkenny, that you had done well. I would think you are an honorable man."

"I've killed men. Too many."

She shrugged. "Perhaps that is bad, but it is the West. I do not believe you ever shot a man from malice, or because there was cruelty in you. Nor do I believe you ever shot one for gain. If you killed, it was because you had to."

"That's the way I wanted it," he said somberly, "but it ain't always been that way. Sometimes you stand in a bar, and you see a man come in, and, when you look at him, you can tell by his eyes and his guns that he's a gunslinger. That's when you should leave. You should get out of there, but you don't, and then sooner or later you have to kill him. You have power when you can sling a gun, but it's an ugly power, and it keeps a man thinkin', worryin' for fear some day he may use it wrong."

"But Kilkenny," Nita said, "surely the West needs good men who can shoot. If there were only the bad men, only the killers, then what chance would honest people have? We need men like you. Oh, I know! Killing is bad, it's wrong. But here in the West men carry guns . . . for wild steers, for rattlesnakes, for Comanches or rustlers . . . and some learn to use them too well. But the West can't grow without them, Kilkenny."

He looked at her for a long moment. "You're a smart girl, Nita. You think, don't you?"

"Is that good, Kilkenny?" The hazel eyes were soft. "I'm not sure that a girl should ever think, or at least she shouldn't let a man know it."

"That's what they say." He grinned suddenly. "But not for me. I want a girl who can think. I want a girl to walk beside me, not behind me."

"Kilkenny," she said, and her hand suddenly came out to touch his, "be careful! He . . . he's deadly, Kilkenny. He's as vicious as a coiled snake, and he's living just for one thing now . . . to kill you! I don't think it is for the reason he gives. I think it is because he hates you for your reputation! I think he's a little afraid, too. He was drinking once, and he told me, when we were standing at the gate, that he wasn't afraid of Hardin. He said he knew he could beat

Hardin or King Fisher. He said in all his life only two men had him bothered. Ben Thompson and you. He's always talking about you when he's drinking. He said Thompson had more nerve than any man he ever knew. And he said that, if you ever fought him, you'd have to be sure he was dead, because if he wasn't and he could walk, he'd come after you again. You bothered him because he said he couldn't place you. You were like a ghost. Nobody could say anything about you except that you were fast and hard-shooting."

Kilkenny nodded. "Yeah, I know what he means. When you're fast with a six-gun, you get to hearin' about others. After a while you get a picture of 'em in your mind, and, when you shoot, you shoot with that picture in mind. Most times you're right, too. But when you don't know about a man, it bothers you. A stranger rides in, wearin' his gun tied down, or mebbe two guns, and he's got a still, cold face, and he drinks with his left hand. Well, you know he's bad. You know he's a gun slick, but you don't know who he is. It leaves you restless and uncertain. Once you know what he is, then you know what you're up against."

They stood there for a while in the warm sun, and a little breeze stirred, and the lilac petals sifted over his shoulders, and he could smell their heavy perfume. He looked up at the girl and felt a strange yearning rise within him. It wasn't merely the yearning of a man for a woman. It was the longing of a man for a home, for a fireside, for the laughter of children and the quiet of night with someone lying beside you. The yearning for someone to work for, to protect, someone to belong to, and some place in life where you fitted in.

It was so different from all he had known these last bitter years. These years of endless watchfulness, of continual awareness, of looking into each man's eyes, and wondering if he was another man you would have to kill, of riding down long trails, always aware that a bullet might cut you down. Yet, even as he thought of that, he knew there was something in his blood that answered to the wild call of the wilderness trails. There was something about riding into a strange town, swinging down from his horse, and walking into a bar, something that gave him a lift, and that gave life a strange zest.

There was something in the pounding of guns, the buck of a .45 in his hand, the leap of a horse beneath him, and the shouts of men, something that awakened everything that was in him. Times bred the men they needed, and the West needed such men, men who could bring peace to a strange, wild land, even while they found death for themselves. The West was won by gunmen no less than it was won by pioneering families, by fur traders and Indian fighters.

"What are you going to do, Kilkenny, when all this is over?" Nita asked softly.

He leaned his elbows on the window sill and pushed his hat back on his head. "I don't rightly know," he said thoughtfully. "I reckon I'll just move on to some other town. Might rustle me a herd of cows and settle down somewheres on a piece of land. Mebbe over in the Big Bend country."

"Why don't you marry and have a home, Kilkenny?" Nita asked softly. "I think you'd make a good man around a home."

"Me?" He laughed, a bit harshly. "All I can do is sling a gun. That ain't much good around a house. Of course, I might punch cows, or play poker?" He straightened suddenly. "Time I was ridin' on. You be careful." Then he paused. "Tell me, Nita. What hold does this man have over you?"

"None. It is as I have said. I like to live, even here, and alone. I know I would die, and quickly, if I talked. Then, after a fashion, he has protected me. Of course, *señor*"—she fell into her old way of speaking—"it is that he wants me for himself. But I belong to no man. Yet."

"You can't tell me who he is?"

"No." She looked at him for a minute. "Perhaps you think I am not helping, but, you see, this is all I have, this place. When it is gone, there is nothing. And the people out there"—she waved a hand toward Botalla—"do not think I am good. There would be no place for me there. I can only say that he will kill you if he can, and you must be careful if you go to the cliff. And do not go by the path."

When he was back on the buckskin, he turned toward Botalla. If Steele and Lord had their men there, he would bring them back to Apple Cañon at once. In his ride to the place he had carefully scouted the approaches.

It had been easy enough to see just what they would be facing in an attack on the stronghold. He could muster about sixty men. There would be at least forty here at the cañon. Sixty wasn't really enough, for the men at the cañon would be fighting on their own ground, and behind defenses. And all were seasoned fighters. Nevertheless, much could be lost by waiting. The time was now. The raid on Apple Cañon, however, might leave the range killer at large.

As Kilkenny rode, his brain dug into the accumulated evidence, little as it was. Yet one idea refused to be denied, and it worried around in his mind until he reached town.

He came up to the Trail House at a spanking trot. Dropping from saddle, he flipped a dollar to a Mexican boy.

"Take that hoss, Pedro," he said, grinning, "and treat him right. Oats, hay, water, and a rub-down."

Pedro dropped his bare feet to the boardwalk and grinned, showing his white teeth.

"*Sí, señor*, it shall be done!"

XIV

Rusty Gates was sitting inside the Trail House, holding himself stiffly, but grinning. Webb Steele was there, too. He looked up keenly as Kilkenny came in.

"Can't keep a good man down!" Rusty said. "Tana bandaged my side, and I wanted to give you a hand with the Brockmans, but she wouldn't let me. She's got a mind of her own, that girl!"

"What happened?" Frame demanded, stepping up.

"Got Abel," said Kilkenny. "Cain got thrown from his hoss. Knocked out, I think. Another *hombre* dragged him around a corner and got him aboard a hoss. They lit out, and I let 'em go."

Frame shook his head, his eyes dark with worry. "Cain will go crazy when he finds out Abel is dead and you're still alive. He'll come gunnin' for you, Kilkenny."

"He might." Kilkenny shrugged. "Got to take that chance. We're after bigger game now. We've got to wipe out that bunch at Apple Cañon. There's at least forty outlaws there."

"Probably more," Steele said. "Clyde Wilder was down there a few days ago, and he says there was anyways fifty, and might have been seventy."

"Don't make no difference," Frame declared. "We're ready. Even Duval at the hotel is goin'. Everybody wants to lend a hand."

Down the main street of Botalla there was suddenly a pounding of hoofs, then a rider threw himself from saddle in front of the Trail House. He thrust the batwing doors open with his shoulder.

"Kilkenny!" he yelled. "Chet Lord's dyin'! Wants to see you, the worst way!"

"What happened?" Steele demanded.

"Gored by a crazy steer. Don't reckon he's got long. Askin' for Kilkenny. Don't know what he wants of him!"

"Steele," Kilkenny said, "get the men together, plenty of arms an' ammunition. Nobody leaves town to warn Apple Cañon. Get set to move, and, when you're ready, start her rollin'!"

He swung into saddle and turned the buckskin toward the Lord Ranch. His mind was working swiftly. What could Chet Lord have to say? That something had been worrying the big rancher for days was obvious enough, for the man had lost weight, he looked drawn and pale, and seemed to be under great strain.

Was he the unknown killer? As soon as that idea occurred, Kilkenny shook his head. The man was not the type. Bluff, outspoken, and direct, he was the kind of man who would shoot straight and die hard, but his shots would be at a man's face, not behind his back.

Kilkenny let the buckskin take his own gait. The long-legged horse knew his rider, and knew the mountains and desert. He knew that on many days he would be called on for long, hard rides, and had learned to pace himself accordingly. While cow ponies were held in light esteem, good as they might be, most cowpunchers had their favorites. Yet they were the gunmen and outlaws, the men whose lives might depend on the horses they rode, who really knew and cared for their horses. It was a time when a few such horses were to acquire almost as much fame as their hard-riding, straight-shooting masters. Sam Bass, for instance, was to become no more famous than the Denton mare he rode. And Black Nell, Wild Bill Hickok's horse with a trick of "dropping quick," was to save Hickok's life on more than one occasion. Kilkenny knew his buckskin, and Buck knew Kilkenny. During the years they had been together, they had learned each other's ways, and Buck had almost human intelligence when it came to knowing what his master wanted of him. He knew the ways of the frontier, and seemed to sense when there he could husband his strength, and when it must be used. Buck's ears were as perfect a guide to danger as a rifle shot. A flicker of movement, even miles ahead, and his ears were up and alert. And when he side-stepped, it was always with reason.

The Lord Ranch was strangely still when the buckskin cantered across the yard and came to a stop before the ranch house. Kilkenny swung to the ground and, leaving Buck ground-hitched, went up the steps at a bound.

Steve met him at the door. The young fellow's eyes were wet, and his face looked pale.

"He wants you," he said. "Wants you bad."

Kilkenny stepped through the door into the room where Chet Lord lay in bed. A sharp-eyed man with a beard stood up when Kilkenny walked in.

"I'm Doc Wentlow," he said softly, then smiled a little wryly. "From Apple Cañon. He wants to talk to you"—he glanced at Steve—"alone."

"Right."

The doctor and Steve went out, and Kilkenny watched them go. He saw Steve hesitate in the door as though loath to leave. Then the young cowboy stepped out, and Kilkenny turned to the old man lying on the bed. Lord's breathing was heavy, but his eyes were open. His face seemed to have aged, and he looked up at Kilkenny for a moment, then reached over and took his hand.

"Kilkenny," he whispered hoarsely, "I got a favor to ask. You got to promise me, for I'm a dyin' man. Promise me you'll do it. It's somethin' you can do."

"Shore," Kilkenny said gently. "If it's anything I can do, I will. You know that."

"Kilkenny," the old man's voice faltered, then his grip tightened on Kilkenny's wrist until the gun expert almost winced with the strength of it, "Kilkenny, I want you to kill my son."

"What?" Kilkenny stared. Then his eyes narrowed slowly. "Why, Lord?"

"Kilkenny, you got to. Kilkenny, I'm an old man, and, wrong or right, I love my boy. I love him like I loved his mother before him, but, Kilkenny, he's a killer! He's insane! I've knowed it for months now! Des told me. Des King told me before Steve killed him. Long time ago, Steve had a bad fall off a buckin' hoss, and was unconscious for days and days. He was kind of queer when he got well, for a spell, then it looked like he was all right again, and didn't take pleasure in torturin' things no more. So when folks began to get killed around here, I never thought of the boy. Then I had a feelin', and one day Des come to me, and said he knowed Steve had done it, and that he'd have to be put away. He couldn't go on killin' folks. But then Des was killed, an' I couldn't bear to put Steve away. He . . . he . . . was all . . . I had, Kilkenny."

Kilkenny nodded slowly, looking down at the old man, seeing the pleading in his eyes, the plea for understanding, for sympathy at least.

"I done wrong. I knowed I was doin' wrong, but I hoped the boy would change. Sometimes he would be a good boy, then he'd get to moonin' around, then off he'd go."

For a long time the old man was silent, then his chest heaved and he turned his head.

"Kilkenny, you got to kill him. I won't be around no more to look after him, and you'll kill him decent, Kilkenny. You'll shoot him, and he won't suffer. I don't want him to suffer, Kilkenny. He's a baby for pain. He can't suffer. I don't want him hung, neither, Kilkenny. Go shoot him down. I left a paper. It's in an envelope, in case I die. Frame has got it. It tells all about it. Kilkenny, you got to kill him. I can't die thinkin' I've left that passel of evil behind me. An' but for that, he's been a good boy."

Kilkenny still stood staring down at old Chet Lord. Yes, it all fitted. Everything fitted. Steve had a Winchester 1873, and he could have done any of the shootings. Kilkenny had suspected something of the kind, which was why he had wired.

Wired?

Kilkenny clapped a hand to his pocket. Why, the wires! He'd had them in his pocket all the time! Hurriedly he dug into his pocket and pulled them out, unfolding the sheets.

The first was from San Antonio, and it was a verification of what Chet Lord had just told him, a few scattered facts about Steve's boyhood actions after his bucking horse accident, before his father had taken him away, all indicative of what might later come. That was unnecessary now. There would be evidence enough. His father's letter with Frame, and a few dates and times would piece it all together.

He unfolded the second message, from El Paso. As its message struck him, his hands stiffened.

TYSON SAW ROYAL BARNES AT APPLE CAÑON. HE KNEW BARNES FROM HAYS CITY AND ABILENE. BARNES MURDERED TYSON'S BROTHER, AND HE HEARD BARNES SWEAR TO KILL YOU FOR GETTING THE WEBERS. BE CAREFUL, KILKENNY, HE'S COLD AS A SNAKE, AND LIGHTNING FAST!

Kilkenny crumpled the message into a ball and thrust it into his pocket. The third message no longer mattered. It had only been an effort to learn what gunslingers were where, in an effort to learn who was at Apple Cañon. Now he knew.

Royal Barnes! The name stood out boldly in his mind, and, even as he turned away from the old man on the bed, he saw that name, the name of a man he had never seen, the name of one of the most ruthless, cold-blooded killers in the West. A man as evil and vicious as any, yet reputed to be handsome, reputed to be smooth and polished, yet known to be a man filled with the lust to kill and of such deadly skill that it was said that Wes Hardin had backed down for him.

Kilkenny opened the door and stepped outside. Instantly Doc Wentlow got up.

"How is he?" he demanded.

"Pretty low." Kilkenny hesitated. "Where's Steve?"

"Steve? That was funny. He stood by the door a minute after you went in. Listening, I guess. Then all of a sudden he turned and got on a horse and took off, riding like the devil."

Despite himself, Kilkenny felt relieved. He had never killed a man unless the man was attempting to kill him. To walk out of the old cattleman's bed chamber and shoot Steve had been the furthest from his thoughts. Just what he had hoped to do, he was not sure. He did know that Steve Lord must be stopped.

Thinking back, he could remember the curious light, the blazing of some inner compulsion, which he had seen in Steve's eyes that first day in the Trail House. Yet Steve had not wanted to shoot it out with him, face to face. The young fellow was a man with an insane urge to kill. It grew from some inner feeling of inferiority. What Steve Lord would do now, Kilkenny could not guess. He knew killers, but the killers he knew were sane men, men whose thoughts could be read, and whose ways could be known. He did know that even the craziest man had his moments of sanity, and he knew that Steve Lord must have listened at the door, probably suspecting what his father intended to tell Kilkenny. So he had mounted and ridden away—to what? Where could he go? Yet even as the question came, he knew its answer. Steve Lord would go to Apple Cañon.

However insane the boy might be, there was some connection between him and the events stemming from the cañon rendezvous. And Kilkenny suspected that Steve had more than a little interest in Nita Riordan. But he would be riding now with fear in his heart, with desperation. For now he was in the open, the place he dreaded to be, where there was no concealment. He must fight, or he must die, and Kilkenny knew that such a man would fight like a cornered rat. Yet he had promised a dying man, and regardless of that it was something that had to be done.

Why should he feel depressed? Steve was a killer, preying upon the lonely and the helpless, a man who shot from ambush, who killed from sheer love of killing. So he must be stopped. It was his own father, the man who sired him, who had passed sentence upon him.

Kilkenny turned off into the thick brush, unrolled his poncho, and was asleep almost as soon as he lay down.

XV

Botalla's Main Street was crowded with horsemen when Kilkenny rode back to the town. They were in for the finish, the lean, hard-bitten, wind- and gun-seasoned veterans of the Texas range. Riders from the Steele and Lord ranches, men who had ridden the long cattle trails north to Dodge and Abilene, men who knew the ways of cows and Indians and guns. Men who had cut their teeth on six-shooters.

Yet, as Kilkenny rode up the street, eyes alert for some sign of Steve Lord, he wondered how many of these men would be alive when another sundown came. For they were facing men as tough as themselves, as good, and as dangerous as cornered rats are always dangerous. Vicious as men can be who find themselves faced at last with justice and the necessity of paying for their misdeeds. They would fight, shrewdly and well. They were not common criminals, these men of Apple Cañon. A few, yes. But many were just tough young men who had taken the wrong trail or liked the hard, reckless life. A different turn of events and they might have been satisfied cowhands, trail bosses, or they might have been Rangers. They would ask no quarter, and they would give none. They would fight this out to the last bitter ditch, and they would go down, guns blazing. They might have taken the wrong trails, but they had courage.

And for him? There was none of that; there was just one man. He had to mount that cliff and take Royal Barnes, the mysterious man in the cliff house. How would he know him? He did not know, but he did know that when he saw the man he would know him. Instinctively he knew that. When a man looked at another across a space of ground, with guns waiting, then he knew whether a man was fast and whether he would kill or not.

This would be different. Lance Kilkenny understood that. The Brockmans had been good but he had timed his chances to nullify their skill as a twin fighting combination. He had killed Abel Brockman as he had killed many another man, and most of them fast. But—and this he knew—he had never drawn against a man like Royal Barnes. Blinding speed. Barnes had that. Barnes had killed Blackie Slade, and Kilkenny recalled Slade only too well. He had seen Slade in action, and the man had been poison. Yet Barnes had shot him down as if he were an amateur.

Yet Kilkenny could feel something building up inside himself, and recognized what it was. It was his own compulsion, his own fire to kill. Every gunman had it. Without it, he was helpless. It was a fiery drive, but with it the cold ruthlessness of a man who knew he must kill, or he must die himself.

He swung down from his horse and walked into the Trail House.

"We're all set," Webb Steele said, walking forward. "All set, and rarin' to go. The boys wanted to wait and see how Chet is."

Kilkenny looked up. "Steele," he said slowly, "Chet's dyin'. He told me about the killin's. It's Steve. Steve's a killer!"

Webb Steele stared, and Frame rubbed the back of his hand across his eyes.

"Huh!" Steele said. "I might of knowed it! He was always a strange 'un."

"That ain't all," Kilkenny said quietly. "The man up in the cliff house is Royal Barnes."

"Barnes?" Rusty Gates's face tightened, then turned gray as he looked at Kilkenny. "One of the slickest *hombres* that ever threw a six-gun."

In the stillness that followed, men stared at one another, and into the mind of each came stories they had heard of Royal Barnes and of the men who had gone down before his roaring guns. In the mind of each was a fear that he might be next.

The silence was shattered by the crashing of a door, and as one man the crowd turned to stare at the rear door of the Trail House. Several steps inside that door, his head thrust forward and his eyes glaring with killing hatred, stood a huge, broad-jawed man in a checked shirt and black jeans stuffed into heavy cowhide boots.

"Cain Brockman!" Frame yelled.

The big man strode forward until he stood only

three paces from Kilkenny. Then, with cold, merciless hatred in his eyes, he unbuckled his belt and shed his guns.

"I'm goin' to kill you, Kilkenny! With my bare hands!"

"No!" Webb burst out, thrusting himself forward. "We got us a job to do, Kilkenny!"

"Keep out of this," Kilkenny said quietly.

Without further word and without taking his eyes from Cain's, he unbuckled his own belt and passed his guns to the big rancher.

With a hoarse grunt, Cain Brockman lunged, swinging a ponderous right fist. Kilkenny stepped inside and snapped a lightning left to the face, then closed with the big man, slamming both fists to his midriff. Cain grabbed Kilkenny and hurled him across the room so that he brought up with a crash against the bar. Cain lunged after him.

Kilkenny pivoted away, stabbing a left that caught the bigger man on the cheek bone, then Brockman swung and caught Kilkenny with a hard right swing that knocked him to his knees. A kick aimed at Kilkenny's shoulder just grazed him as he was starting to rise. He lost balance, toppling over on the floor. He rolled away and came up swinging, and the two sprang together.

Brockman's face was savage with killing fury and an ugly glee at having his enemy and the man who had slain his brother actually in his hands. Another right caught Kilkenny a glancing blow, but he weathered it and stepped under a left, slamming a right to the ribs. Then he hooked a left to the chin, leaping away before Cain could grab him.

It was toe-to-toe, slam-bang fighting, and neither

man was taking any precaution. Both fought like savages, and Kilkenny's face became set in a mask of fierce desperation as he met charge after charge of the huge Brockman. They stood, straddle-legged, in the middle of the floor and swung until the smacking sound of their blows sounded loudly in the room and blood streamed from cut and battered faces. Brockman was a brute for strength, and he was out for a kill, filled with so much fury that he was almost immune to pain.

Kilkenny stepped inside a right and ripped his own right to the heart. He hooked both hands to the body, then they grappled and went to the floor, kicking and gouging. There were no rules here, no niceties of combat. This was fighting to maim, to kill, and there was only one possible end—the finish of one or the other.

Blood streaming from a cut on his cheek, Kilkenny lanced a left to the mouth, then missed a right and took a wicked left to the middle. But he took the punch going in, punching with both hands to the head.

Cain's big head rocked with the force of the blows and he spat a tooth onto the floor, and swung hard to the head, staggering Kilkenny. The gunman came back fast, ripping a right uppercut to the chin, then a left and right to the head. Kilkenny was boxing now. Long ago he had taken lessons from one of the best fighters of the day, and he found now that he needed every bit of his skill.

It was not merely a matter of defeating Cain Brockman. After that, and perhaps soon, he would be meeting Royal Barnes, and his hands must be strong and ready. He stepped inside of a right and smashed a right to the bigger man's body, then hooked a left to the heart, and drummed with both hands against the big man's torso. Body punches stood less chance of hurting his hands, and he must be careful.

He stepped around, putting Brockman off side, and then crossed a right to Cain's bleeding eye, circled farther left, and crossed the right again. Then he stabbed three lefts to the face, and, as Cain lunged, he stepped inside and butted him under the chin with his head.

Brockman let out a muffled roar and crowded Kilkenny to the bar, but Lance wormed away and slugged the big man in the ribs. Brockman was slowing down now, and his face was bloody and swollen. His eyes gleamed fiercely, and he began to move slowly, more cautiously, moving in, watching for his chance.

Cain backed up, backed slowly, trying to keep away from that stabbing left, then suddenly he brought up against the wall. Putting a foot against the wall, he shoved himself off it like a huge battering ram and caught Kilkenny fully in the chest with his big head. Kilkenny went crashing to the floor!

Brockman rushed close, trying to kick him in the ribs, but Kilkenny got to his hands and knees and hurled himself against Brockman's legs. The big man tumbled over him, then spun on the floor with amazing agility and grabbed Kilkenny's head, groping for his eyeballs with his thumbs!

Mad with pain and fear for his eyes, Kilkenny tore loose and lunged to his feet. Brockman came up with him and Kilkenny stabbed a powerful left into that wide granite-hard face. Blood flew in every direction, and he felt the nose bone crunch under his fist. With a cry of pain, Cain Brockman lunged forward, and his mighty blows pounded at Kilkenny's body. But the lighter man blocked swiftly and caught most of the blows on his elbows and shoulders. Driven back, the gun expert swayed like a tree in a gale, fighting desperately to set himself, to stave off that terrific assault. There was the taste of blood in his mouth and he felt his lungs gasping for breath, and their gasping was a tearing pain.

Brockman closed in and thrust out a left that might have ended the fight, but Kilkenny went under it and butted Cain in the chest, staggering the bigger man. Missing a right hook to the head, Kilkenny split Brockman's cheek wide open with his elbow, ripped the elbow back, slamming the big man's head around.

Despite the fierceness of the fighting, Kilkenny was not badly hurt. Most of the bigger man's blows had been wasted. One eye was cut, and he knew his jaw was swollen, but mainly he was fighting to stave off the big man's fierce attacks. They swept forward with tremendous power, but little skill. Yet Kilkenny was growing desperate. His punches seemed to have no effect on the huge hulk of Cain Brockman. The big man's face was bleeding from several cuts. His lips were battered, and one eye was badly swollen, but he seemed to have got his second wind, and was no less strong than when he had thrown his first punch. On his part, Kilkenny had one eye almost swollen shut. He could taste blood from a cut inside his mouth, and his breath was coming in those tearing gasps.

Brockman bored in, swinging. Kilkenny pushed the left swing outward and stepped in, bringing up a hard left uppercut to the wind that stopped Brockman in his tracks. But the big man bowed his head and lunged. Kilkenny dropped an open palm to the head and shoved the fellow off balance, and, as his guard came down for an instant, he stabbed a left to Brockman's cut eye. Then he circled warily.

Cain lunged, kicked at Kilkenny's middle. The lighter man jerked back, then stepped off to the left, and dived in a long flying tackle. He hit Brockman at the knees, grabbed, and jerked hard! Brockman came down with a *thud*, his head bouncing on the wood floor. Kilkenny rolled free and scrambled to his feet. Brockman was getting up, but he was slow. Half up, he lunged in a long dive himself, but Kilkenny jerked his knee into the big man's face. Cain rolled off to one side, his face bloody and scarcely human. Yet even then he tried to get up.

He made it. Kilkenny was sick of the fight, sick of the beating he was giving the bigger man. He stepped in, measured him with a left, and, when Cain tried to lift his hands, Kilkenny slugged him in the solar plexus. The big man went down, conscious, but paralyzed from the waist down.

Kilkenny stepped back, weaving with exhaustion. Grimly he worked his battered, stiffened hands.

"You ain't in shape for that raid now, Kilkenny," Rusty expostulated. "Better call it off or stay behind."

"To thunder with that," Kilkenny replied sharply. "I want Royal Barnes myself, and I'll get him."

Walking back to the wash basin, he dipped up water from the bucket and bathed his cut and bruised face. He turned his head as Frame walked up, his face grave.

"Get me some salts," Kilkenny said.

While he waited, he bathed his hands and replaced his torn shirt with one brought him by Gates.

When he had the salts, he put them in hot water one of the men brought and soaked them. He knew there was nothing better for taking away soreness and stiffness, and it was only his hands he was worried about. He was bruised and battered, but not seriously. Although that one eye was swollen, he could still see through the slit.

Finally he straightened. He turned and looked at the men around him. They would never ride without him, he knew, or, if they did, their hearts wouldn't be in it. He laughed suddenly.

"All-l-l set!" he yelled. "Let's ride!"

XVI

On Buck, Kilkenny headed toward the Apple Cañon trail. He was tired, his muscles were weary and heavy, yet he knew that the outdoor life he had lived, and the rugged existence he had known most of his life would give him the stamina he needed now. Behind him a tight cavalcade of grim, mounted men were riding out to battle.

Rusty Gates rode up alongside Kilkenny in the van of the column.

"You had yourself a scrap," Rusty said. "Can you see?"

"Enough."

"How about your hands?" Gates noticed the swollen knuckles and his lips tightened. "Kilkenny, you can't drag a fast gun with hands like that. Facin' Barnes will be suicide."

"Nevertheless, I'm facin' him," Kilkenny said crisply. "He's my meat, and I'll take him. Besides, my hands ain't as bad as they look, and most of that swelling will be gone soon. It ain't goin' to be speed that'll win, anyway. Both of us are goin' to catch lead. It'll be who can take the most of it and keep goin'." He nodded. "The way I figure it we'll be spotted before we get there. They'll be holed up around the buildin's. The bunkhouse, the livery stable, and blacksmith shop all looked like they was built to stand a siege."

"They were," said Rusty. "Heavy logs or stone, and built solid. Bill Sadler's place, on the same side as the Border Bar, is 'dobe, and it has walls three feet thick. Them windows was built to cover the trail, an' believe me, it ain't a goin' to be no picnic gettin' tough men out of there."

"I know." Kilkenny rubbed Buck's neck thoughtfully. "Got to figger that one out. I'm thinkin' of leavin' you fellers anyway. I'm goin' up to the castle."

"Alone?" Gates was incredulous. "Man, you're askin' for it. He'll be forted up there, and plenty tight."

"I doubt it. I doubt if he ever lets more than one man up there with him. Royal Barnes, as I hear of him, ain't a trustin' soul. No, I'm goin' to try comin' down the cliffs above the castle."

"The what?" Gates swore and spat into the road. "Holy snakes, feller! They're sheer rock! You'd need a rope and a lot of luck. Then he'd see you and get you before you ever got down!"

"Mebbe, I got the rope, and mebbe the luck. Anyway, I'm comin' down from behind where he won't be expectin' me, an' I'm comin' down while you fellers are hard at it in front. Now here . . . the way I see it. . . ."

As Webb Steele, Frame, and Rusty listened, he outlined a brief plan of attack. At the end, they began to grin.

"Might work," observed Steele. "I'd forgot that claim up in the pass. If that stuff is still there. . . ."

"It is. I looked."

Kilkenny had no illusions about the task ahead. With the plan he had conceived, carefully working it out during the previous days, he believed that the fort houses of Apple Cañon could be taken. It meant a struggle, and there would be loss of life. This riding column would lose some faces, and there would be hectic and bloody fighting before that return.

Where was Steve Lord? Had Steve risen to his bait and ridden to the hidden cabin in the box cañon? It would be a place to find him, and there, if Steve should go for a gun, he could end it all. Kilkenny shrank from the task, and only the knowledge that other people would die, brutally murdered from ambush, made him willing to go through with keeping his promise to old Chet Lord. He had that job to do, and luckily the cañon was only a short distance from the route the cavalcade would follow.

There had been no diary left by Des King. The idea had been created in Kilkenny's own mind. It had been bait dropped for the killer, and it had been conceived even before Kilkenny had known that Steve was the man. That he would have discovered it soon, he knew, for slowly the evidence had been mounting, and he had been suspicious of Steve Lord, waiting only for a chance to inspect his guns and check them against the shells he had picked up as evidence.

What would Steve Lord do now? To all intents, he would be outlawed. He knew his father had exposed him, and he must realize there was evidence enough to convict him, or to send him to an asylum. He would be desperate. Would he try to kill Kilkenny? To escape? Or would he go on a killing spree and gun down everything and everybody in sight? Kilkenny couldn't escape the feeling that Steve would go to Apple Cañon. He turned suddenly to Webb Steele.

"I'm ridin' for the shack where I let Steve think Des King hid his diary," he said. "If I ain't back when you get to Apple Cañon, just go to work and don't wait for me. I'm goin' to get Steve Lord. When I find him, I'll come back."

He wheeled the buckskin and took off up a draw into the deeper hills. He had been thinking of this route all the way along. He wasn't sure this route would do it, but knew he could find a way.

The draw opened into a narrower draw, and after a long time he rode out of that to a little stretch of bunch grass that led away to a ridge covered with cedar and pine. It was cool among the trees, and he stopped for a minute to wipe his hatband and check his guns once more. Then he slid his Winchester from the scabbard and took it across the saddle in front if him. His hands felt better than he had expected they would.

He struck a path and followed it through the trees, winding steadily upward. Then the trees thinned, and he entered a region of heaped-up boulders among which the trail wound with all the casualness of cow trails in a country where cows are in no hurry. Twice rabbits jumped up and ran away from his trail, but the buckskin's hoofs made no noise on the pine needles or in the dust of the boulder-bordered trail.

Kilkenny was cutting across a meadow when he

saw the prints of a horse bisecting the trail he was making. In the tall grass of the meadow he could tell nothing of the horse, but on a hunch he turned the buckskin and followed. Whoever the rider was, he was in a hurry, and was moving in as straight a line as possible for his objective.

It had bad features, this trailing of a man native to the country. Such a man would know of routes, of places of concealment of which Kilkenny could know nothing. Such an advantage could mean the difference between life and death in such a country.

Scanning every open space before he moved across it, Kilkenny followed warily. He knew only too well the small amount of concealment it required to prevent a man from being seen. A few inches of grass, clothes that blended with surroundings, and immobility was all that was essential to remain unseen.

Sunlight caught the highest pinnacles of the mountains beyond Forgotten Pass, and slowly the long shadows crept up, and the day crept away down the cañons. Kilkenny rode steadily, every sense alert for trouble, his keen eyes searching the rocks ahead, roving ceaselessly, warily.

The cabin was not far away when he dismounted and faded into the darkness under the gnarled cedars, and looked down through the narrow entrance between the cliffs into the box cañon.

A squat, shapeless structure, built hurriedly by some wandering prospector or hopeful rancher in some distant period. Then in the years that followed it had slowly sagged here and there, the straw roof rotting and being patched with cedar bows, earth, and even heavy branches from the cedars until the roof had become a mound. It was an ancient, decrepit structure, its one window a black hole, its door too low for a tall man. About it the grass was green, for there was a stream nearby that flowed out of the rocks on one side and returned into the cliffs on the other, after diagonally crossing the cañon and watering a meadow in transit.

Outside the shack, under an apple tree, stood a saddled horse, his head hanging.

Well, here we are, Kilkenny, he told himself dryly. *Now to get close.*

Leaving the buckskin in concealment, Kilkenny went at a crouching run to the nearest boulder. Then he ran closer, crouched behind some cedars, watching the cabin.

He was puzzled. There was still no movement. It should take no time to find there was nothing in the cabin, and it was black in there. He should have seen a light by now, for there was no use trying to search in the blackness inside that cabin for anything.

The saddled horse stood, his head low, waiting wearily. A breeze stirred leaves on the cottonwood tree, and they whispered gently. Kilkenny pulled his sombrero lower and, moving carefully with the whispering of the leaves to cover the rustle of his movement, worked along the cliff into the bottleneck entrance. Slowly, carefully he worked inside.

There was no shot, no sound. In dead silence he moved closer, his rifle ready, his eyes searching every particle of cover. The horse moved a little, and began cropping grass absently, as though it had already eaten its fill.

Suddenly he had a feeling that the cabin was empty. There was no reason for him to wait. He would go over to it. He stepped out, his rifle ready, and walked swiftly and silently across the grass toward the cabin.

The horse stopped cropping grass and looked up, pricking its ears at him. Then he stepped up to the cabin.

Was there anyone inside? The blackness of the squat cabin gave off no sound. Despite himself, Kilkenny felt uneasy. It was too still, and there was something unearthly about this lost cañon and the lonely little shack. Carefully he put down his rifle and slipped a six-gun into his hand. The rifle would be a handicap if he had to fight in the close quarters of the shack. Then he looked in.

It was black inside, yet between himself and the hole that passed for a window he could see the vague outline of a sleeping man's head. A man's head bowed forward on his chest.

"All right," he said clearly. "You can get up and come out!"

There was neither sound nor movement. Kilkenny stepped inside quickly, and there was still no move. Taking a chance, he struck a match. The man was dead.

Searching about, he found a stump of candle that some passing rider had left. Lighting it, he looked at the man. He was a stranger. A middle-aged man, and a cowhand by his looks. He had been shot in the right temple by someone who had fired from outside the window. The room had been thoroughly ransacked.

Kilkenny scowled. An innocent man killed, and his fault. If he hadn't told that story, this might not have happened. But at the time he had needed some way for the killer to betray himself. It wasn't easy to do everything right.

He walked out quickly and swung into saddle.

There was nothing to do now but to return. He could make it in time, and morning would be the time to attack. In the small hours, just before daylight.

Buck took the trail with a quickened step as though he understood an end was in sight. Kilkenny lounged in the saddle. Steve would be riding hard now. He would be heading for Apple Cañon.

Weary from the long riding and the fight with Cain Brockman, Kilkenny lounged in the saddle, more asleep than awake. The yellow horse ambled down the trail through the mountains like a ghost horse on a mysterious mission.

There was a faint light in the sky, the barest hint of approaching dawn, when Kilkenny rode up to join the posse. They had stopped in a shallow valley about two miles from Apple Cañon. Dismounted, aside from guards, they were gathered about the fire.

He swung down from his horse and walked over, his boots sinking into the sand of the wash. The firelight glowed on their hard, unshaven faces.

Webb Steele, his huge body looking big as a grizzly's, looked up.

"Find Steve?" he demanded.

"No. But he killed another man." Briefly Kilkenny told of what he had found at the cabin. "Steve's obviously come on here. He's somewhere in there."

"You think he worked with this gang?" Frame asked. "Against his own pa?"

"Uh-huh. I think he knows Barnes. I think they cooked up some kind of a deal. I think Steve Lord has a heavy leanin' toward Nita Riordan, too. That's mebbe why he come here."

Rusty said nothing. He was looking pale, and Kilkenny could see that the ride had been hard on him. He shouldn't have come with that wound, Kilkenny thought. But men like Rusty Gates couldn't stay out of a good fight. And wounded or not, he was worth any two ordinary men.

Not two like Webb Steele, though. Or Frame. Either of them would do to ride the river with. They might be bull-headed, they might argue and talk a lot, but they were men who believed in doing the right thing, and men who would fight in order to be able to do it.

XVII

Glancing around at the others, Kilkenny saw that they looked efficient and sure. All of those men had been through the mill. There probably wasn't a man in the lot who hadn't fought Comanches and rustlers. This was going to be tough, because they were fighting clever men who would kill, and who were fighting from concealment. It is one thing to fight skilled fighting men, who know Indian tactics, and to fight those who battle in the open.

"Well," Kilkenny said, as he tasted the hot, bitter black coffee, "we got to be movin'. The stars are fadin' out a little."

Webb Steele turned to the men.

"You all know what this is about," he said harshly. "We ain't plannin' on no prisoners. Every man who wants to surrender will get his chance. If a man throws down his shootin' iron, take him. We'll try 'em decent, and hang the guilty ones. Although," he added, "ain't likely to be any innocent ones in Apple Cañon."

"One thing," Kilkenny said suddenly. "Leave Nita Riordan's Border Bar and her house alone."

He wasn't sure how they would take that, and he stood there, looking around. He saw tacit approval in Rusty's eyes, and Steele and Frame nodded agreement. Then his eyes encountered those of a tall, lean man with a cadaverous face and piercing gray eyes. The man chewed for a minute in silence, staring at Kilkenny.

"I reckon," he said then harshly, "that if we clear the bad 'uns out of Apple, we better clear 'em all out. Me, I ain't stoppin' for no woman. Nor that half-breed man of her'n, neither!"

Steele's hand tightened, and his eyes narrowed. Kilkenny noticed tension among the crowd. Would there be a split here? He smiled. "No reason for any trouble," he said quietly, "but Nita Riordan gave me a tip once that helped. I think she's friendly to us, an' I think she's innocent of wrong doin'."

The man with the gray eyes looked back at him. "I aim to clear her out of there as well's the others. I aim to burn that bar over her head."

There was cruelty in the man's face, and a harshness that seemed to spring from some inner source of malice and hatred. He wore a gun tied down, and had a carbine in the hollow of his arm. Several other men had moved up behind him now, and there was a curious similarity in their faces.

"Time to settle that," Kilkenny said, "when we get there. But I'm thinkin', friend, you better change your mind. If you don't, you're goin' to have to kill me along with her."

"She's a scarlet woman," the man said viciously, "and dyin's too good for her kind. I'm a-gettin' her, and you stay away."

"Time's a-wastin'," Steele said suddenly. "Let's ride!"

In the saddle, Kilkenny swung alongside of Steele in the van of the column.

"Who is that *hombre?*" he demanded.

"Name of Calkins. Lem Calkins. He hails from West Virginia . . . lives up yonder in the mountains. He's a feuder. You see them around him? He's got three brothers, and five sons. If you touch one of 'em, you got to fight 'em all."

They rode up the rise before coming to Apple Cañon, and then Kilkenny wheeled his horse toward the cliff. Almost instantly a shot rang out, and he wheeled the buckskin again and went racing toward the street of the town.

More shots rang out, and a man at the well dropped the bucket and grabbed for his gun. Kilkenny snapped a shot and the man staggered back, grabbing at his arm. A shot ripped past Kilkenny, scarring the pommel of his saddle as he lunged forward. He snapped another shot, then raced the buckskin between Nita's house and the Border Bar, dropping from the saddle.

He was up the back steps in two jumps, and had swung open the door. Firing had broken out in front, but Kilkenny's sudden attack from the rear of the bar astonished the defenders so much that he was inside the door before they realized what was happening. He snapped a shot at a lean, red-faced gunman in the door. The fellow went down, grabbing at his chest.

The bartender made a grab at the sawed-off shotgun under the bar, and Kilkenny took him with his left-hand gun, getting off two shots. A third man let out a yelp and went out the front door, fast.

Jaime Brigo sat very still, his chair tipped back against the wall. He just watched Kilkenny, his eyes expressionless.

Kilkenny reloaded his pistols.

"Brigo," he said abruptly, "there are some men among us who would harm the *señorita*. Lem Calkins, and his brothers and sons. They would burn this place, and kill her. You savvy?"

"*Sí, señor.*"

"I must go up on the cliff. You must watch over the *señorita.*"

Jamie Brigo got up. He towered above Kilkenny, and he smiled. "Of course, *señor*. I know *Señor* Calkins well. He is a man who thinks himself a good man, but he is cruel. He is also dangerous, *señor.*"

"If necessary, take the *señorita* away. I shall be back when I have seen the man on the cliff."

The firing was increasing in intensity.

"You have seen Steve Lord?" Kilkenny asked Brigo.

"*Sí.* He went before you to the cliff. The *señorita* would not see him. He was very angry, and said he would return soon."

Kilkenny walked to a point just inside the window of the bar and out of line with it. For a time he studied the street. The bulk of the outlaws seemed to be holed up in the livery stable, and they were throwing out a hot fire. Some of the defenders were firing from the pile of stones beyond the town, and others from the bunkhouse. There was no way to estimate their numbers.

Some of the attacking party had closed in and got

into position where they could fire into the face of the building. But for a time at least it looked like a stalemate.

Walking to the back door of the bar, Kilkenny slipped out into the yard and walked over to Buck. Safely concealed by the bar building, he was out of the line of fire of the defenders. Suddenly he heard a low call and, glancing over, saw Nita standing under the roses. An instant he hesitated, then walked over, leading Buck. For a moment he was exposed, but appeared to get by unseen.

Briefly he told her of Lem Calkins. She nodded.

"I expected that. He hates me."

"Why?" Kilkenny asked.

"Oh, because I'm a woman, I think. But he came here once, and had to be sent away. He seemed to think I was somewhat different than I am."

"I see."

"You are going to the cliff?" Her eyes were wide and dark.

"Yes."

"Be careful. There are traps up there, spring guns, and other things."

"I'll be careful."

He swung into saddle and loped the buckskin away, keeping the buildings between him and the firing.

When he cleared her house, a shot winged past him from the stone pile, but he slipped behind a hummock of sand and let the buckskin run. He was going to have to work fast.

Skirting the rocks, he worked down to the stream and walked Buck into it, then turned upstream. The water was no more than a foot deep, flowing over a gravel bottom, clear and bright. For a half mile he walked the horse upstream, then turned up on the bank, and followed a weaving course through a dense thicket of willows that slowly gave way to pine and cedar. After ten minutes more of riding, he rode out on a wide plateau.

Using a high, thumb-shaped butte for a marker, he worked higher and higher among the rocks until he was quite sure he was above and behind the cliff house. Then he dismounted, and dropped the bridle over Buck's head.

"You take care of yourself, Buck," he said quietly. "I've got places to go."

Leaving his carbine in its scabbard, he left the horse and walked down through the rocks toward the cliff edge.

The view was splendid. Far below he could see the scattered houses of Apple Cañon, all of them silent in the morning sun. There were only a few. Around the cluster of buildings that made the town, there were occasional puffs of smoke. From up here he could see clearly what was happening below. The defenders were still holding forth in the livery stable and bunkhouse, and apparently in Sadler's house. His own attacking party had fanned out until they had a line of riflemen across the pass and down close to the town. They were fighting as the plan had been, shrewdly and carefully, never exposing themselves.

Kilkenny had worked out that plan himself. He was quite sure from what he had learned, and from what Rusty and a couple of others who knew Apple Cañon had told him, that the well across from Nita's house was the only source of water. That one bucket was empty, he knew, for it lay there beside the well, and alongside of it the gun that had fallen from the man's hand after Kilkenny had shot him. There were a lot of men defending Apple Cañon, and it was going to be a hot day. If they could be held there, and kept from getting water, and, if during that time he could eliminate Royal Barnes, there would be chance of complete surrender on the part of the rustlers. He believed he could persuade Steele and Frame to let them go if they surrendered as a body and left the country. His only wish was to prevent any losses among his own men while breaking up the gang.

Suddenly, even as he watched, a man dashed from the rear of the bunkhouse and made a run for the well and the fallen bucket. He was halfway to the well before a gun spoke. Kilkenny would have known that gun in a million. It was Mort Davis who was firing.

The runner sprawled face down in the dust. That would keep them quiet for a while. Nobody would want to die that way. It was at least 600 feet to the floor of the valley from where Kilkenny stood. Remembering his calculations, he figured it would be at least fifty feet down to the cliff house and the window he had chosen. Undoubtedly there was an exit back somewhere not far from his horse, or at least somewhere among the boulders and crags either on top or behind the cliff. There had to be at least two exits. But there wasn't time to look for them now.

He had taken his rope from the saddle, and now he made it fast around the trunk of a gnarled and ancient cedar. Then he dropped it over the cliff. Carefully he eased himself over the edge and got both hands on the rope. Then, his feet hanging free, he began to lower himself. His hands gave him no trouble.

He was halfway down when the first shot came, followed by a yell. The shot was from the livery stable, and it clipped the rock wall he was facing. His face was stung with fragments of stone.

Immediately his own men opened up with a hot fire, and he lowered himself a bit more, then glanced down looking for the window. He saw it. A little to the right.

Another shot clipped close to him, but obviously whoever was shooting was taking hurried shots without proper aim or he would not have missed. He was just thanking all the gods that the men behind the stone pile hadn't spotted him when he heard a yell, and almost instantly a shot cut through his sleeve and stung his arm. Involuntarily he jerked, and almost lost his hold. Then, as bullets began to spatter around him, he found a foothold on the window sill, and hurriedly dropped inside.

Instantly he slipped out of line with the window and froze. There was no sound from inside. Only the rattle of rifle fire down below.

The room he was in was a bedroom, empty. It was small, comfortable, and the Indian blankets spread on the bed matched those on the wall. There was a crude table and a chair.

Kilkenny tiptoed across the room and put his hand on the knob. Then slowly he eased open the door.

A voice spoke.

"Come in, Kilkenny!"

XVIII

Quietly Kilkenny swung the door open and stepped into the room, poised to go for a gun.

A man sat in a chair at a table on which there was a dish of fruit. The man wore a white shirt, a broad leather belt, and gray trousers that had been neatly pressed and were tucked into cowhide boots. He also wore crossed gun belts and two guns. He was clean shaven except for a small mustache, and there was a black silk scarf about his neck. It was Victor Bonham.

"So," Kilkenny said thoughtfully, "it's you."

"That's right. Bonham or Barnes, whichever you prefer. Most people call me Royal Barnes."

"I've heard of you."

"And I've heard of you."

Royal Barnes stared at him, his eyes white and ugly. There was grim humor in them, too. "You're making trouble for me again," Barnes said.

"Again?" Kilkenny lifted an eyebrow.

"Yes. You killed the Webers. They were a bungling lot, but they were kinfolk, and people seem to think I should kill you because you killed them. I expect that's as good a reason as any."

"Mebbe."

"You were anxious to die, to come in that way."

"Safer than another way, I think," Kilkenny drawled.

Royal Barnes's eyes sharpened. "So? Somebody talks, do they? Well, it was time I got new men, anyway. You see, Kilkenny, you're a fool. This isn't going to stop me. This is merely a setback. Oh, I grant you it is going to cause me to recruit a new bunch of men. But this will rid me of some of your men, too. Some of the most dangerous men in the Live Oak country will be killed today. The next time, it will be easier. And, you see, I intend to come back, to reorganize, and to carry on with my plans. I'd have succeeded already but for you. Steele will fight, but if he isn't killed today, I'll have him killed within the week. The same for Frame and your friend, Gates. Gates isn't dangerous alone, but he might find someone else to work with, someone as dangerous as you."

The sound of firing had grown in tempo now, but Royal Barnes did not let his eyes shift one instant. He was cool, casual, but wary as a crouched tiger. In the quiet, well-ordered room away from the confusion below, he seemed like someone from another world. Only his eyes showed what was in him.

"You seen Steve Lord?" demanded Kilkenny.

"Lord?" Barnes's eyes changed a little. "He never comes here."

"He worked with you," Kilkenny flatly accused.

Barnes shrugged carelessly. "Of course. I had to use what tools I could find. I held Nita out to him as bait, and power. I told him I would give him the Steele Ranch. He is a fool."

Slowly Kilkenny reached for cigarette papers and began building a smoke, his fingers poised and careful. "You're wrong, Barnes. Steve is crazy. He's crazy with blood lust and a craving for power. He killed Des King. He killed Sam Carter and a half dozen other men. Now he's gunnin' for you, Barnes."

Royal Barnes sat up. "Are you tellin' the truth?" he demanded. "Steve Lord killed those men?"

Kilkenny quietly told him of all that had transpired. Outside, the shooting had settled to occasional shots, no more. A break was coming, and the tension was mounting with every second.

"Now," Kilkenny added, "if you want my hunch, I think Steve figgers to get you. He figgers with you gone, he'll be king bee around here."

Royal Barnes got up, and, for a moment, he stood listening.

"Somebody's on the trail now," he said suddenly.

That would be Steve. Instantly it came to Kilkenny with startling awareness that Barnes was waiting for something, some sound, some signal. If there was a spring gun on the main trail, it would stop Steve in his tracks.

He drew deeply on his cigarette. Somewhere he could hear water dripping slowly, methodically, as though counting off the seconds. Royal Barnes dropped a hand to the deck of cards on the table, and idly riffled them. The spattering sound of the flipping cards was loud in the room.

A heavy crash sounded again. That would be Mort

Davis. Somebody else trying to get water. Somebody who wouldn't try again.

Gravel rattled on the trail, and Kilkenny saw Royal Barnes's face tighten.

Then in the almost complete silence: *Bang!*

Royal Barnes dropped into a crouch and went for his gun with a sweeping movement. At the same instant, he dumped over the table and sent it crashing toward Kilkenny.

Kilkenny sprang aside barely in time to escape the table, and a shot crashed into the wall behind him. His own gun was out, and he triggered it twice with lightning-like rapidity. Through the smoke he could see Royal Barnes's eyes blazing with white light, and his lips parted in a snarl of killing fury.

Then the whole room was swept up in a crashing roar of guns. Something hit him and he was smashed back against the wall. His own guns were bucking and leaping in his hands, and he could see bright orange stabs of flame shot through with crimson streaks. He stepped forward and left, then again left, then back right, and moving in. Barnes had sprung backward through a doorway, and Kilkenny crossed the room, thumbing cartridges into his six-guns.

He went through the door with a leap. A bullet smashed the wall behind him and another tugged sharply at his sleeve. He stepped over, saw Barnes, and fired. The flame blossomed from Barnes's gun and Kilkenny felt his legs give way as he went to his knees. Barnes was backing away, his eyes wide and staring.

Slowly, desperately Kilkenny pulled himself erect and tried to get a gun up. Finally he did, and fired again, but Barnes was gone. Stumbling into the next room, he glared about. He was sick, felt himself weaving on his feet, and blood was running into his eyes.

The room was empty. Then a shot crashed behind him. He turned in a loose, stumbling circle and opened up with both guns on a weaving target. Then he felt himself falling, and he went down, hard.

He must have blacked out briefly, for when he opened his eyes he could smell the acrid smell of gunpowder, and it all came back with a rush. He turned over, and drew his knees under him. Then, catching the door frame, he pulled himself erect.

Royal Barnes, his face bloody and ugly, was propped against the wall opposite, his lips curved back in a snarl. A bullet had gone through one cheek, entering below the nose and coming out under the earlobe. Blood was flowing down his side. Blood was soaking his shirt, too. Barnes was cursing slowly, monotonously, horribly.

"You got me," he mouthed viciously, "but I'm killin' you, too, Kilkenny."

His gun swung up, and Kilkenny's own guns bucked in his hands. He saw Barnes wince and jerk, and the bloody face twisted in pain. Then the outlaw lunged out from the wall, staggering forward, his guns roaring a crescendo of hatred as he reeled toward Kilkenny. His shooting was wild, insane, desperate, and the shots went every which way.

He was toe to toe with Kilkenny when Kilkenny finished it. He finished it with four shots, two from each gun, at three-foot range, pumping the heavy .45 slugs into the outlaw. Barnes fell, and tumbled across Kilkenny's feet.

For what seemed a long time, Kilkenny stood erect, his guns dangling, empty. He stood staring blankly above the dead man at his feet, staring at the curious pattern of the Indian blanket across the room. He could feel his breath coming in great gasps, he could feel the warm blood on his face, and he could feel his growing weakness.

Then suddenly he heard a sound. He had dropped one of his guns. Abruptly he let go everything and fell headlong to the floor, lying there across Royal Barnes, the warm sunlight falling across his bloody face and hair. . . .

A long, long time later he felt hands touching him, and felt his own hand reaching for his gun. A big man loomed over him, and he was trying to get his gun up when he heard a woman's voice, speaking softly. Something in him listened, and he let go the gun. He seemed to feel water on his face, and pain throbbing through him like a live thing. Then he went all away again.

When he finally opened his eyes, he was lying on a wide bed in a sunlit room. Outside there were lilacs, and he could hear a bird singing. There was a flash of red, and a redbird flitted past the window.

The room was beautiful. It was a woman's room, quiet, neat, and smelling faintly of odors he seemed to remember from boyhood. He was still lying there when a door opened and Nita came in.

"Oh, you're awake." Nita laughed, and her eyes grew soft. "We had begun to believe you'd never come out of it."

"What happened?" he mumbled.

"You were badly hit. Six times, in all. Only one of

them serious. Through the body. There was a flesh wound in your leg, and one in your shoulder."

"Barnes?" Kilkenny asked quickly.

"He's dead. He was almost shot to pieces."

Kilkenny was quiet. He closed his eyes and lay still for a few minutes, remembering. In all his experience he had never known any man with such vitality. He rarely missed, and even in the hectic and confused battle in the cliff house he knew he had scored many hits. Yet Royal Barnes had kept shooting, kept fighting.

He opened his eyes again. "Steve Lord?"

"He was killed by a spring gun. A double-barreled shotgun loaded with soft lead pellets. He must have been killed instantly."

"The outlaw gang?"

"Wiped out. A few escaped in the last minutes, but not many. Webb Steele was wounded, but not badly. He's up and around. Has been for three days."

"Three days?" Kilkenny was incredulous. "How long have I been here?"

Nita smiled. "You've been very ill. The fight was two weeks ago."

Kilkenny lay quietly for a while, absorbing that. Then he remembered.

"But Calkins?"

"He was killed. Jaime killed him, and two of his family. Steele put it up to the other Calkins boys to leave me alone and to leave Jaime alone or fight him and all the ranchers. They backed down."

The two weeks more that Kilkenny spent in bed drifted by slowly, and at the end he became restless, worried. He lay in Nita Riordan's bed in her house, cared for by her, and receiving visits daily from Rusty and Tana, from Webb Steele, Frame, and some of the others. Even Lee Hall had come by to thank him. But he was restless. He kept thinking of Buck, and remembering the long, lonely trails.

Then one morning he got up early. Rusty and Tana had come in the night before. He saw their horses in the corral when he went out to saddle Buck.

The sun was just coming up and the morning air was cool and soft. He could smell the sagebrush and the mesquite blossoms. He felt restless and strange. Instinctively he knew he faced a crisis more severe than any brought on by his gunfight. Here, his life could change, but would it be best?

"I don't know, Buck," he said thoughtfully. "I think we'd better take a ride and think it over. Out there in the hills where the wind's in a man's face, he can think better."

He turned at the sound of a footstep, and saw Nita standing behind him. She looked fresh and lovely in a print dress, and her eyes were soft. Kilkenny looked away quickly, and cursed himself under his breath for his sudden weakness.

"Are you going, Kilkenny?" she asked.

He turned slowly. "I reckon, Nita. I reckon out there in the hills a man can think a sight better. I got things to figger out."

"Kilkenny," Nita asked suddenly, "why do you talk as you do? You can speak like an educated man when you wish. And you were, weren't you? Tana told me she picked up a picture you dropped once, a picture of your mother, and there was an inscription on it, something about it being sent to you in college."

"Yes, I reckon I can speak a sight better at times,

Nita. But I'm a Western man at heart, and I speak the way the country does." He hesitated, looking at her somberly. "I reckon I better go now."

There were tears in Nita's eyes, but she lifted her head and smiled at him.

"Of course, Kilkenny. Go, and if you decide you want to come back . . . don't hesitate. And, Buck"—she turned quickly to the long-legged horse—"if he starts back, you bring him very fast, do you hear?"

For an instant, Kilkenny hesitated again, then he swung into saddle.

The buckskin wheeled, and they went out of Apple Cañon at a brisk trot. Once he looked back, and Nita was standing where he had left her. She lifted her hand and waved.

He waved in return, then faced away to the west. The wind from over the plains, fresh with morning, came to his nostrils, and he lifted his head. The buckskin's ears were forward, and he was quickening his pace.

"You an' me, Buck," Kilkenny said slowly, "we ain't civilized. We're wild, and we belong to the far, open country where the wind blows and a man's eyes narrow down to distance."

Kilkenny sat sideward in the saddle and rolled a smoke. Then his voice lifted, and he sang:

> *I have a word to say, boys, only one to say,*
> *Don't never be no cow thief, don't never ride*
> *   no stray.*
> *Be careful of your rope, boys, and keep it on*
> *   the tree,*
> *But suit yourself about it, for it's nothing at all*
> *   to me!*

He sang softly, and the hoofs of the buckskin kept time to the singing, and Lance could feel the air in his face, and a long way ahead the trail curved into the mountains.

A Man Called Trent

1

Smoke lifted wistfully from the charred timbers of the house, and smoke lifted from the shed that had been Moffitt's barn. The corral bars were down and the saddle stock run off, and, where Dick Moffitt's homestead had been in the morning, there was now only desolation, emptiness, and death.

Dick Moffitt himself lay sprawled on the ground. The dust was scratched deeply where his fingers had dug in the agony of death. Even from where he sat on the long-legged buckskin, the man known as Trent could see he had been shot six times. Three of those bullets had gone in from the front. The other three had been fired directly into his back by a man who stood over him. And Dick Moffitt wore no gun.

The little green valley was still in the late afternoon sun. It was warm, and there was still a faint heat emanating from the charred timber of the house.

The man who called himself Trent rode his horse

around the house. Four or five men had come here. One of them riding a horse with a split right rear hoof. They had shot Moffitt down and then burned his layout.

What about the kids? What about Sally Crane, who was sixteen? And young Jack Moffitt, who was fourteen? Whatever had happened, there was no evidence of them here. He hesitated, looking down the trail. Had they been taken away by the killers? Sally, perhaps, but not Jack. If the killers had found the two, Jack would have been dead.

Thoughtfully Trent turned away. The buckskin knew the way was toward home, and he quickened his pace. There were five miles to go, five miles of mountains and heavy woods, and no clear trails.

This could be it. Always, he had been sure it would come. Even when happiest, the knowledge that sooner or later he must sling his gun belts on his hips had been ever present in the back of his mind. Sooner or later there would be trouble, and he had seen it coming here along the rimrock.

Slightly more than a year ago he had built his cabin and squatted in the lush green valley among the peaks. No cattle ranged this high. No wandering cowpunchers drifted up here. Only the other nesters had found homes, the Hatfields, O'Hara, Smithers, Moffitt, and the rest.

Below, in the vicinity of Cedar Bluff, there was one ranch—one and only one. On the ranch and in the town, one man ruled supreme. He rode with majesty, and, when he walked, he strode with the step of kings. He never went unattended. He allowed no man to address him unless he spoke first, he issued orders and bestowed favor like an Eastern potentate, and, if there were some who disputed his authority, he put them down, crushed them.

King Bill Hale had come West as a boy, and he had had money even then. In Texas he had driven cattle over the trails and had learned to fight and sling a gun, and to drive a bargain that was tight and cruel. Then he had come farther West, moved into the town of Cedar Bluff, built the Castle, and drove out the cattle rustlers who had used the valley as a hide-out. The one other honest rancher in the valley he bought out, and, when that man had refused to sell, Hale had told him to sell, or else. And he had cut the offered price in half. The man sold.

Cedar Bluff and Cedar Valley lived under the eye of King Bill. A strong man and an able one, Hale had slowly become power mad. The valley was cut off from both New Mexico and Arizona. In his own world he could not be touched. His will was law. He owned the Mecca, a saloon and gambling house. He owned the stage station, the stage line itself, and the freight company that hauled supplies in and produce out. He owned the Cedar Hotel, the town's one decent rooming house. He owned 60,000 acres of good grazing land and controlled 100,000 more. His cattle were numbered in the tens of thousands, and two men rode beside him when he went among his other men. One was rough, hard-scaled Pete Shaw, and the other was his younger son, Cub Hale. Behind him trailed the gold-dust twins, Dunn and Ravitz, both gunmen.

The man who called himself Trent rarely visited Cedar Bluff. Sooner or later, he knew, there would be someone from the outside, someone who knew him, someone who would recognize him for what and who he was, and then the word would go out.

"That's Kilkenny!"

Men would turn to look, for the story of the strange, drifting gunman was known to all in the West, even though there were few men anywhere who knew him by sight, few who could describe him or knew the way he lived.

Mysterious, solitary, and shadowy, the gunman called Kilkenny had been everywhere. He drifted in and out of towns and cow camps, and sometimes there would be a brief and bloody gun battle, and then Kilkenny would be gone again, and only the body of the man who had dared to try Kilkenny remained.

So Kilkenny had taken the name of Trent, and in the high peaks he had found the lush green valley where he built his cabin and ran a few head of cows and broke wild horses. It was a lonely life, but when he was there, he hung his guns on a peg and carried only his rifle, and that for game or for wolves.

Rarely, not over a dozen times in the year, he went down to Cedar Bluff for supplies, packed them back, and stayed in the hills until he was running short again. He stayed away from the Mecca, and most of all he avoided the Crystal Palace, the new and splendid dance hall and gambling house owned by the woman Nita Riordan.

The cabin in the pines was touched with the red glow of a sun setting beyond the notch, and he swung down from the buckskin and slapped the horse cheerfully on the shoulder.

"Home again, Buck! It's a good feeling, isn't it?"

He stripped the saddle and bridle from the horse and carried them into the log barn, then he turned the buckskin into the corral, and forked over a lot of fresh green grass.

It was a lonely life, yet he was content. Only at times did he find himself looking long at the stars and thinking about the girl in Cedar Bluff. Did she know he was here? Remembering Nita from the Live Oak country, he decided she did. Nita Riordan knew all that was going on; she always had. •

He went about the business of preparing a meal, and thought of Parson Hatfield and his tall sons. What would the mountaineer do now? Yet, need he ask that question? Could he suspect, even for a moment, that the Hatfields would do anything but fight? They were the type. They were men who had always built with their hands and who were beholden to no man. They were not gunfighters, but they were lean, hard-faced men, tall and stooped a little, who carried their rifles as if they were part of them. And big Dan O'Hara, the talkative, friendly Irishman who always acted as though campaigning for public office—could he believe that Dan would do other than fight?

War was coming to the high peaks, and Trent's face grew somber as he thought of it. War meant that he would once more be shooting, killing. He could, of course, mount in the morning and ride away. He could give up this place in the highlands and go once more, but even as the thought came to him, he did not recognize it as even a remote possibility. Like O'Hara and the Hatfields, he would fight.

There were other things to consider. The last time he had been to Cedar Bluff, there had been a letter from Lee Hall, the Ranger.

We're getting along all right here, but I thought you would like to know: Cain Brockman is out. He swears he will hunt you down and kill you for killing his brother and whipping him with your fists. And he'll try, so be careful.

He dropped four slices of bacon into the frying pan, humming softly to himself. Then he put on some coffee water and sat watching the bacon. When it was ready, he took it out of the pan and put it on a tin plate. He was reaching for the coffee when he heard a muffled movement.

Instantly he froze in position. His eyes fastened on the blanket that separated his bedroom from the living room of the two-room cottage. His guns were hanging from a peg near the cupboard. He would have to cross the room to them. His rifle was nearer.

Rising, he went about the business of fixing the coffee, and, when close to the rifle, he dropped his hand to it. Then, swinging it hip high, he crossed the room with a bound, and jerked back the blanket.

Two youngsters sat on the edge of his homemade bed, a slender, wide-eyed girl of sixteen and a boy with a face thickly sprinkled with freckles. They sat tightly together, frightened and pale.

Slowly he let the gun butt down to the floor. "Well, I'll be . . . ! Say, how did you youngsters get here?"

The girl swallowed and stood up, trying to curtsey. Her hair, which was very lovely, hung in two thick blonde braids. Her dress was cheap and cotton and now, after rough treatment, was torn and dirty. "We're . . . I mean, I'm Sally Crane, and this is Jackie Moffitt."

"They burned us out!" Jackie cried out, his face twisted and pale. "Them Hales done it! An' they kilt Pappy!"

"I know." Trent looked at them gravely. "I came by

that way. Come on out here an' we'll eat. Then you can tell me about it."

"They come in about sunup this mornin'," Jack said. "They told Pap he had two hours to get loaded an' movin'. Pap, he allowed he wasn't movin'. This was government land an' he was settled legal, an' he was standin' on his rights."

"What happened?" Trent asked. He sliced more bacon and dropped it in the pan.

"The young 'un, he shot Pap. Shot him three times afore he could move. Then after he fell, he emptied his gun into him."

Something sank within Trent, for he could sense the fight that was coming. The "young 'un" would probably be Cub Hale. He remembered that slim, erect, panther-like young man in white buckskins and riding his white horse, that young, handsome man who loved to kill. Here it was, and there was no way a man could duck it. But, no. It wasn't his fight. Not yet, it wasn't.

"How'd you kids happen to come here?" he asked kindly.

"We had to get away. Sally was gettin' wood for the house, an', when I met her, we started back. Then we heard the shootin', an', when I looked through the brush, I seen the young 'un finishin' Pap. I wanted to fight, but I ain't got no gun."

"Did they look for you?" Trent asked.

"Uhn-huh. We heard one of 'em say he wanted Sally!" Jackie glanced at the girl, whose face was white, her eyes wide. "They allowed there wasn't no use killin' her . . . yet!"

"You had horses?" Trent asked.

"Uhn-huh. We done left them in the brush. We

wasn't sure but what they'd come here, too. But we come here because Pap, he done said if anythin' ever happened to him, we was to come here first. He said you was a good man, an' he figgered you was some shakes with a gun."

"All right." Trent dished them out some food. "You kids can stay here tonight. I got blankets enough. Then in the mornin' I'll take you down to Parson's."

"Let me fix that," Sally pleaded, reaching for the skillet. "I can cook."

"She sure can," Jackie declared admiringly. "She cooked for us all the time."

A horse's hoof *clicked* on a stone, and Trent doused the light instantly. "Get down," he whispered hoarsely. "On the floor. Let's see who this is."

He could hear the horses coming closer, two of them from the sound. Then a voice rang out sharply.

"Halloo, the house! Step out here!"

From inside the door, Trent replied shortly: "Who is it? What d' you want?"

"It don't make a damn who it is! Trent, we're givin' you till noon tomorrow to hit the trail! You're campin' on Hale range! We're movin' everybody off!"

Trent laughed harshly. "That's right amusin', friend," he said dryly. "You go back an' tell King Bill Hale that I'm stayin' right where I am. This is government land, filed on all fittin' an' proper." He glimpsed the light on a gun barrel and spoke sharply. "Don't try it, Dunn. I know you're there by your voice. If you've got a lick of sense, you know you're outlined against the sky. A blind man could get you both at this range."

Dunn cursed bitterly. Then he shouted: "You won't get away with this, Trent!"

"Go back an' tell Hale I like it here, an' I'm plannin' to stay!"

When they had gone, Trent turned to the youngsters. "We'll have a little time now. Sally, you take the bed in the other room, Jackie an' me, we'll bunk out here."

"But . . . ?" Sally protested.

"Go ahead. You'll need all the sleep you can get. I think the trouble has just started. But don't be afraid. Everything is goin' to be all right."

"I'm not afraid." Sally Crane looked at him with large, serious eyes. "You'll take care of us, I know."

He stood there a long minute staring after her. It was a strange feeling to be trusted, and trusted so implicitly. The childish sincerity of the girl moved him as nothing had ever moved him before. He recognized the feeling for what it was, the need within him to protect and care for something beyond himself. It was that, in part, that during these past years had led him to fight so many fights that were not his. And yet, was not the cause of human liberty and freedom always every man's trust?

Jackie was going about the business of making a bed on the floor as though he had spent his life at it. He seemed pleased with this opportunity to show some skill, some ability to do things.

Trent reached up and took down his guns and checked them as he had every night of the entire year in which they had hung from the peg. For a minute after he completed the check, he held them. He liked the feel of them, even when he hated what they meant. Slowly he replaced them on the peg.

II

The early morning sun was just turning the dew-drenched grass into settings for diamonds when Trent was out of his pallet and roping some horses. Yet, early as it was when he returned to the cabin, the fire was going and Sally was preparing breakfast. She smiled at him, but her eyes were red and he could see she had been crying.

Jackie, beginning to realize now the full meaning of the tragedy, was showing his grief through his anger, but was very quiet. Trent was less worried about Jackie than about Sally. Only six years before, according to what Dick Moffitt had told him, Sally Crane had been found hiding in the bushes. Her father's wagons had been burned and her parents murdered by renegades posing as Indians. Since then, Dick had cared for her. Dick's wife had died scarcely a year before, and the girl had tried to take over the household duties, yet even to a Western girl, hardened to a rough life, two such tragedies, each driving her from a home, might be enough to upset her life.

When breakfast was over, he took them out to the saddled horses. Then he walked back to the cabin alone, and, when he returned, he carried an old Sharps rifle. He looked at it a moment, and then he glanced up at Jackie. The boy's eyes were widening, unbelieving, yet bright with hope.

"Jackie," Trent said quietly, "when I was fourteen, I was a man. Had to be. Well, it looks like your pappy dyin' has made you a man, too. I'm goin' to give you this Sharps. She's an old gun, but she can shoot. But Jackie, I'm not givin' this gun to a boy. I'm givin' it to a man. I'm givin' it to Jackie Moffitt, an' he's already showed himself pretty much of a man. A man, Jackie, he don't ever use a gun unless he has to. He don't go around shootin' heedless-like. He shoots only when he has to, an' then he don't miss. This gun's a present, Jackie, an' there's no strings attached, but it carries a responsibility, an' that is never to use it against a man unless it's in defense of your life or the lives or homes of those you love. You're to keep it loaded always. A gun ain't no good to a man unless it's loaded, an', if it's seen settin' around, people won't be handlin' it careless. They'll say 'that's Jackie Moffitt's gun, an' it's always loaded.' It's always guns people think are empty that kill people by accident."

"Gosh!" Jackie stared in admiration at the battered old Sharps. "That's a weapon, man!" Then he looked up at Trent, and his eyes were filled with tears of sincerity. "Mister Trent, I sure do promise! I'll never use no gun unless I have to!"

Trent swung into the saddle and watched the others mount. He carried his own Winchester, one of the

new 1873 models that were replacing the old Sharps
on the frontier. He was under no illusions. If King Bill
Hale had decided to put an end to the nesters among
the high peaks, he would probably succeed. But Hale
was so impressed with his own power that he was not
reckoning with the Hatfields, O'Hara, or himself.

"Y'know, Jackie," Trent said thoughtfully, "there's
a clause in the Constitution that says the right of an
American to keep and bear arms shall not be
abridged. They put that in there so a man would always have a gun to defend his home or his liberty.
Right now there's a man in this valley who is tryin' to
take the liberty an' freedom of some men away from
'em. When a man starts that, and when there isn't
any law to help, you got to fight. I've killed men,
Jackie, an' it ain't a good thing, no way. But I never
killed a man unless he deserved killin' an' unless he
forced me to a corner where it was me or him. This
here country is big enough for all, but some men get
greedy for money or power, an', when they do, the little men have to fight to keep what they got. Your
pappy died in a war for freedom just as much as if he
was killed on a battlefield somewheres. Whenever a
brave man dies for what he believes, he wins more'n
he loses. Maybe not for him, but for men like him
that want to live honest an' true."

The trail narrowed and grew rougher, and Trent
felt a quick excitement within him, as he always did
when he rode up to this windy plateau. They went up
through the tall pines toward the knife-like ridges
that crested the divide, and, when they finally
reached the plateau, he reined in, as he always did
when he reached that spot.

Off over the vast distance that was Cedar Valley

lay the blue haze that deepened to purple against the far-distant mountains. Here the air was fresh and clear, crisp with the crispness of the high peaks and the sense of limitless distance.

Skirting the rim, Trent led on and finally came to the second place he loved, a place he not only loved but which was a challenge to all that was in him. For here the divide, with its skyscraping ridges, was truly a divide. It drew a ragged, mountainous line between the lush beauty of Cedar Valley and the awful waste of the scarred and tortured Smoky Desert.

Always there seemed a haze of dust or smoke hanging in the sky over Smoky Desert, and what lay below it, no man could say, for no known trail led down the steep cañon to the waste below. An Indian had once told him his fathers knew of a trail to the bottom, but no living man knew it, and no man seemed to care, nobody but Trent, drawn by his own loneliness to the vaster loneliness below. Far away were ragged mountains, red, black, and broken like the jagged stumps of broken teeth gnawing at the sky. It was, he believed, the far edge of what was actually an enormous crater, greater than any other of its kind on earth.

"Someday," he told his companions, "I'm goin' down there. It looks like the mouth of hell itself, but I'm goin' down."

Parson Hatfield and his four tall sons were all in sight when the three rode up to the cabin. All were carrying their long Kentucky rifles.

"Alight, Trent," Parson drawled, widening his gash of a mouth into a smile. "We was expectin' 'most anybody else. Been some ructions down to the valley."

"Yeah." Trent swung down. "They killed Dick Moffitt. These are his kids, Parson. I figgered maybe you could make a place for 'em."

"You thought right, son. The good Lord takes care of His own, but we have to help. There's always room for another beneath the roof of a Hatfield."

Quincy Hatfield, oldest of the lean, raw-boned Kentucky boys, joined them. "Howdy," he said. "Did Pap tell you all about Leathers?"

"Leathers?" Trent frowned in quick apprehension. "What about him?"

"He ain't a-goin' to sell anything to us no more." The tall young man spat and shifted his rifle to the hollow of his arm. "That makes the closest store over at Blazer, an' that's three days across the mountains."

Trent shrugged, frowning. "Aims to freeze us out or kill us off." He glanced at Parson speculatively. "What are you plannin'?"

Hatfield shook his head. "Nothin' so far. We sort of figgered we might get together with the rest of the nesters an' try to figger out somethin'. I had Jake ride down to get O'Hara, Smithers, an' young Bartram. We got to have us a confab." Parson Hatfield rubbed his long, grizzled jaw and stared at Trent. His gray eyes were inquisitive, sly. "Y'know, Trent, I always had me an idea you was some shakes of a battler yourself. Maybe, if you'd wear some guns, you'd make some of them gun-slick *hombres* of Hale's back down cold."

Trent smiled. "Why, Parson, I reckon you guess wrong. Me, I'm a peace-lovin' *hombre*. I like the hills, an' all I ask is to be let alone."

"An' if they don't let alone?" Parson stared at him shrewdly, chewing his tobacco slowly and watching Trent with his keen gray eyes.

"If they don't let me alone? An' if they start killin' my friends?" Trent turned to look at Hatfield. "Why, Parson, I reckon I'd take my guns down from that peg. I reckon I'd fight."

Hatfield nodded. "That's all I wanted to know, Trent. I ain't spent my life a-feudin' without knowin' a fightin' man when I see one. O'Hara an' young Bartram will fight. Smithers, too, but he don't stack up like no fightin' man. My young 'uns, they cut their teeth on a rifle stock, so I reckon when the fightin' begins I'll be bloodin' the two young 'uns like I did the two older back in Kentucky."

Trent kicked his toe into the dust. "Don't you reckon we better get the womenfolks off to Blazer? There ain't many of us, Parson, an' Hale must have fifty riders. We better get them out while the gettin' is good."

"Hale's got more'n fifty riders, but the women'll stay, Trent. Ma, she ain't for goin'. You ain't got no woman of your own, Trent, so I don't reckon you know how unpossible ornery they can be, but Ma, she'd be fit to be tied if it was said she was goin' to go to Blazer while we had us a scrap. Ma loaded rifles for me in Kentucky when she was a gal, an' she loaded 'em for me crossin' the plains, an' she done her share of shootin'. Trent, I'd rather face all them Hales than Ma if we tried to send her away. She always says her place is with her menfolks, an' there she'll stay. I reckon Quince's wife feels the same, an' so does Jesse's woman."

Trent nodded. "Parson, we got us an argument when the rest of them get here. They've got to leave their places an' come up here. Together, we could make a pretty stiff fight of it. Scattered, they'd cut us down one by one." He swung into the saddle. "I'm goin' down to Cedar Bluff. I'm goin' to see Leathers."

Without waiting for a reply, Trent swung the buckskin away and loped down the trail. He knew very well he was taking a chance. The killing had started. Dick Moffitt was down. They had burned his place, and within no time at all the Hale riders would be carrying fire and blood through the high hills, wiping out the nesters. If he could but see King Bill, there might be a chance.

Watching him go, Parson Hatfield shook his head doubtfully and then turned to his eldest. "Quince, you rope yourself a horse, boy, an' you an' Jesse follow him into Cedar Bluff. He may get hisself into trouble."

A few minutes later the two tall, loose-limbed mountain men started down the trail on their flea-bitten mustangs. They were solemn, dry young men who chewed tobacco and talked slowly, but they had grown up in the hard school of the Kentucky mountains, and they had come West across the plains.

III

Unknowing, Trent rode rapidly. He knew what he had to do, yet, even as he rode, his thoughts were on the Hatfields. He liked them. Hardworking, honest, opinionated, they were fierce to resent any intrusion on their personal liberty, their women's honor, or their pride.

They were the kind of men to ride the river with. It was such men who had been the backbone of America, the fence-corner soldier, the man who carried his rifle in the hollow of his arm, but the kind of men who knew that fighting was not a complicated business but simply a matter of killing and keeping from being killed. They were men of the blood of Dan Boone, Kit Carson, Jim Bridger, the Green Mountain Boys, Dan Freeman, and those who whipped the cream of the British regulars at Concord, Bunker Hill, and New Orleans. They knew nothing of Prussian methods of close-order drill. They did nothing by the numbers. Many of them had flat feet and many had few teeth. But they fought from cover and they made every shot count—and they lived while the enemy died.

The Hale Ranch was a tremendous power, and it had many riders, and they were men hired for their ability with guns as well as with ropes and cattle. King Bill Hale, wise as he was, was grown confident, and he did not know the caliber of such men as the Hatfields. The numbers Hale had might lead to victory, but not until many men had died.

O'Hara? The big Irishman was blunt and hard. He was not the shrewd fighter the Hatfields were, but he was courageous, and he knew not the meaning of retreat. Himself? Trent's eyes narrowed. He had no illusions about himself. As much as he avoided trouble, he knew that within him there was something that held a fierce resentment for abuse of power, for tyranny. There was something in him that loved battle, too. He could not dodge the fact. He would avoid trouble, but when it came, he would go into it with a fierce love of battle for battle's sake. Someday, he knew, he would ride back to the cattle in the high meadows, back to the cabin in the pines, and he would take down his guns and buckle them on, and then Kilkenny would ride again.

The trail skirted deep cañons and led down toward the flat bottom land of the valley. King Bill, he knew, was learning what he should have known long ago, that the flatlands, while rich, became hot and dry in the summer weather, while the high meadows remained green and lush, and there cattle could graze and grow fat. And King Bill was moving to take back what he had missed so long ago. Had the man been less blinded by his own power and strength, he would have hesitated over the Hatfields. One and all, they were fighting men.

Riding into Cedar Bluff would be dangerous now. Changes were coming to the West, and Trent had hoped to leave his reputation in Texas. He could see the old days of violence were nearing an end. Billy the Kid had been killed by Pat Garrett. King Fisher and Ben Thompson were heard of much less; one and all, the gunmen were beginning to taper off. Names that had once been mighty in the West were already drifting into legend. As for himself, few men could describe him. He had come and gone like a shadow, and where he was now no man could say, and only one woman.

King Bill even owned the law in Cedar Bluff. He had called an election to choose a sheriff and a judge. Yet there had been no fairness in that election. It was true that no unfair practices had been tolerated, but the few nesters and small ranchers had no chance against the fifty-odd riders from the Hale Ranch and the townspeople who needed the Hale business or who worked for him. Trent had voted himself. He had voted for O'Hara. There had been scarcely a dozen votes for O'Hara. One of those votes had been that of Jim Hale, King Bill's oldest son. Another, he knew, had been the one person in Cedar Bluff who he had studiously avoided, the half-Spanish, half-Irish girl, Nita Riordan. Trent had avoided Nita Riordan because the beautiful girl from the Texas-Mexican border was the one person who knew him for what he was—who knew him as Kilkenny, the gunfighter.

Whenever Trent thought of the trouble in Cedar Bluff, he thought less of King Bill but more of Cub

Hale. The older man was huge and powerful physically, but he was not a killer. It was true that he was responsible for deaths, but they were of men who he believed to be his enemies or to be trespassing on his land. But Cub Hale was a killer. Two days after Trent had first come to Cedar Bluff he had seen Cub Hale kill a man. It was a drunken miner, a burly, quarrelsome fellow who could have done with a pistol barrel alongside the head, but needed nothing more. Yet Cub Hale had shot him down ruthlessly, heedlessly.

Then there had been the case of Jack Lindsay, a known gunman, and Cub had killed him in a fair, stand-up fight, with an even break all around. Lindsay's gun had barely cleared its holster when the first of three shots hit him. Trent had walked over to the man's body to see for himself. You could have put a playing card over those three holes. That was shooting. There had been other stories of which Trent had only heard. Cub had caught two rustlers, red-handed, and killed them both. He had killed a Mexican sheepherder in Magdalena. He had killed a gunfighter in Fort Sumner, and gut shot another one near Socorro, leaving him to die slowly in the desert.

Besides Cub, there were Dunn and Ravitz. Both were graduates of the Lincoln County War. Both had been in Trail City and had left California just ahead of a posse. Both were familiar names among the dark brotherhood that lived by the gun. They were strictly cash-and-carry warriors, men whose guns were for hire.

"Buck," Trent told his horse thoughtfully, "if war starts in the Cedar hills, there'll be a power of killin'. I got to see King Bill. I got to talk reason into him."

Cedar Bluff could have been any cow town. Two

things set it off from the others. One was the stone stage station, which also contained the main office of the Hale Ranch; the other was the huge and sprawling Crystal Palace, belonging to Nita Riordan.

Trent loped the yellow horse down the dusty street and swung down in front of Leathers's General Store. He walked into the cool interior. The place smelled of leather and dry-goods. At the rear, where they dispensed food and other supplies, he halted.

Bert Leathers looked up from his customer as Trent walked in, and Trent saw his face change. Leathers wet his lips and kept his eyes away from Trent. At the same time, Trent heard a slight movement, and, glancing casually around, he saw a heavyset cowhand wearing a tied-down gun lounging against a rack of saddles. The fellow took his cigarette from his lips and stared at Trent from shrewd, calculating eyes.

"Need a few things, Leathers," Trent said casually. "Got a list here."

The man Leathers was serving stepped aside. He was a townsman, and he looked worried.

"Sorry, Trent," Leathers said abruptly, "I can't help you. All you nesters have been ordered off the Hale range. I can't sell you anything."

"Lickin' Hale's boots, are you?" Trent asked quietly. "I heard you were, Leathers, but doubted it. I figgered a man with nerve enough to come West an' set up for himself would be his own man."

"I am my own man!" Leathers snapped, his pride stung. "I just don't want your business!"

"I'll remember that, Leathers," Trent said quietly. "When all this is over, I'll remember that. You're forgettin' something. This is America, an' here the people always win. Maybe not at first, but they always win in the end. When this is over, if the people win, you'd better leave . . . understand?"

Leathers looked up, his face white and yet angry. He looked uncertain.

"You all better grab yourself some air," a cool voice suggested.

Trent turned, and he saw the gunhand standing with his thumbs in his belt, grinning at him. "Better slide, Trent. What the man says is true. King Bill's takin' over. I'm here to see Leathers doesn't have no trouble with nesters."

"All right," Trent said quietly, "I'm a quiet man myself. I expect that rightly I should take the gun away from you an' shove it down your throat. But Leathers is probably gun shy, an' there might be some shootin', so I'll take a walk."

"My name's Dan Cooper," the gunhand suggested mildly. "Any time you really get on the prod about shovin' this gun down my throat, look me up."

Trent smiled. "I'll do that, Cooper, an', if you stay with King Bill, I'm afraid you're going to have a heavy diet of lead. He's cuttin' a wide swath."

"Uhn-huh." Cooper was cheerful and tough. "But he's got a blade that cuts 'em off short."

"Ever see the Hatfields shoot?" Trent suggested. "Take a tip, old son, an', when those long Kentucky rifles open up, you be somewhere else."

Dan Cooper nodded sagely. "You got somethin' there, pardner. You really have. That Parson's got him a cold eye."

Trent turned and started for the street, but Cooper's voice halted him. The gunhand had followed him to the door.

"Say," Cooper's voice was curious. "Was you ever in Dodge?"

Trent smiled. "Maybe. Maybe I was. You think that one over, Cooper." He looked at the gunhand thoughtfully. "I like you," he said bluntly, "so I'm givin' you a tip. Get on your horse an' ride. King Bill's got the men, but he ain't goin' to win. Ride, because I always hate to kill a good man."

Trent turned and walked down the street. Behind him, he could feel Dan Cooper's eyes on his back.

The gunman was scowling. "Now, who the hell . . . ?" he muttered. "That *hombre*'s salty, plumb salty."

Three more attempts to buy supplies proved to Trent he was frozen out in Cedar Bluff. Worried now, he started back to his horse. The nesters could not buy in Cedar Bluff, and that meant their only supplies must come by the long wagon trip across country from Blazer. Trent felt grave doubts that Hale would let the wagons proceed unmolested, and their little party was so small they could not spare men to guard the wagons on the three-day trek over desert and mountains.

"Trent!" He turned slowly and found himself facing Price Dixon, a dealer from the Crystal Palace. "Nita wants to see you. Asked me to find you and ask if you'd come to see her."

For a long moment, Trent hesitated. Then he shrugged. "All right," he said, "but it won't do any good to have her seen with me. We nesters aren't looked upon with much favor these days."

Dixon nodded, sober faced. "Looks like a shoot-out. I'm afraid you boys are on the short end of it."

"Maybe."

Dixon glanced at him out of the corner of his eye. "Don't you wear a gun? They'll kill you someday."

"Without a gun you don't have many fights."

"It wouldn't stop Cub Hale. When he decides to shoot, he does. He won't care whether you are packin' a gun or not."

"No. It wouldn't matter to him."

Price Dixon studied him thoughtfully. "Who are you, Trent?" he asked softly.

"I'm Trent, a nester. Who else?"

"That's what I'm wondering. I'm dry behind the ears. I've been dealing cards in the West ever since the War Between the States. I've seen men who packed guns, and I know the breed. You're not Wes Hardin, and you're not Hickok, and you're not one of the Earps. You never drink much, so you can't be Thompson. Whoever you are, you've packed a gun."

"Don't lose any sleep over it."

Dixon shrugged. "I won't. I'm not taking sides in this fight or any other. If I guess, I won't say. You're a friend of Nita's, and that's enough for me. Besides, Jaime Brigo likes you." He glanced at Trent. "What do you think of him?"

"Brigo?" Trent said thoughtfully. "Brigo is part Yaqui, part devil, and all loyal, but I'd sooner tackle three King Bill Hales than him. He's poison."

Dixon nodded. "I think you're right. He sits there by her door night after night, apparently asleep, yet he knows more about what goes on in this town than any five other men."

"Dixon, you should talk Nita into selling out. Good chance of getting the place burned out or shot up if she stays. It's going to be a long fight."

"Hale doesn't think so."

"Parson Hatfield does."

"I've seen Hatfield. He looks like something I'd leave alone." Dixon paused. "I was in Kentucky once, a long time ago. The Hatfields have had three feuds. Somehow, there's always Hatfields left."

"Well, Price"—Trent threw his cigarette into the dust—"I've seen a few fighting men, too, and I'm glad the Hatfields are on my side, an' particularly the Parson."

IV

The Crystal Palace was one of those places that made the Western frontier what it was. Wherever there was money to spend, gambling joints could be found, and some became ornate palaces of drinking and gambling like this one. They had them in Abilene and Dodge, but not so much farther West.

Cedar Bluff had the highly paid riders of the Hale Ranch. It also drew miners from Rock Creek. The Palace was all gilt and glass, and there were plenty of games going, including roulette, faro, and dice. Around the room at scattered tables were at least a dozen poker games.

Nita Riordan, Trent decided, was doing all right. This place was making money and lots of it. Trent knew a lot about gambling houses, enough to know what a rake-off these games would be turning in to the house. There was no necessity for crooked games. The percentage was entirely adequate.

They crossed the room, and Trent saw Jaime Brigo sitting on a chair against the wall as he always sat. The sombrero on the floor was gray and new. He wore dark, tailored trousers and a short velvet jacket, also black. The shirt under it was silk and blue. He wore, as always, two guns.

He looked up as Trent approached, and his lips parted over even white teeth. "*Buenos días, señor,*" he said.

Price stopped and nodded his head toward the door. "She's in there."

Trent faced the door, drew a deep breath, and stepped inside. His heart was pounding, and his mouth was dry. No woman ever stirred him so deeply or made him realize so much what he was missing in his lonely life.

It was a quiet room, utterly different from the garish display of the gambling hall behind him. It was a room to live in, the room of one who loved comfort and peace. On a ledge by the window were several potted plants; on the table lay an open book. These things he absorbed rather than observed, for all his attention was centered upon Nita Riordan.

She stood across the table, taller than most women, with a slender yet voluptuous body that made a pulse pound in his throat. She was dressed for evening, an evening walking among the tables of the gambling room, and she was wearing a black and spangled gown, utterly different from the room in which she stood. Her eyes were wide now, her full lips parted a little, and, as he stopped across the table, he could see the lift of her bosom as she took a deep breath.

"Nita," he said softly. "You've not changed. You're the same."

"I'm older, Lance," she said softly, "more than a year older."

"Has it been only a year? It seems so much longer." He looked at her thoughtfully. "And you are lovely, as always. I think you could never be anything but lovely and desirable."

"And yet," she reminded him, "when you could have had me, you rode away. Lance, do you live all alone in that cabin of yours? Without anyone?"

He nodded. "Except for memories. Except for the thinking, I do. And the thinking only makes it worse, for, whenever I think of you, and all that could be, I remember the Brockmans, Bert Polti, and all those others back down the trail. Then I start wondering how long it will be before I fall in the dust myself."

"That's why I sent for you," Nita told him. Her eyes were serious and worried. She came around the table and took his hands. "Lance, you've got to go. Leave here, now. I can hold your place for you, if that's what you want. If that doesn't matter, say so, and I'll go with you. I'll go with you anywhere, but we must leave here."

"Why?" It was like him to be direct. She looked up into his dark, unsmiling face. "Why, Nita? Why do you want me to go?"

"Because they are going to kill you!" she exclaimed. She caught his arm. "Lance, they are cruel, ruthless, vicious. It isn't King Bill. He's their leader, but what he does he believes to be right. It's Cub. He loves to kill. I've seen him. Last week he killed a boy in the street in front of my place. He shot him down, and then emptied his gun into him with slow, methodical shots. He's a fiend!"

Lance shook his head. "I'll stay, no matter."

"But listen, Lance," she protested. "I've heard them talking here. They are sure you'll fight. I don't know why they think so, but they do. They've decided you must die, and soon. They won't give you a chance. I know that."

"I can't, Nita. These people in the high meadows are my friends. They depend upon me to stand by them. I won't be the first to break and run, or the last. I'm staying. I'm going to fight it out here, Nita, and we'll see who is to win, the people or a man of power and greed."

"I was afraid you'd say that." Nita looked at him seriously. "Hale is out to win, Lance. He's got men. They don't know you're Lance Kilkenny. I've heard them talking, and they do suspect that you're something more than a nester named Trent. But Hale is sure he is right, and he'll fight to the end."

Trent nodded. "I know. When a man thinks he is right, he will fight all the harder. Has anybody tried to talk to him?"

"You can't. You can't even address him. He lives in a world of his own. In his way, I think he is a little insane, Lance, but he does have ability, and he has strength. He's a fighter, too."

Trent studied her thoughtfully. "You seem to know him. Has he made you any trouble?"

"Why do you ask that?" Nita asked quickly.

"I want to know."

"He wants to marry me, Lance."

Trent tightened and then stared at her. "I see," he said slowly. "And you?"

"I don't know." She hesitated, looking away. "Lance, can't you see? I'm lonely. Dreadfully, frighteningly lonely. I have no life here, just a business. I know no women but those of the dance hall. I see no one who feels as I do, thinks as I do. King Bill is strong. He knows how to appeal to a woman. He has a lot to offer. He has a son as old as I, but he's only forty, and he's a powerful man, Lance. A man a woman could be proud of. I don't like what he's doing, but he does think he's right. No," she said finally, "I won't marry him. I'll admit, I've been tempted. He's a little insane, I think. Drunk with power. He got too much and got it too easily, and he believes he is better than other men because he has succeeded. But whatever you do, Lance, don't underrate him. He's a fighter."

"You mean he'll have his men fight?" Trent asked.

"No. I mean *he* is a fighter. By any method. With his fists, if he has to. He told me once in such a flat, ordinary voice that it startled me that he could whip any man he ever saw with his hands."

"I see."

"Shaw, his foreman, tells a story about King Bill beating a man to death in El Paso. He killed another one with his fists on the ranch."

"I've got to see him today. I've got to convince him that we must be left alone."

"He won't talk to you, Lance." Nita looked at him with grave, troubled eyes. "I know him. He'll just turn you over to his cowhands, and they'll beat you up or kill you."

"He'll talk to me."

"Don't go down there, Lance. Please don't."

"Has he ever made any trouble for you?"

"No." She shook her head. "So far, he has listened to me and has talked very quietly and very well. No one has made any trouble yet, but largely because they know he is interested in me. Some men tried to hold me up one night, but Jaime took care of that. He killed them both, and that started some talk. But if King Bill decides he wants this place . . . or me . . . he'll stop at nothing."

"Well,"—he turned—"I've got to see him, Nita. I've got to make one attempt to stop this before anyone else is killed."

"And if you fail . . . ?"

He hesitated, and his shoulders drooped. Then he looked up, and he smiled slowly. "If I fail, Nita, I'll buckle on my guns, and they won't have to wait for war. I'll bring it to Cedar Bluff myself!"

He stopped in the outer room and watched Price Dixon dealing cards, but his mind wasn't on the game. He was thinking of King Bill.

Hale was a man who fought to win. In this little corner of the West, there was no law but that of the gun. Actually there were but two trails in and out of Cedar Valley. What news left the valley would depend on Hale. The echoes of the war to come need never be heard beyond these hills. Only one trail led into Cedar Bluff, and one led out. Most of the traffic went in and out on the same route. The other trail, the little-used route to Blazer, was rough and bad. Yet in Blazer, too, Hale owned the livery stable, and he had his spies there as all around.

Hale himself lived in the Castle, two miles from Cedar Bluff. He rode into town once each day and stopped in at the Mecca for a drink and again at the Crystal Palace. Then he rode out of town. He went nowhere without his gunmen around him. Thinking of that, Trent decided on the Mecca. There would be trouble unless everything happened just right. He didn't want the trouble close to Nita.

He knew what Nita meant when she said she was lonely. There had never been a time when he hadn't been lonely. He had been born on the frontier in Dakota, but his father had been killed in a gun battle, and he had gone to live with an uncle in New York, and later in Virginia.

Trent walked out on the street. It was late now, and the sun was already gone. It would soon be dark. He walked down to the buckskin and led him to a watering trough. Then he gave him a bundle of hay and left him tied at the hitching rail.

There were few people around. Dan Cooper had left the store and was sitting on the steps in front now. He watched Trent thoughtfully. Finally he got up and walked slowly down the walk. He stopped near the buckskin.

"If I was you, Trent," he said slowly, "I'd get on that horse an' hit the trail. You ain't among friends."

"Thanks." Trent looked up at Cooper. "I think that's friendly, Cooper. But I've got business. I don't want a war in Cedar Bluff, Cooper. I want to make one more stab at stopping it."

"An' if you don't?" Cooper studied him quizzically.

"If I don't?" Trent stepped up on the boardwalk. "Well, I'll tell you like I've told others. If I don't, I'm going to buckle on my guns and come to town."

Dan Cooper began to roll a cigarette. "You sound all-fired sure of yourself. Who are you?"

"Like I said, old son, I'm a nester, name of Trent."

He turned and strolled down the walk toward the Mecca, and, even as he walked, he saw a small cavalcade of horsemen come up the road from the Castle. Four men, and the big man on the bay would be King Bill Hale.

Hale got down, and strode through the doors. Cub followed. Ravitz tied King Bill's horse, and Dunn stood for a moment, staring at Trent, who he could not quite make out in the gathering gloom. Then he and Ravitz walked inside.

V

Walking up, Trent pushed open the swinging doors. He stopped for an instant inside the door. The place was jammed with Hale cowhands. At the bar, King Bill was standing, his back to the room. He was big— no taller than Trent, and perhaps an inch shorter than Trent's six one, but much heavier. He was broad and powerful, with thick shoulders and a massive chest. His head was a block set upon the thick column of a muscular neck. The man's jaw was broad, his face brown and hard. He was a bull. Looking at him, Trent could guess that the stories of his killing men with his fists were only the truth.

Beside him, in white buckskin, was the slender, cat-like Cub Hale. And on either side of the two stood the gunmen, Dunn and Ravitz.

Trent walked slowly to the bar and ordered a drink. Dunn, hearing his voice, turned his head slowly. As his eyes met Trent's, the glass slipped from his fingers and crashed on the bar, scattering rye whiskey.

"Seem nervous, Dunn," Trent said quietly. "Let me buy you a drink."

"I'll be hanged if I will!" Dunn shouted. "What do you want here?"

Trent smiled. All the room was listening, and he knew that many of the townspeople, some of whom might still be on the fence, were present.

"Why, I just thought I'd ride down an' have a talk with King Bill," he said quietly. "It seems there's a lot of war talk, an' somebody killed a harmless nester the other day. It seemed a man like King Bill Hale wouldn't want such things goin' on."

"Get out!" Dunn's hand hovered above a gun. "Get out or be carried out!"

"No use you makin' motions toward that gun," Trent said quietly. "I'm not heeled. Look for yourself, I'm makin' peace talk, an' I'm talkin' to King Bill."

"I said . . . get out!" Dunn shouted.

Trent stood with his hands on his hips, smiling. Suddenly Dunn's hand streaked for his gun, and instantly Trent moved.

One hand dropped to Dunn's gun wrist, while his right whipped up in a short, wicked arc and exploded on Dunn's chin. The gunman sagged, and Trent released his gun hand and shoved him away so hard he fell headlong into a table. The table crashed over, and among the scattered cards and chips Bing Dunn lay, out cold.

In the silence that followed, Trent stepped quickly up to King Bill.

"Hale," he said abruptly, "some of your men killed Dick Moffitt, shot him down in cold blood, and then burned him out. Those same men warned me to move out. I thought I'd come to you. I've heard you're a fair man."

King Bill did not move. He held his glass in his fingers and stared thoughtfully into the mirror back of the bar, giving no indication that he heard. Cub Hale moved out from the bar, his head thrust forward, his eyes eager.

"Hale," Trent said sharply, "this is between you an' me. Call off your dogs! I'm talkin' to you, not anybody else. We want peace, but if we have to fight to keep our land, we'll fight! If we fight, we'll win. You're buckin' the United States government now."

Cub had stepped out, and now his lips curled back in a wolfish snarl as his hand hovered over his gun.

"What's the matter, Hale?" Trent persisted. "Making a hired killer of your son because you're afraid to talk?"

Hale turned deliberately. "Cub, get back. I'll handle this!"

Cub hesitated, his eyes alive with eagerness and disappointment.

"I said," Hale repeated, "to get back." He turned. "As for you, you squatted on my land. Now you're gettin' off, all of you. If you don't get off, some of you may die. That's final!"

"No!" Trent's voice rang out sharply. "It's not final, Hale! We took those claims legal. You never made any claim to them until now. You got more land now than you can handle, and we're stayin'. I filed my claim with the United States, so did the others. If we don't get justice, we'll get a United States marshal in here to see why."

"Justice!" Hale sneered. "You blasted nesters'll get

all the justice you get from me. I'm givin' you time to leave . . . now get!"

Trent stood his ground. He could see the fury bolted up in Hale, could see the man was relentless. Well, maybe. . . . Suddenly Trent smiled. "Hale," he said slowly, "I've heard you're a fightin' man. I hope that ain't a lie. I'm callin' you now. We fight, man to man, right here in this barroom, no holds barred, an', if I win, you leave the nesters alone. If you win, we all leave."

King Bill wheeled, his eyes bulging. "You challenge *me?* You dirty-necked, nestin' renegade. No! I bargain with no man. You nesters get movin' or suffer the consequences."

"What's the matter, Bill?" Trent said slowly. "Afraid?"

For a long moment, there was deathly stillness in the room, while Hale's face grew darker and darker. Slowly, then, he unbuckled his gun belt. "You asked for it, nester," he sneered. "Now you get it."

He rushed. Trent had been watching, and, as Hale rushed, he side-stepped quickly. Hale's rush missed, and Trent faced him, smiling.

"What's the matter, King. I'm right here!"

Hale rushed, and Trent stepped in with a left jab that split Hale's lips and showered him with blood. In a fury, Hale closed in and caught Trent with a powerful right swing that sent him staggering back on his heels. Blood staining his gray shirt, King Bill leaped at Trent, swinging with both hands. Trent crashed to the floor, rolled over, and got up. Another swing caught him, and he went down again, his head roaring with sound.

King Bill rushed in, aiming a vicious kick, but

Trent rolled out of the way and scrambled up, groggy
and hurt. Hale rushed, and Trent weaved inside of a
swing and smashed a right and left to that massive
body. Hale grabbed Trent and hurled him into the bar
with terrific power, and then sprang close, swinging
both fists to Trent's head. Trent slipped the first
punch, but took the other one, and started to sag.
King Bill set himself, a cold sneer on his face, and
measured Trent with a left, aiming a ponderous right,
but Trent pushed the left aside and smashed a wicked
left uppercut to Hale's wind.

The bigger man gasped and missed a right, and
Trent stabbed another left to the bleeding mouth.
Hale landed a right and knocked Trent rolling on the
floor. Somebody kicked him wickedly in the ribs as
he rolled against the feet of the crowd, and he came
up staggering as Hale closed in. Hurt, gasping with
pain, Trent clinched desperately and hung on.

Hale tore him loose, smashed a left to his head that
split his cheekbone wide open, and then smashed him
on the jaw with a powerful right. Again Trent stabbed
that left to the mouth, ducked under a right, and
bored in, slamming away with both hands at close
quarters. Hale grabbed him and threw him, and then
rushed upon him, but, even as he jumped at him,
Trent caught Hale with a toe in the pit of the stomach
and pitched him over on his head and shoulders.

King Bill staggered up, visibly shaken. Then Trent
walked in. His face was streaming blood and his head
was buzzing, but he could see Hale's face weaving before him. He walked in, deliberately lanced that
bleeding mouth with a left, and then crossed a right
that ripped the flesh over Hale's eye.

Dunn started forward, and with an oath Hale

waved him back. He put up his hands and walked in, his face twisted with hatred. Trent let him come, feinted, and then dropped a right under the big man's heart. Hale staggered, and Trent walked in, stabbed another left into the blood-covered face, and smashed another right to the wind.

Then he stood there and began to swing. Hale was swinging, too, but his power was gone. Trent bored in, his head clearing, and he slammed punch after punch into the face and body of the tottering rancher. He was getting his second wind now, although he was hurt, and blood dripped from his face to his shirt. He brushed Hale's hands aside and crossed a driving right to the chin. Hale's knees buckled, but, before he could fall, Trent hit him twice more, left and right to the chin. Then Hale crashed to the floor.

In the instant of silence that followed the fall of the King, a voice rang out. "You all just hold to where you're standin' now. I ain't a-wantin' to shoot nobody, but sure as my name's Quince Hatfield, the one to make the first move dies!"

The long rifle stared through the open window at them, and on the next window sill they saw another. Nobody in the room moved.

In three steps, Trent was out of the room. The buckskin was standing at the edge of the walk with the other horses. Swinging into the saddle, he wrenched the rifle from the boot and with two quick shots sent the chandelier crashing to the floor, plunging the Mecca into darkness. Then, the Hatfields at his side, he raced the buckskin toward the edge of town. When they slowed down, a mile out of town, Quince looked at him, grinning in the moonlight.

"I reckon you all sure busted things wide open now."

Trent nodded soberly. "I tried to make peace talk. When he wouldn't, I thought a good lickin' might show the townspeople the fight wasn't all on one side. We're goin' to need friends."

"You done a good job!" Jesse said. "Parson'll sure wish he'd been along. He always said what Hale needed was a good whuppin'. Well, he sho' nuff had it tonight."

Nothing, Trent realized, had been solved by the fight. Taking to the brush, they used every stratagem to ward off pursuit, although they knew it was exceedingly doubtful if any pursuit would be started against three armed men who were skilled woodsmen. Following them in the dark would be impossible and scarcely wise.

Three hours later, they swung down at the Hatfield cabin. A tall young man with broad shoulders stepped out of the darkness.

"It's us, Saul," Jesse said, "an' Trent done whipped King Bill Hale with his fists!"

Saul Hatfield strode up, smiling. "I reckon Paw will sure like to hear that!"

"They gone to bed?"

"Uhn-huh. Lijah was on guard till a few minutes back. He just turned in to catch hisself some sleep afore mornin'."

"O'Hara get here?" Quince asked softly.

"Yeah. Him an' Smithers an' Bartram are here. Havin' a big confab, come mornin'."

VI

The morning sun was lifting over the pines when the men gathered around the long table in the Hatfield home. Breakfast was over, and the women were at work. Trent sat quietly at the foot of the table, thoughtfully looking at the men around him. Yet even as he looked, he could not but wonder how many would be alive to enjoy the fruits of the victory, if victory it was to be.

The five Hatfields were all there. Big O'Hara was there, too, a huge man with great shoulders and mighty hands, a bull for strength and a good shot. Bartram, young, good-looking, and keen, would fight. He believed in what he was fighting for, and he had youth and energy enough to be looking forward to the struggle. Smithers was middle-aged, quiet, a man who had lived a peaceful life, avoiding trouble, yet fearless. He was a small man, precise, and an excellent farmer, probably the best farmer of the lot.

Two more horsemen rode in while they were sitting down. Jackson Hight was a wild-horse hunter, former cowhand, and buffalo hunter; Steven Runyon was a former miner.

Parson Hatfield straightened up slowly. "I reckon this here meetin' better get started. Them Hales ain't a-goin' to wait on us to get organized. I reckon they's a few things we got to do. We got to pick us a leader, an' we got to think of gettin' some food."

Trent spoke up. "Parson, if you'll let me have a word. We all better leave our places an' come here to yours. We better bring all the food an' horses we got up here."

"Leave our places?" Smithers objected. "Why, man, they'd burn us out if we aren't there to defend 'em. They'd ruin our crops."

"He's right," O'Hara said. "If we ain't on hand to defend 'em, they sure won't last long."

"Which of you feel qualified to stand off Hale's riders?" Trent asked dryly. "What man here could hold off ten or twenty men? I don't feel I could. I don't think the Parson could, alone. We've got to get together. Suppose they burn us out. We can build again, if we're alive to do it, an' we can band together and help each other build back. If you ain't alive, you ain't goin' to build very much."

"Thet strikes me as bein' plumb sense," Hight said, leaning forward. "Looks to me like we got to sink or swim together. Hale's got too much power, an' we're too scattered. He ain't plannin' on us gettin' together. He's plannin' on wipin' us out one at a time. Together, we got us a chance."

"Maybe you're right," O'Hara said slowly. "Dick Moffitt didn't do very well alone."

"This place can be defended," Trent said. "Aside from my own place, this is the easiest to defend of them all. Then, the house is the biggest and strongest. If we have to fall back from the rocks, the house can hold out."

"What about a leader?" Bartram asked. "We'd better get that settled. How about you, Parson?"

"No." Parson drew himself up. "I'm right flattered, right pleased. But I ain't your man. I move we choose Trent, here."

There was a moment's silence, and then O'Hara spoke up. "I second that motion. Trent's good for me. He whipped old King Bill."

Runyon looked thoughtfully at Trent. "I don't know this gent," he said slowly. "I ain't got any objections to him. But how do we know he's our man? You've done a power of feudin', Parson. You should know this kind of fightin'."

"I do," Parson drawled. "But I ain't got the savvy Trent has. First, lemme say this here. I ain't been here all my life. I was a sharpshooter with the Confederate Army, an' later I rid with Jeb Stuart. Well, we was only whipped once, an' that was by a youngster of a Union officer. He whipped our socks off with half as many men . . . an' that officer was Trent here."

Trent's eyes turned slowly to Parson, who sat there staring at him, his eyes twinkling.

"I reckon," Hatfield went on, "Trent is some surprised. I ain't said nothin' to him about knowin' him, specially when his name wasn't Trent, but I knowed him from the first time I seen him."

"That's good enough for me," Runyon said flatly. "You say he's got the savvy, I'll take your word for it."

Trent leaned over the table. "All right. All of you

mount up and go home. Watch your trail carefully. When you get home, load up and get back. Those of you who can, ride together. Get back here with everything you want to save, but especially with all the grub you've got. But get back, and quick." He got to his feet. "We're goin' to let Hale make the first move, but we're goin' to have a Hatfield watchin' the town. When Hale moves, we're goin' to move, too. We've got twelve men. . . ."

"Twelve?" Smithers looked around. "I count eleven."

"Jackie Moffitt's the twelfth," Trent said quietly. "I gave him a Sharps. He's fourteen. Many of you at fourteen did a man's job. I'll stake my saddle that Jackie Moffitt will do his part. He can hit squirrels with that gun, an' a man's not so big. He'll do. Like I say, we've got twelve men. Six of them can hold this place. With the other six, or maybe with four, we'll strike back. I don't know how you feel, but I feel no man ever won a war by sittin' on his royal American tail, an' we're not a-goin' to."

"That's good talk," Smithers said quietly. "I'm not a war-like man, but I don't want to think of my place being burned when they go scotfree. I'm for striking back, but we've got to think of food."

"I've thought of that. Lije an' Saul Hatfield are goin' out today after some deer. They know where they are, an' neither of them is goin' to miss any shots. With the food we have, we can get by a few days. Then I'm goin' after some myself!"

"You?" O'Hara stated. "Where you figger on gettin' this grub?"

"Blazer." He looked down at his hands on the

table, and then looked up. "I'm not goin' to spend three days, either. I'm goin' through Smoky Desert."

There was dead silence. Runyon leaned forward, starting to speak, but then he sat back, shaking his head. It was Smithers who broke the silence.

"I'll go with you," he said quietly.

"But, man!" Hight protested. "There ain't no way through that desert, an', if there was. . . ."

"The Indians used to go through," Trent said quietly, "and I think I know how. If it can be done, I could reach Blazer in a little over a day an' start back the same night." He looked over at Jesse Hatfield. "You want to watch Cedar Bluff? I reckon you know how to Indian. Don't take any chances, but keep an eye on 'em. You take that chestnut of mine. He's a racer. You take that horse, an', when they move, you take the back trails for here."

Jesse Hatfield got up and slipped from the room.

Then Trent said: "All right, start rolling. Get back here when you can."

He walked outside and saddled the buckskin. Jackie sauntered up, the Sharps in the hollow of his arm.

"Jackie," Trent said, "you get up there in the eye, an' keep a lookout on the Cedar trail." Mounting, he rode out of the hollow at a lope and swung into the trail toward his own cabin.

He knew what they were facing, but already in his mind the plan of campaign was taking shape. If they sat still, sooner or later they must be wiped out, and sooner or later his own men would lose heart. They must strike back. Hale must be made to learn that he could not win all the time, that he must lose, too.

All was quiet and green around the little cabin, and

he rode up, swinging down. He stepped through, hurriedly put his grub into sacks, and hung it on a pack horse. Then he hesitated. Slowly he walked across to the peg on the cupboard. For a long minute he looked at the guns hanging there. Then he reached up and took them down. He buckled them on, heavy-hearted and feeling lost and empty.

It was sundown when he hazed his little band of carefully selected horses through the notch into the Hatfield hollow and, with Jackie's help, put them in the corral. All the men were back, and the women were working around, laughing, pleasant. They were true women of the West, and most of them had been through Indian fights before this.

Hight was the last one in. He came riding through the notch on a spent horse, his face drawn and hard.

"They burned me out," he said hoarsely, sweat streaking his face. "They hit me just as I was a-packin'. I didn't get off with nothin'. I winged one of 'em, though."

Even as he spoke, Smithers caught Trent's arm. "Look!" he urged, and pointed. In the sky they could see a red glow from reflected fire. "O'Hara's place," he said. "Maybe they got him, too."

"No." O'Hara walked up, scowling. "They didn't get me. I got here twenty minutes ago. They'll pay for this, the wolves."

Jesse Hatfield on the chestnut suddenly materialized in the gloom. "Two bunches ridin'," he said, "an' they aim to get here about sunup. I heard 'em talkin'."

Trent nodded. "Get some sleep, Jesse. You, too, Jackie. Parson, you an' Smithers better keep watch. Quince, I want you an' Bartram to ride with me."

"Where you all goin'?" Saul demanded.

"Why, Saul"—Trent smiled in the darkness—"I reckon we're goin' to town after groceries. We're goin' to call on Leathers, an' we'll just load up while we're there. If he ain't willin', we may have to take him along, anyway."

"Count me in," Saul said. "I sure want to be in on that."

"You'd better rest," Trent suggested. "You got three antelope today, you an' Lije."

"I reckon I ain't so wearied I'd miss that ride, Captain, if you all say I can go."

"We can use you."

Suddenly there was a burst of flame to the south. "There goes my place!" Smithers exclaimed bitterly. "I spent two years a-buildin' that place. Had some onions comin' up, too, an' a good crop of potatoes in."

Trent had started away, but he stopped and turned. "Smithers," he said quietly, "you'll dig those potatoes yourself. I promise you . . . if I have to wipe out Hales personally so's you can do it."

Smithers stared after him as he walked away. "Y'-know," he remarked thoughtfully to the big Irishman, "I believe he would do it. O'Hara, maybe we can win this fight after all."

VII

Cedar Bluff lay, dark and still, when the four horsemen rode slowly down the path behind the town. Trent, peering through the darkness, studied the town carefully. Taking the trail might have been undue precaution, for there was small chance the road would be watched. There had been, of course, the possibility that some late cowpuncher might have spotted them on the trail.

It was after three, and the Crystal Palace and the Mecca had closed their doors over an hour earlier. Trent reined in on the edge of the town and studied the situation. King Bill, secure in his power even after the beating he had taken, would never expect the nesters to approach the town. He would be expecting them to try the overland route to Blazer for supplies, and in his monumental conceit he would never dream that they would come right to the heart of his domain.

"Bartram," Trent whispered, "you an' Saul take the pack horses behind the store. Keep 'em quiet. Don't try to get in or do anything. Just hold 'em there." He turned to the older Hatfield. "Quince, we're goin' to get Leathers."

"Why not just bust in?" Saul protested. "Why bother with him? We can find what we need."

"No," Trent said flatly. "He's goin' to wait on us, an' we're goin' to pay him. We ain't thieves, an' we're goin' to stick to the legal way. I may hold him up an' bring him down there, but we're goin' to pay him, cash on the barrel head, for everything we take."

Leaving their horses with the others behind the store, Trent took Quince and soft-footed it toward the storekeeper's home, about 100 yards from the store. Walking along the dark street, Trent looked around from time to time to see Quince. The long, lean Hatfield, six foot three in his socks, could move like an Indian. Unless Trent had looked, he would never have dreamed there was another man so close.

Trent stopped by the garden gate. There was a faint scent of lilacs in the air, and of some other flowers. Gently he pushed open the gate. It creaked on rusty hinges, and for an instant they froze. All remained dark and still, so Trent moved on, and Quince deftly took the gate from him and eased it slowly shut.

The air was heavy with lilac now, and the smell of damp grass. Trent stopped at the edge of the shadow and motioned to Quince to stand by. Ever so gently, he lifted one foot and put it down on the first step. Lifting himself by the muscles of his leg, he put down the other foot. Carefully, inch by inch, he worked his way across the porch to the house.

Two people slept inside. Leathers and his wife. His

wife was a fat, comfortable woman, one of those in the town who idolized King Bill Hale and held him up as an example of all the West should be and all a man should be. King Bill's swagger and his grandiose manner impressed her. He was, she was convinced, a great man. Once, shortly after he had first come to Cedar Bluff, Trent had been in this house. He had come to get Leathers to buy supplies after the store had been closed. He remembered vaguely the layout of the rooms.

The door he was now opening gently gave access to the kitchen. From it, there were two doors, one to a living room, rarely used, and one to the bedroom. In that bedroom, Leathers would be sleeping with his wife.

Once inside the kitchen he stood very still. He could hear the breathing of two people in the next room, the slow, heavy breathing of Elsa Leathers and the more jerky, erratic breathing of the storekeeper. The kitchen smelled faintly of onions and of home-made soap.

Drawing a large handkerchief from his pocket, he tied it across his face under his eyes. Then he slid his six-gun into his hand and tiptoed through the door into the bedroom. For a moment, Elsa Leathers's breathing caught, hesitated, and then went on. He heaved a sigh of relief. If she awakened, she was almost certain to start screaming.

Alongside the bed, he stooped and put the cold muzzle of his gun under the storekeeper's nose. Almost instantly the man's eyes opened. Even in the darkness of the room, Trent could see them slowly turn upward toward him. He leaned down, almost breathing the words.

"Get up quietly."

Very carefully, Leathers eased out of bed. Trent gestured for him to put on his pants, and, as the man drew them on, Trent watched him like a hawk. Then Trent gestured toward the door, and Leathers tiptoed outside.

"What's the matter?" he whispered, his voice hoarse and shaking. "What do you want me for?"

"Just a little matter of some groceries," Trent replied. "You open your store an' give us what we want, an' you won't have any trouble. Make one squawk an' I'll bend this gun over your noggin."

"I ain't sayin' anythin'," Leathers protested. He buckled his belt and hurried toward the store with Trent at his heels. Quince Hatfield sauntered along behind, stopping only to pluck a blue cornflower and stick it in an empty buttonhole of his shirt.

Leathers fumbled for the lock on the door. "If my wife wakes up an' finds me gone, mister," he said grumpily, "I ain't responsible for what happens."

"Don't you worry about that," Trent assured him dryly, "you just fill this order an' don't make us any trouble."

He motioned to Saul, who came forward. "As soon as you get four horses loaded, you let Bartram take 'em back to the trail an' hold 'em there. Then, if anything happens, he can take off with that much grub."

As fast as Leathers piled out the groceries, Saul and Quince hurried to carry them out to the horses. Trent stood by, gun in hand.

"You ain't goin' to get away with this," Leathers stated finally. "When Hale finds out, he's a-goin' to make somebody sweat."

"Yeah," Trent said quietly, "maybe he will. From all

I hear, he'd better wait until he gets over one beatin' afore he starts huntin' another. An', while we're talkin', you better make up your mind, too. When this war is over, if Hale doesn't win, what d'you suppose happens to you?"

"Huh?" Leathers straightened, his face a shade whiter. "What d'you mean?"

"I mean, brother," Trent said harshly, "that you've taken sides in this fuss. An' if Hale loses, you're goin' out of town . . . but fast!"

"He ain't a-goin' to lose!" Leathers brought out a sack of flour and put it down on the floor. "Hale's got the money, an' he's got the men. Look what happened to Smithers's place today, an' O'Hara's. An' look what happened to. . . ."

"To Dick Moffitt?" Trent's voice was cold. "That was murder."

Quince stepped into the door. "Somebody's comin'," he hissed. "Watch it."

"Let 'em come in," Trent said softly, "but no shootin' unless they shoot first."

Trent thrust a gun against Leathers. "If they come in," he whispered, "you talk right, see? Answer any questions, but answer 'em like I tell you, because if there is any shootin', Elsa Leathers is goin' to be a widow, but quick."

Two men walked up to the door, and one tried the knob. Then, as the door opened, he thrust his head in.

"Who's there?" he demanded.

"It's me," Leathers said, and as Trent prodded him with the gun barrel, "fixin' up an order that has to get out early."

The two men pushed on inside. "I never knew you

to work this late afore. Why, man, it must be nearly four o'clock."

"Right," Quince stepped up with a six-gun. "You *hombres* invited yourself to this party, now pick up them sacks an' cart 'em outside."

"Huh?" The two men stared stupidly. "Why . . . ?"

"Get movin'!" Quince snapped. "Get them sacks out there before I bend this over your head!" The man hesitated and then obeyed, and the other followed a moment later.

It was growing gray in the east when the orders were completed. Quickly they tied up the two men while Leathers stood by. Then, at a motion from Trent, Saul grabbed Leathers and he was bound and gagged. Carrying him very carefully, Trent took him back into his cottage and placed him in bed, drawing the blankets over him. Elsa Leathers sighed heavily, and turned in her sleep. Trent stood very still, waiting. Then her breathing became even once more, and he tiptoed from the house.

Quince was standing in the shadow of the store, holding both horses. "They've started up the trail," he said. Then he grinned. "Gosh a'mighty, I'll bet old Leathers is some sore."

"There'll be a chase, most likely," Trent said. "We'd better hang back a little in case."

Bartram was ahead, keeping the horses at a stiff trot. He was a tough, wiry young farmer and woodsman who had spent three years convoying wagon trains over the Overland Trail before he came south. He knew how to handle a pack train, and he showed it now. Swinging the line of pack horses from the trail, he led them into the shallow water of Cedar

Branch and walked them very rapidly through the water. Twice he stopped to give them a breather, but kept moving at a good pace, Saul riding behind the string, his long Kentucky rifle across his saddle.

"You pay Leathers?" Quince asked, riding close.

"Yeah." Trent nodded. "I stuck it down between him an' his wife after I put him in bed. He'll be some surprised."

Using every trick they knew to camouflage their trail, they worked steadily back up into the hills. They were still five miles or more from the Hatfield place when they heard shots in the distance.

Quince reined in, his features sharpened. "Looks like they've done attacked the place," he said. "What d'you think, Trent? Should we leave this to Saul an' ride up there?"

Trent hesitated, and then shook his head. "No. They can hold 'em for a while. We want to make sure this food is safe." Suddenly he reined in. "Somebody's comin' up our back trail. Go ahead, Saul. But don't run into the attackin' party."

Saul nodded grimly, and Trent, taking a quick look around, indicated a bunch of boulders above the trail. They rode up and swung down, and Quince gave an exclamation of satisfaction as he noted the deep arroyo behind the boulders—a good place for their horses and good for a getaway, if need be.

The horsemen were coming fast now. Lying behind the boulders, they could see the dust rising above them as they wound their way through the cedars and huge rocks that bordered the narrow trail. Only yards away they broke into the open.

"Dust 'em!" Trent said, and fired.

Their two rifles went off with the same sound and

two puffs of dust went up in front of the nearest horse. The horse reared sharply and spun halfway around. Trent lowered his rifle to note the effect of their shots, and then aimed high at the second horseman and saw his sombrero lift from his head and sail into the brush. The men wheeled and whipped their horses back into the brush.

Quince chuckled and bit off a chew. "That'll make 'em think a mite . . . say!" He nodded toward a nest of rocks on the other side. "What'll you bet one of them rannies ain't a-shinnyin' up into that nest of rocks about now?"

There was a notch in the rocks and a boulder beyond, not four feet beyond by the look of it. Quince Hatfield lifted his Kentucky rifle, took careful aim, and then fired. There was a startled yell, and then curses.

Quince chuckled a little. "Dusted him with granite off that boulder," he said. "They won't hurry to get up there again."

Trent thought swiftly. If he took the arroyo and circled back, he could then get higher up on the mountain. With careful fire, he could still cover the open spot and so give Quince a chance to retreat while he held them. Swiftly he told Hatfield. The big mountaineer nodded.

"Go ahead. They won't move none till you get there."

It took Trent ten minutes to work his way out of the arroyo and up the mountain. As distance went, he wasn't so far, being not more than 400 yards away. He signaled his presence to Quince Hatfield by letting go with three shots into the shelter taken by their pursuers. From above, that shelter was scarcely more than concealment and not at all cover.

In a few minutes Quince joined him. They each let go with two shots, and then, mounting, rode swiftly away, out of view of the men in the brush below.

"They'll be slow about showin' themselves, I reckon," Quince said, "so we'll be nigh to home afore they get nerve enough to move."

When they had ridden four miles, Quince reined in sharply. "Horses ahead," he advised. "Maybe they're ours."

Approaching cautiously, they saw Bartram with the eight pack horses. He was sitting with his rifle in his hands, watching the brush ahead. He glanced around at their approach, and then with a wave of the hand, motioned them on.

"Firing up ahead. Saul's gone up. He'll be back pretty soon."

Low voiced, Trent told him what had happened. Then, as they talked, they saw Saul Hatfield coming through the brush on foot. He walked up to them and caught his horse by the bridle.

"They got 'em stopped outside the cup," he said. "I think only one man of theirs is down. He's a-lyin' on his face in the open not far from the boulders where O'Hara is. There must be about a dozen of them, no more."

"Is there a way into the cup with these horses?" Trent asked.

Saul nodded. "Yeah, I reckon if they was busy over yonder for a few minutes, we could run 'em all in."

"We'll make 'em busy, eh, Quince?" Trent suggested. "Bart, you an' Saul whip 'em in there fast as soon as we open up." He had reloaded his rifle, and the two turned their horses and started skirting the rocks to outflank the attackers.

Trent could see what had happened. The Hatfield place lay in a cup-like depression surrounded on three sides by high, rocky walls and on the other by scattered boulders. Through the cliffs, there were two ways of getting into the cup. One of these, now about to be attempted, lay partly across an open space before the cut was entered. The attackers were mostly among the scattered boulders, but had been stopped and pinned down by O'Hara and someone else. Two men there could hold that ground against thirty. Obviously some of the others were up in the cliffs above the cup, waiting for any attack.

Approaching as they were, Trent and Quince were coming down from the south toward the west end of the cup, where the scattered boulders lay. By working up close there, they could find and dislodge the attackers, or at least keep them so busy the pack animals could get across the open to the cup.

About three acres of land lay in the bottom of the cup. There was a fine, cold spring, the barn, horse corrals, and adequate protection. The cliffs were ringed with scattered cedar and rocks, so men there could protect the approach to the boulder. However, if a rifleman got into those rocks on the edge of the cup, he could render movement in the cup impossible until he could be driven out. It was the weak spot of the stronghold.

When they had ridden several hundred yards, the two men reined in and dismounted. Slipping through the cedars, Indian fashion, they soon came to the edge of the woods overlooking the valley of boulders. Not fifty yards away, two men lay behind boulders facing toward the Hatfield cup.

Trent lifted his Winchester and let go with three

fast shots. One, aimed at the nearest man's feet, clipped a heel from his boot; the others threw dust in his face, and with a yell the fellow scrambled out of there. Trent followed him with two more shots, and the man tumbled into a gully and started to run.

The other man started to get up, and Quince Hatfield made him leap like a wild man with a well-placed shot that burned the inside of his leg. Scattering their shots, the two had the rest of the attackers scattering for better cover.

VIII

Parson Hatfield walked out to meet them as they rode in. He grinned through his yellowed handlebar mustache.

"Well, I reckon we win the first round." He chuckled. "Sure was a sight to see them 'punchers dustin' out of there when you all opened up on 'em!"

"Who was the man we saw down?" Trent asked.

"Gunhand they called Indian Joe. A killer. He wouldn't stop comin', so O'Hara let him have it. Dead center."

They walked back to the cabin.

"We got grub to keep us for a few days, but we got a passel of folks here," Parson said, squatting on his haunches, "an' I don't reckon you're goin' to be able to hit Cedar Bluff again."

Trent nodded agreement. "We've got to get to Blazer," he said. "There isn't any two ways about it. I wish I knew what they'd do now. If we had a couple of days' leeway. . . ."

"You know anythin' about the celebration Hale's figurin' on down to Cedar Bluff? They's been talk about it. He's been there ten years, an' he figures that's reason to celebrate."

"What's happenin'?" Trent asked.

"Horse races, horseshoe pitchin', wrestlin', footraces, an' a prize fight. King Bill's bringing in a prize fighter. Big feller, they called him Tombull Turner."

Trent whistled. "Say, he is good! Big, too. He fought over in Abilene when I was there. A regular bruiser."

"That may keep 'em busy," Quince said. He had a big chunk of corn pone in his hand. "Maybe we'll get some time to get grub."

Trent got up. "Me, I'm goin' to sleep," he said. "I'm fairly dead on my feet. You'd better, too," he added to Quince Hatfield.

It was growing dusk when Trent awakened. He rubbed his hand over his face and got to his feet. He had been dead tired, and no sooner had he lain down on the grass under the trees than he had fallen asleep.

Walking over to the spring, he drew a bucket of water and plunged his head into it. Then he dried himself on a rough towel Sally handed him.

"Two more men came in," Sally told him. "Tot Wilson from down in the breaks by the box cañon, and Jody Miller, a neighbor of his."

Saul looked up as he walked into the house. "Wilson an' Miller were both burned out. They done killed Wilson's partner. Shot him down when he went out to rope him a horse."

"Hi." Miller looked up at Trent. "I've seen you afore."

"Could be." Trent looked away.

This was it. He could tell by the way Miller looked at him and said: "I'd have knowed you even if it wasn't for that *hombre* down to the Mecca."

"What *hombre*?" Trent demanded.

"Big feller, bigger'n you. He come in there about sundown yesterday, askin' about a man fittin' your description. Wants you pretty bad."

"Flat face? Deep scar over one eye?"

"That's him. Looks like he'd been in a lot of fights, bad ones."

"He was in one," Trent said dryly. "One was enough."

Cain Brockman! Even before he'd heard from Lee Hall, he had known this would come sooner or later. All that was almost two years behind him, but Cain wasn't a man to forget. He had been one of the hard-riding, fast-shooting duo, the Brockman twins. In a fight at Cottonwood, down in the Live Oak country, Trent, then known by his real name, had killed Abel. Later, in a hand-to-hand fight, he had beaten Cain Brockman into a staggering, punch-drunk hulk. Now Brockman was here. As if it weren't enough to have the fight with King Bill Hale on his hands!

Parson Hatfield was staring at Trent. Then he glanced at Miller. "You say you know this feller?" He gestured at Trent. "I'd like to . . . myself!"

"The name," Trent said slowly, "is Lance Kilkenny."

"Kilkenny!" Bartram dropped his plate. "You're Kilkenny."

"Uhn-huh." He turned and walked outside and stood there with his hands on his hips, staring out toward the scattered boulders at the entrance to the Hatfield cup. He was Kilkenny. The name had come back again. He dropped his hands, and almost by magic the big guns leaped into them, and he stood there, staring at them. Slowly, thoughtfully he replaced them.

Cain Brockman was here. The thought made him suddenly weary. It meant, sooner or later, that he must shoot it out with Cain. In his reluctance to fight the big man there was something more than his hatred of killing. He had whipped Cain Brockman with his hands; he had killed Abel. It should be enough. If there was to be any killing—his thoughts skipped Dunn and Ravitz, and he found himself looking again into the blazing white eyes of a trim young man in buckskin, Cub Hale.

He shook his head to clear it and walked toward the spring. What would King Bill do next? He had whipped Hale. Knowing what he had done to the big man, he knew he would still be under cover. Also, Hale's pride would be hurt badly by his beating. Also, it was not only that he had taken a licking. He had burned out a few helpless nesters, only to have those nesters band together and fight off his raiding party, and in the meantime they had ridden into his own town and taken a load of supplies, supplies he had refused them.

The power of any man is built largely on the belief of others in that power. To maintain leadership, he must win victories, and King Bill had been whipped and his plans had been thwarted. The answer to that seemed plain—King Bill must do something to retrieve his losses. But what would he do? Despite the victories the nesters had won, King Bill was still in the driver's seat. He knew how many men they had. He knew about what supplies they had taken from the store, and he knew the number they had at the Hatfields' could not survive for long without more food. Hale could, if he wished, withdraw all his men and just sit tight across the trail to Blazer and wait until the nesters had to move or starve. He might do that. Or he might strike again, and in greater force.

Kilkenny—it seemed strange to be thinking of himself as Kilkenny again, he had been Trent so long— ruled out the quick strike. By now Hale would know that the Hatfields were strongly entrenched. The main trail to Blazer led through Cedar Bluff. There was a trail, only occasionally used, from the Hatfields' to the Blazer mountain trail, but Hale knew that, and would be covering it. There was a chance they might slip through. Yet even as he thought of that, he found himself thinking again of the vast crater that was the Smoky Desert. That was still a possibility.

O'Hara walked out to where he was standing under the trees. "Runyon an' Wilson want to try the mountain trail to Blazer," he told him. "What do you think?"

"I don't think much of it," Kilkenny said truthfully, "yet we've got to have grub."

"Parson told 'em what you said about Smoky Desert. Wilson says it can't be done. He said he done tried it."

Jackson Hight, Miller, and Wilson walked out.

"We're all for tryin' the mountain trail," Wilson said. "I don't believe Hale will have it watched this far up. What do you say, Kilkenny?"

Kilkenny looked at his boot toe thoughtfully. They wanted to go, and they might get through. After all, the Smoky Desert seemed an impossible dream, and even more so to them than to him. "It's up to you," he said finally. "I won't send a man over that trail, but if you want to try it, go ahead."

It was almost midnight when the wagon pulled out of the cup. Miller was driving, with Wilson, Jackson Hight, and Lije Hatfield riding escort. Kilkenny was up to watch them go, and, when the sound of the wagon died away, he returned to his pallet and turned in.

Twice during the night he awakened with a start, to lie there listening in the stillness, his body tense, his mind fraught with worry, but despite his expectations there were no sounds of shots, nothing.

When daybreak came, he ate a hurried breakfast and swung into the saddle. He left the cup on a lope and followed the dim trail of the wagon. He followed it past the charred ruins of his own cabin and past those of Moffitt's cabin, yet, as he neared the Blazer trail, he slowed down, walking the buckskin and stopping frequently to listen. He could see by the tracks that Lije and Hight had been riding ahead, scouting the way. Sometimes they were as much as a half mile ahead, and he found several places where they had sat their horses, waiting.

Suddenly the hills seemed to fall away and he saw the dim trail that led to Blazer, more than forty miles away. Such a short distance, yet the trail was so bad that fifteen miles a day was considered good. There was no sign of the wagon or of the men. There were no tracks visible, and that in itself was a good thing. It meant that someone, probably Lije, was remembering they must leave no trail.

He turned the buckskin then and rode back over the trail. He took his time, and it was the middle of the afternoon before he reached the ledge where he could look down into the awful haze that hung over the Smoky Desert. Once, in his first trip up over this route, it had been clearer below, and he had thought he saw a ruined wagon far below. Kilkenny found the place where he had stood that other day, for long since he had marked the spot with a cairn of stones. Then slowly and with great pains he began to seek. Time and again he was turned back by sheer drops of hundreds of feet, and nowhere could he find even the suggestion of a trail.

Four hours later, with long fingers of darkness reaching out from the tall pines, he mounted the buckskin and started down toward the cup. Jackson Hight could be correct. Possibly he was mistaken and the Indians were wrong, and there was no trail down to the valley below and across that wasteland. In his long search he had found nothing.

Parson met him as he rode through the notch. Ma Hatfield had come to the door and was shading her eyes toward him.

"They got through to the trail," Kilkenny said. "Maybe they'll make it."

Sally was working over the fireplace when he walked inside. Young Bartram was sitting close by, watching her. Kilkenny glanced at them and smiled grimly. Sally caught his eye and flushed painfully, so he walked outside again and sat down against the house.

Quince had gone after deer into the high meadows, and Saul was on guard. Runyon was sleeping on the grass under the trees, and Jesse Hatfield was up on the cliffs somewhere. Kilkenny sat for a long time against the house, and then he took his blankets over to the grass, rolled up, and went to sleep.

Shortly after daybreak he roped a black horse from his string, saddled up, and with a couple of sandwiches headed back toward the Smoky Desert. There must be a route. There had to be one.

When he reached the rim of the cliff again, he dismounted and studied the terrain thoughtfully. He stood on a wide ledge that thrust itself out into space. The desert below was partially obscured, as always, by clouds of dust or smoke, yet the rim itself was visible for some distance.

Actually, studying the rim, he could see that it bore less resemblance to the crater he had previously imagined than to a great sink. In fact, it looked as though some internal upheaval had caused the earth to subside at this point, breaking off the rock of the ledge and sinking the plateau several hundred feet. For the most part the cliffs below the rim were jagged but almost sheer, yet at places the rim had caved away into steep rock slides that led, or seemed to lead, to the bottom. This great rift in the plateau led for miles, causing the trail to Blazer to swing in a wide semicircle to get around it. Actually, as best he could figure, Blazer was almost straight across from the ledge where he now stood.

Again he began to work with painstaking care along the rim. The Indians had said it could be crossed, that there was a way down, and Lance Kilkenny had lived in the West long enough to know that what the Indians said was usually right.

It was almost noon before he found the path. It was scarcely three feet wide, so he left his horse standing under the cedars and started walking. The path dipped through some gigantic slabs of ragged-edged rock and then ran out to the very edge of the cliff itself. When it seemed he was about to step right off into space, the path turned sharply to the right and ran along the face of the cliff.

He hesitated, taking off his hat and mopping his brow. The path led right along the face of the cliff, and at times it seemed almost broken away, but then it continued on. One thing he knew—this was useless for his purpose, for no man could take a horse, not even such a sure-footed mountain horse as the buckskin, along this path. Yet he walked on.

The end was abrupt. He started to work his way around a thread of path that clung to the precipice, but when he could see around the corner, he saw the trail had ended. An hour of walking had brought him to a dead-end. Clinging to the rock, he looked slowly around. Then his eyes riveted. There, over 300 feet below, on what even at this distance was obviously a trail, he could see a wagon wheel.

Leaning out with a precarious handhold on a root, he could distinguish the half-buried wagon from which the wheel had been broken. Of the rest of the trail, he could see nothing. It vanished from sight under the bulge of the cliff. He drew back, sweating.

The trail was there. The wagon was there. Obviously someone, at some time, had taken a wagon or wagons over that trail. But where was the beginning?

Had the shelf upon which it ran broken off and ruined the trail for use?

Taking a point of gray rock for a landmark, he retraced his steps along the path. By the time he reached the buckskin again, his feet hurt from walking over the rough rock in his riding boots, and he was tired, dead tired. He had walked about six miles, and that was an impossible distance to a horseman.

IX

When he rode into the cup that night, Parson looked up from the rifle that he was cleaning. "Howdy, son! You look done up!"

Kilkenny nodded and stopped beside the older man. He was tired, and his shirt stuck to his back with sweat. For the first time he wondered if they would win. For the first time, he doubted. Without food they were helpless. They could neither escape nor resist. He doubted now if Hale would ever let them go, if he would ever give them any chance of escape.

They ate short rations that night. He knew there was still a good deal of food, yet fourteen men, if he included those who were gone, and six women had to eat there. And there were nine children. Yet there was no word of complaint, and only on the faces of those women who had men with the food wagon could he distinguish the thin gray lines of worry.

"Any sign from Hale?" he asked O'Hara.

The Irishman shook his head. "Not any. He's got men out in the rocks. They ain't tryin' to shoot nobody. Just a-watchin'. But they're there."

"I don't think he'll try anything now until after the celebration," Bartram said. "He's plannin' on makin' a lot of friends with that celebration. It means a lot to him, anyway."

Jesse Hatfield pushed back his torn felt hat. "I took me a ride today," he said. "Done slipped out through the brush. I got clean to Cedar Bluff without bein' seen. I edged up close to town, an' I could see a lot of workin' around. They got 'em a ring set up out in front of the livery stable near the horse corral. Ropes an' everythin'. Lots of talk around, an' the big wonder is who's goin' to fight Tombull Turner."

Kilkenny listened absently, not caring. His thoughts were back on that ragged rim, working along each notch and crevice, wondering where that road reached the top of the plateau.

"This here Dan Cooper was there, an' he done some talkin'. He looked powerful wise, an' he says Turner ain't been brought here by accident. He's been brought to whip one man . . . Kilkenny!"

"Did he say Kilkenny?" Kilkenny looked around to ask. "Do they know who I am?"

"He said Trent," Jesse drawled. "I don't reckon they know."

Tombull Turner to beat him? Kilkenny remembered the bullet head, the knotted cauliflower ears, the flat nose and hard, battered face of the big bare-knuckle fighter. Tombull was a fighter. He was more; he was a brute. He was an American who had fought much in England, and against the best on both continents. He had even met Joe Goss and Paddy Ryan. While he, Kilkenny, was no prize fighter.

An idle rumor. It could be no more, for he was not in Cedar Bluff, nor was he likely to be. Studying the faces of the men around him, he could see what was on their minds. Despite their avoidance of the subject, he knew they were all thinking of the wagon on the road to Blazer.

The food was necessary, but four men were out there, four men they all knew, men who had shared their work, their trials, and even the long trip West from their lands in Kentucky, Pennsylvania, and Missouri. Lije Hatfield was gone, and, knowing the family, Kilkenny knew that, if he were killed, no Hatfield would stop until all the Hales were dead or the Hatfields wiped out.

Knowing the route, he could picture the wagon rolling slowly along over the rocky road, horsemen to the front and rear, watching, hoping, fearing. They, too, if still alive and free, would have their worries. They would know that back here men and women were getting close to the end of their food supply, that those men and women were depending on them.

On the morning of the third day, Kilkenny mounted again and started for the rim. He saw Parson Hatfield staring after him, but the old man said nothing.

This time Kilkenny had a plan. He was going back where he had been the day before, and by some means he was going down the face of the cliff to the wagon. Then he would backtrack. If there was no trail back, he would have to come up the cliff. Well, that was a bridge to be crossed later. Somewhere in that jumble of broken cliffs, great slabs of jagged rock, and towering shoulders of stone, there must be a trail down which that wagon had gone.

It was almost seven o'clock in the morning before he found himself, two ropes in his hands, at the tapering edge of the trail along the face of the cliff. Lying flat, he peered over the edge. The rock on which he lay was a bulge that thrust out over the face of the cliff, and, if he dropped over here, he must use the rope purely as a safety precaution and work down with his hands. There were cracks and knobs that could be used. The depth below was sickening, but partially obscured by the strange thickness of the air.

A gnarled cedar grew from the face of the rock, and he tested it for strength. The thing seemed as immovable as the rocks themselves. Making his first rope fast to the cedar, Kilkenny knotted the other end in a bowline around himself. Then he turned himself around and backed over the edge, feeling with his feet for a toehold.

For a time, he knew, he would be almost upside down like a fly on a ceiling. Unless he could find handholds where he could get a good grip and, if necessary, hang by them, there was small chance of making it. But there were, he had noticed, a number of roots, probably of rock cedar, thrusting out through the rock below.

Forcing himself to think of nothing but the task at hand, he lowered himself over the edge, and, when he got the merest toehold, he swung one hand down and felt around until he could grasp one of the roots. Then he let go with his left hand and let himself down until he was half upside down, clinging by a precarious toehold and his grip on the root.

Finding another hold for his left hand, he took a

firm grasp, and then pulled out his left toe and felt downward. He found a crack, tested it with his toe, and then set the foot solidly. Carefully he released a handhold and lowered his hand to another root, lower down. Then, sweating profusely, he lowered his weight to the lower foot.

He resolutely kept his thoughts away from the awful depths below. He had a chance, but a very slim one. Slowly and with great care he shifted himself down the bulging overhang. Every time he moved a foot or hand, his life seemed about to end. He was, he knew, wringing with perspiration, his breath was coming painfully, and he swung himself precariously toward the sheer cliff below. Even that great height of straight up and down cliff seemed a haven to this bulge of the overhang.

Clinging to a huge root and pressing himself as tightly to the face as he could, he turned his head right, and then left, searching the face of the bulge. There were handholds enough here. The roots of the cedars that had grown on the ledge above thrust through the bulge. Yet that very fact seemed to indicate that at some time in the past huge chunks of rock had given way, leaving these roots exposed. It had happened once, and it could happen again.

Far out in the blue sky a buzzard whirled in great, slow circles. His fingers ached with gripping, and he lowered himself away from the face of the cliff and looked down between his legs. A notch showed in the rock, and he worked his toe loose, and then lowered it with care until he could test the notch. He tried it.

Solid. Slowly, carefully he began to settle weight on the ball of his foot. There was a sudden sag beneath his foot and then a rattle of stones, and the notch gave way under him, forcing him to grip hard with his hands to catch the additional weight.

His right foot hung free. Carefully he began to feel with his toe for another foothold. He found it, tried, and rested his weight again, and the stone took it. Slowly he shifted hands again, and then lowered himself down a little more.

Glancing down again, he found himself looking at a stretch of rock at least fifteen feet across that was absolutely smooth. No single crack or crevice showed, no projection of stone, no root. His muscles desperate with weariness, he stared, unbelieving—to come this far and fail.

Forcing himself to think, he studied the face of the cliff. There was, some twenty feet below and almost that far to the left, a gnarled and twisted rock cedar growing out of the mountainside. It was too far to the right, and there was no way of reaching it. Yet, as he stared, he could see that a crevice, deep enough for a good foothold, ran off at an angle from the cedar. If he could reach it—but how?

There was a way. It hit him almost at once. If he released his grip on the roots, he would instantly swing free. As he had worked himself far to the right of the cedar to which his lariat was tied, his release would swing him far out from the cliff, and then, as he swung back, for an instant he would be above the clump of cedar. On each succeeding swing he would fall shorter and shorter, until finally he was suspended in mid-air, hanging like a great pendulum from the cedar above.

Then all his efforts would be vain, for he would have to catch the rope over his head and go up it, hand over hand, to the cedar above, and he would have failed. On the other hand, if he could release himself above the cedar, he would fall into it, and unless some sharp branch injured him, the chances were the limbs would cushion his fall.

He had his knife, and it was razor sharp. Even as these thoughts flitted through his mind, he was drawing the knife. Luckily, before leaving his horse, he had tied a rawhide thong over each six-shooter, so his guns were secure. Yet the rope was rawhide and tough. Could he slash through at one blow?

The answer to that was simple. He had to. If he swung out over the void below on half or less of the strength of the lariat, there was small chance it would not break at the extreme end of the swing, and he would go shooting out over the deadly waste of the Smoky Desert to fall, and fall—over and over into that murky cloud that obscured the depths.

He let go and shoved hard with both feet and hands. His body swept out in a long swing over the breathtaking depths below. Then, hesitating but an instant as the rope tore at his sides, he swept back like a giant pendulum, rushing through the air toward the cliff! It shot toward him, and he raised his arm, and, seeing the cedar below and ahead, he cut down with a mighty slash.

He felt himself come loose, and then he was hurled forward at the cedar. He hit it, all doubled into a ball, heard a splintering crash, slipped through, and felt the branches tearing at his clothes like angry fingers. Then he brought up with a jolt and lay, trembling in every limb, clinging to the cedar.

How long he lay there, he did not know. Finally he pulled himself together and crawled out of the tree and got his feet on the narrow foothold. He worked his way along until the ledge grew wide enough for him to walk. His breath was coming with more regularity now. He felt gingerly of his arms and body where the rawhide rope had burned him.

The path, if such it might be called, slanted steeply away from him, ending in some broken slabs. He stopped when he reached them. He was, at last, on the Smoky Desert.

X

Lance Kilkenny stood on a dusty desert floor littered with jagged slabs of rock, obviously fallen from the cliff above. There was no grass here, no cedar, nothing growing at all, not even a cactus. Above him, the dark, basalt cliff lifted toward the sky, towering and ugly. Looking off over the desert, he could see only a few hundred yards, and then all became indistinct. The reason was obvious enough. The floor of the desert was dust, fine as flour, and even the lightest breeze lifted it into the air, where it hung for hours on end. A strong wind would fill the air so full of these particles as to make the air thick as a cloud, and the particles were largely silicate.

One thing he knew now. Crossing the Smoky Desert, even if there was a trail, would be a frightful job. Unfastening the thongs that had held his guns in place, he walked on slowly. It was still, only a little murmur from the wind among the rocks, and nothing else.

The cliff lifted on his right, and off to the left stretched the awful expanse of the desert, concealed behind that curtain of dust. He stepped over the dead and bleached bones of an ancient cedar, fallen from above, and rounded a short bend in the cliff. As he walked, little puffs of dust lifted from his boot soles, and his mouth grew dry. Once he stopped and carefully wiped his guns free of dust, and then lowered them once more into the holsters.

Then he saw the white scar of the road, tracks of vehicles filled with fine white dust, and the rough, barely visible marks of what had been a fairly good road, dwindling away into the gray, dusty vagueness that was the desert. He looked up and saw the trail winding steeply up the cliff's face through a narrow draw.

Turning, he began to climb the trail. Several times he paused to roll boulders from the path. He was already thinking in terms of a wagon and a team. It could be done. That is, it could be done if there was still a way of getting a team onto this trail. That might be the catch. What lay at the end?

Sweat rolled down his face, making thin rivulets through the white dust. White dust clung to the hairs on the backs of his hands, and once, when he stopped to remove his sombrero and wipe the sweat from his brow, he saw his hat was covered with a thin gray coat of it.

He looked ahead. He could see the road for no more than 100 yards, but the cliff to his right was now growing steeper, and, glancing down, he could see the trail was already far above the valley floor. He walked, making heavy work of it in his riding boots, sweat soaking his shirt under the film of gray dust, and the draw was narrowing.

The rock under the trail sloped steeply away into a dark, shadowy cañon now over 200 feet down. He walked on, plodding wearily. For over an hour he walked, winding around and around to follow the curving walls of the cañon. Then he halted suddenly.

Ahead of him the trail ended. It ended and explained his difficulties in one instant. A gigantic pine, once perched upon the edge of the cliff, had given way, its roots evidently weakened by wind erosion. The tree had blown down and fallen across the trail. Pines had sprung up around it and around its roots until the trail was blocked by a dense thicket that gave no hint of the road that had once run beneath it.

Crawling over the pine, Kilkenny emerged from the thicket and walked back to his horse. Mounting, he rode slowly homeward, and, as he rode, he thought he had never been so utterly tired as he was now. But there was coolness in the breeze through the pines, and some of their piney fragrance seemed to get into his blood. He looked up, feeling better as he rode slowly along the grassy trail, through the mountain meadows and down through the columned trunks of the great old trees toward the Hatfield cup.

Yes, it was worth fighting for, worth fighting to keep what one had in this lonely land among the high peaks. It was such a country as a man would want, a country where a man could grow and could live, and where his sons could grow. Even as he thought of that, Kilkenny found himself remembering Nita. King Bill Hale wanted her. Well, what would be more understandable? Certainly she was beautiful, the most beautiful woman in Cedar Valley and many

other valleys. And what did she think? Hale had
everything to offer: strength, position, wealth. She
could reign like a queen at the Castle.

And Hale himself? He was a handsome man. Cold,
but yet, what man ever sees another man as a woman
sees him? The side of himself that a man shows to
women is often much different from that seen by
men. Worry began to move through him like a drug.
Nita nearby was one thing, but Nita belonging to
someone else, that was another idea. He realized suddenly it was an idea he didn't like, not even a little
bit. Especially he did not want her to belong to the
arrogant King Bill.

Hale wanted her, and, regardless of what she
thought, he could bring pressure to bear, if his own
eloquence failed him. He was king in Cedar Valley.
Her supplies came in over the road he controlled. He
could close her business. He could even prevent her
from leaving. He might. Jaime Brigo was the reason
why he might not succeed. Brigo and himself,
Kilkenny.

King Bill's lack of action disturbed him. Hale had
been beaten in a fist fight. Knowing the arrogance of
the man, Kilkenny knew he would never allow that to
pass. He had refused them supplies, and they had
come and taken them from under his nose. Was Hale
waiting to starve them? He knew how many they
were. He knew the supplies they had were not
enough to last long. And he held the trail to Blazer.
Did he know of the trail through the Smoky Desert?
Kilkenny doubted that. Even he did not know if it
were passable. The chances were Hale had never
even dreamed of such a thing. Aside from the Indian

to whom he had talked, Kilkenny had heard no mention of it.

Saul Hatfield walked down from among the trees as he neared the cup. "Anything happen?" Kilkenny asked.

Saul shook his head, staring curiously at the dust-covered Kilkenny. "Nope. Not any. Jesse took him a ride down to town. They sure are gettin' set for that celebration. Expectin' a big crowd. They say Hale's invited some folks down from Santa Fé, some big muckety-mucks."

"From Santa Fé?" Kilkenny's eyes narrowed. That was a neat bit of politics, a good chance to entertain the officials, and then tell them casually of the outlaws in the mountains, the men who had come in and tried to take away valuable land from King Bill. Lance knew how persuasive such a man could be. And he would entertain like royalty, and these men would go away impressed. That King Bill didn't intend to strengthen his position very much would be foolhardy to imagine. Hale would know how to play politics, how to impress these men with his influence and the power of his wealth.

The audience would all be friendly, too. They would give the visiting officials the idea that all was well in Cedar Valley. Then, when the elimination of some outlaws hiding in the mountains was revealed, if it ever was, the officials would imagine it was merely that and never inquire as to the rightness or wrongness of Hale's actions.

In that moment, Kilkenny decided. He would go to Cedar Bluff for the celebration. Yet, even as the thought occurred to him, he remembered the thick neck and beetling brow of Tombull Turner. For the first time he began to think of the prize fighter. He had seen the man fight. He was a mountain of muscle, a man with a body of muscle and iron. His jaw was like a chunk of granite. His flat nose and beetling brow were fearsome.

Kilkenny rode down into the cup and swung from his horse. Parson walked slowly toward him, Jesse and O'Hara beside him. They stared at the dust on his clothes.

"Looks like you been places, son," Parson drawled.

"I have." Kilkenny removed the saddle and threw it on the rail. "I've been down into the Smoky Desert."

"The Smoky Desert?" O'Hara stepped forward. "You found a way?"

"Uhn-huh. Take a little axe work to clear it."

"Could a wagon get across?"

Kilkenny shrugged, looking up at the big Irishman. "Your guess is as good as mine. I know I can get a wagon into the desert. I know there used to be a trail. I could see it. There's parts of a wagon down there. Somebody has been across. Where somebody else went, we'll go."

"How about gettin' out?" Parson drawled.

"That," Kilkenny admitted, "is the point. You put your finger right on the sore spot. Maybe there's a way, maybe there isn't. There was once. But I'm a-goin'. I'm goin' over, an' with luck I'll get back. We'll have to take water. We'll have to tie cloths over our faces and over the nostrils of the horses. Otherwise that dust will fix us for good."

"When you goin'?" Jesse demanded.

"Right soon. We got to make a try. If we could

make it soon enough, we might bring the others back that way. I'll start tomorrow."

"Leave us short-handed," Parson suggested.

"It will." Kilkenny nodded agreement. He looked at the old mountaineer thoughtfully. "The trouble is, Hale has time, an' we haven't. I'm bankin' that he won't try anything until after the celebration. I think this is not only his tenth anniversary but a bit of politics to get friendly with them down at Santa Fé. He'll wait until he's solid with them before he cleans us out."

"Maybe. Ain't nobody down to town goin' to tell our side of this. Not a soul," Hatfield agreed.

"There will be." Kilkenny stripped off his shirt and drew a bucket of water from the well. His powerful muscles ran like snakes beneath his tawny skin. "I'm goin' down."

"They'll kill you, man!" O'Hara declared. "They'd shoot you like a dog."

"No, not while those Santa Fé officials are there. I'll go. I hear they want me to fight Tombull Turner. Well, I'm goin' down an' fight him."

"What?" Runyon shouted. "That man's a killer. He's a ringer."

"I know." Kilkenny shrugged. "But I've seen him fight. Maybe I'm a dang' fool, but I've got to get down there an' see those Santa Fé men. This is my chance."

"You think you can do any good against Hale?" Parson asked keenly. "He'll be winin' and dinin' them folks from Santa Fé. He won't let you go nowhere close to 'em."

"But they'll be at the fight," Kilkenny told him. "I'm countin' on that."

* * *

At daybreak the labor gang had reached the thicket of pines covering the entrance to the road. Axes in hand, they went to work. Other men began bucking the big fallen tree into sections to be snaked out of the way with ox teams.

Once, during a pause when he straightened his back from the saw, Quince looked over at Kilkenny. "They should be there today," he drawled slowly. "I sure hope they make it."

"Yeah." Lance straightened and rubbed his back. It had been a long time since he'd used a cross-cut saw. "You know Blazer?"

"Uhn-huh." Hatfield bit off a chew of tobacco. "Man there named Sodermann. Big an' fat. Mean as a wolf. He's Hale's man. Got a gunman with him name of Rye Pitkin."

"I know him. A two-bit rustler from the Pecos country. Fair hand with a six-gun."

"There's others, too. Ratcliff an' Gaddis are worst. We can expect trouble."

"We?" Kilkenny looked at him. "You volunteerin' for the trip?"

"Sure." Quince grinned at him. "I need me a change of air. Gettin' old, a-settin' around. Reckon the bore of that Kentucky rifle needs a bit of cleanin', too."

They worked on until dark, and, when they stopped, the road was open. O'Hara, who had done the work of two men with an axe, stood on the edge of the cañon in the dimming light and looked across that awful expanse toward the distance, red ridges touched now with light from a vanished sun. "It don't look good to me, Kilkenny," he said. "It sure don't look good."

XI

The wagon was loaded with water—not heavily, but three good kegs of it. With Bartram on the driver's seat, they started. Kilkenny led the way down the steep trail, Quince behind him. He reined in once and watched the wagon trundle over the first stones and past the ruin of the great tree. Then he continued on. For better or worse, they were committed now.

He led the way slowly, stopping often, for it was slow going for the wagon. He watched it coming and watched the mules. They were good mules; Hale himself had no better. They would need to be good.

At the bottom of the road he swung down, and, standing there with Quince Hatfield, he waited, listening to the strange, lonely sighing of the mysterious wind that flowed like a slow current through the dusty depths of the sink.

Bartram was a hand with mules. He brought the wagon up beside them, and Kilkenny indicated the mules. "Soak those cloths in water an' hang one over the nose of each of them. We better each wear a handkerchief over the nose and mouth, too."

He was riding the buckskin, and he got down and hung a cloth over the horse's nostrils, where it would stop part of the dust at least without impeding the breathing. Then they started on.

From here, it was guesswork. He had a compass, and, before leaving the cliff top, he had taken a sight on a distant peak. How closely the trail would hold to that course he did not know, or if any trail would be visible once they got out into the desert. Walking the buckskin, he led off into the dust. The wind did not howl. It blew gently but steadily, and the dust filled the air. Much of it, he knew, was alkali. Behind him, Quince Hatfield rode a raw-boned roan bred to the desert.

Fifteen minutes after leaving the cliff, they were out of sight of it. Overhead the sky was only a lighter space dimly visible through a hanging curtain of dust. Dust arose in clouds from their walking horses and from the wagon, fine, powdery, stifling dust. Over and around them the cloud closed in, thick and prickly when the dust settled on the flesh. Glancing at Quince during one interval, Kilkenny saw the man's face was covered with a film of dust; his eyelashes were thick with it; his hair was white.

When they had been going an hour, he reined in and dismounted. Taking a damp cloth, he sponged out the buckskin's nostrils and wiped off the horse's head and ears. Quince had drawn abreast and was doing likewise, and, when the others came up, they worked over the mules.

The dust filled the air and drew a thick veil around

them, as in a blizzard. Saul drew closer. "What if the wind comes up?" he asked.

Bartram's face was stern. "I've been thinking of that," he said. "If the wind comes up, in all of this, we're sunk."

"Where are we now?" Jackie asked, standing up on the wagon.

"We should have made about three or four miles. Maybe more, maybe less. We're right on our course so far."

They rested the mules. The wagon was heavy, even though it was not carrying a load now. The dust and sand in places were a couple of feet deep, but usually the wheels sank no more than six inches into the dust. The animals would all need rest, for the air was heavy with heat, and there was no coolness here in the sink. The dust made breathing an effort.

Kilkenny swung into the saddle and moved out. The flatness of the desert floor was broken now, and it began to slant away from them toward the middle. Kilkenny scowled thoughtfully, and rode more slowly. An hour later, they paused again. This time there was no talking. All of the men were feeling the frightful pressure of the heat, and, glancing at the mules, Kilkenny could see they were breathing heavily. Streaks marred the thick whiteness of the dust on their bodies.

"We'll have to stop more often," he told Bartram, and the farmer nodded.

They rode on, and almost another hour had passed before the buckskin stopped suddenly. Lance touched him gently with a spur, but Buck would not move. Kilkenny swung down. Ahead of him—and he could see for no more than fifty feet—was an even, unbroken expanse of white. It was not even marred by the blackish upthrust of rock that had occasionally appeared along the back trail.

Quince rode up and stopped. "What's wrong?" he asked. Then he swung down and walked up.

"Don't know," Kilkenny said. "Buck won't go on, something wrong." He stepped forward and felt the earth suddenly turn to jelly under his feet. He gave a cry and tried to leap backward, but only tripped himself.

Quince helped him up. "Quicksand," he said, "an' the worst I ever see. Must be springs under."

The wagon drew up, and then Saul and Jackie. "Stay here," Lance told them. "I'll scout to the left."

"I'll go right," Quince suggested. "Might be a way around."

Kilkenny turned the buckskin and let him have his head. He walked at right angles to the course and then, at Kilkenny's urging, tried the surface. It was still soggy. They pulled back and rode on. In a half hour he reined in. There was still no way around, and the edge of the quicksand seemed to be curving back toward him. Only the sagacity of Buck had kept them out of it. He rode back.

"Any luck?" he shouted as he saw Quince waiting with the wagon.

"Uhn-huh. It ends back there about two mile. High ground, rocky."

They turned the wagon and started on once more. They would lose at least an hour more, perhaps two, in skirting the quicksand.

Hour after hour they struggled on. Weariness made their limbs leaden. The mules were beginning to weave a bit now, and Kilkenny found himself sagging in the saddle. His sweat-soaked shirt had become something very like cement with its heavy coating of white dust. They stopped oftener now, stopped for water and to sponge the nostrils of the mules and horses.

At times the trail led through acres upon acres of great, jagged black rocks that thrust up in long ledges that had to be skirted. All calculations on miles across were thrown out of kilter by this continual weaving back and forth across the desert. Time had ceased to matter, and they lived only for the quiet numbness of the halts.

All of them walked from time to time now. Time and again they had to get behind the wagon and push, or had to dig out rocks to roll them aside to clear the only possible trail. The world had become a nightmare of choking, smothering, clinging dust particles, a nightmare of sticky heat and stifling dust-filled air. Even all thought of Hale was gone. They did not think of food or of family, but only of getting across, of getting out of this hell of choking white.

Kilkenny was no longer sure of the compass. Mineral deposits might have made it err. They might be wandering in circles. His only hope was that the ground seemed to rise now, seemed to be slanting upward. Choking, coughing, they moved on into the dust blizzard, hearing the lonely sough of the wind. Dazed with heat, dust, and weariness, they moved on. The mules were staggering now, and they moved only a few yards at a time.

The black upthrust of the cliff loomed at them suddenly, when all hope seemed gone. It loomed, black and sheer, yet here at the base the dust seemed a little less, a little thinner.

Kilkenny swung down and waited until the rest came up. "Well," he said hoarsely, "we're across. Now to get up."

They rested there under the cliff for a half hour, and then his own restlessness won over his weariness. He had never been able to stop short of a goal; there was something in him that always drove him on, regardless of weariness, trouble, or danger. It came to the surface now, and he lunged to his feet and started moving.

He had walked no more than 100 yards when he found it. He stared at the incredible fact, that through all their weaving back and forth they had held that close to their destination. The road looked rough, but it was a way up, and beyond the hills, but a little way now, lay Blazer.

It was dusk when they reached the top of the cliff and drew up under the pines. Digging a hole in the ground among some rocks, they built a fire in the bottom and warmed some food and made coffee. The hole concealed the flames, and using dry wood they would make no smoke.

Kilkenny drank the strong black coffee and found his hand growing lax and his lids heavy. He got up, staggered to his blankets, and fell asleep. He slept like he was drugged until Saul Hatfield shook him from his slumber in the last hours of the night to take over the watch.

Lance got up and stretched. Then he walked over to the water casks, drew water, and bathed himself, washing the dust from his hair and ears. Stripping to the waist, he bathed his body in the cold water. Refreshed, he crossed to the black bulk of the rocks and seated himself.

In the darkness thoughts come easily. He sat there, his eyes open and staring restlessly from side to side, yet his thoughts wandering back to Cedar Bluff. They wanted him to fight Tombull Turner. He had decided to take the fight. Sitting here in the darkness with the wind in the pines overhead, he could think clearly. It was their only chance of getting to the Santa Fé officials. He knew how men of all sorts and kinds admire a fighting man. The Santa Fé officials, especially if one of them was Halloran, would be no exception. He would be going into the fight as the underdog. Hale wanted him whipped, but King Bill's power was destroying his shrewdness.

Halloran, or whoever came, would know about Tombull. The man had been fighting, and winning, all through the West. Any man who went against him would be the underdog, and the underdog always has the crowd with him. Kilkenny knew there was scarcely a chance that he would do anything but take a beating, yet he believed he could stay in there long enough to make some impression. And between rounds—that would be his chance.

If ever, he would have a chance to talk then. King Bill would have his guests in ringside seats. He would be expecting a quick victory. Coldly Kilkenny appraised himself. Like all fighting men, he considered himself good. He had fought many times in the rough and tumble fistfights of the frontier. As a boy he had fought many times in school. During the days when he was in the East, he had taken instruction from the great Jem Mace, the English pugilist, who was one of the cleverest of all bare-knuckle fighters. Mace was a shrewd fighter who used his head for something aside from a parking place for two thick ears.

King Bill did not know that Kilkenny had ever boxed. Neither would Tombull know that. Moreover, Kilkenny had for years lived a life in the open, a life that required hard physical condition and superb strength. He had those assets, and above all he had his knowledge of Turner, whereas Turner knew nothing of him. Turner would be overconfident. Nevertheless, in all honesty, Kilkenny could find little hope of victory. His one hope was to make a game fight of it, to win the sympathy and interest of the officials before he spoke to them, as he would.

He would rest when he returned to the cup. He would soak his hands in brine, and he would wear driving gloves in the ring. Some of the younger fighters were wearing skintight gloves now, and Mace had told him of their cutting ability.

There was no sound but the sound of the forest, and he relaxed, watching and awaiting the dawn. When it came, they ate a hurried breakfast. They were rested and felt better. Kilkenny cleaned his guns carefully, both pistols and his rifle. The others did likewise.

"Quince," Kilkenny said as he holstered his guns. "You know Blazer. What d'you think?"

Hatfield shrugged. "I reckon they won't be expectin' us from hereabouts. I been takin' some bearin's, an' I reckon we will come into town from the opposite side. We got us a good chance of gettin' in afore they know who we are."

"Good!" Kilkenny turned to Bartram. "You know the team. You stay by the wagon an' keep your gun handy. Stay on the ground where you can either mount up or take cover. Saul, you an' Jackie hustle the grub out to the wagon, an' Quince will stand by to cover you."

"How about you?" Bartram asked, looking up at him.

"I'm goin' to look around for sign of the other wagon. I want to know what happened to Lije an' them. They may be all right, but I want to know." As they mounted up, he turned in his saddle. "Quince, you ride with me. Saul an' Jackie will bring up the rear."

They started out, and less than a mile from where they had come from the desert they rode down into the trail to Blazer. As Quince Hatfield had suggested, they were coming in from the opposite side.

Two rows of ramshackle saloons, cheap dance halls, and stores made up the town of Blazer. These two rows faced each other across a river of dust that was called a street. The usual number of town loafers sat on benches in front of the Crossroads, the Temple of Chance, and the Wagon Wheel.

It was morning, and few horses stood at the hitching rail. There was a blood bay with a beautifully handworked saddle standing in front of the Crossroads, and two cow ponies stood three-legged before the Wagon Wheel.

XII

Lance Kilkenny rode past the Perkins General Store and swung down in front of the Wagon Wheel. Bartram stopped the wagon parallel to the hitching rail and began to fill his pipe. His rifle leaned against the seat beside him.

Saul and Jackie walked into the store, and Quince leaned against the corner of the store and lighted a cigarette. His rifle lay in the wagon, but he wore a huge Walker Colt slung to his belt.

A horseman came down the trail and swung down in front of the Wagon Wheel and walked inside. Quince straightened and stared at him, and his eyes narrowed. The man was big and had red hair and a red beard. Kilkenny stared at the man, and then, as Quince motioned with his head, he idled over toward him.

"That *hombre* was wearin' an ivory-handled Colt

with a chipped ivory on the right side," Hatfield said. His narrow face was empty and his eyes bitter.

"A chipped ivory butt?" Kilkenny frowned, and then suddenly his face paled. "Why, Jody Miller had a gun like that. An' Jody was with the first wagon."

"Uhn-huh. I reckon," Hatfield said, "I better ask me a few questions."

"Wait," Kilkenny said. "I'm goin' in there. You keep your eyes open. Remember, we need the grub first. Meantime, I'll find out somethin'."

He turned and walked over to the Wagon Wheel and ambled inside. Two cowpokes sat at a table with the bartender and a man in a black coat, a huge man, enormously big and enormously fat. That, he decided, would be Sodermann.

The red-bearded man was leaning on the bar. "Come on, Shorty," he snapped. "Give us a drink! I'm dry."

"Take it easy, Gaddis," Shorty barked. He was a short, thick-set man with an unshaven face. "I'll be with you in a minute."

Kilkenny leaned against the bar and looked around. It didn't look good. If the big man was Sodermann—and there was small chance of there being two such huge men in any Western town—that placed Sodermann and Gaddis. The cowpokes might be mere cowhands, but they didn't look it. One of the men might be Ratcliff. And there was still Rye Pitkin. But he knew Rye, and the rustler was not present.

Judging by appearances, Shorty could be counted on to side Sodermann, and, if that was Jody Miller's gun, it meant that the other wagon had been stopped, and the chances were that the men who accompanied it had been wiped out.

Slow rage began to mount in Kilkenny at the thought of those honest, sincere men who asked only the right to work and build homes, being killed by such as these. He was suddenly conscious that Sodermann was watching him.

Shorty got up and sauntered behind the bar. "What'll you have?" he asked, leaning on the hardwood. His eyes slanted from Gaddis to Kilkenny.

"Rye," Gaddis said. He turned abruptly and gave Kilkenny a cool glance, a glance that suddenly quickened as he noticed the dusty clothing and the tied-down guns. He stared at Kilkenny's face, but Lance had his hat brim low, and this man had never seen him before, anyway.

"Make mine rye, too," Kilkenny said. He turned his head and looked at Sodermann. "You drinkin'?"

"Maybe." The fat man got up, and he moved his huge bulk with astonishing lightness. Kilkenny's eyes sharpened. This man could move. "Maybe I will. I always likes to know who I'm drinkin' with, howsoever."

"Not so particular where I come from," Kilkenny said softly. "A drink's a drink."

"I reckon." Sodermann nodded affably. "You appear to be a stranger hereabouts. I reckon every man who wears a gun like you wear yours knows Doc Sodermann."

"I've heard the name." Kilkenny let his eyes drift to the table. One of the men was sitting up straight rolling a smoke, the other idly riffling the cards. Either could draw fast. Red Gaddis had turned to face them.

The whole setup was too obviously ready to spring. He was going to have to relax them a little. He would have to relieve this tension.

"Heard there might be a job up this way for a man," he said slowly, "an' I could use a job up here where it's quiet."

"Away from the law, you mean?" Sodermann laughed until he shook all over. Kilkenny noticed there was no laughter in his eyes.

"Uhn-huh. Away from everythin'."

"We got law here. King Bill Hale runs this country."

"Heard of him."

"You hear a lot," Gaddis suggested. His eyes were mean.

"Yeah." Kilkenny turned a little and let his green eyes stare from under his hat brim at the red-headed man. "Yeah, I make it my business to hear a lot."

"Maybe you hear too much!" Gaddis snapped.

"You want to show me how much?" Kilkenny's voice was level. He spoke coolly, yet he was sure there would be no shooting here, yet. He was wondering if Sodermann knew Hatfield was outside beside the window.

Gaddis stepped away from the bar, and his jaw jutted. "Why, I think you're. . . ."

"Stop it!" Sodermann's voice was suddenly charged with anger. "You're too anxious for trouble, Gaddis. Someday you'll get yourself killed."

Gaddis relaxed slowly, his eyes ugly. Yet, watching the man, Kilkenny could sense a certain relief in him, also. Gaddis was a killer, but not a gunman in the sense that he was highly skilled. He was a paid killer, a murderer, the sort of man who would dry-gulch men around a wagon. And he wore a chipped gun.

"Your friend's right proddy," Kilkenny said softly. "He must have a killin' urge."

"Forget it," Sodermann said jovially. "He's all right. Just likes to fight, that's all."

Kilkenny stared at Gaddis. "Seems like you should be somebody I know," he drawled slowly. "I don't recognize that face, but I do know you. But then, I never remember a face, anyway. I got my own methods of knowin' a man. I look at the only thing that's important to me."

"What's that?" Sodermann asked. He was studying Kilkenny, curiosity in his eyes and some puzzlement.

"I always remember a man's gun. Each gun has its own special look, or maybe it's the way a man wears a gun. Take that one now, with that chipped ivory on the side of the butt. A man wouldn't forget a gun like that in a hurry."

Gaddis stiffened, and his face turned gray. Then the tip of his tongue touched his lips. Before he could speak, Sodermann looked straight into Kilkenny's eyes.

"An' where would you see that gun?"

"In Santa Fé," Kilkenny drawled, remembering that Miller had once lived there. "It was hangin' to a man they said was comin' West to farm. His name was Jody Miller."

"You talk too much!" Gaddis snarled, his face white and his lips thin.

"It was in Santa Fé." Kilkenny was adding a touch now that he hoped would worry Sodermann. Only a word, yet sometimes. . . . "Miller stopped off in Santa Fé to see some folks at the fort there an' to talk to Halloran an' Wallace. Seems they was old friends of his."

Sodermann's face sharpened, and he turned. His raised hand made Gaddis draw back a little.

"You're talkin' a lot, stranger," he said smoothly. "You say this Miller knowed Halloran an' Wallace?"

"Uhn-huh." Kilkenny motioned to Shorty to refill his glass. "Seems he knowed them back East. One of 'em married a sister of his, or somethin'. I heard 'em talkin' in a saloon once. Heard Halloran say he was comin' out here to visit Miller." Kilkenny glanced at Gaddis, his face expressionless. "I reckon you'll be plum glad to see him, Miller. It's mighty nice to have an official, big man like that for a friend."

Lance could have laughed if he hadn't known what he knew now, that the wagon had been waylaid and that Miller was probably dead. There would be no other reason for Gaddis's looking as he did. The man was obviously afraid. Sodermann was staring, keen-eyed, yet there was uncertainty in the big man. When that uncertainty ended, there would be danger, Kilkenny knew.

"Funny," Kilkenny said softly, "I don't remember Miller havin' red hair. Seemed to me it was black. That's what it was. Black."

"It was yel . . . !" Gaddis began.

"Yellow. That's right. It was yellow. Strange, I couldn't remember that. But you, stranger, you've got Jody Miller's gun. How d'you explain that?"

Suddenly the door behind Kilkenny opened. He felt the flesh along the back of his neck tighten. He dared not turn. He had been deliberately baiting them, hoping for more information, yet baiting them, too. Now, suddenly, there was a man behind him.

Sodermann seemed to make up his mind. Assurance returned to him, and he spoke low, almost amused. "Why, howdy, Rye! I reckon you should come in an' meet our friend, here. Says he recognizes this gun Red's a-wearin'."

Rye Pitkin walked past Kilkenny and then turned.

His jaw dropped as though he had seen a ghost, and he made an involuntary step backward, his face slowly going white. "You!" he gasped. "You!"

"Why, yes," Kilkenny said. "It's me, Pitkin. Long ways from the Pecos country, isn't it? An' a sight farther from the Brazos. Now, Pitkin, I'll tell you somethin'. I'm not real anxious to kill anybody right here an' now. If I start shootin', two of you are goin' to die. That'll be you, Rye, and Sodermann here. I couldn't miss him. An' if I am still shootin', as I will be, I'm goin' to take care of Gaddis next. Gaddis because he killed Jody Miller. But that comes later. Right now I'm leavin', an' right now you better impress it on your friends that reachin' for an iron won't do any good."

He stepped back toward the door, and his eyes shifted under the hat brim from one face to the other. Sodermann's eyes were narrowed. Pitkin's obvious fear put doubt in the big man. Who was the stranger? Red Gaddis shifted toward the center of the room, his eyes watchful.

Rye stiffened as Red moved. "Don't, Red! That's Kilkenny!"

Gaddis stopped, and his face turned blank with mingled astonishment and fear. Then glass tinkled from the front of the room, and a long Kentucky rifle barrel slid into the room. Kilkenny stepped back to the door.

"Now, if you *hombres* are smart, you'll just hole up here for the time bein'. We don't want trouble, but we may have it!"

Kilkenny stepped through the door and glanced quickly up and down the street. Bartram was on the wagon seat, his rifle across his knees. Jackie Moffitt was standing by his horse, his rifle in his hands, and Saul was across the street. Kilkenny smiled in narrow-eyed apprehension. They were fighters, these men.

"Start the wagon," he said, "down the Cedar trail. Jackie, stay with Bartram."

He walked out and swung into the saddle, and then slid a rifle from the boot. "All right, slide!"

He wheeled the buckskin and whipped down the street. A shot rang out from behind him, and he twisted to look. Saul was mounted, but Quince had turned and thrown up his rifle. He fired. A man staggered from the shelter of the Wagon Wheel and spilled on his face in the dust. The next instant there was a fusillade of shots from the Wagon Wheel and nearby buildings. The gunmen had slipped out the back way and were getting into action.

Kilkenny reined in behind the last building and swung to the ground. Then, with careful fire, he covered the Hatfields as they raced up the street to join him.

Quince was smiling, his eyes hard. "That was Red Gaddis," he said coolly. "He won't take no more dead men's guns."

"Give the wagon a start," Kilkenny said. "We three are going to make some buzzard bait! We have to come back to this town, and we might as well let them know what the score is."

Every time a head moved, one of them fired. While they stayed where they were, no man dared enter that street, and no man dared try the back way in this direction.

Leaving the two Hatfields, Kilkenny sprinted down behind the buildings toward the Wagon Wheel. The men there were killers. He did not know what had happened to the other wagon, but he meant to find out. It was his reason for taking the Blazer trail. He was hoping they might not all be dead. At least, he could bury those that were.

XIII

The rear door of the saloon was open, and there was no one in sight. He stood behind the next building and watched for an instant. He wanted Pitkin or Ratcliff. He would get nothing from Sodermann unless the fat man elected to tell him.

Several old boards lay on the ground behind the saloon, dry and parched. On a sudden inspiration, he moved swiftly from the shelter of the building and, holstering his gun, hurriedly piled them together. Then, using a piece of old sacking and some parched grass, he lit the fire.

It was away from the buildings, but the wind would blow the smoke into the saloon. He hoped they would think he was burning them out, the last thing he wanted to do, as they needed the town as a supply base. As the boards caught fire, he stepped back quickly.

There was a startled exclamation as the fire began

to crackle and wood smoke blew in the back of the saloon. A second later a man stepped to the door, thrust his head out, and then stared at the fire. He seemed puzzled. Out of sight, Kilkenny waited.

Then the man stepped out and kicked the boards apart. "All right!" Kilkenny snapped. "Don't move!"

It was Ratcliff, and the man froze. "What's up, Kilkenny? I never done nothin' to you."

"Start this way, walk careful, an' watch your hands."

Ratcliff was a weasel-faced man with shifty eyes. He started moving, but shot a glance at the doorway. He held his hands wide. When he was six feet away, Kilkenny stopped him.

"All right, talk. I want to know what happened to that other wagon."

Ratcliff sneered. "You think I'll tell? Guess again. You don't dare shoot. If you do, they'll be out, but fast."

With one quick step, Kilkenny grabbed the man by the throat and slammed him back against the building. Then he lifted the pistol.

"Want a pistol-whipping, man?" he asked harshly. "If I start on you, you'll never look the same again!"

"Leave me be," Ratcliff pleaded, his face yellow. "I'll talk."

"Get at it then."

"They done loaded up with grub. We let 'em get out of town. Then Sodermann ambushed 'em. Had about six men, I think."

"Who was killed?"

"We lost a man. We got Miller an' Tot Wilson in the first blast. It was Hatfield got our man. Nailed him dead center between the eyes."

"What happened to Hatfield an' Hight?"

"They got Hight. I seen him go down. He was shot two, maybe three times. We got Hatfield, too. But he got up, an' he dragged Hight into some rocks. We couldn't get to 'em."

"Then what?"

A voice roared from the saloon. It was Sodermann. "Ratcliff! What in time are you doin' out there?"

"Answer me!" Kilkenny snapped. "Then what?"

"Sodermann said it'd serve 'em right. Leave 'em there to die with two men to see they didn't move out of them rocks. They been there two days now."

"On the Blazer trail?"

"Yeah, almost to the turn-off to the peaks."

With a swift movement, Kilkenny flipped Ratcliff's pistol from its holster. "All right, get goin'!" he snapped.

With a dive, Ratcliff started for the saloon door. And just at that instant, Sodermann thrust his huge bulk into the open space. He glimpsed Kilkenny as he released Ratcliff and, with a swift motion, palmed his gun and fired.

He fired from the hip, and he wasn't a good hip shot. His first bullet caught Ratcliff squarely in the chest, and the weasel-faced rider stopped dead still, and then dropped. Kilkenny's gun swept up, and, straddle-legged in the open, he fired.

Sodermann's gun went off at the same instant, but Kilkenny's bullet hit him right above the belt buckle in the middle of that vast expanse. The blow staggered Sodermann, and his bullet clipped slivers from the building above Kilkenny's head and whined angrily away into the grass back of the saloon.

The big man looked sick, and then suddenly his

knees gave way and he toppled face downward upon the steps. The pistol fell from fingers that had lost their life, and rattled on the boards below.

Kilkenny walked toward the saloon, keeping his gun in his hand. Stepping up beside the door, he saw Rye Pitkin and the short bartender, rifles in hand, crouched by the front window.

"Drop 'em!" Kilkenny snapped. He stepped quickly inside. "Unbuckle your belts and let those guns down quick!"

Surprised into helplessness, the men did as they were told. "Rye, I've given you a break before. I'm givin' you one again. The same for Shorty. You two mount and ride. If I ever see either of you again, I'll kill you. I'll be back to Blazer, an' you be dog-gone sure you aren't here."

Backing them away, he scooped up the guns and then backed out the door. He hurried to the corner where the Hatfields waited. Quince was chewing on a straw. He looked at the weapons, grinned a little, and started for his horse.

"Lije may be alive," Kilkenny told him. Then he explained quickly.

Quince narrowed his eyes. "You won't be needin' us," he said. "We'll ride on."

"Go ahead," Kilkenny said, "an' luck with you."

With a rush of hoofs, Saul and Quince Hatfield swept off down the trail. Kilkenny watched them go. The Hatfields were hard to kill. Lije might be alive. It was like him to have thought of Hight, even when wounded. Those lean, wiry men were tough. He might still be alive.

He rode up to the wagon and saw Bartram's face

flush with relief. Jackie was riding beside the wagon, his old Sharps ready. His face was boyishly stern.

"What is it?" Bartram asked. "What happened?"

"We've won another round," Kilkenny said. "We can come to Blazer for supplies now."

Dust devils danced over the desert, and the mules plodded slowly along the trail. The wagon rumbled and bumped over the stones in the road, and Bartram dozed on the wagon seat. To the left the mountains lifted in rocky slopes with many upthrust edges of jagged rock. To the right the ground sloped away toward Cedar Branch, which lay miles away beyond the intervening sagebrush and mesquite.

Jackie Moffitt rode silently, looking from time to time at Kilkenny. Lance knew the youngster was dying to ask him about what had happened in Blazer, and he was just as loath to speak of it. He could understand the youngster's curiosity.

He moved the buckskin over alongside the boy. "Trouble back there, Jack," he said after a minute. "Men killed back there."

"Who was it? Did you kill 'em?" Jackie asked eagerly.

"One. I had to, Jack. Didn't want to. Nobody ever likes to kill a man unless there's something wrong with him. I had to get news out of somebody. I got it from Ratcliff, and then turned him loose, but, in tryin' to get me, Sodermann shot him. Then I shot Sodermann."

"What about the others?"

"Let 'em go. I told Pitkin an' Shorty to get out of the country. I think they'll go."

"We asked 'em in the store, but they was scared.

They wouldn't talk, no how. Saul, he asked 'em. They was afraid. But they was right nice with us."

They rode on through the heat. Occasionally they stopped to rest the mules. It was slower this way, as the road was longer, but there was no dust, and they had to come this way to make sure about Lije and the others.

Again and again Kilkenny found his thoughts reverting to Nita. How was she faring with Hale? Would she marry him? The thought came to him with a pang. He was in love with Nita. He had admitted that to himself long before this, but he knew too well what it would mean to be the wife of a gunman, a man who never knew when he might go down to dusty death in a lead-spattered street.

A man couldn't think only of himself. A few men seemed to be able to leave it all behind, but they were few. Of course, he could go East, but his whole life had been lived in the West, and he had no source of income in the East. He had been a gambler at times and had done well, but it was nothing to build a life upon.

His thoughts moved ahead to the Hatfields. What would they find? Would the men left behind have murdered the wounded Lije? Had Hight been dead? How many more would die before this war was settled? Why did one man see fit to push this bloody fight upon men who wanted only peace and time to till their fields? Why should one man desire power so much? There was enough in the world for all to have a quiet, comfortable living, and what more could a man desire?

The wagon rumbled over the rocks, and he lifted his eyes and let them idle over the heat-waved distance. After the fire and blood there would be peace, and men could come to this land and settle these hills. Perhaps someday there would be water, and then grass would grow where now there were only cacti and sagebrush. Cicadas whined and sang in the mesquite until the sound became almost the voice of the wastelands.

They camped that night in a hollow in the hills and pushed on at dawn toward the joining of the trails. The country was rockier now. The distance closed in, pushing the mountains nearer, and there was less breeze. The air was dead and still.

Jackie traded places with Bartram and handled the mules. Bartram rode on ahead, riding carefully. Kilkenny watched him go, liking the easy way the farmer rode, and liking his clean-cut honesty.

It was morning of the third day when Kilkenny saw a horseman drawing near. He recognized him even before he came up with him. It was Saul.

"Found 'em," Saul said briefly, "both alive. Hight's plumb riddled. Lije was hit three times, one time pretty bad. They was holed up in some rocks, more dead than alive."

"Anybody around?"

"Yeah. One man. He was dead. Lije must've got him, bad off as he was. The other took out. Lije'll live. We Hatfields are tough."

When they reached the cluster of rocks, they pulled the wagon close. Quince had both men stretched out and had rigged a shelter from the sun. Kilkenny knelt over the men. That Hight was breathing was a marvel, although all his wounds showed signs of care. Lije, wounded as he was, had cared for the other man. His wounds had been bathed and crudely bandaged. His lips seemed moist, and he had evidently not lacked for water.

Lije Hatfield was grimly conscious. There was an unrelenting look in his eyes, enough to show them that Lije meant to face death, if need be, as sternly and fearlessly as he faced life and danger.

His lips were dry and parched. Even the water that Quince had given him failed to reduce the ravages brought on by several days of thirst. Obviously, from the condition of the two men, Lije had been giving the little water they had to Jackson Hight.

The two men were lifted carefully and placed in the wagon, with groceries piled around them and sacks and blankets beneath them. Another blanket was placed over two barrels to form a crude awning over their faces. Then, with Bartram handling the mules, they started once more.

XIV

It was quiet in the Hatfield cup when the little group rode in. The Hatfield women did not cry. They gathered around, and they watched when the two men were lifted from the wagon and carried within.

Parson waited, grim-faced, for Kilkenny. "That's two more, Kilkenny. Two more good men gone, an' two that are like to die! I'm tellin' you, man, I'm a-goin' to kill Bill Hale!"

"Not now. Wait." Kilkenny kicked a toe into the dust. "Any more trouble here?"

"Smithers ain't come back."

"Where'd he go?"

"To look at his crop. He sets great store by that crop. Says he'll be back to harvest it."

"When did he leave?"

"Yesterday mornin'. Shouldn't keep him that long, no-ways. I reckon he might hole up in the hills somewhere."

Talking slowly, Lance recounted all that had transpired. He told of the bitter crossing of the Smoky Desert, of the fight at Blazer, and of the death of Gaddis and the others.

"We can cross the desert anytime unless the wind is blowin' strong," he concluded. "They can't bottle us up. It's a miserable trip, an', if a man was to try it an' get caught in a windstorm, there's a good chance you'd never hear of him again. The same if he got into that quicksand."

"I knowed that Gaddis was a bad one. Glad he's gone. The same for Sodermann."

"There's something else," Kilkenny suggested after a moment. "We've proved we could get across, an' we slipped by their guards comin' back by the Blazer trail, but it won't take them much time to figure what happened. They may try comin' in our back door by that way."

Parson nodded shrewdly. "I was thinkin' of that. We'll have to be careful."

When morning came and Lance rolled out of his blankets, he looked quickly at the house. Then he saw Saul. The tall, lean boy was walking away from the house, and he looked sick and old. They saw each other at almost the same instant.

"Saul?" Kilkenny said. "Is . . . ?"

"He's dead. Lijah's dead."

Kilkenny turned away, and for the first time something like despair welled up inside of him. One of the Hatfields had died. It seemed as though something of the mountains themselves had gone, for there was in those lean, hard-headed, raw-boned men something that lived on despite everything. And Lije had died.

O'Hara came out to him later, and the big Irishman's face was sullen and ugly. "An' that doc down to Cedar Bluff. We sneaked in an' tried to get him to come. He wouldn't come, an' he set up a squall when we tried to take him. We was lucky to get away."

"We'll remember that," Kilkenny said quietly. "We can't use a doctor who won't come when he's called, not in this country."

Parson looked at him thoughtfully, and then he looked away. "Lance, you ever think maybe we won't win? That maybe they'll wipe us out? Suppose you can't talk to them Santa Fé men? Supposin', if you do, they won't listen?"

Kilkenny looked down at the ground, and then slowly he lifted his head. "There's a man behind this, Parson," he said slowly, "a man who's gone mad with power-cravin'. His son's a-drivin' him. Parson, I've seen men murdered because they wanted homes. There was no harm in Jody Miller, nor in Tot Wilson. They were hard-workin' men an' honest ones. Lije, well, he was a fine boy, a real man, too. He had strength, courage, an' all that it takes to make a man. There at the last, when they were holed up in the rocks, he cared for Hight when he must've been near dead himself. He must've had to drag himself to Hight's side . . . he must've had to force himself to forget his own pain. Those men are dead, an' they are dead because of one man, maybe two. Maybe I'm wrong, Parson, but if all else fails, I'm ridin' to Cedar Bluff, an' I'll kill those two men."

"An' I'll go with you," Parson stated flatly. His old face was grim and hard. "Lije was my son, he. . . ."

"No, Parson, you can't go with me. You'll have to stay here, keep this bunch together, an' see they make the most of their land. I want homes in these high meadows, Parson. Homes, an' kids around 'em, an' cattle walkin' peaceful in the evenin'. No, it'll be my job down there. We all . . . we who live by the gun . . . we all die in the end. It's better for me to go alone an' live or die by what happens then. At least, it'll be in a good cause."

He lay in the shade of a huge Norway pine, resting and thinking of what lay ahead of him, thinking of the fight with Tombull Turner. Lying there with his eyes shut, he could hear the sound of the shovels as Runyon and Jesse Hatfield dug a grave for Lije. In his mind he was taking himself back to the times when he had seen Turner fight. He was remembering, not the battered men who went down before Turner, but every move the big man made. No man was without a fault. Kilkenny had been taught well. He knew how he must plan, and he ran over and over in his mind the way the big man held his hands, the way his feet moved when he advanced or retreated, the way they moved when he punched, and what Turner did when hit with a left or right. Each fighter develops habits. A certain method of stopping or countering a punch is easy for him, so he uses that method most, even though he may know others. A smooth boxer, walking out into the ring and expecting a long fight, will feel out an opponent, find how he uses a left, how he blocks one. Then he knows what to do. If he lasted in this fight, Kilkenny knew, he would last only because of brains, only because he could think faster, better, and more effectively than Turner or those who handled him.

Yet again and again, as he lay there thinking, his mind reverted to Nita Riordan. The dark, voluptuous beauty of the Irish and Spanish girl at the Crystal Palace was continually in his mind. There was something else, too. In the back of his mind loomed the huge, ominous Cain Brockman. On that desperate day back in Cottonwood, in the Live Oak country, he had killed Abel, and Cain had been thrown from his rearing horse and knocked unconscious. Later, in the Trail House, he had slugged it out and whipped Cain in a bitter knock-down-and-drag-out fistfight. Cain had sworn to kill him. And Cain Brockman was in Cedar Bluff.

When night came, Kilkenny threw a saddle on a slim, black horse and rode out of the cup. He was going to see Nita. Even as he rode, he admitted to himself there was little reason to see her except that he wanted to. He had no right to take chances with his life when it could mean so much to the cause he was aiding, yet he had to see Nita. Also, he could find out what Hale was doing, what he was planning.

He rode swiftly, and the black horse was eager for the trail. It wasn't Buck, but the horse was fast, with speed to spare.

It was late when he rode down to the edge of Cedar Bluff, and his thoughts went back to Leathers, aroused out of a sound sleep and made to put up groceries, and to Dan Cooper, the tough cowhand and gunman who had watched Leathers's store. Cooper was a good man on the wrong side. Leathers was a man who would be on any winning side, one of the little men who think only of immediate profits and who try to ride with the powers that be. Well, the pay-off for Leathers was coming.

Leaving his horse in the shadows of the trees beyond the Crystal Palace, Kilkenny moved up into the shadows of the stable, and his eyes watched the Palace for a long time. Finally he moved, ghost-like, across the open space back of the gambling hall. Tip-toeing along the wall, he came to the door he sought. Carefully he tried the knob. It was locked.

Ahead of him a curtain blew through an open window, waving a little, and then sagging back as the momentary breeze died. He paused beneath the window, listening. Inside, he could hear the steady rise and fall of a man's breathing. It was the only way in. Hesitating only a minute, he put his foot through the open window and stepped inside.

Almost at once there was a black shadow of movement, and a forearm slipped across his throat in a stranglehold. Then that forearm crushed back into his throat with tremendous power. Setting the muscles in his neck, he strained forward, agonizing pain shooting through the growing blackness in his brain. He surged forward and felt the man's feet lift from the floor. Then suddenly the hold relaxed, and he felt a hand slide down to his gun and then to the other gun. Then he was released.

"Brigo?" he said.

"Sí, señor," Brigo answered in a whisper. "I did not know. But only one man is so powerful as you. When you lifted me, I knew it must be you. Then I felt your guns, and I know them well."

"The señorita is here?"

"Sí." Brigo was silent for a moment. "Señor, I fear for her. This Hale, he wants her very much. Also, the Cub of the bear. He wants her. I fear for her. One day they will come to take her."

Kilkenny could sense the worry in the big man's voice. "But you, Brigo?"

He could almost see the Yaqui shrug. "I see the two *hombres*, Dunn an' Ravitz. They watch me always. Soon they will try to kill me. The *señorita* says I must not go out to kill them, but soon I must."

"Wait, if you can," Kilkenny said. "Then act as you must. If you feel the time has come, do not wait for the *señorita* to say. You do not kill heedlessly. If there is no other way, you are to judge."

"*Gracias, señor*," Brigo said simply. "If you will come with me?"

Kilkenny followed him through the darkness down the hall to another door, and there Brigo tapped gently. Almost at once, he heard Nita's voice. "Jaime?"

"*Sí*. The *señor* is here."

The door opened quickly, and Brigo vanished into the darkness as Kilkenny stepped in. Nita closed the door. Her long dark hair fell about her shoulders. In the vague light he could see the clinging of her nightgown, the rise and fall of her bosom beneath the thin material.

"Kilkenny, what is it?" Her voice was low, and something in its timbre made his muscles tremble. It required all the strength that was in him not to take her in his arms.

"I had to see you. You are all right?"

"*Sí*. For now. He has given me until after the celebration to make up my mind. After that, I shall have to marry him or run."

"That celebration," he said bitterly, "is the cornerstone of everything now." Briefly, dispassionately he told her of all that had happened. Of the trip across the Smoky Desert, of the deaths of Miller, Wilson, and Lije Hatfield, and then of the death of Sodermann and the others of Hale's men.

"Does he know of that yet?" he asked.

"I doubt it. He told me there had been an attempt to get food over the Blazer trail and that the men who made it had been wiped out. I don't think he knew more than that."

"I am going to fight Turner," he said.

She caught her breath suddenly. "Oh, no! Kilkenny, he is a brute! I have seen him around the Palace. So huge. And so strong. I have seen him bend silver dollars in his fingers. I have seen him squat beside a table, take the edge in his teeth, and lift it clear off the floor."

"I know, but I must fight him. It is my only chance to get close to Halloran." He explained quickly. "If we can just let them know that we aren't outlaws. If they could only realize what is happening here, that these are good men, trying only to establish homes. To fight him is my only chance."

"I heard you would. Brigo told me the word had come that you would fight him."

"What did Brigo say?" Kilkenny suddenly found he was very anxious to know. The big Yaqui had an instinct for judging the fighting abilities of men. Powerful, fierce, and ruthless himself, he knew fighting men, and he had been long in lands where men lived by courage and strength.

"He says you will win." She said it simply. "I cannot see how anyone could defeat that man, but Brigo is sure. He has made bets. And he is the only one who dares to bet against Turner."

"Nita, if there's a chance, say something to Halloran."

"There won't be. Hale will see to that. But if there is, I surely will."

"Nita, when the fight is over, I'll come for you. I'm going to take you away from this. Will you go?"

"Need you ask?" She smiled up at him in the dimness. "You know I will go, Kilkenny. Wherever you go, I will go, Kilkenny. I made my choice long ago."

Kilkenny slipped from the house and returned to his horse. The black stood patiently, and, when Lance touched his bridle, he jerked up his head and was ready to go. Yet, when he reached the turn, Lance swung the black horse down the street of Cedar Bluff.

Walking the horse, he rode slowly up to the ring. It had been set up in an open space near the corrals. Seats had been placed around, with several rows close to the ringside. That would be where King Bill would sit with his friends. The emperor would watch the gladiators. Kilkenny smiled wryly.

A light footstep sounded at the side of the ring, and Kilkenny's gun leaped from its holster. "Don't move," he whispered sharply.

"It's all right, Kilkenny." The man stepped closer, his hands held wide. "It's Dan Cooper."

"So you know I'm Kilkenny?"

Cooper chuckled. "Yeah, I recognized your face that first day, but couldn't tie it to a name. It came to me just now. Hale will be wild when he hears."

"You're a good man, Cooper," Kilkenny said suddenly. "Why stay on the wrong side?"

"Is the winnin' side the wrong side? Not for me it ain't. I ain't sayin' as to who's right in this squabble, but for a gunhand the winnin' side is the right one."

"No conscience, Cooper?" Kilkenny questioned, trying to see the other man's eyes through the darkness. "Dick Moffitt was a good man. So were Jody Miller, Tot Wilson, an' Lije Hatfield."

"Then Lije died?" Cooper's voice quickened. "That's not good, for you or us. The Hales, they don't think much of the Hatfields. I do. I know 'em. The Hales will have to kill every last Hatfield now, or die themselves. I know them."

"You could have tried a shot at me, Cooper," Kilkenny suggested.

"Me?" Cooper laughed lightly. "I'm not the kind, Kilkenny. Not in the dark, without a warnin'. I ain't so anxious to get you, anyway. I'd be the *hombre* that killed Kilkenny, an' that's like settin' yourself up in a shootin' gallery. Anyway, I want to see the fight."

"The fight?"

"Between you and Tombull. That should be good." Cooper leaned against the platform of the ring. "Between the two of us, I ain't envyin' you none. That *hombre*'s poison. He ain't human. Eats food enough for three men. Still"—Cooper shoved his hat back on his head—"you sure took King Bill, an' he was some shakes of a scrapper." Cooper straightened up. "Y'know, Kilkenny, just two men in town are bettin' on you."

"Two?"

"Uhn-huh. One's that Yaqui gunman, Brigo. The other's Cain Brockman."

"Cain Brockman?" Kilkenny was startled.

"Yeah. He says he's goin' to kill you, but he says you can whip Turner first. He told Turner to his face that you was the best man. Turner was sure mad." Dan Cooper hitched up his belt. "Almost time for my relief. If I was you, I'd take out. The next *hombre* might not be so anxious to see a good fight that he'd pass up five thousand dollars."

"You mean there's money on my head?" Kilkenny asked.

"Yeah. Five thousand. Dead or alive." Cooper shrugged. "Cub didn't like the idea of the reward. He figures you're staked out for him."

"OK, Dan. Enjoyed the confab."

"Thanks. Listen, make that fight worth the money, will you? An' by the way . . . watch Cub Hale. He's poison mean and faster than a strikin' rattler."

Kilkenny rode out of town and took to the hills. The route he took homeward was not the same as that by which he had approached the town. Long ago he had learned it was very foolhardy to retrace one's steps. Once at the Hatfields', he bedded down about daylight and slept until early afternoon.

So Cain Brockman was betting on him. For a long time, Kilkenny sat in speculation. He lived over again that bitter, bloody afternoon in the Trail House when he had whipped the huge Cain. It had seemed that great bulk was impervious to anything in the shape of a human fist. Yet he had brought him down, had beaten him into helplessness.

Parson and Quince strolled over and sat down. Their faces were grave. It was like these men to hide their grief, yet he knew that under the emotionless faces of the men there was a feeling of family and unity stronger than any he had ever known. These men loved each other and lived for each other.

"Kilkenny, you set on fightin' this Turner?" Parson inquired.

"Yes, I am," Kilkenny said quietly. "It's our big chance. It is more than a chance to talk to Halloran, too. It's a chance to hit Hale another wallop."

"To hurt him, you got to beat Turner," Quince said, staring at Kilkenny. "You got to win."

"That's right," Kilkenny agreed. "So I'm goin' in to win. I've changed my mind about some things. I was figurin' just on stayin' in there long enough to talk to the officials from Santa Fé, but now I am goin' in there to win. If I win, I make friends. People will like to see Hale beat again. Halloran is an Irishman, an' an Irishman loves a good fighter. Well, I got to win."

They were silent for a few minutes and Parson chewed on a straw. Then he looked up from under his bushy gray eyebrows. "It ain't the fight what worries me. If the good Lord wants you to win, you'll win. What bothers me is after . . . win or lose, what happens then? Think Hale will let you go?"

Kilkenny smiled grimly. "He will, or there'll be blood on the streets of Cedar Bluff. Hale blood!"

XV

The crowds had started coming to Cedar Bluff by daylight. The miners had come, drifting over for the rodeo and the fight. The gold camps had been abandoned for the day, as there was rarely any celebration for them, rarely any relief from the loneliness and the endless masculinity of the gold camps. The cowhands from the Hale Ranch were around in force. The bars were doing a rushing business even before noon, and the streets were jammed with people.

Kilkenny rode into town on the buckskin when the sun was high. For over an hour he had been lying on a hillside above the town, watching the movement. It was almost certain that King Bill would avoid trouble today. There were too many visitors, too many people who were beyond his control. He would be on his good behavior today, making an impression as the upright citizen and free-handed giver of celebrations.

A rider under a flag of truce had appeared in the

cup the evening before with an invitation to Kilkenny and the actual challenge for the fight. Word of Kilkenny's willingness for the fight had seeped into town by the grapevine several days before, so no tricks were needed. Kilkenny was to report to a man named John Bartlett, at the Crystal Palace.

Kilkenny, accompanied by Parson Hatfield and Steve Runyon, rode down to the Palace and dismounted. Quince Hatfield and O'Hara had already arrived in town, and they moved up outside the Palace and loafed where they could watch the horses. Only a few of the Hale riders actually knew them by sight.

Pushing open the batwing doors, Kilkenny stepped inside, Parson at his elbow. The place was crowded, and all the games were going full blast. Kilkenny's quick eyes swept the place. Jaime Brigo was in his usual chair across the room, and their eyes met. Then Kilkenny located Price Dixon. He was dealing cards at a nearby table.

There was a warning in Dixon's eyes, and then Price made an almost imperceptible gesture of his head. Turning his eyes, Kilkenny felt a little chill go over him. Cain Brockman was standing at the bar, and Cain was watching him. Slowly, as though subtly aware of the tension in the room, eyes began to lift. As if by instinct they went from the tall, broad-shouldered man with the bronzed face, clad completely in black, to the towering bruiser in the checked shirt and the worn Levi's.

Then, his hands hanging carelessly at his sides, his flat-brimmed hat tipped just a little, Kilkenny started across the room toward Cain Brockman. A deadly hush fell over the room. Cain had turned, his wide unshaven face still marked by the scars of his former battle with Kilkenny, marked with scars he would carry to his grave. Through narrow eyes the big man looked at Kilkenny, watching his slow steps across the floor, the studied ease, the grace of the man in black, the two big guns at his hips. Unseen, Nita Riordan had come to the door of her room, and, eyes wide, she watched Kilkenny walk slowly among the tables and pause before Cain Brockman.

For a minute the two men looked at each other. Then Kilkenny spoke. "I hear you've come to town to kill me, Cain," he said quietly. Yet in the deathly hush of the room his voice carried to each corner. "Well, I've another fight on my hands, with Tombull Turner. If we shoot it out, I'm going to kill you, but you're a good man with a gun, and I reckon I'll catch some lead. Fighting Tombull is going to be enough without carrying a crawful of lead when I do it. So how about a truce until afterward?"

For an instant, Cain hesitated. In the small gray eyes, chill and cold, there came a little light of reluctant admiration. He straightened. "I reckon I can wait," Cain drawled harshly. "Let it never be said that Cain Brockman broke up a good fight."

"Thanks." Abruptly Kilkenny turned away, turning his back fully on Cain Brockman, and with the same slow walk crossed the room to Price Dixon. A big red-headed man stood at the table near Price.

As he walked up to the table, the batwing doors pushed open and four men walked in. Kilkenny noticed them and felt the flash of recognition of danger go over him. It was King Bill Hale, Cub Hale, and the gold-dust twins, Dunn and Ravitz.

Ignoring them, Kilkenny walked up to the red-headed man. "You're John Bartlett?" he asked. "I'm Kilkenny."

"Glad to meet you." Bartlett thrust out a huge hand. "How'd you know me?"

"Saw you in Abilene. Again in New Orleans."

"Then you've seen Turner fight?" Bartlett demanded keenly. He glanced up and down Kilkenny with a quick, practiced eye.

"Yes. I've seen him fight."

"An' you're not afraid? He's a bruiser. He nearly killed Tom Hanlon."

Kilkenny smiled. "An' who was Tom Hanlon? A big chunk of beef so slow he couldn't get out of his own way. I see nothing in Turner to fear."

"You'll actually fight him, then?" Bartlett was incredulous.

"Fight him?" Kilkenny asked. "Fight him? I'm going to whip him."

"That's the way to talk!" a big, black-bearded miner burst out. "I'm sick of this big bull of a Turner struttin' around. My money goes on Kilkenny."

"Mine, too," another miner said. "I'd rather he was a miner, but I'll even bet on a cowhand if he can fight."

Kilkenny turned and looked at the miner, and then he grinned. "Friend," he said, "I've swung a single-jack for many a day and tried a pan on half the creeks in Arizona."

Bartlett leaned forward. "This fight is for a prize of one thousand dollars in gold, put up by King Hale. However, if you want to make a side bet . . . ?"

"I do," Kilkenny said. He unbuttoned his shirt and took out a packet of bills. "Five thousand dollars of it."

"Five thousand?" Bartlett swallowed and saw Hale frown. "I don't think we can cover it."

"What?" Kilkenny looked up, and his eyes met those of King Bill. "I understood that Hale was offering three to one, and no takers. That's the money I want. Some of that three to one that Bill Hale is offering."

"Three to one?" Hale demanded. "Why, I never. . . ." The astonishment in his voice was plain enough, but Kilkenny knew he had him, and every move was calculated to win the crowd, not for himself, but for the men he represented. To back down would mean loss of prestige to Hale; to declare he knew of no three-to-one offer would make many believe he had welshed on his bet. And if Kilkenny won, Hale would never dare order him killed because all would think it was revenge for losing the bet. And if Kilkenny lost, it would still put Hale in a bad light if he were suddenly murdered.

"What's the matter, Hale?" Kilkenny demanded sharply, and his voice rang loudly in the crowded room. "Are you backing down? Have you decided the man who whipped you on your own ground can whip Turner, too? Didn't you bring Tombull Turner here to whip me or to force me to back down? I'm calling you, Hale. Put up or shut up! I'm betting five thousand against your fifteen thousand that I win. I'm betting all I own, aside from that little claim you're trying to take away from me, against a mere fifteen thousand. Are you backing down?"

"No, by the Lord Harry, I'm not!" Hale's face was purple with anger. "I'm not going to let any fence-crawling nester throw money in my face. I'm covering you."

Kilkenny smiled slowly. "Looks like an interesting

afternoon," he said cheerfully. Then he turned and walked slowly from the room, conscious that at every step he took the white cold eyes of Cub Hale followed him, their hatred almost a tangible thing.

When they got outside, Parson stared at him. "You sure made King Bill look bad in there. You made some friends."

"You mean *we* made friends," Kilkenny said quietly. "That's the point. We've got to make friends, we've got to get the sympathy of these miners and the outside people Hale can't touch. If we can get enough of them, we've got a fighting chance. Hale can't get too raw. There's law in this country now, an' he can win only so long as he can make what he's doin' seem right. If it stopped right here, an' he got me killed or took my land, a lot of people would be asking questions. They'll remember what I said. You see, Parson, we're little people buckin' a powerful an' wealthy man. That makes us the underdogs. I'm the smaller man in this fight, too. I'm a cowhand and a miner fightin' a trained prize fighter with my fists. A good part of that crowd is goin' to be with me for that reason, even some of Hale's cowhands."

It was mid-afternoon when Kilkenny walked down to the ring. The corral fence was covered with cowhands and miners, and the intervening space was filled with them. They were crowded along roofs and in every bit of space. Scanning the crowd, Kilkenny's eyes glinted. The miners were out in strength, and with them had come a number of gamblers, cowhands from outside the valley, and a few odds and ends of trappers.

The cluster of seats near the ring was empty, and two men guarded them. Kilkenny walked down to the ringside and stripped to the waist. He slipped off his boots and pulled on a pair of Indian moccasins that fitted snugly.

There was a roar from the crowd, and he saw Tombull Turner leaving the back door of Leathers's store and striding toward the ring, wrapped in a blanket. As he climbed through the ropes and walked to his corner, King Bill Hale, Cub Hale, and two men in store clothes left the Mecca and started toward the ring. Behind them walked Dunn and Ravitz.

Then, escorted by Jaime Brigo, Nita Riordan left the Palace and walked slowly through the crowd toward the ring. She was beautifully dressed, in the very latest of fashion, and carried her chin high. Men drew aside to let her pass, and those along the way she walked removed their hats. Nita Riordan had proved to Cedar Bluff that a woman could run a gambling joint and still remain a lady. Not one word had ever been said against her character. Even the most skeptical had been convinced, both by her own lady-like manner and by the ever-watchful presence of Brigo.

Price Dixon walked down to Kilkenny's corner. He hesitated, and then stepped forward. "I've had some experience as a handler," he said simply, "if you'll trust a gambling man."

Kilkenny looked at him, and then smiled. "Why, I reckon we're all gambling men after a fashion, sir. I'd be proud to have you."

He glanced around quickly. John Bartlett was to referee, and the big red-headed man was already in the ring. Parson Hatfield, wearing a huge Walker Colt, lounged behind Kilkenny's corner. Runyon was a short distance away, and near him was Quince Hatfield. O'Hara was to work in Kilkenny's corner, also.

XVI

Kilkenny climbed quickly into the ring and slipped off the coat he had hung around his shoulders. He heard a low murmur from the crowd. He knew they were sizing him up.

Tombull Turner was the larger by thirty pounds. He was taller, broader, and thicker, a huge man with a round bullet head set on a powerful neck and mighty shoulders. His biceps and forearms were heavy with muscle, and the deltoid development on the ends of his shoulders was large. His stomach was flat and solid, his legs columns of strength.

Kilkenny was lean. His shoulders were broad and had the strength of years of living in the open, working, fighting, and struggling. His stomach was flat and corded with muscle and his shoulders splendidly muscled, yet beside the bigger man he appeared much smaller. Actually he weighed 200 pounds. Yet scarcely a man present, if asked to guess his weight, would have made it more than 180.

Bartlett walked to the center of the ring and raised a huge hand. "The rules is no punches below the belt. Hit as long as they have one hand free. No gouging or biting allowed. Holding and hitting is fair. When a man falls, is thrown, or is knocked to the floor, the round ends. The fight is to a finish." He strode back, glancing with piercing eyes from Turner to Kilkenny.

The call of time was made, and the two men came forward to the scratch. Instantly Tombull rushed, swinging with both hands. Kilkenny weaved inside and smashed hard with a right and left to the body. Then Turner grabbed him and attempted to hurl him to the canvas, but Kilkenny twisted himself loose and struck with a lightning-like left to the bigger man's mouth.

Turner set himself and swung a left that caught Kilkenny in the chest and knocked him back against the ropes. The crowd let out a roar, but, unhurt, Kilkenny slipped away from Turner's charge and landed twice to the ribs. The big man closed in, feinted a left, and caught Kilkenny with a wicked overhand right that hit him on the temple.

Groggy, Kilkenny staggered into the ropes, and Turner charged like a bull and struck twice, left and right, to Kilkenny's head. Lance clinched and hung on tightly. Then, slipping a heel behind Turner's ankle, he tripped him up and threw him hard to the canvas!

He walked to his corner, seeing through a mist. They doused him with water, and at the call of time he came out slowly until almost up to the scratch. Then he lunged forward and landed with a hard left to the side of the neck. Tombull took it flat-footed and walked in, apparently unhurt. Kilkenny evaded a right and then lashed back with both hands, staggering the big man again.

Turner lunged forward, hitting Kilkenny with a short right, and then, slipping Kilkenny's left, he grabbed him and threw him to the canvas. The third round opened with both men coming out fast, and, walking right together, they began to slug. Then Kilkenny blocked Turner's left and hit him in the body with a right. They broke free, and, circling, Kilkenny got a look at the two men sitting with Hale.

One was Halloran. The other was a leaner, taller man. Lance evaded a rush, and then clipped Turner with a right. He had been doing well, but he was no fool. Turner was a fighter, and the big man had not been trying yet, was just getting warmed up now. He was quite sure Tombull was under orders to beat him, to pound him badly, but to keep him in the ring as long as possible. Hale was to have his revenge, his bloodletting.

Tombull Turner moved in, landing a powerful left to the head and then a right to the body. Kilkenny circled away from Turner's heavy-hitting right. Turner bored in, striving to get his hands on the lighter man and to get his fists where he could hit better. He liked to use short punches when standing close. Kilkenny slid away, stabbed a long left to Turner's mouth, feinted, and, when Tombull swung his right, stepped in and smashed both hands to the body.

For all the effect the punches had he might have been hitting a huge drum. Turner rushed, crowding Kilkenny against the ropes, where he launched a storm of crashing, battering blows. One fist caught

Kilkenny over the eye, and another crashed into the pit of his stomach. Then a clubbing right hit Kilkenny on the kidney. He staggered away, and Turner, his big fists poised, crowded closer.

He swung for the head, and Kilkenny ducked the right but caught a chopping blow from the left that started blood flowing from a cut over one eye. Kilkenny backed away, and Turner rushed and floored Kilkenny with a smashing right.

Dixon worked over the eye rapidly and skillfully. Kilkenny found time to be surprised at his skill. "Watch that right," O'Hara said. "It's bad."

Kilkenny moved up to scratch and then side-stepped just in time to miss Turner's bull rush. He stepped in and stabbed a left to the head, and then Tombull got in close and hurled him to the canvas again.

Taking the rest on the stool, Kilkenny relaxed. Then at the call, he came to the scratch again, and, suddenly leaping in, he smashed two rocking punches to Turner's jaw. The bigger man staggered, and, before he could recover, Kilkenny stepped in, stabbed a hard left to the mouth, and then hooked a powerful right to the body. Turner tried to get his feet under him, but Kilkenny was relentless. He smashed a left to the mouth and a right to the body, and then landed both hands to the body as Turner hit the ropes.

Tombull braced himself and, summoning his tremendous strength, bulled in close, literally hurling Kilkenny across the ring, and then followed with a rush. The crowd was on its feet now. Kilkenny feinted, and then smashed a powerful right to the ribs. Turner tried a left, and, pushing it aside,

Kilkenny stepped in with a wicked left uppercut to the wind. Turner staggered.

The crowd, still on its feet, was yelling for Kilkenny. He shook Turner with a right, but Tombull set himself and threw a mighty right that caught Kilkenny coming in and flattened him on the canvas.

When he got to his corner, he could see the crowd was excited. He was badly shaken, but not dazed by the blow. Suddenly he was on his feet, and before anyone could realize what was happening, he had stepped across to the ringside where Hale sat with the two officials.

"Gentlemen," he said swiftly, "I've little time. I am fighting here today because it is the only way I could get to speak to you. I am one of a dozen nesters who have filed on claims among the peaks, claims from which Hale is unlawfully trying to drive us. One man has been cruelly murdered. . . ."

The call of time interrupted. He wheeled to see Tombull charging, and he slid away along the ropes. Then Turner hit him and he staggered, but Turner lunged close, unwilling to let him fall. Shoving him back against the ropes, Turner shoved a left to his chin and then clubbed a powerful right.

Blasting pain seared across Kilkenny's brain. He saw that right go up again and knew he could never survive another such punch. With all his strength, he jerked away. Turner intended to kill him now.

In a daze, he could see Hale was on his feet, as were the officials. Cub Hale had a hand on his gun, and Parson Hatfield was facing him across the ring. Then Kilkenny jerked loose.

But Turner was on him like a madman, clubbing, striking with all his mighty strength, trying to batter

Kilkenny into helplessness before the round ended. The crowd was in a mighty uproar, and in a haze of pain and waning consciousness Kilkenny saw Steve Runyon had slipped behind Cub Hale and had a gun on him.

Somebody was shouting outside the ring, and then Turner hit him again and he broke away from Tombull and crashed to the canvas.

O'Hara carried him bodily to his corner, where Dixon worked over him like mad. The call of time came, and Kilkenny staggered to his feet and had taken but one step toward the mark when Tombull hit him like a hurricane, sweeping him back into the ropes with a whirlwind of staggering, pounding, battering blows. Weaving, swaying, slipping, and ducking punches, Kilkenny tried to weather the storm.

Somehow he slipped under a right to the head and got in close. Spreading his legs wide, he began to slug both hands into the big man's body. The crowd had gone mad now, but he was berserk. The huge man was fighting like a madman, eager for the kill, and Kilkenny was suddenly lost to everything but the battering fury of the fight and the lust to put the big man down and to keep him down.

Slipping a left, he smashed a wicked right to the ribs and then another and another. Driving in, he refused to let Turner get set and smashed him with punch after punch. Turner threw him off, but he leaped in again, got Tombull's head in chancery with a crude headlock, and proceeded to batter blow after blow into the big man's face before Turner did a back somersault to break free and end the round.

Panting, gasping for every breath when each stabbed like a knife, Kilkenny swung to the ropes.

"We've been refused food in Cedar Bluff!" Kilkenny shouted hoarsely at the officials. "We sent a wagon to Blazer, and three men were waylaid and killed. On a second attempt, we succeeded in getting a little, but only after a pitched battle."

The call of time came and he wheeled. Turner was on him with a rush, his face bloody and wild. Kilkenny set himself and struck hard with a left that smashed Turner's nose, and then with a wicked right that rocked Turner to his heels. Faster than the big man, he carried less weight and was tiring less rapidly. Also, the pounding of his body blows had weakened the bigger man.

Close in, they began to slug, but here, too, despite Turner's massive strength, Kilkenny was the better man. He was faster, and he was beating the big man to the punch. Smashing a wicked left to the chin, Kilkenny stepped in and hooked both hands hard to the body. Then he brought up an uppercut that ripped a gash across Turner's face. Before Tombull could get set, Kilkenny drove after him with a smashing volley of hooks and swings that had the big man reeling.

Everyone was yelling now, yelling like madmen, but Turner was gone. Kilkenny was on him like a panther. He drove him into the ropes and, holding him there, struck the big man three times in the face. Then Tombull broke loose and swung a right that Kilkenny took in his stride. He smashed Turner back on his heels with a right of his own.

The big man started to fall, and Kilkenny whipped both hands to his face with cracking force! Turner went down, rolled over, and lay still.

In an instant, Kilkenny was across the ring. Grabbing his guns, he strapped them on. His fists were battered and swollen, but he could still hold a gun. He caught a quick glimpse of Nita and saw Brigo was hurrying her from the crowd. Parson and Quincy Hatfield closed in beside him, guns drawn.

"I'll have to go with you," Dixon said. "If I stay now, they'll kill me."

"Come on," Kilkenny said grimly. "We can use you."

Backing after them, Runyon kept Cub Hale at the end of his gun. The younger Hale's face was white. Then, as the Hale cowhands began to gather, a mob of miners surged between them.

"Go ahead!" a big miner shouted. "We'll stand by you!"

Kilkenny smiled suddenly, and, swinging away from his men, he walked directly toward the crowding cowhands. Muttering sullenly, they broke ahead of him, and he strode up to King Bill Hale. The big rancher was pale, and his eyes were cold as ice and bitter. Halloran stood behind him, and the tall, cool-eyed man stood nearby.

"I will take my fifteen thousand dollars now," Kilkenny said quietly.

His face sullen and stiff, Hale counted out the money and thrust it at him.

Kilkenny turned then, bowed slightly to Halloran and the other man, and said quietly: "What I have told you here, gentlemen, is true. I wish you would investigate the claims of Hale to our land, and our own filings upon that land."

Turning, he walked back to the miners, mounted, and rode off with the Hatfields, O'Hara, and Runyon close about him.

"We'll have to move fast!" Kilkenny said. "What happens will happen quick now!"

"What can he do?" Runyon asked. "We got our story across."

"Supposin', when they come back to investigate, there aren't any of us left?" Kilkenny demanded. "What could anybody do about that? There'd be no witnesses, an', even if they asked a lot of questions, it wouldn't do us any good. The big fight will come now."

They rode hard and fast, sticking to little-known trails through the brush. They threaded the bottom of a twisted, broken cañon and curled along a path that led along the sloping shoulder of a rocky hill among the cedars.

Kilkenny rode with his rifle across the saddle in front of him and with one hand always ready to swing it up. He was under no misapprehension about King Bill. The man had been defeated again, and he would be frantic now. His ego was being sadly battered, and to prove to himself that he was still the power in the Cedar Valley country he must wipe this trouble from the earth. He would have lost much. Knowing the man, and knowing the white lightning that lay beneath the surface of Cub Hale, he knew the older man must more than once have cautioned the slower, surer method. Now Cub would be ranting for a shoot-out. Kilkenny knew he had gauged that young man correctly. He was spoiled. The son of a man of power, he had ridden, wild and free, and had grown more arrogant by the year, taking what he wanted and killing those who thwarted him. Dunn and Ravitz would be with him, he knew. That trio was poison itself. He was no fool. He believed he could beat Hale. Yet he had no illusions about beating all three. There was, of course, the chance of catching them off side as he had caught the Brockmans that day in Cottonwood. The Brockmans! Like a flash he remembered Cain. The big man was free to come gunning for him now!

XVII

Winding around a saddle trail leading into a deep gorge, they came out on the sandy bottom, and he speeded their movement to a rapid trot. Despite himself, he was worried. At the cup, there were only Jesse and Saul Hatfield, Bartram, and Jackie Moffitt. Suppose Hale had taken that moment to sweep down upon them and shoot it out? With luck, the defenders might hold the cup, but if the breaks went against them . . . ?

He turned his horse up a steep slope toward the pines. Ahead of him, suddenly, there was a rifle shot, just one. It sounded loudly and clearly in the cañon, yet he heard no bullet. As if by command, the little cavalcade spread out and rode up through the trees. It was Kilkenny who swept around a clump of scrub pine and saw several men scrambling for their horses. He reined in and dropped to the ground.

A rifle shot chunked into the trunk of the pine be-

side him, but he fired. One of the riders dropped his
rifle and grabbed for the saddle horn, and then they
swept into the trees. He got off three carefully spaced
shots, heard Runyon, off to his left, opening up, and
then, farther along, Parson himself.

He wheeled the buckskin and rode the yellow horse
toward the cañon, yelling his name as he swept into
the cup. What he saw sent his face white with fear!
Jesse Hatfield lay sprawled full length on the hard-
packed ground of the cup, a slow curl of blood trick-
ling from under his arm, a bloody gash on his head.

As he reined in alongside Jesse, the door of the
house burst open and Jackie Moffitt came running
out. "They hit us about two hour ago!" Jackie said excitedly. "They nicked Bart, too!"

Kilkenny dropped to his knees beside Hatfield and
turned him gently. One bullet had grazed his scalp;
another had gone through his chest, high up. He
looked at the wound and the bubbling froth on the
man's lips, and his jaws tightened.

Price Dixon swung down beside him. Kneeling
over Hatfield, he examined the wound. Kilkenny's
eyes narrowed as he saw the gambler's fingers working over him with almost professional skill. He
quickly cut away the cloth and examined the wound.

"We'll have to get him inside," he said gravely.
"I've got to operate."

"Operate?" Parson Hatfield stared at him. "You a
doc?"

Dixon smiled wryly. "I was once," he said. "Maybe
I still am."

Ma Hatfield came to the door, bearing a rifle. Then,
putting it down, she turned and walked back inside,
and, when they brought the wounded man in, a bed

was ready for him. Her long, thin-cheeked face was grave, and only her eyes showed pain and shock. She worked swiftly and without hysteria. Sally Crane was working over a wound in Bartram's arm, her own face white.

Kilkenny motioned to Parson and stepped outside. "I've got to go back tonight an' get Nita," he said quietly. "I'll go alone."

"You better take help. There's enough of us now to hold this place. You'll have you a fight down to Cedar Bluff. An' don't forget Cain Brockman."

"I won't. By night I can make it, I think. This is all comin' to a head, Parson. They can't wait now. We've called their hand an' raised 'em. They never figured on me talkin'. They never figured on me winnin' that fight."

"All right," Parson said, "we'll stand by." He looked down at the ground a moment. "I reckon," he said slowly, "we've done a good day's work. I got me a man back on the trail, too. Jackie says Jesse got one up on the rim. A couple more nicked. That's goin' to spoil their appetite for fightin', an' spoil it a heap."

"Yeah," Kilkenny agreed. "I'm ridin' at sundown, Parson."

Yet it was after sundown before he got started. Jesse Hatfield was in a bad way. Price Dixon had taken a compact packet of tools from his saddlebags, and his operation had been quick and skilled. His gambler's work had kept his hands well, and he showed it now. Kilkenny glanced at him, curiosity in his eyes. At one time this man had been a fine surgeon.

He was never surprised. In the West you found strange men—noblemen from Europe, wanderers from fine old families, veterans of several wars, schoolboys, and boys who had grown up along the cattle trails. Doctors, lawyers, men of brilliance, and men with none, all had thronged West, looking for what the romantic called adventure and the experienced knew was trouble, or looking for a new home, for a change, or escaping from something. Price Dixon was one of these. The man was observant, shrewd, and cultured. He and Kilkenny had known each other from the first, not as men who came from the same life, but men who came from the same stratum of society. They were men of the lost legion, the kind who always must move.

Despite his lack of practice, Dixon's moves were sure and his hands skilled. He removed the bullet from dangerously near the spine. When he finished, he washed his hands and looked up at Parson.

"He'll live, with rest and treatment. Beef broth, that's what he needs now, to build strength in him."

Parson grinned behind his gray mustache. "He'll get it," he said dryly. "He'll get it as long as King Bill Hale has a steer on the range."

Sally Crane caught Kilkenny as he was saddling the little gray horse he was riding that night. She hurried up to him and then stopped suddenly and stood there, shifting her feet from side to side. Kilkenny turned and looked at her curiously from under his flat-brimmed hat.

"What's the trouble, Sally?"

"I wanted to ask. . . ." She hesitated, and he could sense her shyness. "Do you think I'm old enough to marry?"

"To marry?" He stopped, startled. "Why, I don't know, Sally. How old are you?"

"I'm sixteen, 'most nigh seventeen."

"That's young," he conceded, "but I've heard Ma Hatfield say she was just sixteen when she married, an' down in Kentucky and Virginia many a girl marries at that age. Why?"

"I reckon I want to marry," Sally said shyly. "Ma Hatfield said I should ask you. Said you was Daddy Moffitt's friend, an' you was sort of my guardian."

"Me?" He was thunderstruck. "Well, I reckon I never thought of it that way. Who wants to marry you, Sally?"

"It's Bart."

"You love him?" he asked. He suddenly felt strangely old, and yet, looking at the young girl standing there so shyly, he felt more than ever before the vast loneliness there was in him, and also a strange tenderness such as he had never known before.

"Yes." Her voice was shy, but he could sense the excitement in her, and the happiness.

"Well, Sally," he said slowly, "I reckon I'm as much a guardian as you've got now. I think, if you love Bartram an' he loves you, that's all that's needed. I know him. He's a fine, brave, serious young fellow who's goin' to do right well as soon as this trouble clears up. Yes, I reckon you can marry him."

She was gone, running.

For a few minutes he stood there, one foot in the stirrup. Then he swung his leg over the gray horse and shook his head in astonishment. *That's one thing, Lance,* he told himself, *you never expected to happen to you!*

But as he turned the horse into the pines, he remembered the Hatfields digging the grave for their brother. Men died, men were married, and the fighting and living and working went on. So it would always go. Lije Hatfield was gone, Miller and Wilson were gone, and Jesse Hatfield lay near to death in the cabin in the cup. Yet Sally was to marry Tom Bartram, and they were to build a home. Yes, this was the country, and these were its people. They had the strength to live, the strength to endure. In such a country men would be born, men who loved liberty and would ever fight to preserve it.

The little gray was as sure-footed as a mountain goat. Even the long-legged yellow horse could walk no more silently, no more skillfully than this little mountain horse. He talked to it in a low whisper and watched the ears flick backward with intelligence. This was a good horse.

Yet, when he reached the edge of Cedar Bluff, he reined in sharply. Something was wrong. There was a vague smell of smoke in the air, and an atmosphere of uneasiness seemed to hang over the town. He looked down, studying the place. Something was wrong. Something had changed. It was not only the emptiness left after a crowd is gone, it was something else, something that made him uneasy.

He moved the gray horse forward slowly, keeping to sandy places where the horse would make no sound. The black bulk of a building loomed before him, and he rode up beside it and swung down. The smell of wood smoke was stronger. Then he peered around the corner of the building. Where the Mecca had stood was only a heap of charred ruins.

Hale's place—burned! He scowled, trying to imagine what could have happened. An accident? It could be, yet something warned him it was not that, and more, that the town wasn't asleep.

Keeping to the side of the buildings, he walked forward a little. There was a faint light in Bert Leathers's store. The Crystal Palace was dark. He went back to the gray horse and, carefully skirting the troubled area, came in from behind the building, and then swung down.

A man loomed ahead of him, a huge bulk of man. His heart seemed to stop, and he froze against the building. It was Cain Brockman!

Watching, Kilkenny saw him moving with incredible stealth, slip to the side of the Crystal Palace, work for an instant at the door, and then disappear inside. Like a ghost, Kilkenny crossed the alley and went in the door fast. There he flattened against the wall. He could hear the big man ahead of him, but only his breathing. Stealthily he crept after.

What could Brockman be doing here? Was he after Nita? Or hoping to find him? He crept along, closed a door after him, and lost Brockman in the stillness. Then suddenly a candle gleamed, and another. The first person he saw was Nita. She was standing there, in riding costume, staring at him.

"You've come, Lance?" she said softly. "Then it was you I heard?"

"No," he spoke softly, "it wasn't me. Cain Brockman's here."

A shadow moved against the curtain at the far side of the big room, and Cain Brockman stepped into the open. "Yeah," he said softly, "I'm here."

He continued to move, coming around the card tables until he stood near, scarcely a dozen feet away. The curtains were drawn on all the windows, thick drapes that kept all light within. If he lived to be a thousand, Lance Kilkenny would never forget that room. It was large and rectangular. Along one side ran the bar; the rest, except for the small dance floor where they stood now, was littered with tables and chairs. Here and there were fallen chips, cards, cigarette butts, and glasses. A balcony surrounded the room on three sides, a balcony with curtained booths. Only the candles flickered in the great room, candles that burned brightly but with a wavering, uncertain light. The girl held the candles—Nita Riordan, with her dark hair gathered against the nape of her neck, her eyes unusually large in the dimness.

Opposite Kilkenny stood the bulk of Cain Brockman. His big black hat was shoved back on his huge head. His thick neck descended into powerful shoulders, and the checkered shirt was open to expose a hairy chest. Crossed gun belts and big pistols completed the picture, guns that hung just beneath the open hands. Cain stood there, his flat face oily and unshaven in the vague light, his stance wide, his feet in their riding boots seeming unusually small.

"Yeah," Cain repeated. "I'm here."

Kilkenny drew a deep breath. Suddenly a wave of hopelessness spread over him. He could kill this man. He knew it. Yet why kill him? Cain Brockman had come looking for him, had come because it was the code of the life he had lived and because the one anchor he had, his brother Abel, had pulled loose. Suddenly Kilkenny saw Cain Brockman as he had never seen him before, as a big man, simple and earnest, a man who had drifted along the darker trails because of some accident of fate, and whose one tie, his brother, had been cut loose. He saw him now as big, helpless, and rather lost. To kill Kilkenny was his only purpose in life

Abruptly Kilkenny dropped his hands away from

his guns. "Cain," he said, "I'm not going to shoot it out with you. I'm not going to kill you. I'm not even goin' to try. Cain, there's no sense in you an' me shootin' it out. Not a mite."

"What d'you mean?" The big man's brow was furrowed, his eyes narrowed with thought as he tried to decide what deception was in this.

"I don't want to kill you, Cain. You an' your brother teamed up with the wrong crowd in Texas. Because of that, I had to kill him. You looked for me, an' I had to fight you an' whip you. I didn't want to then, an' I don't now. Cain, I owe somethin' to those people up there, the Hatfields an' the rest. They want homes out here. I've got a reason to fight for them. If I kill, it'll be for that. If I die, it'll be to keep their land for them. There's nothin' to gain for you or me by shootin' it out. Suppose you kill me? What will you do then?"

Cain hesitated, staring, puzzled. "Why, ride out of here. And go back to Texas."

"An' then?"

"Go to ridin', I guess.

"Maybe, for a while. Then some *hombre*'ll come along, an' you'll rustle a few cows. Then you'll rob a stage, an' one time they'll get you like they got Sam Bass. You'll get shot down or you'll hang. I'm not goin' to shoot you, Cain. An' you're too good a man to draw iron on a man who won't shoot. You're a good man, Cain. Just a good man on the wrong trail. You've got too much good stuff in you to die the way you'll die."

Cain Brockman stared at him, and, in the flickering candlelight, Kilkenny waited. He was afraid for the first time, afraid his words would fail, and the big man would go for his gun. He didn't want to kill him, and he knew that his own gunman's instinct would make him draw if Cain went for a gun.

Cain Brockman stood stockstill in the center of the room, and then he lifted a hand to his face and pawed at his grizzled chin.

"Well, I'll be damned," he muttered. "I'll be eternally damned."

He shook his head, turned unsteadily, and lurched into the darkness toward the door.

XVIII

Kilkenny stepped back and wiped the sweat from his brow. Nita crossed the room to him, her face radiant with relief.

"Oh, Lance!" she exclaimed. "That was wonderful! Wonderful!"

Kilkenny grinned dazedly. "It was awful . . . just plain awful." He glanced around. "What's happened here? Where's Brigo?"

"He's in my room, Lance," Nita said quickly. "I was going to tell you, but Brockman came. He's hurt, very badly."

"Brigo? Hurt?" It seemed impossible. "What happened?"

"It was those two gunmen of Hale's. Cub sent them here after me. Brigo met them right here, and they shot it out. He killed both Dunn and Ravitz, but he was hit three times, once through the body."

"What happened to the Mecca? What happened in town?"

"That was before Dunn and Ravitz came. Some miners were in the Mecca, and they were all drinking. A miner had some words with a Hale gunman about the fight and about the nesters. The miner spoke very loudly, and I guess he said what he thought about Hale. The gunman reached for a gun, and the miner hit him with a bottle, and it was awful. It was a regular battle, miners against the Hale hands, and it was bloody and terrible. Some of the Hale riders liked your fight and your attitude, and they had quit. The miners drove the others out of the Mecca and burned it to the ground. Then the miners and the Hale riders fought all up and down the streets. But no one was killed. Nobody used a gun then. I guess all of them were afraid what might happen."

"And the miners?" Kilkenny asked quickly.

"They mounted up and got into wagons and rode out of town on the way back to their claims. It was like a ghost town then. Nobody stirred on the streets. They are littered with bottles, broken windows, and clubs. Then everything was quiet until Dunn and Ravitz came."

"What about Hale? King Bill, I mean?"

"We've only heard rumors. Some of the cowhands who quit stopped by here to get drinks. They said that Hale acts like a man who'd lost his mind. He had been here after the fight, before he went home. He asked me to marry him, and I refused. He said he would take me, and I told him Brigo would kill him if he tried. Then he went away. It was afterward that Cub sent the gunmen for me. He wanted me for himself. Something has happened to Hale. He doesn't even look like the same man. You won fifteen thousand dollars from him, and he paid you. He lost money to the miners, too, and to Cain Brockman. It hit him hard. He's a man who has always won, always had things his own way. He isn't used to being thwarted, isn't used to adversity, and he can't take it. Then before he left, Halloran told him he would have to let the law decide about the nesters, and Hale declared that he was the law. Halloran told him he would find out he was not and that, if he had ordered the killing of Dick Moffitt, he would hang."

"And then?"

"He seemed broken. He just seemed to go to pieces. I think he had ruled here these past ten years and that he actually believed he was king, that he had the power and that nothing could win against him. Everything had gone just as he wanted until you came along."

"You mean," Kilkenny said dryly, "until he tried to turn some good Americans out of their homes."

"Well, anyway, you'd managed to get food from here right under his nose. Then, when the attempt along the Blazer trail was tried, and he practically wiped your men out, he was supremely confident. But his attack on the cup failed. What really did it all was your defeat of Turner, and at the moment, when he had finished paying off, he was told for the first time of the death of Sodermann at Blazer. Then some of the cowhands who quit took the opportunity to drive off almost a thousand head of cattle. These defeats and what Halloran told him have completely demoralized the man."

"What about Cub?"

"He's wild. He hated you, and he was furious that some of the men quit. He doesn't care about Halloran, for he's completely lawless. He's taken a dozen of the toughest men and gone after the stolen cattle."

"Good! That means we have time." Kilkenny took her by the arms. "Nita, you can't stay here. He might just come back. You must go to the cup and send Price Dixon down here. He can do something for Brigo. Tell him to get here as fast as he can. And you'll be safe there."

"But you?" Nita protested.

He smiled gently and put his hand on her head. "Don't worry about me, Nita. I've lived this way for years. I'll do what I can for Jaime. But hurry."

She hesitated only an instant. Then, suddenly on tiptoe, she kissed him lightly on the lips and turned toward the door.

"Just take my horse," he said. "It'll be quicker. The little gray. Give him his head and he'll go right back to the cup. I got him from Parson Hatfield."

Nita was gone.

Kilkenny turned swiftly and took a quick look around the darkened room. Then he walked through the door and over to the bed where Brigo lay.

The big Yaqui was asleep. He was breathing deeply, and his face was pale. When Kilkenny laid a hand on his brow, it was hot to the touch. Yet he was resting and was better left alone.

Kilkenny walked back into the main room and checked his guns by the candles. Then he got Brigo's guns, reloaded them, and hunted around. He found two more rifles, a double-barreled shotgun and many shells, and two more pistols. He loaded them all and placed the pistols in a neat row on the bar. One he thrust into his waistband, leaving his own guns in their holsters.

Then he doused the candles and sat down in Brigo's chair by the door. It would be a long time until morning.

Twice during the long hours he got up and paced restlessly about the great room, staring out into the vague dimness of the night at the ghostly street. It was deathly still. Once, something sounded outside, and he was out of his chair, gun in hand. But when he tiptoed to the window, he saw it was merely a lonely burro wandering aimlessly in the dead street.

Toward morning he slept a little, only restlessly and in snatches, every nerve alert for trouble or some sound that would warn of danger. When it was growing gray in the street, he went in to look at the wounded man. Brigo had opened his eyes and was lying there. He looked feverish. Kilkenny changed the dressing on the wound after bathing it, and then checked the two flesh wounds.

"¿*Señor*? Is it bad?" Brigo asked, turning his big black eyes toward Kilkenny.

"Not very. You lie still. Dixon is coming down."

"Dixon?" Brigo was puzzled.

"Yeah, he used to be a doctor. Good, too."

"A strange man." Sudden alarm came into Brigo's eyes. "And the *señorita*?"

"I sent her to the cup, to the Hatfields. She'll be safe there."

"*Bueno*. Cub, he has not come?"

"No. You'd better rest and lay off the talk. Don't worry if they come. I've got plenty of guns."

He put the water bucket close by the bed, and a tin cup on the table. Then he went out into the saloon.

In the gray light of dawn it looked garish and tawdry. Empty glasses lay about, and scattered poker chips. Idly he began to straighten things up a little. Then, after making a round of the windows, he went to the kitchen and started a fire. Then he put on water for coffee.

Cub Hale would come. It might take him a few hours or a few days to find the herd. He might grow impatient and return here first. He would believe Nita was still here, and his gunmen had not returned. Or he might send some men. Nita would not go over the trail as fast as he or the Hatfields. If all was well at the cup, the earliest Price could get here would be midday.

No one moved in the street. The gray dawn made it look strange and lonely in its emptiness. Somewhere, behind one of the houses, he heard the squeaking of a pump handle, and then the clatter of a tin pail. His eyelids drooped and he felt very tired. He shook himself awake and walked to the kitchen. The water was ready, so he made coffee, strong and black.

Brigo was awake when he came in and the big man took the coffee gratefully. "*Bueno,*" he said.

Kilkenny noticed the man had somehow managed to reach his gun belt and had his guns on the table.

"Any pain?" he asked.

Brigo shrugged, and, after a look at him, Kilkenny walked out. Out in the main room of the saloon, he looked thoughtfully around. Then he searched until he found a hammer and nails. Getting some loose lumber from the back room, he nailed boards over the windows, leaving only a narrow space as a loophole from which each side of the building might be observed. Then he prepared breakfast.

The work on breakfast showed him how dangerously short of food they were. He thrust his head in the door and saw Brigo's eyes open.

"We're short of grub an' might have to stand a siege. I'm goin' down to Leathers's store."

The street was empty when he peered out of the door. He took a step out onto the porch. One would have thought the town was deserted. There was no sound now. Even the squeaky pump was still. He stepped down into the street and walked along slowly, little puffs of dust rising at every step. Then he went up on the boardwalk. There was still no sign of life.

The door to Leathers's store was closed. He rattled the knob, and there was no response. Without further hesitation, he put his shoulder to the door, picked up on the knob, and shoved. It held, but then he set himself and lunged. The lock burst and the door swung inward. Almost instantly, Leathers appeared from the back of the store.

"Here!" he exclaimed angrily. "You can't do this!"

"When I rattled the door, you should have opened it," Kilkenny said quietly. "I need some supplies."

"I told you once I couldn't sell to you," Leathers protested.

Kilkenny looked at him with disgust. "You're a yellow-belly, Leathers," he said quietly. "Why did you ever come West? You're built for a neat little civilized community where you can knuckle under to authority and crawl every time somebody looks at you. We don't like that in the West."

He picked up a slab of bacon and thrust it into a sack, and then he began piling more groceries into the burlap sack, until it was full. He took out some money and dropped it on the counter. He turned then to go. Leathers stood watching him angrily.

"Hale will get you for this," he snapped out.

Kilkenny turned patiently. "Leathers, you're a fool.

Can't you realize that Hale is finished? That whole set-up is finished and you sided with him, so you're finished. You're the kind that always has to bow to authority. You think money is everything and power is everything. You've spent your life living in the shadows and cringing before bigger men. A good part of it's due to that sanctimonious wife of yours. If King Bill smiled at her, she'd walk in a daze for hours. It's because she's a snob and you're a weakling. Take a tip from me. Take what cash you've got, load up some supplies, and get out of here . . . but fast."

"An' leave my store?" Leathers wailed. "What do you mean?"

"What I say." Kilkenny's voice was harsh. "There's going to be some doin's in this town before another day. Hale's riders are comin' back, an' Cub Hale will be leadin' 'em. You know how much respect he has for property or anythin'. If he doesn't clear you out, the Hatfields will. There's no place for you in Cedar Bluff any more. We want to build from the ground up here, an' we want men who'll fight for what they believe. You won't, an' you were against us, so get out!"

He walked back down the silent street, went into the saloon, and stored his grub. Despite himself, he was worried. The morning was early yet, and he was expecting some of the Hale riders, and soon. The longer he waited, the more worried he became.

Brigo needed medical attention, and Doc Pollard, the Hale henchman, had gone to the Hale Ranch. He was little better than useless, anyway.

Seated at a table, he riffled the cards, and the sound was loud in the room. No one moved in the deserted street, and he played silently, smoking endless cigarettes and waiting. Again and again his thoughts returned to Nita. After all, should he wait? Supposing he was killed eventually? Why not have a little happiness first? He knew without asking that she was the girl for him, and he knew she would marry him in an instant and be completely happy to live in a house built among the high peaks. She was lovely, tender, thoughtful. A man could ask no more of any woman than she had for the giving. Yet he remembered the faces of other gunmen's wives when word came that their men had died. He remembered their faces when their men went down into the streets, when they waited through every lonely hour, never sure whether they would come back or not. Bartram had Sally Crane. He remembered her sweet, youthful face, flushed with happiness. It made him feel old and lonely.

He slipped his guns out and checked them once more. Then he took up the cards and shuffled them again. Suddenly an idea came to him. He got up and went to the back door, took a quick look around, and slipped out to the stable. There were still horses there. He had a hunch he might need them, and saddled two.

Then he went back inside and closed the door. The place was deathly still and the air close and hot. It felt like a storm was impending. He brushed the sweat from his brow and crossed to have a look at Brigo. The big man was sleeping, but his face was flushed and feverish. He looked poor.

He glanced out the door at the empty street. Clouds were building up around the peaks. If it rained, it was going to make it tough to move Jaime Brigo. Thunder rumbled like a whimper of far-off trumpets, and then deeper like a rolling of gigantic casks along the floor of a cavern. He walked back inside, and sat down.

XIX

They came down the dusty street at high noon, a tight little cavalcade of men expecting no trouble. They rode as tired men ride, for there was dust on their horses and dust on their clothing and dust on their wide-brimmed hats. It was only their guns that had no dust. There was no humor in them, for they were men for whom killing was the order of business. The softer members of the Hale outfit were gone. These were the pick of the tough, gun-handy crew.

Lee Wright was in the lead, riding a blood bay. At his right and a bit behind was Jeff Nebel, and a bit behind him were gun-slick Tandy Wade and Kurt Wilde. There were ten in all, ten tough, gun-belted men riding into Cedar Bluff when the sun was high.

Dunn and Ravitz had not returned. What that meant, they could not know, nor did they care. They had come to get a woman, and, if Dunn and Ravitz had decided to keep her, these men would take her away. If those two had failed in their mission, they were to take her from the protection of Brigo. They had their orders and they knew what to do.

Near Leathers's store the group broke, and three men rode on down to the Crystal Palace. Lee Wright, big, hard-faced, and cruel, was in the lead. With him were Kurt Wilde and Tandy Wade.

His eyes slanting up the street at the scattering men, Kilkenny let the three come on. When they reined in and were about to swing down, Kilkenny stopped them.

"Hold it!" he said sharply. "What do you want, Wright?"

Wright froze, and then settled back in the saddle. "Who is that?" he demanded, peering to see under the darkness of the sheet-metal awning and into the vagueness of the doorway.

"It's Kilkenny," he said. "What do you want?"

"We've come for that woman. Cub wants her," Wright said harshly. "What are you doin' here?"

"Me?" Kilkenny chuckled quietly. His eyes were cold and watchful. He knew these men were uncertain. They hadn't expected him. Now they did not know what the situation was. How many men were inside? Was Brigo there? The Hatfields? Kilkenny knew their lack of knowledge was half his strength. "Why, I've been waitin' for you boys to show up. Wanted to tell you that I'd slope, if I were you. The Hales are through."

"Are they?" Wright's eyes swept the building. Those boarded windows bothered him. "We came after the woman. We'll get her."

Kilkenny began building a smoke. "With only ten men? It ain't enough, Wright." He touched his tongue to the paper. "You're a fightin' man, Wright. Ever try to take a place like this with no more men than you got?"

"You're bluffin'!" Wright said. "You're alone."

Kilkenny chuckled. "You reckon I'd come down here alone? Or that the Hatfields would let me? They are right careful of me, Wright."

"Where are they?" Wright declared. "You. . . ." The words died on his lips as there was a tinkle of glass from down the building. Wright looked, and Kilkenny saw his face darken. It could mean but one thing. Brigo had gotten out of bed and thrust a rifle through the window at the right moment. But how long could he stand there? The man was weak. . . .

Kilkenny laughed. "Well, you can start comin' any time you want, Wright, but a lot of you boys are goin' to die for nothin'. If you think Hale can pay off now, you're wrong."

Kurt Wilde had been sitting quietly. Now he exploded suddenly: "To hell with this! Let's go in there!" He jumped his horse to one side and grabbed for his gun.

Kilkenny's hand swept down, and his gun was barking before it reached belt high. The first shot cut the rearing horse's bridle at the bit and whined off into the street. The second took Wilde in the shoulder and knocked him, sprawling, into the dust.

At the same instant, Brigo fired, and Tandy Wade's horse backed up suddenly and went down. Wade leaped clear and sprinted with Lee Wright for the shelter of the nearest building. From up the street, there was a volley of shots, but Kilkenny was safely inside.

With one quick look, he dodged away from the door and ran to Brigo in the other room. The big man's face was deathly pale, and his movements had started his wounds bleeding.

"Lie down, damn it!" Kilkenny commanded. "You did your part. You fooled 'em. Now lie down!"

"No, *señor*, not when you fight."

"I can hold 'em now. Lie down an' rest till I need you. When they rush, I'll need help."

Brigo hesitated, and then sank back on the bed. From where he lay, he could see through a crack in the boards without moving. Lance grabbed a box of shells and dropped them on the bed beside him and handed him another rifle. Then he went back and made a round of the loopholes. He fired from one, skipped one, and fired from the next. He made the rounds, hunting for targets, but trying to keep the shots mixed so they would be in doubt.

Wilde was getting up. Kilkenny watched him, letting him go. Suddenly the man wheeled and blasted at the door, and Brigo, lying on his bed, drilled him through the chest!

One down, Kilkenny told himself, *an' nine to go!*

He was under no illusions. They could trade shots for a while, and he could fool Wright and the Hale riders for a few hours, perhaps. But they were much too shrewd to be fooled for long. Sooner or later they would guess, and then under cover of an attack from one direction, they would drive from the other, and the whole thing would end in a wicked red-laced blasting inside the Palace.

Kilkenny found a good place near a window where he could watch up the street toward Leathers's store. The dusty street was empty. He waited, and suddenly he saw a man slip around the corner of the store and dart for the door. He fired quickly, twice.

The first shot hit the man about waist high, but on the outside and probably near his holster. He staggered, and Kilkenny fired again and saw the fellow go to one knee. He crawled through the door. The first shot had not been a disabling one, he was sure, but the second, when he aimed at the thigh, had brought the man down.

He got up restlessly and started for the back of the saloon. There was no movement, but when he moved to the door, a bullet clipped the doorjamb right over his head, and, had he not been crouched, it would probably have been dead center. No chance to get to the horses then, not by day, anyway.

The afternoon wore on, and there were only occasional shots. They came with a rush finally. It had been quiet. Then suddenly a volley blasted at the back of the store. Taking a chance, Kilkenny rushed to the front just in time to see a half dozen men charging across the street. He dropped his rifle, whipped out both guns, and leaped into the doorway.

His first shot was dead center, a bullet fired from the hip that hit the Hale man and knocked him rolling. His guns roaring and blasting, he smelled the acrid odor of gunpowder, felt a red-hot whip laid across his cheek, and knew he'd been grazed. Then he blasted again, felt a gun go empty, and, still triggering the first gun, jerked out his belt gun and opened up again.

They fell back, and he saw two men were down. He knew neither of them. His cheek bone was burning like fire and he lifted a hand. It came away bloody. He sopped the wound with his handkerchief, and then dropped it and began reloading his guns. This time he brought the shotgun up to the door and stuffed his pockets with shotgun shells. The waiting was what got a man. He didn't want to wait. He wanted to go out there.

There was no firing now. The attacking party was down to seven, and one of those was wounded. They would hesitate a little now. And he still had the shotgun. That was his pay-off weapon. He knew what it would do to a man and hated to use it. At close range a shotgun wouldn't just make a wound. It would blast a man in two.

He showed himself at a window and got no action. He could hear loud voices in Leathers's store. There was some kind of an argument. After all, what had they to gain? Suddenly Kilkenny had an idea. He wheeled and went into the bedroom. Brigo was lying on the bed, breathing hoarsely. He looked terrible.

"Lie still an' watch," Kilkenny said. "I'm goin' out."

"Out?" Brigo's eyes fired. "You after them?"

"*Sí*. With this." He touched the shotgun. "They are all in Leathers's store. I'm goin' to settle this once an' for all."

He went to the door. For a long time he studied the terrain. He was worried. Price Dixon should be here by now. The Hale men probably knew he had joined Kilkenny and the Hatfields, so, if he came back, they would shoot him. And if Jaime Brigo was to live, he would need Dixon's attention.

Kilkenny waited. The sun was making a shadow under the awning, even if not much of a one. He eased outside, listening to the loud voices, and then he left the porch with a rush.

There was no shot. He got to the side of Leathers's store. From here it was four good steps to the door, and there was no window to pass. He stepped up on the porch, knowing that, if they had a man across the street, he was a gone gosling.

He took another step, and waited. Inside, the voices continued, and he could hear Lee Wright's voice above all the others. "Cub'll pay off, all right. If he don't, we can always take some cows ourselves!"

"Blazes!" somebody said disgustedly. "I don't want any cows! I want money! An'," he added, "I want out of this with a whole skin!"

"Personally," a voice drawled, "I don't see no percentage in gettin' a hide full of lead because some other *hombre* wants a woman. I'll admit that Riordan gal is somethin' to look at, but I think, if she wanted to have a Hale, she'd take one. I think the gal's crazy for this Kilkenny, an' for my money she's got the best of the lot."

"What's it to you, Tandy?" Wright demanded. "Hale's got the money. He pays us. Besides, that Kilkenny figgers he's too durned good."

Tandy laughed. "Why, Lee, I reckon, if you'd go out there an' tell him you wanted a shoot-out, he'd give it to you."

"Say!" Wright jumped to his feet. "That's it! That's the way we'll get him. I'll go out and challenge him. Then when he comes out, pour it into him."

There was a moment of silence, but Kilkenny was just outside the screened door now. "Lee, that sure is a polecat's idea. You know durned well I wouldn't have no part of that. I'm a fightin' man, not a murderer."

"Tandy Wade, someday you'll . . . !" Wright began, angrily.

"Suppose," Kilkenny said, "that I take over from here?" Wright froze, his mouth open, his face slowly turning white. Only Tandy turned, and he turned very slowly, keeping his hands wide. He looked at the double-barreled shotgun for just an instant.

"Well, Kilkenny," he said softly, "I reckon that shotgun calls my hand."

"Shotgun?" Wright gasped. Kilkenny let him turn. He knew how ugly a double-barreled shotgun can seem when seen at close quarters.

"Buckshot in it, too," Kilkenny said lazily. "I might not be able to get more'n four or five of you *hombres*. Might be even one or two, but I'm sure goin' to get them good. Who wants a hot taste of buckshot?"

Wright backed up, licking his lips. He didn't want any trouble now. You could see it in his eyes that he knew that shotgun was meant for him, and he didn't want any part of it.

"Leathers!" Kilkenny's voice cracked like a whiplash. "Come around here and get their guns. Slap their shirts, too. I don't want any sneak guns."

The storekeeper, his face dead white, came around and began lifting the guns, and no one said a word. When the guns were collected and all laid at Kilkenny's feet, he stood there for a moment, looking at the men.

"Wright, you wanted to trick me an' kill me. Didn't you?"

Lee Wright's eyes were wide and dark in the sickly moon of his face. "I talked too much," he said, tight-lipped, "I wouldn't've had nerve enough for that."

"Well. . . ."

There was a sudden rattle of horses' hoofs in the street, and Kilkenny saw Lee Wright's eyes brighten, but, as he looked at Kilkenny, his face went sick.

"Careful, Lee!" Kilkenny said quietly. "Don't get uneasy. If I go, you go with me."

"I ain't movin," Wright said hoarsely. "For heaven's sake, don't shoot!"

XX

Now the horses were walking. They stopped before the Crystal Palace. Kilkenny dared not turn. He dared not look. Putting a toe behind the stack of guns, he pushed them back. Then, still keeping his eyes on the men, he dragged them back farther. Then he waited.

Sweat came out on his forehead, and he felt his mouth go dry. They could slip up and come in. They could just walk up. And he dared not turn, or one of these men would leap and have a gun. His only way out was to go out fighting. Looking at the men before him, he could see what was in their minds. Their faces were gray and sick. A shotgun wasn't an easy way to die, and, once that gun started blasting, there was no telling who would get it. And Kilkenny, with an empty shotgun, was still closer to the guns on the floor than they were.

The flesh seemed to crawl on the back of Kilkenny's neck, and he saw Wright's tongue feeling his dry lips. Only Tandy Wade seemed relaxed. The tension was only in his eyes. Any moment now might turn this room into a bloody bit of hell. The shotgun was going to. . . . A door slammed at the Crystal Palace.

Had Brigo passed out? There was no sound, but Kilkenny knew someone was crossing the dusty space between the buildings. He was drawing closer now. The sound of a foot on the boardwalk made them all jump. Suddenly Leathers slipped to the floor in a dead faint. Tandy looked down amusedly, and then lifted his eyes as a board creaked.

Any moment now. When that door opened, if a friendly voice didn't speak. . . .

The door creaked just a little. That was only when it opened wide. Kilkenny remembered that door. He had eased through a crack himself. He lifted the shotgun slightly, his own face gray.

Suddenly he knew that, if this was Cub Hale, he would turn this store into a shambles. Kilkenny was going to go out taking a bloody dozen with him. He had these guns, and, if the first shot didn't get him, he wasn't going alone. He clicked back the hammers.

"No!" He didn't know who spoke. "No, Kilkenny! My God, no!"

These men who could stand a shoot-out with perfect composure were frightened and pale at the gaping muzzles of the shotgun.

"Kilkenny?" The voice was behind him, and it was Parson Hatfield.

"Yeah, Parson. I got me a few restless *hombres* here."

Hatfield came in, and behind him were Bartram and Steve Runyon. "Where's Cub?" Parson demanded sharply.

"He cut off for the ranch. He figured Dunn would have the girl there."

"We didn't find him," Parson said. "He must've stopped off on the way. Hale shot hisself."

"He did?" Kilkenny turned. "What happened at the place?"

"She was plumb deserted," Runyon offered. "Not a soul around. Looks as if they all deserted like rats from a sinkin' ship. He was all alone, an', when he seen us comin', he shot hisself."

"What happened then?" Kilkenny asked.

"We set fire to the place. Too big for any honest rancher. It's burnin' now."

"What happens to us?" Tandy demanded.

Kilkenny looked at them for a minute, but, before he could speak, Parson spoke up. "We want Jeff Nebel an' Lee Wright. They done murdered Miller, Wilson, an' Lije. They got Smithers, too. Jeff Nebel killed him. An' they was in on the killin' of Dick Moffitt. We got a rope for 'em!"

"Take them, then," Kilkenny said. He looked at Tandy Wade. "You're too good a man to run with this owlhoot crowd, Wade. You better change your ways before they get a rope on you. Get goin'!"

Wade looked at him. "Thanks, man," he said. "It's more'n I deserve."

"You," Kilkenny said to the others, "ride! If you ever come into this country again, we'll hang you."

They scrambled for the door. The Hatfields were already gone with Wright and Nebel. Kilkenny turned away and looked at Leathers, who had recovered from his faint. "You got twenty-four hours," he said quietly. "Take what you can an' get out of here. Don't come back."

He walked out of the store into the dusty street. A man was coming down the street on a rangy sorrel horse. He looked, and then looked again. It was Dan Cooper. A short distance behind him, another man rounded the corner. It was Cain Brockman. They rode straight on until they came up to Kilkenny.

Cooper reined in and began to roll a smoke. "Looks like I backed the wrong horse," he said slowly. "What's the deal? Got a rope for me? Or do I draw a ticket out of here?"

"What do you want?" Kilkenny demanded sharply. He had his thumbs in his belt, watching the two men.

"Well," Dan said, looking up at Kilkenny, "we talked it over. We both won money on your fight, an' we sort of had an idea we'd like to join you-all an' take up some claims ourselves."

"Right pretty places up in them meadows," Cain suggested. He sat his horse, looking at Kilkenny.

For a long minute Kilkenny glanced from one to the other. "Sure," he said finally. "You might find a good place up near mine, Cain. And the Moffitt place is empty now."

He turned and walked back to the Palace. He had forgotten Brigo. Yet, when he entered the place, his worry left him. Price Dixon had come, and Nita had returned with him. She met Kilkenny at the door.

"He's asleep," she whispered. "Dixon got the bullet out, and he's going to be all right."

"Good." Kilkenny looked at the girl, and then he took her in his arms. He drew her close and her lips melted into his, and for a long time they stood there, holding each other.

"Oh, Lance," she whispered, "don't let me go. Keep me now. It's been so long, and I've been so lonely."

"Sure," he said quietly, "I'll keep you now. I don't want to let you go . . . ever!"

Slowly, in the days that followed, the town came back to itself. Widows of two of the nesters moved into the Leathers' house and took over the store. Kilkenny and Bartram helped them get things arranged and get started. The ruins of the Mecca were cleared away. Van Hawkins, a former actor from San Francisco, came in and bought the Crystal Palace from Nita. Kilkenny started to build a bigger, more comfortable house on the site of the old one that the Hales had burned for him.

Yet, over it all, there was restlessness and uneasiness. Kilkenny talked much with Nita in the evenings and saw the dark circles under her eyes. She was sleeping little, he knew.

The Hatfields carried their guns all the time, and Steve Runyon came and went with a pistol strapped on. It was because of Cub Hale. No one ever mentioned his name, yet his shadow lay over them all. He had vanished mysteriously, leaving no trace, nothing to tell them of where he had gone, what he planned to do, or when he would return.

Then one day Saul Hatfield rode up to Kilkenny's claim. He leaned on the saddle horn and looked down at Lance.

"How's things?" he asked. "Seems you're doin' right well with the house."

"Yeah," Kilkenny admitted. "It's goin' up." He looked up at Saul. "How's your dad?"

"Right pert."

"Jesse goin' to dig those potatoes of Smithers's?"

"I reckon."

"He'd like it. He was a savin' man." Kilkenny straightened and their eyes met. "What's on your mind, Saul?"

"I was ridin' this mornin', down on the branch," Saul said thoughtfully. "Seen some tracks where a horse crossed the stream. I was right curious. I followed him a ways. Found some white hairs on the brush."

Cub Hale always rode a white horse. An albino, it was.

"I see." Kilkenny rubbed his jaw. "Which way was he headin'?"

"Sort of circlin'. Sizin' up the town, like."

Kilkenny nodded. "I reckon I better go down to Cedar Bluff," he said thoughtfully. "I want to stick around town a while."

"Sure." Saul looked at him. "A body could follow them tracks," he suggested. "It was a plain trail."

"Dangerous. He's a bad one. Maybe later. We'll see."

Kilkenny mounted the long-legged yellow horse and headed for town. Cub Hale was mean. He wasn't going to leave. It wasn't in him to leave. He was a man who had to kill, even if he died in the process. Kilkenny had known that. He knew that some of the men believed Cub had lit out and left the country. He had never believed that. Cub was prowling, licking his wounds, waiting. And the hate in him was building up.

Kilkenny rode the yellow buckskin to the little cottage where Nita Riordan and Sally Crane were living together while Sally prepared for her wedding with Bartram. Nita came to the door, her sewing in her hand.

"Lance," she said quickly, "is it . . . ?"

"He's close by." He swung down from the horse. "I reckon you've got a guest for dinner."

Sitting by the window with a book, he glanced occasionally down the street. He saw two Hatfields ride in—Quince and Saul. They dismounted at the store, and then Steve Runyon rode in and, after him, Cain Brockman.

Brockman rode right on to the Palace, dismounted, and went in for a drink. Then he came out and loafed on a bench by the door. He was wearing two guns.

The room was bright and cheery with china plates and curtains at the windows. Nita came in, drying her hands on an apron, and called him to lunch. He took a last look down the street, and then got up and walked in to the table. Sally's face was flushed and she looked very pretty, yet he had eyes only for Nita.

He had never seen her so lovely as now. Her face looked softer and prettier than he had ever seen it. She was happy, too, radiantly happy. Even the news of the nearness of Cub Hale had not been able to wipe it from her face.

Bartram came in and joined them. He grinned at Kilkenny. "Not often a man gets a chance to try his wife's cooking as much as I have before he marries her!" He chuckled. "I'll say this for her, she can sure make biscuits!"

"I didn't make them!" Sally protested. "Nita did!"

"Nita?" Kilkenny looked up, smiling. "I didn't know you could cook."

There was a low call from the door. "Kilkenny?" It was Cain Brockman. "He's comin'. Shall I take him?"

"No." Kilkenny touched his mouth with a napkin and drew back from the table. "It's my job." His eyes met Nita's across the table. "Don't pour my coffee," he said quietly. "I like it hot."

He turned and walked to the door. Far down the street he could see Cub Hale. He was on foot, and his hat was gone, his yellow hair blowing in the wind. He was walking straight up the center of the street, looking straight ahead.

Kilkenny stepped down off the porch. The roses were blooming, and their scent was strong in his nostrils. He could smell the rich odor of fresh earth in the sunlight, and somewhere a magpie shrieked. He opened the gate and, stepping out, closed it carefully behind him. Then he began to walk.

He took his time. There was no hurry. There was never any hurry at a time like this. Everything always seemed to move by slow motion, until suddenly it was over and you wondered how it all could have happened. Saul Hatfield was standing on the steps, his rifle in the hollow of his arm. He and Quince were just there in case he failed.

Failed? Kilkenny smiled. He had never failed. Yet, they all failed soon or late. There was always a time when they were too slow, when their guns hung or missed fire. The dust smelled hot, and in the distance thunder rumbled. Then a few scattered drops fell. Odd, he hadn't even been aware it was clouding up.

Little puffs of dust lifted from his boots when he walked. He could see Cub more clearly now. He was unshaven, and his face was scratched by brush. His fancy buckskin jacket was gone. Only the guns were the same, and the white eyes, eyes that seemed to burn.

Suddenly Hale stopped, and, when he stopped, Kilkenny stopped, too. He stood there perfectly relaxed, waiting. Cub's face was white, dead. Only his eyes seemed alive, and that burning white light was in them. "I'm goin' to kill you!" he said, his voice sharp and strained.

It was all wrong. Kilkenny felt no tension, no alertness. He was just standing there, and in him suddenly there welled up a tremendous feeling of pity. Why couldn't they ever learn? There was nothing in a gun but death.

Something flickered in those white, blazing eyes, and Kilkenny, standing perfectly erect, slapped the butt of his gun with his palm. The gun leaped up, settled into a rock-like grip, and then bucked in his hand, once, twice. The gun before him flowered with flame, and something stabbed, white hot, low down on his right side. The gun flowered again, but the stabbing flame wasted itself in the dust and Cub's knees buckled and there was a spot of blood on his chest, right over the heart. He fell face down and then straightened his legs, and there was silence in the long dusty street of Cedar Bluff.

Kilkenny thumbed shells into his gun, holstered it, and then turned. Steadily, quietly, looking straight ahead, he walked back up the hill toward the cottage. It was just a little hill, but it suddenly seemed steep. He walked on, and then he could see Nita opening the gate and running toward him.

He stopped then, and waited. There was a burning in his side, and he felt something wet against his leg. He looked down, puzzled, and, when he looked, he fell flat on his face in the dust.

Then Nita was turning him over, and her face was white. He tried to sit up, but they pushed him down.

Cain Brockman came over, and with Saul Hatfield they carried him up the hill. It was only a few steps, and it had seemed so far.

He was still conscious when Price Dixon came in. Dixon made a brief examination, and then shrugged.

"He's all right. The bullet went into his side, slid off a rib, and narrowly missed his spine. But it's nothing that we can't fix up. Shock, mostly . . . and bleeding."

Later, Nita came in. She looked at him and smiled. "Shall I put the coffee on now?" she asked lightly. Her eyes were large and dark.

"Let Sally put it on," he said gently. "You stay here."

ABOUT THE EDITOR

Jon Tuska is the author of numerous books about the American West, as well as editor of several short story collections, *Billy the Kid: His Life and Legend* (Greenwood Press, 1994) and *The Western Story: A Chronological Treasury* (University of Nebraska Press, 1995) among them. Together with his wife Vicki Piekarski, Tuska cofounded Golden West Literary Agency, which primarily represents authors of Western fiction and Western Americana. They edit and co-publish forty titles a year in two prestigious series of new hardcover Western novels and story collections, the Five Star Westerns and the Circle V Westerns. They also coedited the *Encyclopedia of Frontier and Western Fiction* (McGraw-Hill, 1983), *The Max Brand Companion* (Greenwood Press, 1996), *The Morrow Anthology of Great Western Short Stories* (Morrow, 1997), and *The First Five Star Western Corral* (Five Star Westerns, 2000). Tuska has also been editing an annual series of short story collections, *Stories of the Golden West*, of which there have so far been seven volumes.

LOUIS L'AMOUR

THE SIXTH SHOTGUN

No writer is associated more closely with the American West than Louis L'Amour. Collected here are two of his most exciting works, in their original forms. The title story, a tale of stagecoach robbery and frontier justice, is finally available in its full-length version. Similarly, the short novel included in this volume, *The Rider of the Ruby Hills*, one of L'Amour's greatest range war novels, was published first in a magazine, then expanded by the author into a longer version years later. Here is a chance to experience the novel as it appeared in its debut, as L'Amour originally wrote it.

Dorchester Publishing Co., Inc.
P.O. Box 6640   ___5580-5
Wayne, PA 19087-8640 $6.99 US/$8.99 CAN

Please add $2.50 for shipping and handling for the first book and $.75 for each additional book. NY and PA residents, add appropriate sales tax. No cash, stamps, or CODs. Canadian orders require an extra $2.00 for shipping and handling and must be paid in U.S. dollars. Prices and availability subject to change. **Payment must accompany all orders.**

Name: _____

Address: _____

City: _____ State: _____ Zip: _____

E-mail: _____

I have enclosed $_____ in payment for the checked book(s).

For more information on these books, check out our website at www.dorchesterpub.com.
____ Please send me a free catalog.